Tutored in Love

BARBARA J. ADAMSON

Tutored in Love

A NOVEL

COVENANT

Cover image: *Couple Holding Hands* © PHUOC LE, Unsplash.com

Cover design by Tara Leong
Cover design copyright © 2023 by Covenant Communications, Inc.

Published by Covenant Communications, Inc.
American Fork, Utah

Library of Congress Cataloging-in-Publication Data

Name: Barbara J. Adamson
Title: Tutored in love / Barbara Adamson
Description: American Fork, UT : Covenant Communications, Inc. [2023]
Identifiers: Library of Congress Control Number 2023931186 | ISBN 9781524424060
LC record available at https://lccn.loc.gov/2023931186

Printed in the United States of America
First Printing: December 2023

29 28 27 26 25 24 23   10 9 8 7 6 5 4 3 2 1

to Sue,
who sent the email

Without you this journey
would never have begun.

Praise for

BARBARA J. ADAMSON

"I just couldn't put Tutored in Love down once I started reading it. This novel gave me a few enjoyable late nights, and I would not have had it any other way. The love story between Grace and Noah is authentic and enjoyable. I have to applaud Barbara J. Adamson and her humor. I found myself laughing out loud a few times. Grace is such a relatable character, you can't help but root for her and Noah to get together. I loved how the author incorporated religion into the story without making it overpowering but still putting it out there for Christians to enjoy. This is Adamson's first published novel, and I just can't wait for the next one."

—*Readers' Favorite* five-star review

"I really enjoyed the excellent mental health representation and how therapy was shown in a positive light. Neither character was so broken that they couldn't be healed, but they had to be whole before moving on with their lives and loves. I loved how the two main characters were opposites! Grace sees the bright side to everything and can find humor in the worst situation. Noah is a grump with a good heart and a difficult history. I really enjoyed the twists and turns and, of course, the happily ever after. This is a romance with depth and heart."

—Samantha Hastings, author of *Secret of the Sonnets*

"Tutored in Love offers a reality check on single life, dating, and the chance encounters that can lead to more. Grace and Noah take us on a journey of introspection and growth, and we are cheering for them all along the way. A strong debut from Barbara J. Adamson."

—Chalon Linton, author of the Flying in Love series

Acknowledgments

I NEVER IMAGINED THAT JOINING a writing group would lead me here. Thank you, Russ, for supporting me, believing I can do whatever new thing I want to try, and smoothing out the rough edges when times are tough. Many thanks to my stalwart Ridge Writers. Sue, Michelle, and Leona, your encouragement, friendship, and kind but honest feedback are priceless. I would never have made it this far without you all!

To my family, thank you for answering way too many random questions, reading passages over and over again, and buoying my confidence when it drooped. I love you and appreciate your patience when I'm staring into space for the answer to some plot hole or another. Lisa, thanks for helping me find the answers. Carly, thanks for helping me with my English and reading the manuscript more times than anyone but me. Max, thanks for lending your medical expertise.

Jennifer Jenkins, thank you for sharing your knowledge of the art and the industry and for sticking your neck out to help a friend.

Thank you to Covenant Communications for the opportunity to send my words out into the world.

And, most of all, thanks to God, who made this wonderful world and all the amazing things in it. If only words could do them justice.

Part One

Chapter 1

THE GREAT SHAME

"GRACE!" MY SISTER, CLAIRE, GALLOPS out of her tiny house with a giggling baby on her hip. That she is already a wife and mother at the ripe age of twenty makes it increasingly difficult for me to maintain my oldest-sibling mindset, especially during the few weeks of summer when we share the same age. I'll pull ahead in years again next week, but she has far surpassed me in adulting.

Baby squeals from behind a slobbery fist soften the tightness in my chest and reassure me that this weekend trip to Denver will be worthwhile, even if it does include Claire setting me up on a date. Little Ava is the only reason I agreed to the torture.

I relieve my sister of her cherub and nuzzle Ava's belly with my face. "Smells like someone needs a diaper change," I say over baby giggles.

"Oh, sorry," Claire says, reaching to take her back.

"No way." I kiss Ava's head and breathe in the much sweeter smell I find there. It sends a wave of longing through my heart. *Someday*, I think. For now, I'll content myself with being the world's best aunt. "I crossed the Continental Divide to see her and I'm not sharing. Tell me your AC works."

"Yes, thank heaven. I'd be dying if it didn't, having this little heater on my lap all the time." She tickles Ava and receives a happy squeal in return. "C'mon," she says, shooing me toward her home. "You don't want to get all sweaty before your date."

I'd rather ignore this reminder of why I was invited to visit, but as I kneel on the floor to change Ava's diaper, Claire insists on telling me all about the guy and how he and my brother-in-law met building wells in Ghana. I tune out, focusing on the baby and stifling the irritation I feel at my younger sister's insistence on setting me up. She knows I'd do anything for her, but in addition to the family issues I've been dealing with and the fact that literally no one enjoys a setup, I have yet to recover from the last guy.

Granted, it wasn't an actual relationship, but still. I have a major crush on this guy, Alec, who recently moved into my apartment complex. In addition to his general attractiveness and the fact that he exceeds by several inches my minimum height requirement of six feet, he's smart, nice, and even plays the divine sport: volleyball. Besides being the most civilized of sports—no Neanderthal maulings, just a gentlemanly game of smashing the ball into your opponent's face, players neatly separated by a net—it's also the sport most easily adapted to coed play. Definite bonus. I mean, I can appreciate the sight of an attractive man volleying in the sand as well as the next girl, but I prefer participation to observation.

I've dropped hints to Alec about our shared enjoyment of the sport for weeks, checked the sand courts at our complex religiously, even managed to give him a glimpse of my ball as I brought it into my apartment one day, but nothing developed from my semistalking. Alec evidently prefers the spectator type of female, as proven by his rapid acquisition of the most unathletic arm candy in our college-student neighborhood.

But. They've only been together a few weeks. I allow myself to wonder how long it will take him to realize his mistake and—

The front door opens, admitting two male voices just as I blow another round of raspberries into Ava's silky-soft tummy. It is not, perhaps, the best first impression I've ever made, considering my backside is raised stink-bug style toward the door.

I quickly reseat myself on the floor, scooping up the giggling baby and pasting what I hope is a carefree smile over my embarrassment before I dare to look up. I'm pleasantly surprised when I do.

Dark, straight hair worn long enough to brush my date's ears and collar, olive skin similar to my own, build slightly on the too-lean side of slender. His eyes crinkle at the corners with an inviting smile, and tightly groomed stubble enhances his square jawline. He definitely fits the "cute" and "nice" Claire promised, though the three-day beard makes his look gravitate rogue.

My brother-in-law, Ryan, gives me a hand up, takes the baby, and says, "This is my sister-in-law, Grace."

More interested than I care to admit, I make it to my feet and stretch to my full height, meeting his eyes. Nice eyes, hazel, that look into my boring browns and draw me in—until an alarm goes off in the back of my head. I am looking directly into his eyes. Not up. Straight in.

This guy—I don't even catch his name, though Ryan's voice sounds in the background—is barely my height. And since I'm wearing flats, that puts him in the neighborhood of five foot ten—decidedly less than my minimum of six feet tall.

Renewed and amplified annoyance at Claire axes any attraction I may have imagined. What the heck is she thinking? She knows about the requirement, and it's not like it's completely unreasonable. That a woman of height wants a tall husband must be as universally acknowledged a truth as Austen's "single man in possession of a good fortune" wanting a wife. And it goes both ways, as evidenced by all the boys from my youth who refused to consider interest in a girl—aka, me—who was taller than them.

My date's smile falters, and I wonder what about me he's found disappointing. I have a long list of shortcomings, but even with my disinterest it hurts a little that he's already noticed. Maybe it's my height. Turnabout is fair play, I guess. While we shake hands and murmur some socially acceptable niceties, I manage to simultaneously throw dagger eyes at Claire. She pretends not to notice since she's giving the newly arrived babysitter a rundown on Ava's routine, but even a pointed whisper about my height requirement draws no reaction from her as we walk to the car.

We drive somewhere for dinner, the conversational flow in the car left to Claire's management as I stew on the best way to get even. Hitting a volleyball at her sounds pretty therapeutic, and that steers my thoughts back to more pleasant territory. Fanciful images of Alec and me on the sand court—me setting him a perfect ball to smash, his blond hair against my dark curls as we enjoy a victory hug—carry me all the way through the car ride.

Carne asada wafting out the restaurant door awakens my ravenous appetite and brings me back to the present. My date holds the door open for all of us to enter and waits for another group to exit before joining us inside. I'm about to voice my thanks when none other than Mandy Miller sidles up to our group. Pain slices through my chest, white-hot anger on its heels.

"Hi, Grace," she drawls, not even bothering to look my way as she checks out my date.

I draw in a breath and take one step her way, but Claire's fingers digging into my elbow save Mandy from a verbal barrage. Or a bloody nose.

"Mandy," Claire says with a curt nod, steering me away. "Not worth it," she hisses into my ear as she shoves me toward a booth in the back.

"But if she hadn't—"

"She wasn't even with Benson that night. It's in the past. Drop it." Claire seals off her own disquiet and replaces it with a smile as the guys join us. I envy that ability—accepting things as they are and moving on. I used to think she didn't feel things as deeply as I do, but that isn't it.

Maybe it's just Ryan's influence. Mellow and forgiving as ever, I overhear him dismissing Mandy as "just a girl from back home" while my date slides in next to me. The scoff I offer in response—in addition, no doubt, to the fire still smoldering in my expression—must encourage my date to leave extra space between us on the bench. Not that I mind. In fact, the seating arrangement is perfect because I won't have to look at him at all.

Thankfully, Mandy was on her way out, and by the time we place our orders I nearly have my emotions back in line. I'm handing the waiter my menu when a group of late-teenage boys comes in. Spent anger no longer covering my pain, I watch the group. I'll never see Benson like that with his buddies again. Oblivious to the conversation at my own table, I focus on the tallest boy as the group settles in. Unfortunately, their table is diagonal from our booth, giving me a full view. He doesn't look much like Benson but sports a similar hairstyle and confidence.

Claire kicks me in the shin under the table. I blink myself back.

"You know, the guy in the new Spider-Man movie?" she cues me.

"Oh," I say. Not-Benson is laughing at something his buddy said. His laugh is different from Benson's. Or is it? I'm desperately scouring my memory for that sound when Claire's shoe strikes my shin again, a little harder this time.

"Spider-Man?" she repeats.

"I'm sorry," I say, "I haven't seen it."

Her eyes narrow, but she allows me to slip back into silence. I almost wish she wouldn't. Even manufactured visions of Alec can't chase away the crushing realization that I can't recall Benson's laugh.

Thankfully, the service at the restaurant is quick, and though my appetite has diminished, I force myself to eat. Steaming fajitas and rising blood sugar do what Alec-vision could not, dampening the shock of seeing Mandy and Not-Benson. The more I watch Not-Benson, the more familiar he seems.

My date laughs at something Ryan says. Another shin kick prompts a gasp turned half-hearted chuckle from me, though I didn't hear the joke.

"Guess you had to be there," Ryan's buddy says, his laughter extinguished.

Arrival of the waiter with an offer of dessert menus preempts my apology.

"I'm sorry," Claire says. "Not tonight."

"No worries," he says. "I'll be right back with your check."

"I hope you don't mind having dessert at the house," Claire says to the rest of us. "I have to get back to Ava."

The waiter returns quickly, and we head to the cashier to pay. Pain surges in my gut as I take a last look at Not-Benson. The sideways what-are-you-looking-at disdain the kid throws my way convinces me to stop, but even that teenage grumpiness reminds me of what I've lost.

"How were the fajitas?" my date asks as I move past him and out the door.

"Uh, really good," I manage, though I hardly tasted them. Claire and Ryan are ahead of us on the way to the car, so I make a lame attempt at conversation. "What about your . . . ?" I can't even remember what he ordered, so I correct myself with a belated *s* and end up buzzing like an idiot bee.

I swear he suppresses an eye roll at my obvious ignorance, answering with a token "Fine" before surrendering us both to silence.

I murmur a thank-you when he opens the car door for me, but my words bounce back at me as he shuts it. Firmly.

Claire, already seated, seizes the opportunity in the brief moment we're alone in the car. "Could you at least *try?*"

My face heats at her scolding, but there's no time to process my swirling emotions before the guys are back in the car with us.

Claire covers her irritation with an overly happy expression and tone, maybe hoping she can make up for my deficiencies. "Sorry we can't stay out longer, but I thought maybe a movie?"

She *has* to be kidding. But she's not. I steel myself for a couple more hours of torture. At least she didn't suggest—

"Or we could play games!" she says.

"No," I say a little too forcefully, and my date stiffens beside me. "We should definitely watch a movie." I try to soften my response with a smile at him, but he keeps his eyes straight ahead. I've really dug a hole for myself here, and I can't see a way out.

Back at the house I try to make up for my distraction by dishing up the brownies while Claire pays the babysitter and sees her out. The guys' conversation flows easily while they're getting the movie queued up in the other room, allowing me to find a little respite from the pressure.

Unfortunately, they've picked a comedy that just happens to be an old favorite. As in Benson's favorite. Claire and I share a look when she realizes, but I shrug it off. I have to get over these memories sometime. Might as well rip the Band-Aid off now.

Except that it's stuck. Really stuck.

The familiar film resurrects Benson's laugh loud and clear in my head, and it's all I can do to pretend-laugh at the right parts as I throw every effort into forcing my real emotions back into their box. I finally resort to leaning back against the cushions and closing my eyes.

Not a good idea, considering how poorly I'm sleeping these days. When the others' laughter startles me awake, I'm surprised to see that we're already halfway through the movie and vow that I'll be attentive for the duration. Vow or not, my eyelids feel like lead.

It's not long before my date speaks up.

"Sorry to bail," he says, edging his way off the couch, "but I need to get going. Early morning tomorrow at work."

"No problem," Ryan says, pausing the movie and standing to shake his hand.

My sleep fog is eagerly counting the seconds until it can complete its hostile takeover when Claire clears her throat and gives a tight-lipped nod to the door.

Duh. I should definitely walk my date out.

He already has the front door open when I catch up.

"So hey," I say, cringing at my middle school–level awkwardness, "thanks for coming, and for dinner."

He turns, and our eyes meet squarely for the second time this evening. His jaw clenches, irritation and something else flashing in his eyes during a lengthy pause. "Nice to meet you, *Grace.*"

I don't know if he's caught on to my not knowing his name, but there's definitely something extra in the way he emphasizes mine. He turns on his heel, lifting a hand half-heartedly when I manage to say goodbye. He doesn't look back.

I shut the door softly, relief floating to the top of my other emotions.

Until I get back to the living room.

Unfortunately, Claire is perched angrily on the couch that will be my bed tonight. "What the heck was that?" she whisper-yells over the sleeping baby in her arms. Ava exhibits an admirable startle reflex with the only limb not swaddled.

Wide-eyed, Ryan manages a careful transfer of the whimpering baby, a hurried good-night, and a dash for safety behind the closed door of the only bedroom before I answer.

"What?" I will some innocence into my voice, wishing I could escape like Ryan did.

Claire's not buying it. "*That.*" She jerks her chin toward the front door.

"Uh . . ."

"He's one of Ryan's *best friends*, Grace!"

My fajitas churn uncomfortably.

"You hardly spoke to him; didn't look at him once during dinner, though you seemed to find the other tables interesting; missed several questions he asked you directly; clung to your end of the couch like he was leprous; *fell asleep* during the movie; and you weren't even going to walk him to the door!" She shakes her head, rubbing her hand across tired new-mom eyes. "I know you're struggling. We all are since—"

"Don't." I stop her before she can finish the sentence, say *it* out loud.

Her shoulders slump, sympathy mixing with her anger, but she yields to my objection. "That's no excuse to treat a person the way you did tonight."

I swallow against the rising tide in my eyes, willing it down, away, while knowing I only delay the inevitable.

Though the tears don't roll, my battle softens Claire. "He's a nice guy," she says. "He made an effort, paid for your dinner, and received nothing more than indifference and distraction in return."

"You knew I didn't want a setup," I say. One pitiful last-ditch attempt at defense.

"I know. There's already a guy."

For half a second I think she might let me off the hook, but no.

"Let me guess. He's very tall," she says, her tone leaving no question of her feelings on my height requirement, "handsome, athletic . . ." She pauses for dramatic effect. "And he's never spoken a word to you beyond 'hello.'"

She's waiting for a contradiction, but I have none. "He's nice," I protest.

"Doubtless. Also completely unattainable and therefore risk-free." She gets off the couch and meets me where I stand locked in my struggle. "What happened tonight? That wasn't the Grace I know." Her gentle hand on my crossed arms nearly obliterates my defenses. "You have to move on," she says, leaving me to my tortured thoughts with the quiet closing of her bedroom door.

My behavior ensured the date was a disaster, but I know she's talking about more than that. I've been thoughtless, unfeeling, oblivious. In spite of my issues—*because* of them—I should have been kind. I've never felt so ashamed.

Mourning silently in the limited privacy of Claire's living room, I decide it's best to take a break from dating until I can figure myself out. Until the pain of losing Benson doesn't cloud my every interaction. Eventually I try to sleep, but every time I get close some painful detail from tonight's failure shames me awake.

I should have been present. I should have been nice. It's not like Claire was asking me to marry him. I could have at least tried to see him as a friend.

Chapter 2

SOCIALLY EXHAUSTED

Three years later

I HATE DATING.

It's exhausting.

I'm socially exhausted.

My thumbs peck at my phone's screen as though it is to blame for my many social failings.

Maybe it is.

I reread my text, add, *Maybe I should join a convent*, and tap Send before lying back on my sunlit pillow. I stare at my screen and will my roommate and closest friend, Ivy, to give an immediate response. Three blinking dots appear in a conversation bubble and bring a smile to my face.

Ivy: *You'd have to change religions . . .*

Me: *Hmm . . .*

Ivy: *That bad?*

Me: *Worse.*

Last night's first date was so depressing that even the prospect—not that I have any—of another first date makes me want to throw up. Or eat a full pint of Häagen-Dazs.

Ivy: *Wow. Need to talk?*

Me: *Maybe. Still in class?*

Ivy: *Yeah, but Prof. Plum is winding down. Meet for lunch?*

I chuckle and wonder what my roommate's professor has done to earn *that* nickname. There's probably a good story behind it—there usually is, with Ivy.

Me: *Yes, please.* Anything to take my mind off my misery. *I'll attempt to drum up an appetite. And put on some actual clothes. See you in a few.*

Thank heaven for Ivy—and no early classes.

A glance at the time propels me out of bed and into the bathroom, where I stuff my dark curls into a messy bun as protection from a speed shower. I locate my favorite jeans on the closet floor as I dry off and snatch a top at random from among the hangers, forgoing makeup and deciding the bun looks presentable enough for campus.

In ten minutes flat I bounce out of our apartment and head up Campus Hill by way of the tree tunnel, thankful for the branches arching across the paved trail and the welcome shade they provide for the climb. The air holds the excitement of a new semester, the stress of papers and testing still a week or two away. Summer leaves have yet to yield to autumn colors in the high mountain valley that is home to Oak Hills, Colorado, and the small university that bears its name. It will be hard to say goodbye to this beautiful area once I graduate in December.

Not as hard as coming back in January would be.

I shove the disturbing thought aside and pick up my pace, forcing a smile as I pass a fellow student going the opposite direction. *No way can she be eighteen*, I think, feeling every one of my twenty-four years. One more reason I do *not* want another semester.

Reaching the student center, I push through the outer doors and speed-walk down the wide hallway that leads to the food court, relieved to narrowly beat the chaos that will ensue when eleven-o'clock classes let out. Still, there are already plenty of noisy students staking claim to lunch tables. After an assessment of the various lines and a quick consultation with my nose, I decide on a beef burrito for brunch, work my way through the rabble to pay, then scan the growing throng for Ivy.

"Grace!"

My eyes turn at the sound of my name, and find Ivy tucked away in the coveted corner booth. Auburn hair pulled half back in a Dutch braid and cascading over one shoulder, my elfin friend throws me a look of triumph around a long, skinny carrot, greens intact.

"How?" I demand once I navigate through the crush.

She lifts a shoulder, wielding her vegetable like Audrey Hepburn's cigarette holder in *Breakfast at Tiffany's*. "Skill."

I set down my tray, shrug off my backpack, and scoot in across from her, my long legs not fitting nearly as easily as her shorter limbs. "Three and a half years here, and I've *never* scored the corner booth. Sometimes I think you're magic."

"Totally magic." Ivy's bright-green eyes sparkle with mischief. "I left class right after you texted. I'd had enough talk of *movements*."

"Movements?"

With a sigh of disgust, Ivy spills. "She can't stop extolling the virtues of prunes. Antioxidants, yes. Blood-sugar stabilizers, true. But, honestly, if she mentions her digestive issues one more time . . ."

"Thus, you have christened her Professor Plum." I laugh. "What did you expect in a class called Nutrition through the Life Cycle?"

"A little more discussion of the rest of the cycle, that's what! You'd think she would save the geriatrics for the end of the semester. I mean, what happened to natural chronology? Just because *she's* a centenarian—"

"Oh, the trials of a nutritional science major. Looks like you're low on protein today. Want some of my burrito?"

Ivy cringes at my forkful of steaming, red-sauce-dripping shredded beef, then pulls a box of organic almonds from her waxed-canvas lunch bag.

"Don't you ever miss meat?"

"Honestly? No. But I'll keep the dairy."

"Right? Much as I love beef, I'd have a way harder time giving up ice cream." I swallow a bite of burrito and wipe off any evidence with a napkin. "Anyway, don't you want to hear my latest date fail?"

"Sorry I was asleep when you came in," she says, but I wave off her apology. We both knew she would be as soon as I left last night. "Was he a complete oaf?"

I blow a curl off my forehead and wonder yet again what is wrong with me. "He was completely *not* an oaf. Nice, cute, smart, even tall." Not that I'm too picky about the tall thing anymore. The Great Shame, as I labeled it, taught me better than that.

Ivy's face scrunches in confusion. "So what was the problem?"

"Just . . . I don't know. No chemistry."

"Chemistry? Did he try to kiss you?"

"Please. I'm sure he felt the nonreaction as vividly as I did."

Ivy frowns. "Hmm."

"Seriously, I can't remember the last time I struggled so hard to make conversation. And he was trying too. We just had nothing in common."

"Nothing?"

"Well, nothing exciting. He assumed I would enjoy talking sports since I'm in rec management, and in desperation I went right along. Once he started in on the college football scene, all I had to do was *hmm* or nod every few minutes."

Which is why I'm now riddled with guilt. Regardless of the work I've done in therapy and all the progress I tell myself I've made since that most epic date fail brought awareness to the depth of my issues, I failed again last night. I may not have been rude like I was back then—I maintained eye contact and threw in enough comments to keep the conversation flowing, albeit like molasses—but I didn't really listen, didn't manage to really *see* him like I vowed to after I realized how thoughtless I'd become.

"Seriously, Ivy. What is wrong with me? Why am I a noble gas when it comes to romantic reactivity? Am I destined to be alone?"

"Oh, come on. You've been attracted to plenty of guys!"

"Yeah, none of whom were attracted to me. And the ones who were?" I shudder around my last bite. It's close enough to class time for me to escape the depressing conversation before she probes any deeper. Ivy knows about my Great Shame, so she can fully comprehend my guilt but has a nasty tendency toward reminding me to forget about it. As if it were that easy.

"Anyway, thanks for meeting me for lunch," I say, "and for making my collegiate experience complete."

"Huh?"

"Between Professor Plum's movements and finally sitting in the corner booth, I am unconditionally fulfilled. I don't even need to finish the semester now."

Ivy's carrot stops halfway to her mouth, her eyes narrowing. "Oh yes you do. How's math?"

I deny a flicker of panic and wish I had chosen my words more carefully. If only I had more burrito to distract me or another topic to distract Ivy. Instead I have to deflect her challenge head-on. "I refuse to speak of The Unmentionable outside of class."

"Have you turned anything in yet?"

I glare at her.

"Didn't think so. Hired a tutor?"

"You're engaging my fight-or-flight response!"

"Good, because we're fighting," she says, completely calm. "Besides, you can deal with that in stress management. Not that you'll need it after your golf class."

"Hey, be nice! It's my last semester. I had to fill it with *something*."

"Let's remember that the only reason you're still here, in your last semester, is to *pass math*."

I grit my teeth and stand to gather my things.

"Grace. Don't you want to graduate?"

No comment.

Ivy makes a sound between a sigh and a growl, digging into her stylish faux-leather tote bag and eventually pulling out her phone. I collect the garbage on my tray and, while she thumbs and scrolls, retrieve Trusty, the well-loved generic-blue backpack Benson gave me, along with its name, when I left for college. I hope she'll let the subject drop and pray she isn't calling my mom. As soon as she sets her phone down, mine buzzes in my back pocket. I pull it out and open her message.

"What's this?" I ask, looking at the contact she sent me. "Who is Lupe Navarro? Are you trying to set me up?"

"Yes—"

"I haven't even recovered from the last one!"

"Not on a date. *She's* the math tutor who helped me get through stats last year, and she's amazing."

"Does she speak stupid?"

Ivy takes a deep breath. "Would I have passed stats if she didn't? Stop *acting* stupid, and give her a call."

"I *am* stupid when it comes to math."

"Well, I'm not much better off than you, and she pulled me through. Give her a try. You really don't want to lose your dream job because you didn't even *attempt* to pass math."

I stare at the contact information on my phone, knowing Ivy is right, knowing I have to try. "All right," I say. "I'll give it a shot."

Ivy sits back with a smug smile. "You can do this, Gracie. I know you can. And you *aren't* stupid. Just—"

"I know, I know: *mathematically challenged*," I say, recalling the term Dad had once used in a lame attempt to shore up my junior high ego. The years haven't done anything to increase its efficacy.

Chapter 3

ARITHMOPHOBIA

I'm NOT SCARED OF SNAKES, heights, tight spaces, spiders, or germs. I've been skydiving and spelunking, camped in the wilderness with no tent or sleeping bag, and lived for a year with random strangers in a third-world country. None of that gave me anxiety.

However, there is a single word that makes my blood pressure skyrocket, my palms sweat, and my stomach churn: algebra.

Arithmophobia is an actual thing, although I'm not sure it's the correct label for my problem. I always enjoyed math in elementary school, but then— horror of horrors—they went and added *letters*.

I've heard it was Satan himself.

Some kindred spirits have gone to the trouble of printing this theory on T-shirts and coffee mugs, although I personally don't choose to advertise my deficiency.

Which is why I am pursuing a career that will involve much less frightening things, like spending the night with insects creeping over my limbs or army-crawling through a pitch-black tunnel that barely accommodates my shoulders or jumping out of an airplane at thirteen thousand feet. Recreation therapy and me? A match made in heaven.

Unfortunately, the powers that be have decreed that one must attain a certain level of math proficiency before one may graduate from Oak Hills. I managed to bypass the higher-math classes by ignoring the recommended statistics course and using Spanish skills honed during my year volunteering in Peru for the languages of learning requirement. I breezed through the rest of my generals, excelled in my major, enjoyed the social scene—other than dating—and pretended to forget about math.

Which is why in this, my theoretically last semester of college, my schedule includes only one class required for graduation: quantitative reasoning.

If I pass, I graduate and claim the perfect job waiting for me, moving into the realm of true adulting.

If I don't pass? No job, no money, no life.

No pressure.

Mom told me repeatedly that I shouldn't wait to take this class—mostly, I think, so that I'd be able to repeat it if I failed. She has such faith in my skills. But I ignored her, and now my entire future rests on my ability to pass the one class for which my failure is predestined.

Mom says she'll pay for a tutor.

I will not ignore her.

Like a dutiful friend and daughter, I called Lupe Navarro as soon as I finished classes yesterday. We connected immediately—she's from Peru, though not the area where I worked—and spent half the conversation in Spanish. Fortunately, she had one opening left.

I've been struggling all morning to repress the memory of yesterday's math lecture, which rendered me sweatier and more disoriented than the marathon I ran last year. That bucket-list item is definitely something I don't want to do twice. Kind of like quantitative reasoning.

"Nice swing," my golf instructor says as he walks by, watching my drive fly. His name is Ethan, and he's kind of cute with his lankiness and sandy-blond hair and clipboard and official-looking fancy-casual golf attire. He's completely professional, but there's something in his tone that draws my eyes back to him a little more than necessary. It's enough to keep me from thinking about what's next on my schedule, but it also makes the class fly by.

The sun is shining in a clear-blue, deceptively happy sky, and before I know it I'm on my way up Campus Hill to the doom I can no longer delay. I journey alone to the gates of perdition itself: math lab. Here I will be required to actually *do* math—as opposed to sitting in the lecture hall among the other math losers and striving for anonymity in my confusion as I aspire to nod at the appropriate times. Hopefully, having Lupe as my tutor will make it all better.

Through the outer doors of the math building and past the auditorium, I mosey, casually noting room numbers as I pass and pretending confidence. I turn a corner and see a wall of glass stretching before me—windows into a world I've avoided like the plague. Inside, sparsely occupied chairs surround a multitude of round tables, several rows of computer desks stretch along the back of the room, and whiteboards cover the walls. I take the plunge and open the door with a shaky hand.

A pungent ambiance of anxiety and superior intellect assails me as I walk in, but I cover my butterflies with a smile and pretend I'm comfortable here. I'll assess my environment like I would if I were stranded in a desert and left for dead.

I'd have a better chance of survival there.

Most of the people in the room bend over their homework or stare at computer screens. A couple of workers in light-green vests and name tags meander amid the low hum of conversation, watching for hands and swooping in to help the poor souls who raise them. The only anomaly is a stocky guy wearing glasses in the corner, leaning back in his chair and scrolling on his phone.

An unoccupied vested woman takes pity on me as I stand stupidly near the door. "Can I help you?" she asks.

"Hi, um, Ashley," I say after a glance at the name tag pinned to her vest. "I'm looking for Lupe Navarro."

Ashley looks at me like I'm crazy. Maybe I'm in the wrong room.

"She's a math tutor." I lower my voice. "I'm supposed to meet her here."

"Oh, um . . ." She glances around the room. "I'm sorry, but I don't think there's anyone by that name working today."

My jitters have expanded into sweaty palms, and my heartbeat is surely audible. I scan the room again, hoping for a comforting Lupe to pop up from behind a computer and wash away my anxiety, but the only face looking my way bears the curious gaze of Glasses Guy in the corner. As a cover for my discomfort, I touch up my smile and turn back to my helper, but not before I notice how the guy's eyes have narrowed at me.

Ashley looks as thoroughly confused as I feel. Maybe, hopefully, it's her first day on the job and she has no idea what she's talking about.

"You must have some record of her," I say, barely keeping the tremor out of my voice. "She helped my roommate with stats last year. Do you have a list or something you can check?"

Understanding lights Ashley's face. "I'll bet she's one of the private tutors. Did you try texting her?"

Duh. "Thanks," I say, pulling out my phone as I berate myself for being an idiot. "I wasn't thinking. She's probably just running late." I thumb in a quick text and send it as I talk.

Ashley smiles and stays at my side, complimenting my phone case and making me wonder if she's done some sensitivity training to help her empathize with the mathematically challenged.

A deep voice sounds behind me. "Did you say Lupe Navarro?"

I'm staring at my phone, willing it to display *Delivered* and the three dots that will let me know the tutor who's supposed to salvage my graduation is responding, but the progress bar is stuck.

Ashley answers him for me. "Yeah, do you know her?"

"I do," the man at my back says.

At this, I wince. What does he have to do with my tutor? More importantly, why isn't she answering my text?

He answers my unvoiced question. "She had a family emergency and asked me to take over her student list."

Shock spins me around to face him, but his eyes are glued to his phone, so all I see is thick, short black hair and the bold rims of his glasses. A pleasant whiff of shampoo or gel or something informs me I'm standing too close, so I back up a step.

"Where is it?" he mutters, scrolling through the Notes app on his phone. "Ah, here we go. I'm supposed to be meeting a Tracy Burt here right now. Is that you?" He looks up with a small smile that immediately vanishes.

Can he already tell I'm beyond help? Just from a glance? I remind myself that I have survival skills like Bear Grylls and put on a brave face. "I *am* supposed to meet Lupe Navarro here, but my name is Grace Ebert."

He flinches as I put out my hand to shake. His thick brows furrow, nearly meeting in the middle. He looks down at his phone again and mumbles, "Tracy Burt."

He must be so good at math that he never conquered social skills, because I have to reel in my unshaken hand and pretend to tuck a curl behind my ear with it. Summoning my inner empath, I decide to help him through the awkwardness. Somehow his bumbling eases my math-lab angst, and I chuckle as I realize what has probably caused the confusion. "Tracy Burt, huh?" I ask him.

He nods, though he's still looking down.

"Must have been a bad connection. Grace Ebert. Tracy Burt." I force another chuckle.

His eyes stay on his phone as he mutters something under his breath about why she couldn't have texted.

Biting back a sigh and the feeling that my chances of graduation have significantly diminished, I forge onward. "You're the replacement tutor?" I shift Trusty on my shoulders. "I wish she would have let me know about the change. It would have made this a lot easier."

His head pops back up, angry. He must have an ego the size of Texas if he's offended at being called a replacement, especially when he is one.

"Her brother died. She's on a plane to Peru."

Oh. My heart sinks. "I'm so sor—"

"She didn't have time to contact everyone personally, so she just told me her schedule"—his voice is clipped, irritated—"which, obviously, I had difficulty understanding over the phone. She was cutting in and out."

"Well, that's totally understandable," I say in what I hope is a comforting tone, pushing away the sharp pang of grief I'm feeling for Lupe. This guy's curtness is throwing me, but if I'm to have any chance of succeeding in math, I have to make this work. I take a deep breath, knowing I don't have time to find another tutor. "Look, I'm so sorry about her brother and the confusion, but I have quite a few questions on an assignment that's due at midnight. So, if you don't mind, I'd really like to get started."

He stares at me through those thick black frames as if he has no idea what I'm talking about. Serious social problems here. Well, maybe I can help him with his people skills while he helps me with my math.

"Maybe it would be best if we just start over. Hi," I say, forcing some cheerfulness into my voice and blatantly offering my hand again. "My name is Grace Ebert, and I could really use your help with my math homework."

He stares at me for the longest three seconds of my life, as his eyes shift from confused to something I can't quite place.

"Noah Jennings." He delivers a handshake that is slightly longer than normal and several degrees beyond firm, holding my eyes in a bit of a dare.

An uncomfortable laugh bubbles out before I can stop it, triggering an answering one from him that definitely has sadistic undertones.

Oh, please, don't let him be mean.

My tutor takes a seat at the nearest table, Ashley having abandoned me for some other hapless wretch. I'm still standing where they left me, clutching Trusty like a life preserver and contemplating alternative career paths. Maybe the taco shop I worked for in high school is hiring.

"So. Quantitative reasoning." Noah leans back in his chair like this is the most comfortable thing ever.

I swallow in a futile effort to quench the dryness at the back of my throat and approach the table with the care I give every cliff edge. Settling into my chair gives me more angst than the first step back in a three-hundred-foot rappel—without the adrenaline rush.

Might as well jump in. Or off. Whatever. I pull out my assignments and set them on the table. They're both unmarked, other than a slight rumpling at the corners from residing in my backpack.

Anticipating Noah's judgment as he inevitably finds the lapsed due date on the first, I start to unzip my backpack's laptop compartment—a little too forcefully, judging by the tearing sound it produces.

"Trusty!" I gasp when I see the little split I've created in the zipper's seam. "Oh no." I manage to reverse the zipper past the loose threads that caught and led to the rip, forcing back thoughts of Benson, hoping I haven't ruined the last thing he gave me.

"Trusty?" Noah says, watching my struggle.

"My backpack," I say.

"You named your backpack?" I see mockery in his eyes.

"My brother did." I say it as flat as I can, lifting my chin and daring him to make fun of me. He takes the hint and goes back to reading over my assignments.

I take my time extracting my laptop, reassuring myself that Trusty will hold together if I'm careful, and pull from the pens pocket a brand-new mechanical pencil—the one thing about this moment that brings me some semblance of enjoyment. I'm pretty sure it makes me *look* smarter, even if it can't change my brain.

His eyes catch on the due date. He clears his throat. "Syllabus?" One hand snaps out, palm up, as he continues to thumb through the pages without looking at me.

"She, uh, didn't hand out a hard copy."

The thumbing stops. He looks up, and a muscle jumps in his jaw. "Pull it up, please?" he says, gesturing at my laptop with a forced smile.

"Right," I say, wishing I could slap the idiocy out of myself. I try for some positive self-talk instead, reassuring junior high Grace that all is well and she can go back to long-term memory. I swear there's a glint in his eyes, hinting that he's only just able to hold back the disparaging comments brewing behind them.

The clicking of my keyboard sounds loud in my ears as he waits for me to find the document. His "May I?" when the page finally loads sounds polite, though I can't help but think his impatience is barely contained.

I hand over my laptop, holding my breath as he skims the material I have yet to read and wondering—thanks to his furrowed brows—how badly that missing assignment is going to affect my future. My angst upgrades to full stomachache in anticipation.

"Well," he finally says, aiming my laptop back toward me, "it looks like she doesn't accept anything late, so the first assignment is a loss—"

"One less to do, heh heh," I say in an attempt to humor my way out, smiling over my regret.

He continues as if I haven't spoken. "—for credit, but you'll still need to complete it."

I stifle a groan.

"Math is cumulative." His fake smile reemerges, and though his tone is not condescending, I manage to interpret his words that way. "You'll need to master those concepts before you can move on to the next section."

Great.

"And it would be best if you try the assignment on your own before we meet next week."

Double great. I mean, I didn't really expect him to do the work for me, but a girl can hope.

"Questions?" he asks.

So many I don't even know what to ask. "Uh . . ."

"We'll just start at the beginning."

I drop Trusty on the kitchen table, and Ivy nearly jumps out of her skin, as intended.

"What happened?" she asks.

Flopping into the wooden chair across from hers, I let out a groan and plop my head onto my hands. "He died."

Ivy springs out of her chair to my side. "What? Who?"

"Lupe Navarro's brother."

Her hand stops making comforting circles on my back. "Huh?"

I sigh and ramble off the basics. "He died, and she's on her way back to Peru, so she found me a replacement tutor, and he's a sadist." I pause for effect before pressing on. "And now I'll never pass math or graduate, and my job will go to someone else."

"And it's all my fault and you're never speaking to me again?" She reclaims her seat and the rabbit-food meal I've so rudely interrupted.

"Clearly."

"Hmm. That's tragic because I was about to give you some good news."

My head lifts off my hands.

"But first you have to give me the undramatized version of events. That's terrible about Lupe's brother. Did she really go back to Peru? And she found you another tutor?"

I sit up and resist the urge to sigh again. "Yes and yes. I felt terrible when he told me about her brother, but he didn't offer any details. There was a mix-up at first, so it was kind of confusing. He had my name all garbled because she gave it to him over the phone, but we got that figured out, and then we sat down at a table and he helped me get caught up."

"Wait. I thought he was sadistic."

"He is."

"But . . . he helped you?"

"Oh yeah. He's really good at it—using terms I understand and making sense of all the stupid jargon."

"And that's somehow sadistic?"

I get up from the table and open the freezer, pulling out some taquitos and preheating the oven. "It was weird, Ivy. I swear he was a complete social idiot when we were sorting out the mix-up, but when we were working on my math, he seemed pretty normal."

She folds her arms and squints at me. "So normal is sadistic?"

"No, it's just . . . the whole time he was helping me, I felt like he was really irritated about something, or maybe derisive."

"Did he laugh at you?" Her eyebrows shoot up like a dog's hackles.

"No," I say with a shake of my head to diffuse her protective instincts. Not even when he found out my backpack is named. "And he never said or did anything demeaning—you know I wouldn't have been able to concentrate if he had—but there was something in his eyes at times that made me wonder."

"Well, whatever it was, hopefully it's harmless enough to ignore through December." Ivy gives me a pointed look. "You are going to keep seeing him, right?"

"You make it sound like we're dating. But yes, we finalized everything."

"Longest relationship you've had in ages."

"Yeah. Too bad I have to pay him to stay in it."

Ivy's cheeks dimple beautifully as she smiles around her food, making me marvel for not the first time that no man has yet convinced her to take pity on him and settle down. Not that they haven't tried.

The oven beeps its readiness, so I pop my taquitos in, set a timer on my phone, and change the subject. "So," I say, "what's your good news?"

She swallows her mouthful of greens, and the dimples deepen along with her smile. "Guess who has a date for Friday night?"

"That's your good news?" First week of the semester, second week in our latest apartment, and already the vultures are circling. This is no surprise to me. If anything, it's a little late. "You always have a date."

"Not always! Besides, it isn't so much that I have a date but *who* it's with." She pokes at her salad for a few seconds before she continues. "Also, I asked *him*."

Now *that* is news. Between the dimples and the flowy hair and the elfin physique, Ivy is one of the lucky few girls who never has to beg for a date.

"You? Asked a guy out?"

"Yep."

"Who?"

"Remember the guy that led Bible study last week?"

My brain flips through faces from the Christian singles group the local pastor has organized and comes up with a fuzzy picture of a fairly nerdy, stocky guy. Sort of cute, but Ivy typically scores dates with the super attractive guys all the other girls—myself, I reluctantly admit, occasionally included—are unsuccessfully chasing. This guy is seriously average-looking.

"Uh, yeah. Blond?"

Ivy sees through my lame attempt at excitement. "His name is Dave Sapir, and he's very nice, so stop looking at me like I'm an alien."

I wipe the shock off my face and try to imagine Dave as someone I would be excited about dating. "So how did this come about? I didn't think you knew each other."

"Well, yesterday after lunch, I ran into him at the bookstore and told him how much I enjoyed his insights on Sunday, and we talked for a bit. And then he said he had to get going and I told him I was going home, too, so we walked together. He lives in the Moore Apartments—"

"As in '*Less* is Moore'?"

She completely ignores the reference to our running slight on the extremely rundown complex that borders ours. She's also refusing to look at me as she hastily clears her meal. Interesting.

"I mentioned having to attend the musical Friday," she continues, "and he seemed interested, so I asked him if he'd like to come."

Ivy throws away her trash and leans against the counter, drawing some much-needed air and meeting my eyes with what appears to be a request for approval. From me? This is new. As picky as she is about guys, anyone she's this interested in must be amazing. Far be it for me to object.

"That's great! I'm assuming he accepted?"

She nods, smiles bigger.

Very interesting.

Chapter 4

SWING

THE NEXT DAY I'M STUFFING my notebook back into Trusty after another incomprehensible math lecture when Ivy's text buzzes.

Ivy: *Help!*

Me: *What's up?*

Ivy: *This date is freaking me out. Double me?*

Good grief. *I hate musicals*, I remind her.

My phone buzzes with an incoming call as I'm walking out of the lecture hall. I'm expecting Ivy, but it's my mom. Maybe she can save me.

"Hey, Mom!" I say, exiting the building and finding a bit of shade under a cluster of aspens.

"Gracie, darlin'," she says, the lilt of her Southern accent bringing a smile to my face. "How are you? Did I catch you at a bad time?"

"I have a minute," I say. "What's up?"

She gives me a rundown on my brothers and Claire, including my three-year-old niece, Ava's, latest antics with her new baby brother.

"Maybe I'll come home this weekend," I say, thinking that would be a great way to avoid Ivy's musical setup torture.

"I'd love that," she says, "but we're headed to Durango for Kaden's football game—you know how Zach loves to go and watch. Another weekend?"

"That works. How's Kaden doing?" I ask.

"Oh, you know," she says, "he doesn't play much, but he enjoys it while he's waiting for basketball season."

"Good friends?" I ask, the question loaded. I really should reach out to him more.

"He's doin' just fine." Her gentle tone reassures me more than her words, and I blink away the sting in my eyes. I hear my dad calling to her in the background. "Looks like your dad's home for lunch. You want to say hi?"

"Nah, I need to get to class," I say, "but give him a hug for me."

Another text from Ivy buzzes in as we say goodbye, and I gladly trade the worry triggered by Mom's phone call for irritation with Ivy. It's not like I have a boyfriend I can hoodwink into being my plus-one for this stupid musical. She's asking for the moon and she knows it, but I can already feel myself giving in. Still, I open her text with no small amount of annoyance.

Ivy: *I'll buy the tickets. And I'll find your date*, she adds, as if she's reading my mind.

Me: *I hate setups more than musicals.*

Ivy: *I know. And with good reason.* ☺ *But you gotta move on someday. Please, please, please, Grace. I need you! Maybe one of Dave's roommates? I'll make sure he knows it's casual, friends, no pressure.*

I'm trying to formulate a sufficiently caustic reply without resorting to profanity when another text comes through.

Ivy: *And ice cream. I'll get you your own pint to consume as post-date therapy.*
Me: *Häagen-Dazs?*
Ivy: *Does Grace eat any other?*
Me: **Sigh* . . . Okay, I'm in.*

She sends me an entire screen of happy faces, and though I'm happy to help her, I wish it could be in some other, less painful way. Like maybe I could donate a kidney. Or a leg. Anything but another setup.

I use every moment of the half hour I have to get to the community golf course adjacent to campus, strolling between the buildings and savoring the fresh air as I wait to cross the street. It's a warm day for mid-September, puffy clouds in an azure sky setting off the mountains and the changing leaves. It's therapeutic, as it always is when I'm outdoors, but it isn't enough.

Meandering through the dark wood-paneled interior of the clubhouse to the storage room set aside for our use, I grab my clubs and lug them out to the driving range. I squeeze into one of two remaining spots and start hitting balls, but I'm so worried about Ivy finding me a date and my currently failing math grade that my swing is off for most of class. This triggers several odd looks from instructor Ethan. My swing, while not stellar, is usually consistent.

"Everything okay?" he asks, taking a minute to check on me. Normally, he spends all his time with the novices.

I straighten from my stance and lean on my driver, free hand on my hip. "Lots on my mind today."

He smiles knowingly and settles onto his heels, wrapping his long arms around his clipboard. "It's a mental game. Want to talk about it?"

"It's nothing," I say, not wanting him to go therapist on my game. Or my life. "Really."

"Okay, but sometimes talking can loosen up your swing."

I lift one eyebrow, trying not to be taken in by his attention and height and general attractiveness. This is about golf. Just golf.

"What's bugging you?" he prods.

I sigh and figure I've got nothing to lose. Every ball I've hit today would have been two fairways over if we weren't on the driving range. "My roommate needs me to double with her Friday, but I don't have a date, so she's going to find me one, and I absolutely hate setups. Plus we're going to a musical, which I also hate, and my math class is stressing me out." I tilt my head and dare him to fix my problems.

He chuckles and adjusts the crisp visor that's shading his blue eyes. "I don't think I can help you with the math."

I mumble a few incomprehensible words conveying my love for the subject and ease back into my stance, drawing another laugh from him.

"But . . . as I have just been notified that my Friday plans are toast, and as I also hate musicals . . . I could accompany you tomorrow night."

I look up and he's fully smirking at me. Is he joking?

"It would be a purely professional arrangement." He goes mock-serious. "I feel it my duty, as your golf instructor, to help you conquer the mental element of the game."

"By sitting through a stupid musical?"

"We could have a competition to see who can pretend to enjoy the show most while simultaneously being the most miserable."

Who is this guy? I've only talked to him a few times, and only in class, but he seems pretty laid back. I mean, he's a golf instructor, so he must be fairly chill, right? I'm smiling in spite of myself.

He does a little bow with his head. "I pride myself on going the extra mile for my students. What do you say?"

Would I rather take this offer or have Ivy beg a date for me on the street? No contest. "I wouldn't want my game to suffer."

His smile broadens. "Then it's a . . . not a date, because I can't date students, you know . . . how about 'appointment'?"

"Perfect," I say. And it is. No pressure. No expectations.

"Now, let's see that swing."

When class is over, I drive across town to the elementary school where I volunteer in an after-school program twice a week. I'm impatient to share my news with Ivy, but I can't call because she's still in class and texting would take too long. The kids deserve my full attention while I'm here. Not that they'd accept anything less.

Jace nearly bowls me over with a lightning-fast around-the-waist hug when I walk into the classroom.

"What's up, man?" I ask him, but he's already past greetings, pulling me toward his desk.

He sits down and points me into the adjacent chair. "Mrs. Harris said if I finish this paper, you'll shoot hoops with me."

I glance at the teacher who runs the program, a tiny woman with a gorgeous halo of curly white-gray hair against her dark skin.

Mrs. Harris narrows her eyes at him. "Only if . . . ?" she prompts.

"If Ms. Ebert is willing," he says in a decidedly practiced cadence.

His teacher humphs. "And?"

Jace sighs, then squares his rounded shoulders, presents me with a striving-for-angelic smile, and asks, "Ms. Ebert, will you help me with my—"

"*Please,*" Mrs. Harris insists.

"—*please* help me with my paper and play basketball after?" He breaks eye contact with me long enough to see the nod of approval from Mrs. Harris.

"I would love to. Let's see what you have."

The worksheet Jace shoves my way is unmarked. He offers me a pencil, and I'm reminded how much I wanted my own tutor to do my work for me.

"Not my job," I say, hands up. "Dig in."

The face he pulls looks like the one I use when taking out the overripe trash. He fiddles with the pencil, glaring down at the page.

"Did you know I have someone who helps me with my math in college?" I say.

That perks him right up. "You need help with math?"

Ah, the faith of a child. If only I could muster one-tenth that amount of confidence in my math skills. "Sure," I say. "Everyone has things they're really good at and other stuff they need some help with."

Jace mulls that over for a minute. "You'll play ball when I'm finished?"

"I'm here for the hoops, bro. And the sooner you're done with English—"

"The longer we play!" he finishes for me, diving right into his work.

My time at the school flies by. Jace completes his homework with plenty of time left to beat me and several of the other kids soundly in a game of HORSE before parents start showing up. Once the kids have filtered back home and my shift is over, I send a text to Ivy before I start my drive home: *Don't bother getting me a date.*

She text-bombs me the entire way home, but I don't bother responding. Let her stew on it for ten minutes. Serves her right.

She gives up the texting and actually calls me as I approach the front door, but I don't answer. Instead I holler a cheery, "Honey, I'm home!" as I walk in, and she bowls me over with her distress before the door has closed.

"Is your phone dead? Why aren't you answering my texts? Please, please don't bail on me!"

"Don't freak out," I say, hanging Trusty on my hook by the door and aiming for the kitchen. "I'm coming."

"What? You said not to get you a date. Don't you think it'll be awkward if it's just the three of us?"

"Your faith in my abilities is astounding," I say, rummaging in the freezer.

"You found your own date?"

"Always with the surprise."

She backpedals. "It's not that you can't—you just usually . . . don't. And you're amazing! I don't know why they don't—"

An exaggerated eye roll around the freezer door cuts her off. "I was teasing, not asking for validation. Anyway . . . I have a date. Except, not a date, but I'm bringing someone. Or meeting him there. Or something."

"Huh?"

I've completely confused her now, so I have to recount the whole golf incident—somewhat embellished—while my pot pie spins in the microwave.

"Well, that's nice of him. Do you think he's interested?"

"Absolutely not. He made it abundantly clear that he can't date students, and that's fine with me. I'm much more comfortable with guys in a non-dating scenario."

Ivy weighs this and decides to agree. Sort of.

"But is he attractive?"

"Ivy, leave it. He's my instructor, so I couldn't date him if I wanted to. Which I don't."

"Definitely attractive."

Sometimes this girl drives me crazy. "He could be," I say. "Possibly. But that's not how it is, so I'm just going to pretend he's my golf buddy—which he is, sort of—and leave it at that."

She smirks in triumph, so I steer her toward our couch and turn the tables. "Now, tell me why my dating-queen roommate is all worked up about a simple first date."

Though Ivy refuses to admit anything, she takes the hint and stops pressuring me about Ethan. Thank heaven. I'm having enough trouble managing my expectations as it is.

Chapter 5

SUPER

I'VE WORKED IT OUT WITH Ethan to meet at my apartment so we can all drive to the show together. Ivy is seriously nervous—which never happens—but no matter how hard I press, she won't say anything more about Dave. All I can figure is that she might actually like this guy.

Promptly at 6:15 there's a knock on our door, and I am unceremoniously shoved toward the stairs as Ivy bolts back into her room. Like water on a duck, I let her nerves wash off me and slowly descend our town-house stairs to the front door. We wouldn't want them to think we're anxious.

Dave is about like I remember from church, and I wonder again what has Ivy so uptight, but she's back out of her room before Dave has accepted my invitation to come in. "Hey, Dave," she says, cranking up the charm. "Thanks again for coming with us."

"Oh, no problem." His oblivion knows no bounds. "Everyone in my family sings, so I've been to plenty of musicals. What is it tonight?"

With that they launch into a discussion of song and dance that is the camping equivalent of hiking the entire Pacific Coast Trail. I have no idea what they're talking about—partially because I avoid musicals like algebra but mostly because I'm too busy watching the nonverbal communication. Dave is confident, pleased to be here, and engaged in the conversation, but there are two glaring differences from Ivy's usual dates. First, he seems completely indifferent to her appearance. And second, she is seriously affected by his. She tends to bowl over most males of our acquaintance with her gorgeousness, so I'm amazed that Dave seems unaffected by her auburn waves, tiny waist, and shapely legs—not to mention the knockout smile and the almost hungry look in her emerald eyes.

That's different. She rarely gives her dates a second look—and, believe me, they're always worth looking at—but with Dave she can't look anywhere else. She is laughing with him, checking out his hair and shoulders, offering him a seat on the couch next to her.

And, apparently, I'm gawking, because now Ivy's giving me a strange look and so is Dave.

"Are you going to get the door?" Ivy asks me.

Did someone knock? "Yes. Definitely getting the door." I am rewarded for my intuitiveness with a tall, blond, handsome Ethan at the door wearing his usual golfish attire and a rather attractive smirk.

"Are you ready for this?" he asks.

"As I'll ever be," I say, thinking to myself that the no-dating-students rule is a gift I'll happily embrace in lieu of the awkwardness that would be plaguing me otherwise, especially considering the enticingly subtle smell of his cologne.

The evening passes with relative ease, Ivy and Dave enthralled by our college theater company's production of *Mary Poppins* while Ethan and I pretend to be. Honestly, *pretending* to like the show almost makes me enjoy it, even though the musical numbers drag the story out for way too long and have me glancing at my watch in spite of the pleasant company.

Ivy and Dave want ice cream after the show, but as that feels a bit too date-like, we have them drop us back at my apartment before they go. Ethan sees me to my door with his best Bert impression, singing "It's a jolly holiday with Gracie" on a hitherto unknown melody.

"I think you should consider a career in musical theater," I tease through my laughter.

"Really?" He gives up the song and leans against the side of my building. "Just when I was starting to get comfortable with golf."

"This could be your true calling. You don't want to miss the boat."

"Maybe I could just do it as a hobby."

"Whatever you decide, I'm sure the stage is your destiny."

He laughs a deep belly laugh, and the outside lights sparkle in his blue eyes. The comfort I've taken in the no-dating rule dissolves in an instant, and I'm suddenly anxious to be inside before I do or say something that crosses the line.

"Hey, so," I say, "I really appreciate you doing this."

"My pleasure." He brushes off my thanks and looks into my eyes, his smile settling into a smolder worthy of Flynn Rider.

For half a second, I wonder . . .

Then he walks away.

I choose to keep smiling, refusing to allow one half-second's lapse in mental discipline to ruin the most enjoyable evening of musical theater I've ever experienced—the most enjoyable evening I've had in a long time, period.

Inside the apartment, I trade my jeans and sweater for leggings and a hoodie and retrieve my reward from the freezer.

I'm sitting at the table, numbing my mouth and mind with Häagen-Dazs cookies and cream when I hear voices at the door. I'm considering whether I should remove myself to my bedroom when Ivy slips inside with a happy sounding "Good night" and promptly slides to the floor, beaming.

The ice cream has recovered me enough from my non-date that she doesn't notice I might be crushing on my golf instructor. Or maybe she's too preoccupied with her own sunshine.

"Did he kiss you?" I am nothing if not subtle.

Ivy scoffs but keeps the smile. "No, thank heaven. That would have ruined everything."

I'd wondered if her interest in Dave would loosen her no-kissing-on-the-first-date policy. Apparently not. A contented sigh floats her up the stairs to her room, leaving me alone at the table with my ice cream and my thoughts.

Chapter 6

SLIDE

I'M A LITTLE KEYED-UP WHEN my next golf class approaches, trying to crush the crush that's strategically assaulting the no-dating-teachers barrier. While my more reasonable half knows Ethan fits squarely in the No zone, the lonely/silly/hopeful half keeps lobbing thoughts like, *Class only lasts half a semester* and *But you're the same age* and *What are they going to do, kick you out? It's your last semester!*

That last one makes me laugh—until I remember the math quiz I failed yesterday. The sobering fact that I might actually *require* another semester reinforces the seawall I'm constructing against the threat of Ethan's charm. Risking my graduation on a silly crush would be beyond stupid. I can appreciate his attention without getting attached.

Right?

I mentally smack myself in the forehead—I don't want to make a spectacle as I arrive at the driving range—and hope the effect is sufficient to keep my barrier intact.

It's not unusual that Ethan isn't here before class starts, so I grab my driver and start swinging, enjoying the heat on my back and the intermittent pings and thwacks of irons and woods around me. At five after the hour, he still hasn't arrived. Surveying the area while I'm teeing up another ball, I notice a middle-aged woman coming our way. It's like she's walked straight out of the framed picture in the clubhouse—the one right next to the plaque bearing the name Patti Johnson and the list of top finishes she had on the LPGA tour.

"I'm Patti," she says as if we didn't know. "Sorry I'm late—got stuck on a phone call."

"Where's Ethan?" the girl to my left—the same girl who needed Ethan's extensive help last week with her grip and swing—asks, looking and sounding like someone stole her puppy. Maybe if she hadn't been batting her eyelashes so forcefully, she would have hit the ball more than half the time. I should think of her as a woman, but honestly, she looks a little young for my brother Kaden—and he's not quite done with high school. Anyway, I'm thankful she asks before I can make a similar fool of myself.

"Tournament this week in Phoenix. He'll be back Monday." Patti says this with a compassionate smirk at Eyelashes—who, I remind myself, I need to make an effort to get to know. Her name would be a good start. Patti clearly understands and doesn't seem to mind that she is the second-choice instructor, which makes me instantly like her. "Get out your 7-iron and let's see where we are."

We spend the whole hour with that club, Patti moving efficiently from student to student, making suggestions and small corrections and offering encouragement. She really is a golf genius. I should be thrilled at the prospect of semiprivate lessons with her for the rest of the week, and a part of me is. A very small part. Which forces me to admit that the sturdy barrier I've been building against Ethan's charm is more like one of those bead curtains from the 1970s—and that my enjoyment of this class thus far has more to do with Ethan than the course itself.

Is it shallow of me to miss his attention? Whether or not it is, I do miss it. Him?

Irritation—with Ethan for not mentioning his upcoming absence, with myself for caring—dogs me all the way to math lab and mixes with an increasingly realistic fear of failure in math. Not, perhaps, the best mindset to promote learning.

Noah waits at the same table as last week. "How was the quiz?" he asks.

"Super!" I say, pushing false cheer through my irritation as I open my laptop and log in. "I was nearly perfect!"

His expression lifts like he's surprised I did so well, which fuels the fire. I pull up the file and turn my screen so he can see the carnage for himself, watching as his brows sink from mild surprise into a deep furrow of confusion. "Perfect? This is awful."

"Yeah, well," I say, tightening my grip on the emotional reins as my irritation slides toward anger, "I somehow managed to get the last question right and ruin the perfect zero, but it's hard to be sure with true and false."

The furrow stays, though his confusion morphs into something else. He doesn't say anything.

"That was called *sarcasm*," I say, my voice dripping with it. "I didn't *actually* intend to get a zero, or I would have answered false on the last one."

He doesn't even flinch. "So what happened with the rest?"

"No idea," I say, my comfortable blanket of sarcasm slipping. "I thought I did pretty well, considering my panic."

"Why would you panic?" he asks, as if I actually meant to.

"I don't know," I say, dangerously close to dissolving into tears as I dig my fingernails into my palms, focusing on the bite of pain. Must. Stay. Mad.

Either he doesn't notice my instability, or he ignores it. "Well, let's go through it and see what happened."

We rework all the questions and find each mistake—stupid things like missed negative signs and transcription errors. It's ridiculous, and I no longer have to struggle to maintain irritation. I *do* know this stuff.

"The good news is I can see that you understood the concepts. You just need to be more careful."

I scoff. "And the bad news?"

"The bad news is . . . you're out of second chances. You'll need to average above a C on everything else to pass."

I'm sliding again, straight past anger and into despair.

"You can give up now."

My slide comes to a halt. Only *I* am allowed to disparage my abilities. He's actually being *paid* to help me, and he wants me to give up? I take a deep breath of the math lab–scented air, ready to tell him off.

"Or you can get to work." He leans back in his chair and crosses his arms, a challenge in his eyes. "Your call."

I glare at him, but his flat expression holds. Is he using reverse psychology? Appealing to my competitive nature? Or does he really want me to give up and walk out? My opinion leans to the last option, but the competitor in me won't give up. Whatever his motive, my downward spiral has screeched to a stop, and I figure I'll have to concede the staring match if we're going to get anything done.

"Fine," I say, snatching my laptop away from him and pulling up today's assignment.

Betraying neither dismay nor satisfaction, Noah sits forward and we get to work, slogging through problems until he's satisfied I won't embarrass myself again on the next quiz. My emotions are steadier when we've finished, probably because my brain is fried.

"So," I say, not ready to thank him for his heavy-handed methods but willing to admit they worked with a conversational peace offering. "How was your weekend?"

He looks at me like I've asked if I can chew on his shoe. "It was fine," he says.

"I was thinking about going home," I say, closing my laptop and loading it into Trusty, "but my brother Kaden—he's a senior—had an away game and they decided to make a trip out of it."

Noah doesn't offer anything in return, just sits there with his mouth in a thin line, which makes mine take off like he's asked for a full rundown of the clan.

"And then there's Zach. He's twelve, and I think he took all the math genes. He could do this in his sleep," I say, picking up this week's assignment and tucking it into my bag. "Do you have siblings?"

"I gotta go," he says, picking up his stuff and bolting out of the room.

Alrighty then.

Chapter 7

CAPRICE

THE WEEK WITHOUT ETHAN PASSES slowly, and another typically lackluster weekend crawls into Monday with sluglike constancy. The excess free time my empty calendar presented—thanks to Ivy abandoning me to "study" with Dave and another away game for Kaden—eventually convinced me to spend some time reworking math problems in preparation for the next quiz. It only took me a hundred tries each to be able to work through them without referring back to Noah's step-by-step instructions. Even with the extra practice, I'm a hot mess of nerves when I get to the cavernous lecture hall.

"Please leave at least one empty seat between yourself and others," my professor says, her expression stern. Though she's never asked this of us before, we all comply.

There's a touch of anger in her voice as she continues. "Several of your classmates cheated last time, so we'll be doing things the old-fashioned way from now on. They won't be rejoining us. There are several versions of the quiz, so don't bother trying to see what your neighbor is doing." She takes a moment to level us all with a glare. "Any instance of cheating will earn that student an immediate fail. My TAs and I will be watching." Her cheeks lift briefly in a thin smile, but only to facilitate the death rays coming from her eyes.

A bead of sweat dribbles its way down my spine, the hard plastic auditorium chair squeaking in protest as I try to get comfortable and drawing several sets of proctoring eyes. Awesome. I pull the spiral hair tie off my wrist and contain my mass of curls in a fruitless effort to restore brain function. All I can think about in the silence is how *not* to appear like I'm cheating. The fact that I'm not—never intended to—matters as little as my not being a terrorist when I go through airport security; innocent or not, the angst is real.

I can barely read the stupid numbers on the page, and my handwriting looks like a five-year-old's, but I soldier my way through the problems. It helps that several of them are structured exactly like the ones I worked over the weekend. Checking and double-checking my steps, I look for stupid mistakes like I made last time, but don't find any. Either I've done well or I'm too dumb to catch my own errors. Too soon the quizzes are collected and my professor starts explaining the next concept, but the lecture flies over my addled brain.

Noah won't be pleased.

Even the mostly sunny sky and the smell of fresh-cut grass as I walk to the golf course don't dispel the pit in my stomach. What if I bombed again? Mechanically, I retrieve my clubs, check the whiteboard for today's location, and head to the practice green. Did I just guarantee myself a solid fail? Hope dwindling, I'm caught off guard when Ethan looks up from helping another student and sends what feels like a flirtatious grin my way. I smile back, and he holds my gaze for several counts longer than instructorly interest would dictate. My smile deepens, and I notice my stress levels inch down a hair. It feels good to see him again.

We're working on long rolls and hitting out of the bunkers today, and that protracted eye contact has me wishing I had him to myself. Anticipation provides a nice distraction from more serious matters, but class is half spent before he comes my way. I spot him in my peripheral vision, clipboard held to his lean chest, while I'm lining up a long putt on the green. My heart rate climbs in a much more pleasant way than it does in math, and I sink the shot.

"Looking good," he says, obviously talking about my putt, though his tone convinces my hormones otherwise. He holds my eyes, navigating toward me without walking into anyone's line.

I smile back, soaking up the attention while admiring his stride and debating what to say, to flirt or not to flirt. He passes close enough to brush my shoulder. The slight contact sends a flutter of awareness down my arm before he moves on to the next student, leaving me with only the slightest hint of his cologne.

Well.

It's our only direct interaction during the whole class. My golf game has plenty of room for improvement, so his inattention leads me to believe that I imagined any romantic interest on his part. I've almost convinced myself, until he catches my eye as I'm leaving.

He stokes his smolder and turns his full attention to me. "See you tomorrow," he says like he can't wait.

So maybe not imagined?

Ethan's mixed signals are similarly confusing on Tuesday, and it takes my entire walk from golf to math lab to squash the flutters and remind myself he isn't really interested.

Unless he is.

A grumble of frustration escapes as I yank open the math lab door.

Noah greets me from his usual chair with a raised eyebrow. "Score?" he asks.

Deep in rumination on the caprice of men, I wonder briefly if he's referencing my love life. "I'm not . . . what?" I say, buying time for my thoughts to switch from romance—or the lack thereof—to logic.

Annoyance flashes briefly in his eyes, but I find my feet before he can chew me out for not being invested in my academics or any of the other obnoxious things about me I can see swirling behind his cold front.

"Oh, the quiz," I say. "I don't think they've posted scores, but I'll check." This is only a tiny blurring of the truth that I haven't yet dared to look. His finger taps a moderate tempo against the tabletop as I log in and find the newly posted pitiful score, along with an image of the graded quiz. Someone bled all over mine. To cover my disappointment I'm about to make a wisecrack about how I more than doubled my score from the last one, but that tapping finger warns me against it. I swallow a sigh and turn my screen so he can see.

"Hmm," he says, more puzzled than disappointed. "Why is this on paper? Wasn't the first online?"

"Some people cheated," I answer, thankful for the aside. "She told us they wouldn't be coming back and said she'd fail anyone else who got caught."

His chin lifts a hair. "And how did you take that?"

"How do you think I took it? I can't afford to fail this class just because one of her TAs thinks I'm cheating. I freaked out!"

"Ah," he says, as if this explains everything. He taps a few more times for good measure. "Do you know any breathing exercises?"

I scoff. "Of course I do." He knows my major. It may say *recreation*, but it's mostly about therapy. Why would he— "Oh."

He nods, know-it-all that he is, when he sees I've made the connection. Every therapist needs a therapist indeed. I just didn't think Noah was the type to appreciate that kind of thing.

"I *panicked*," I say, understanding the truth as I speak it. "Both times, completely destroying any chance I had at clear thinking."

"So?" he says, allowing me to write my own prescription.

"So next time I calm myself down before I start the quiz, and maybe I won't be such a screwup."

He frowns a bit at my phrasing but doesn't comment.

"Do I still have a chance at passing?" I ask. Much as I want to pass, there's no point in trying if it isn't numerically possible.

He references the scoring rubric in my syllabus and does a few calculations. "It's possible, but every point matters. You'll need near-perfect scores on all your assignments and above-average scores on the rest of the assessments."

There's no need to worry about the assignments since Noah checks everything before I turn it in. As for the assessments, above average shouldn't sound so hard, but considering I'm currently hovering around 30 percent . . .

"So?" he asks again.

I meet his eyes, surprised to see a different hardness there, like maybe he actually thinks I can do this and doesn't want me to give up.

"Let's get to work," I say.

He doesn't nod, doesn't tell me I'm a good soldier, but there's something in his expression that I find encouraging. We attack the quiz, diving into the little mistakes and how not to make them, and then he explains the incomprehensible lecture in language that actually makes today's assignment seem simple. Too bad for everyone else that he isn't teaching the class.

"You're a really good teacher," I say, putting my laptop away and shouldering my backpack. "Is that what you're going into?"

He freezes, and his expression—a mixture of confusion and distaste—reminds me so much of that first day in the lab that I nearly laugh out loud. We worked so well together today that I nearly forgot how socially awkward he can be.

"Accounting," he says, his posture like a deer in the headlights.

I save him from having to bolt again by leaving first. He's still sitting there when I reach the door and turn to wave goodbye.

Chapter 8

TERRIBLE TUESDAY

"Why do we have to name the days of the week?"

Ivy squints at me like I'm the loon I am.

"Seriously, it carries either a stigma or a basketful of unrealistic expectations." I toss Trusty onto the couch and continue walking to the far end of our tiny living room, where I am forced to reverse right as I'm hitting my stride.

"Is this going to be an extended rant?" she asks, looking up from one of several textbooks surrounding her.

I ignore her and keep talking. And pacing. "Wednesday, for example. Hump day! So pretentious! Just because it's the middle of the week, I'm supposed to have a much better day? Whatever."

Ivy sets aside her textbook and settles into the cushions without comment, her eyes following me as I wear a runway into the brownish carpet.

"Thursday: exciting only because it is the day before Friday. Friday and Saturday? I'm supposed to look forward to them all week long, but mostly I dread their lofty, unfulfilled expectations."

Her nod registers in my periphery.

"Sunday is fine, I suppose, but there's always Monday, dread of dreads, looming on the horizon, so Sunday night is awful."

I pause my pacing to look out our back windows onto the central courtyard of our apartment complex. There's nothing happening out there except a few colorful leaves fluttering down in the still sunshine. It doesn't *look* like an awful day. How deceptive.

When I turn back around, Ivy's arched eyebrows accost me. "Are you going somewhere with this? Because I have a huge paper due this week. Do you actually require attention, or can I get back to work and throw you an occasional mm-hmm?"

Flopping down next to Trusty, I get to the root of my problem. "I used to *like* Tuesdays. No pressure of a looming week or an empty weekend. Such an unassuming and underrated day."

"You've given this some thought."

"Shunned by the weekend, overshadowed by gloomy Monday, ignored by hump day. I always enjoyed a humble Tuesday."

"Past tense?" she asks.

I nod my confirmation. "Now Tuesday is worse than Monday. It's like . . . the day of terrible, torturous torment."

"Ah, I see where you're going with your fancy alliteration skills. Tutoring day, isn't it?"

"Yeah." Joking aside, it's all I can do to keep from tearing up. "It's terrible Tuesday."

"It can't be that bad," she says.

It is. Three weeks have passed, and I'm still within an inch of failing the only class I have to pass. I did okay on the last quiz, but those early scores have left me no wiggle room.

I *hate* math.

Ivy reads my thoughts and moves from her couch to mine. "Aw, Lou." I must look pitiful for her to stoop to using my childhood nickname. We didn't even know each other as kids. "Are you lost?"

"No," I say. "Noah's really good at figuring out where I don't understand things and helping me see them in ways that make sense." So good I've started using some of his methods when I'm volunteering. I've even been able to help some of the kids with their math, of all things.

"But?" Ivy says.

Sigh. "My math midterm is Friday."

"And you're not ready?"

"He says I am. But I don't feel like it." I grimace against the root of my problem. "What if I don't pass, Ivy? What if, even with all this help, I freak out and bomb it like I did on those quizzes? I've wasted years of my life and my parents' money pursuing a degree that I can't finish because I'm a math idiot."

"Did you tell Noah you don't feel ready?"

I scoff. "I'm not allowed to *feel* in there. He's like the coach from that women's baseball movie. There's no crying in math lab! I'm pretty sure he would refuse to tutor me anymore if I stopped doing exactly what he says like a little soldier. I don't think he even has emotions. Or a life outside of his equations."

Ivy stifles her laughter. "Why is that?"

"We've been meeting for, what? Seven weeks?"

She shrugs.

"Seven weeks, and I know nothing more about him than I learned the first day."

"Why?"

"He refuses to talk about anything but math!"

"Isn't that what you're paying him for?"

"Ha. My mother is paying him."

"So ask him some questions."

"Believe me, I've tried. I asked him what brought him to Oak Hills, and he said, 'Scholarship. You missed a significant figure on problem four.'"

"Hmm," Ivy says, holding back a laugh.

"Also, I don't think he can stand me."

"Oh, come on. Everyone likes you." She gives my shoulder a squeeze. "You're the fun friend, always game for anything, even when you hate it."

"Except math. And that's apparently the only language he speaks. Remarkably well, but still. Any time I mention anything about myself or anything nonmathematical or ask him about himself, he clams up and gets all awkward like he was on that first day. It's weird."

"Is he married? Maybe he's uncomfortable tutoring a woman."

"No idea. I don't think so. No ring, but you never know if a guy's just not wearing one."

"Maybe he's engaged or has a girlfriend. Wait, I know. What if he's attracted to you and doesn't know how to deal with it?"

Finally, Ivy has struck on a theme that brings me out of my doldrums. I can't stop laughing. "Attracted? To me?" I shake my head. "He's a robot. I mean, maybe if *you* walked in, he might react. But I'm just a source of income, and a distasteful one at that."

"Distasteful?" she says, her voice reflecting the flavor of the word.

"I get the feeling he only agreed to the tutoring as a favor for Lupe. Tragic circumstances and all that."

"Does he have other students?"

I shrug. "I told you—we talk of nothing but my assignments."

"Huh." Ivy finally grasps the futility of this thread and changes tack. "Didn't you golf today too? Was Ethan there? Is your swing off again?"

"Ethan was there, and my swing is fine. Well, as fine as it will ever be, considering this is our last week of class."

"Did he . . . ?" She leaves the question hanging, but I know what she's getting at.

"You know he can't ask me out, even if he wants to." At least, not until our class is finished. Several semiflirtatious comments he aimed my way today beg for my attention, but he dishes it out to every female in the class. "He's entertaining, but I seriously doubt he has any genuine interest."

"But your class is almost over, so . . ."

"That only means Tuesdays just got worse. After this week, I won't even have golf to distract me." Or Ethan.

Ivy's phone chimes, and she grins as she checks it.

"Dave?" I ask.

She nods absently, thumbs flying.

"Did he kiss you yet?"

She frowns and keeps texting.

"Hold your hand?"

Her phone slaps into the couch and she faces me. "It's not like that. We're just friends."

They might be, but I can't help teasing her. I've never seen her like this with a guy. Or a guy like this about her. Maybe they *are* just friends. All I know is that Ivy is happier when she's with him or texting him or talking about him. Guys usually just make her irritable.

Weird.

The thing is, if they're just friends, why is she spending so much time with him and so little time with me?

Chapter 9

DODGE

COOL AUTUMN SUNLIGHT DANCES ALONG the western horizon as I put on my jacket and step out of the university's building of centralized torture—otherwise known as the testing center—and back into the real world.

I can't believe it.

I cannot believe what just happened. The slip of paper in my hand is tangible proof, but I'm in shock.

I passed my math midterm!

More than passed.

I look again at my 80 percent and laugh out loud. I still have to score well on everything that remains in order to pass the class, but I'm more excited about this B minus than I've ever been about an A in any other class. The burst of energy and relief has me wanting to twirl, dance, run, maybe even sing my way down the long bank of stairs that leads off campus. I'm reassessing my skepticism about musicals when I indulge in a little twirl that sends me right into someone coming the other way.

"Sorry!" I say, laughing even more when I see that it's Ethan that I've nearly bowled over. He catches me by the waist and keeps us both from falling, laughing with me and holding me closer than strictly necessary.

"What's got you so happy?"

"I got an eighty on my math midterm!"

"That's cause for celebration!" he says, pulling me even closer. "What should we do?"

I chuckle and lift a brow at his forwardness. "We?"

He nods flirtatiously, reminding me that our last class was yesterday and sending a different kind of thrill through me.

"Aren't you going somewhere?" I give a meaningful tug on his backpack.

"Nowhere important." He does a one-eighty and takes my hand, leading me down the stairs. "Have you eaten?"

With that, Ethan whisks me away. His car—a nice one—is waiting in the parking lot at the bottom, and he keeps my hand until he opens the passenger door and sees me safely seated.

He keeps me laughing all the way to a fast-casual restaurant, feeds my ego throughout the meal, and touches me at every opportunity. Elbow, hand, waist, hair. I can't remember the last time I received so much attention. It's intoxicating enough to squash the niggle of hesitation supplied by the more logical part of my brain.

After dinner he drives to an elementary school in a residential area east of campus and pushes me on probably the last existing really good elementary school swing in existence—a great hexagonal arrangement that dares me to reach my feet out and touch the top center ring at the height of my swing.

The sun has long since set and my hands are nearly numb when Ethan pulls me out of my swing and into a hug.

"This has been so fun!" I say, hugging him back. "Thank you for celebrating with me. I haven't felt this relaxed in ages."

"My pleasure," he says, and in a moment the friendly hug has morphed into something more. His hands move to my waist, and he pulls back a bit, his eyes dropping to my lips. I barely have time to question whether this is what I want before he leans in. My neck muscles decide for me, landing his lips squarely on my cheek.

Awkward.

"Ouch," he says, pulling back with a grimace. "A swing and a miss. Did I read that wrong?"

"Ethan, I'm sorry." I don't know how to explain this thing that I don't understand yet myself, but maybe it has something to do with watching Ivy and Dave's friendship grow—without the physical aspect to confuse or rush things.

Ethan's still holding me, though the romance of the moment is gone. "What are we doing here?" I ask.

"I thought that was pretty obvious." He smirks at me, confidence unscathed. "I mean, it's just for fun, right?" His eyes drop briefly to my lips in question.

"I don't usually . . . kiss guys I'm not dating." I wince. "Are we dating?"

"Well, we went to dinner . . ."

I can't help but chuckle. He's incorrigible. "So we're dating now?" I say.

"Uh . . ."

"I didn't think so." I move out of his arms, and he looks worried.

"Grace, listen." He recaptures my hand to stop my retreat. "I didn't mean to . . . I thought you needed a pick-me-up."

"You were right." I give his hand a squeeze. "I did, and I appreciate you taking me to dinner, and I had a fantastic time—"

"But I took it a little too far." He sighs deeply, lets go of my hand to ruffle his stylishly messy hair, and manages to look sheepish. "Still friends?"

"Still friends," I say, and I mean it. Just not with benefits.

When I get back to the apartment, Ivy is worried out of her mind. "Where have you been? How was your test?"

I sigh and she assumes the worst.

"Maybe you can retake—"

"I got an eighty."

"What? That's fantastic!"

Her enthusiasm dies as I slink into the couch and close my eyes. "Why is that not fantastic?"

She's confused, so I relate the whole Ethan fiasco to her, and as I do, I realize why I couldn't let him kiss me. In spite of how enjoyable and entertaining it is to be around handsome, athletic, funny Ethan, he isn't the one I would have chosen to share the good news with.

I don't tell Ivy that, but the person I really wanted to share the good news with is a dark-haired, bespectacled, surly math guru.

Chapter 10

MENTAL TOUGHNESS

I'VE HAD THREE AND A half days to figure out what brand of insanity has me thinking I would prefer to share good news with Noah over Ethan, and the only rational conclusion I can come up with is that math has made me crazy. So instead of arithmophobia, I now have arithmomania. Or maybe both. I must be mathematically bipolar, because I have no other reason to want to share this news with Noah.

We aren't even friends.

Still, I feel remarkably mellow on my first terrible Tuesday without golf to bolster me through another tutoring session. My now-free hour between human development and tutoring is not long enough to do much, so I take advantage of the warmer-than-usual October afternoon and claim a sunny spot on the grass outside the math lab. Sitting against the trunk of a gorgeous maple, my jacket functioning as padding and insulation against the damp, I pull out my laptop and plug away at my life story—an assignment for my human-development class that I've been avoiding—until a shadow covers my screen.

"You're never early."

I resist the urge to look up at Noah's deep voice. "No more golf. It's a block class, and we finished up last week."

"Well, that should really reduce your load for the second block."

"Yeah, I'm pretty relieved." I shut my screen, grateful for another excuse to put off the life-story baggage, and start loading Trusty. "I mean, skills tests, all those rules, and trying to remember what the numbers on all those different clubs mean? Plus, adding up your strokes and figuring out which direction to go after each hole? It's been a struggle."

"I'm sure," he says, holding the door for me as we make our way into the building. "It's classes like that that give college a bad rap." Our eyes meet as I pass, and I swear the corner of his mouth lifts a little.

"Thanks," I say to his show of chivalry, not sure what to make of the banter.

He reverts right back to business. "How did the midterm go?"

"Well, I missed a couple of points on the essay about infancy, but I still got an A."

"Infancy?" His brows furrow.

"Oh," I say with a vapid smile. "Did you mean my *math* midterm?"

There's that tick in his scowl again. What would it take to get him to really smile—the kind that involves the entire face?

"I'll assume you did well since you aren't crying about it," he says.

"You really think I'd cry over math?" His expression tells me he knows I have, but I refuse to confirm it. "I would never. But since you know so much, why don't you tell me my score?"

His eyes narrow, unnerving me with their perceptiveness. "Based on your understanding of the material, I'd say you got a solid B, unless you panicked." He takes my silence for the confirmation that it is and motions for me to take a seat.

"No congratulations?" I'm shamelessly fishing, but I can't help myself.

"I knew you'd pass," he says in the same analytical tone he always employs during my lessons. "Do well, even, as long as you stayed calm. You knew the material. Besides," he adds, "you developed all that mental toughness in your golf class, so there was nearly zero chance of failure."

Mental toughness indeed. I can't help but smile, but Noah moves on without so much as a blink at his own joke.

"What questions do you have from Monday's lecture?" he asks.

He knew I wouldn't fail. I guess that's as close to congratulations as the phlegmatic Noah Jennings gets.

So why does that mean more to me than Ethan's exuberance?

Chapter 11

FRIENDBOY

THERE'S NOTHING WORSE THAN A roommate with a boyfriend. Even when he isn't really a boyfriend.

It's been more than a month since Ivy and Dave's first date, and I hardly see the girl anymore. Sure, she's at the apartment sometimes, but when she is, Dave is usually with her. He's even brought his guitar over a few times to play for Ivy, everything from Dan Fogelburg oldies and a few of his own compositions to the latest country hits, not that I would recognize them. Country isn't my thing, but if I had a guy singing to me like Dave does for Ivy, I'd consider adapting.

When she's not with him, she's studying hard to make up for time lost to her not-boyfriend. One would think they were committed, if it weren't for the fact that he hasn't even held her hand, let alone kissed her. I'm not sure who that's making crazier, me or Ivy. Not that she's said anything to me, but I can tell she's dying for some show of affection.

I've picked up some extra shifts volunteering with the after-school kids to fill the empty hours, but I'm getting desperate for company. So when I spot Ivy staring into space at the kitchen table on this Friday afternoon, I pounce. "Hey! Want to go see a movie?"

She startles out of her glazed stare and moves a hand to her idle laptop. "I should study."

Her phone buzzes, and she reads the text with a spreading smile, then jumps up and clears her things off the table.

"Where are you going?" I ask.

"Dave wants some help with a song he's working on."

"I thought you had to study."

"I said I *should* study. There's a difference. I can do that later."

I try not to feel frustrated at being passed over again for a friendboy. "What's up with you guys, anyway?"

"What do you mean?"

"I mean you're always together, and you don't date anyone else. Have you defined the relationship? Are you exclusive?"

Worry lines her forehead. "No. I mean, we're not even dating, really, so there's nothing to define. We're just friends."

"Just friends? I hardly see you anymore."

She flushes. "Dave doesn't like me that way."

"You're devoting a lot of time to a guy who only wants to be friends. Don't you want more than that?"

"Of course I want more than that!" she snaps.

Whoa. Ivy isn't a snapper. There's a glint in her expression that dims against my silence.

"I'm sorry." She sighs, plops back into her chair, and runs a hand through her untamed curls. "He doesn't find me attractive."

I'm dumbfounded. Ivy unattractive? Not possible. "If that's true, he's an idiot. Is he seeing someone else?"

"I don't know when he would."

I can certify that truth.

I think back on the last few times I've seen them together. Dave is always the gentleman, opening her doors and that kind of thing, and when they're together, they both light up. Maybe I need to do some sleuthing.

With another heavy sigh, Ivy gets up again. "It's whatever. I need to go get ready."

"Is he coming to pick you up?"

"Yeah. Let me know when he gets here?"

A plan takes shape as I agree. As soon as I hear the water running in the bathroom, I take up a post in the courtyard outside our apartment. Mr. Platonic shows up a few minutes later.

"Hey, Dave," I say.

He shares the smile he was already wearing and gives me a wave, slowing enough not to be rude but still making straight for our apartment.

"How's it going?" I ask.

He slows further with a glance at our door. It's obvious he'd rather be talking to Ivy than me, but he's polite enough to stay and answer. "Pretty good. You?"

"Not too shabby. Glad to have midterms over. Haven't seen much of Ivy lately though . . ."

His smile brightens. "Yeah, sorry about that."

He's not sorry. At all.

"So what's up with you two?"

"Up?" His eyes go shifty.

"I'm pretty much her family here, so I have to watch out for her. You know." I do a fake chuckle that he matches with a nervous one. "You like her?"

The panic is getting real, but he swallows and tries to cover. "Just friends. You know." He clears his throat and tosses another look at our door.

"Oh good," I say with another chuckle to ease his nerves as I move to the door. "I'm not ready to lose her to a boyfriend."

His relief is tangible, but his eyes are cautious. I take him into our living room and tell him I'll go check on Ivy, but just then I hear her coming out of the bathroom upstairs.

"Dave's here, Ivy," I holler, busying myself with tidying up the room to disguise my motives while I observe. He forgets about me as soon as he hears her voice.

"Hey, sorry. I'm almost ready—just looking for my keys," she says.

He watches her walk all the way down the stairs—mostly the toned calves showing below her capris, if I'm reading the angle of his eyes correctly. Right before she looks up from digging through her purse, he throws a wall of shutters in front of the appreciation in his eyes.

"Hey," he says with as much enthusiasm as most people reserve for a passing acquaintance.

"Hi!" She gives him a full smile, tosses her curls over her shoulder without artifice and searches her purse one more time.

His defenses take a major hit from her hair and perfume, but he recovers quickly. He glances my way to see if I've noticed, but I turn my back.

"I think your keys are over here." I fetch them from the kitchen and bring them to Ivy.

She thanks me on her way out the door that Dave has opened for her. He watches her go through, then casts a wary look at me.

I offer him a vacant smile, but I can see that he knows I'm not fooled. He's head over heels for my roommate.

Ivy's desertion leaves me antsy and irritable and alone. I could seek out some company, but the most recent additions to our complex are all fresh from the dorms. That doesn't sound promising as a solution for irritability, and thanks to my taking a year off for Peru, pretty much all of my close friends have moved on from the college scene. Since it looks like the *alone* portion of the equation is fixed, I'll have to do something to change the *antsy* and *irritable*.

New episodes of the series I'm addicted to won't be out for six months, and I have no desire to delve further into my life story assignment. In desperation I don my trail shoes and running shorts. I don't really like running, but it's a means to an end. The endorphins will be good for me.

I choose a route that will take me through the tree-named streets and up Lookout Mountain. The air is crisp and the leaves are fabulous, blanketing the ground in red and gold and enabling me to ignore the *Homo sapiens* I spy playing or lounging along my route past the park. I hit the mostly empty trailhead parking lot at not quite a mile, my warm-up officially over as I make my way from asphalt onto Lookout Trail.

My feet appreciate the change to packed dirt, but my quads and calves burn as I zigzag up the mountain. I push through each switchback and enjoy the milder slopes in between, grateful I have yet to pass another soul, though I've seen some antlike humans milling about near the lookout above. Judging by the three or four cars in the parking lot, I'll most likely run into someone somewhere on the trail. I'm hoping I won't. This kind of solitude—with the autumn air and palette—is beautifully therapeutic.

When I reach the side trail leading to the lower lookout, I spot a small group ahead moving that way. I push harder, knowing it's only about a hundred more vertical feet to the upper lookout, and reach the top in a rush, legs and lungs afire. Allowing myself a much-needed rest, I bend over my knees, close my eyes, and gulp in the crisp smell of fall. Once my lungs have caught up, I pull a tiny water bottle from my running belt, deciding I've earned a few minutes of sight-seeing from the top.

I never tire of this view. Looking out over the Colorado Plateau to the west, I fancy I can see the curvature of the earth from this height. Below me, Oak Hills Reservoir has adopted a bluish tint in lieu of its usual green, thanks to the cloudless sky. A bead of sweat trickling down my back reminds me that I need to get moving, so I loft a prayer of gratitude heavenward and start back. Maybe I can get past the lower-lookout group before they return to the main trail.

Watching my footing, I avoid the worst of the loose rocks and push my pace on the glorious downhill. I don't hear the group until we nearly collide at the intersection of trails. With a smile and an apology for startling them, I make my way past several pairs of ill-chosen footwear and some giggling before I hear a deep voice say my name.

"Grace?"

Trail shoes skidding to a full stop, I turn and find Noah watching me.

"In a hurry?" he asks, a cute little blonde sidling up to him.

A bright, fake smile takes possession of my face. "Nah, just getting a run in."

"You *run* this?" the blonde asks.

"Sometimes," I say, noting that she barely reaches past Noah's shoulder, even in her thick-soled, spindly strapped flip-flops.

"I thought I was going to die coming this far, but Noah insists we have to go to the top." She pouts and gives him a shoulder bump that hits his elbow.

"Oh," he says, "Amy, this is Grace. I've been tutoring her in math."

Amy grins knowingly. "Noah's an absolute genius, isn't he?" She looks back to Noah and nudges him again. "Too bad I didn't know you when *I* was taking calculus." She laughs, high-pitched and annoying, and I feel my endorphins slipping away. "Isn't it awful?"

Noah's brows furrow as I consider how to respond to that. As if I'd ever attempt calculus. Ha.

"I'm not—" I begin, but Noah talks over me.

"We'd better get up to the top before it cools off anymore." He motions Amy and her fashionably useless shoes up the trail ahead of him and tosses an unreadable glance over his shoulder as he follows. "Enjoy your run."

I mumble a thanks as Amy bids an enthusiastic farewell, and I resume my descent.

I get back to my apartment in record time, but somehow the post-running rush is AWOL.

Chapter 12

DAVE'S DEAL

AFTER ANOTHER UNEVENTFUL WEEKEND SPENT studying and wondering why people crave alone time, I'm still trying to figure out what Dave's deal is. I watched him and Ivy at church together a few days after I cornered him, and they're as attentive as any real couple—minus the nauseating PDA. I did see him steer her through a crowd with his hand on the small of her back, and I can't help but think that Ivy's happier-than-usual mood after church was related. So what's holding him back?

The benefit of having so much alone time is that I've finally been forced to work on my life story project for human development. I've summarized my infancy and toddlerhood, recapped elementary school, and painfully relived every I'm-taller-than-every-male-my-age moment of junior high. High school wasn't quite as bad, as my peers finally started catching up to me and my height became an asset, thanks to sports. It was much more socially acceptable to be the tall girl who was decent at sports than just plain tall.

The downside of progress is the early-twenties chapters that loom ever nearer. I vowed never to relive some things, and now I'm going to have to.

Luckily, I can procrastinate that since Tuesday equals math lab. It's too cool today to sit under a tree and wait, so I go into the lab with thirty minutes to spare and sit at an empty table. Editing the early chapters of my life story keeps me occupied until Noah appears, five minutes early, as usual. If only I could go back and edit my early twenties.

He sits down without salutation and taps the table for my assignment.

"I am having a great day, Noah," I say with a grin. "Thank you for asking. How are you?"

"Fine," he says. "Your assignment?" He taps the table again, and his words are a little clipped, but something in his eyes tells me he's . . . not quite joking but also not entirely serious.

I hold out my assignment—more than half of which I was able to solve on my own—and narrow my eyes at him. "You know what I think is odd?" Our eyes meet and hold for a moment. My breath catches, and now I'm almost sure he's pulling my leg with his dogged stoicism.

He breaks the connection and takes the paper. "Numbers that can't be divided by two," he deadpans.

It takes me a second to catch on to his words, and then a loud laugh breaks free before I can stop it. This earns me a number of stern glares from the other occupants of the lab, including Noah.

I get a handle on the volume, but I'm still laughing. "Noah! You made a joke!"

"I stated a fact," he says, still deadpan, and returns to my calculations.

"I think it's odd," I say, returning to my point and pressing my luck against this lighter mood, "that you've been helping me for all this time and I know nothing more about you than I did the first day."

He turns the page on my assignment as if I haven't spoken, but I see the muscle in his jaw tick. I try some wait time, like I do with my after-school kids, to see if the awkward silence will persuade him to answer. He clears his throat, swallows, and opens his mouth to speak. At long last, the perplexing Noah Jennings is going to shine some light on his life outside this lab. I hold utterly still in anticipation.

"You dropped the negative sign on this coefficient," he says, lightly circling the problem with his pencil and moving on to the next.

What?

I was so sure he'd finally tell me something about himself that this non-answer renders me speechless. I want to call him on it—I *know* he was joking around, letting a side of himself peek out from that thick shell he always wears—but he doesn't give me a chance, working through the rest of the assignment and teaching me how to correct the errors he finds, barely leaving me time to breathe between problems. In a blink, we're done and he's gone, leaving me even more frustrated with his remoteness than before.

Now I know there's a sense of humor behind that stony front, but I didn't even get a chance to rib him about his ditzy date.

It's looking like another long evening in which I should tackle my paper, but I'm relieved to find Ivy home when I walk through the door. She's staring at the TV and doesn't say anything to me even when I sit next to her on the couch. That wouldn't be terribly unusual, except that the TV is off and her eyes are red-rimmed and puffy.

"Hey," I say.

She sniffs.

"You okay?"

She shrugs.

"Family okay?"

She nods.

"Dave?"

Another shrug. Some welling up.

"What happened?"

"I ruined everything. I kissed him."

"What? Why is that bad? Did he kiss you back?"

She smiles, sad yet smug. "Yeah."

"Was it . . . ?"

Her eyes close and her smile deepens. "So good."

I'm so confused. "Then why did that ruin everything? Did he not think it was good?"

"He only wanted to be friends and now he can't even be my friend anymore because I stupidly, arrogantly assumed that if I could just get him to kiss me, he'd see we're perfect for each other." She blows out a gust of frustration. "He said he's too attracted to me."

Wait. What? "Is that even a thing? Too attracted? Attraction is a *good* thing, especially when you're already friends like you two!"

"Agreed," she says, "but he doesn't see it that way. I should have known better. He's told me about his family, his mom. It's pretty messed up. Apparently she stepped out on his dad and has bounced around a ton of relationships since, all based solely on physical attraction. I think he's determined that he won't date or marry for attraction because he doesn't want to end up like his parents."

"So he won't date you *because* he's attracted to you?"

Another nod. "And we can't spend any more time together because I ruined our platonic friendship with *lustfulness*." The word drips with disdain.

"Is that what he said? That you were lustful?" I ask, mama-bear hackles raised.

She scoffs. "No, but he implied it. And more about himself than me." Her hands fiddle with a loose thread on the blanket enveloping her. "It was just a kiss, Gracie. A really good one, but still."

"I'm going to—"

"Don't, Grace." She grabs my knee to keep me on the couch. "Don't say anything to him. Promise."

I acquiesce, reluctantly, but man, would I love to give this guy a talking-to. Or a slapping.

"It's so ironic," she says. "All this time I've been searching for someone who would appreciate me for who I am instead of how I look." She goes back to toying with the loose thread and lets out a cynical little laugh. "And now I've found him, but my looks have ruined it for me anyway. Everyone says beauty is a blessing, but for me it's a curse."

I have a few curses of my own I'd like to try on Dave.

Three days go by without a word from Dave. Ivy spends all her time outside of class with me now, but she's really only here in body. Her mind is solely occupied with Dave. At first, I was glad to have my Ivy back, but she's so miserable I'm feeling guilty for that sentiment.

Also violent.

It's Friday afternoon, and I'm killing an hour between classes while I eat my lunch. I pull my jacket tighter around me, chewing a bland mouthful of peanut-butter sandwich. I'd rather have ham, but that would require effort and an ice pack. I'm people watching, relishing the nip in the air and the October sun on my dark jeans when I see Dave approaching.

He hasn't spotted me yet, which isn't surprising, considering his brow is furrowed like the Grand Canyon. I try to squelch my mama-bear response with limited success before he reaches me. If this isn't a divine opportunity, I don't know what is.

"Hey, Dave."

He jumps and blinks, seeing me, where he was just navigating the crowd before. "Oh. Hey, Grace." The furrows deepen, drawing the corners of his mouth down. "How's . . . it going?"

Hmm. He might be almost as miserable as Ivy. Idiot. "It's going," I say, then take the plunge and kick my promise to Ivy to the curb. "I've missed seeing you around the apartment."

He looks up at the sky, which offers no deliverance from me. "Yeah."

"Have a seat, Dave."

Fear creeps into his worry.

"C'mon. I'll be nice."

He sighs himself onto the bench I've claimed and stares out at the milling crowd—a small gathering of political activists campaigning for next week's congressional election, but mostly they're stalling traffic—leaving me free to examine him.

"You look miserable."

He grunts, keeping his eyes on the people. "What happened to nice?"

"It's a good thing you're miserable since I was pretty tempted to punch you. But since you're already suffering . . ."

No response.

"She's pretty down too."

He swallows.

I switch to people-watching. "You seemed happy before, with Ivy. Seems like if you were both happier together, maybe you should *be* together."

"I can't. She's . . . I can't."

Maybe I *will* punch him. I choose words instead because I am that mature. "You know, Dave, I've gone out with a lot of guys. Some I've been attracted to but they weren't attracted to me, others were good friends but I wasn't attracted to them. I've watched you and Ivy, and frankly, what you have is special. You're great friends, you enjoy being together, and from what Ivy said about that kiss"—he flinches—"you've got the attraction part down too. Attraction is a gift. If I ever meet a guy who can be a great friend *and* take my breath away, you can bet your best guitar I won't be running away from him at the first hint of emotional danger." My eyes are stinging, so I busy myself with collecting my lunch and anger. Thankfully, he's inspecting his hands, so I don't have to meet his eye. "It's a gift, Dave, not a sin. Don't throw it away."

Chapter 13

HALLOWEEN

I'M WORRIED IVY WILL DETECT my treachery, but she's too mired in neglected studies and romantic misery to notice. At first, I'm expecting every minute for Dave to come over or call. But a whole day goes by without any sign of him coming to his senses. It's Friday, Halloween, and I'm facing down another boring weekend. That would be fine, except I'm worried about Ivy. She really needs to get out. Thus, I gird myself for battle and launch a warning shot off her starboard bow.

"Hey."

Ivy lifts her frazzled head and looks at me over a teetering stack of books and papers. I'm not sure when she showered last. She's been watching classes online and submitting everything electronically. "Hey."

"We should do something," I say. "Are you willing to play wingman? Woman? Whatever?"

Her eyes trace the piles surrounding her, burying her, and land on a whole red bell pepper sitting near the edge of the table. She picks it up and bites it like it's an apple. The crunch is a little disturbing. She wipes a dribble of red juice from the corner of her mouth on her sleeve.

"You need a change of scene, my friend. I won't expect you to have fun, but can we just get out for a bit?"

"And do what?"

"Uhh . . ."

An insistent knock at the door buys me some time to come up with an idea. It's Tiffany, our energetic young neighbor.

"Hey, guys!" she says as I open the door, her perfectly straightened hair shimmering golden in the afternoon sunlight.

Ivy squints against the glare and takes another chomp out of her pepper, seeds scattering among the papers. I offer my own hello, but Tiffany silences me with a verbal barrage.

"A bunch of us are going to the Halloween party at the student center tonight and thought it would be so fun to be the Seven Dwarfs, but Brittney and Amanda got asked out, so now we only have five, and I was wondering if you two would come and round us out since we're not going all-out, just T-shirts and beanies and if you have a pair of black jeans or something, but we really need a couple extras. Can you come?"

Finally, she draws a breath. I do not love Halloween, and I'm formulating my excuses when Ivy speaks from the table of gloom.

"Only if I can be Grumpy."

I'm so shocked that Ivy volunteered for this that we arrive at the party before I can lodge any of my own complaints. First of all, I've drawn the short straw of having to wear a bright-orange T-shirt that is at least one size too small, not to mention it has the word *BASHFUL* blazoned across the most, um, prominent area. I am a walking oxymoron, bashfully, brazenly here to coax my dear friend from her doldrums by watching her embrace her Grumpy-ness in the presence of several hundred crazed collegians. The music is loud enough to render conversation difficult at best, and the other five Dwarfs have long since abandoned our group for the mosh pit in the middle of the student center parking lot. Safely positioned near the outer rim of hay bales that endeavors to contain the milling crowd, Grumpy is steady at my side but so immersed in her character that I have no expectation of breaking her out. At least it's a dry campus. At least we're out of the house.

I revise my earlier assessment of not loving Halloween to a deep loathing.

The only saving grace—no pun intended—is that they let me wear my favorite shorts and socks and hiking boots. Apparently, my hiking attire is Disney animation approved, though they did loan me some suspenders and a beanie in addition to the lovely shirt. And, if I'm entirely honest with myself, I must say I'm quite pleased with the way Tiffany fixed my hair, taming my unruly curls into some amazing waves flowing out from under the beanie with that deceptively effortless look I can never produce.

Thankfully, the party is outside and the night is absolutely splendid, with a clear sky and a bright first-quarter moon approaching its zenith. I draw the cool air into my lungs, hold it for a moment while I admire the lunar seas, and nearly succeed in blocking out the too-loud music until someone bumps into me.

I turn to find Amy—Noah's hiking buddy—giggling through an apology and clinging to Noah's arm. I tell her it's all good and throw an eyebrow Noah's way. I never would have pegged him as one who enjoys a giggler, but here they are together, again. He meets my brow raise with a tight smile, and I bite back a laugh. So maybe he isn't a fan.

"It's so funny that we'd meet you here!" Amy is saying, her high voice reaching new heights to be heard over the music. "I didn't think you were a"— her eyes drop to my BASHFULness and widen before jumping back to my face and hair—"*party* kind of girl, but you never know, right, Noah?"

"Nnnope," he says, straight-faced and drawing out the *n*.

Amy squeezes his arm and grins as if he's paid her the highest of compliments. I use the break in conversation to introduce Ivy, who offers a grumpy look and a slight head bob in response.

Amy leans in so she can marginally reduce her shouting. "She's really into this, isn't she?"

I nod enthusiastically, adopting Amy's tone as my own. "She's very into theater, so Halloween is, like, her favorite holiday."

In my peripheral vision Noah looks away and coughs into his hand.

"Oh! Right! That's so great!" Amy gestures to the matching black *Happy Halloween* shirts she and Noah are wearing. "I wanted to dress up, but I couldn't come up with anything Noah would agree to, so we just went with these." She leans in again. "Actually, I'm surprised I even talked him into this. I don't think he really likes dressing up."

Noah has found something very interesting on the other side of the parking lot.

"But I love your costumes! Where did you get them?" Amy glances again at BASHFUL, and I'm tempted to clock her. Or myself. I'm suddenly grateful for whatever Noah is interested in over there. Why, why did I allow myself to be talked into this?

Ivy throws some Grumpy-ness our way, saving me from responding. "Our neighbors needed someone to fill out their seven."

"If only it had been *The Magnificent Seven*," I mutter. I would much rather be dressed for the Wild West than in this awful shirt.

"Denzel Washington or Yul Brynner?" Noah asks, his attention suddenly back on me.

Interesting. I wouldn't have pegged him as a fan of Westerns.

"Love Denzel," I say, "but I have to go with Yul. Assuming, of course, you're only talking about that title. Now, if we're talking cowboys in general, nobody beats John Wayne."

Noah's eyes narrow. He opens his mouth to say something, but Amy's giggle cuts him off.

"Well it's been nice chatting with you again, but we'd better get going. Noah *promised* he'd dance if he didn't have to dress up."

The muscle in his jaw clenches as Amy uses her death grip on his arm to steer him away, tossing a "Nice to meet you" at Grumpy over her shoulder as they leave.

Noah? Dancing? This I have to see.

I turn to conspire with Grumpy on how best to follow them without being obvious, but one look at her face scuttles that idea. When she catches me watching her, she wipes a tear away and does her best to reinstate Grumpy.

"Let's get out of here," I say, refusing to be disappointed at missing Noah's dance. I can't even begin to imagine him cutting loose, but Ivy is more important than satisfying my curiosity. "You're miserable."

"I'm fine," she insists, but even if I were excited to be at this party, I wouldn't ask her to stay any longer. It takes only a nudge to get her moving in the direction of the parking lot.

"Movie?" I offer.

"Sure," she says.

As we make our way through the crowd and back to my car without so much as a glimpse of Noah or his date, I can't help wondering how the dancing went. And whether Noah would pick Denzel over Yul Brynner.

Chapter 14

CHANCE

Ivy and I blunder our way through the rest of the weekend on a steady diet of ice cream and classic cowboy films. Ivy doesn't love old movies, but when given the choice between guns and chick flicks, she chooses wisely. Watching other people's happily ever afters would just rub salt in her wound.

Of course, mooning over cowboys isn't much better.

Sunday proves to be a challenge, as Ivy spends extra time trying to look irresistibly unattractive in hopes of regaining Dave's attention. How he manages to escape either one of us spotting him at church has both of us perplexed, until a mutual friend spills that he left Friday to go home for the weekend.

Coward.

Knowing that he chose to hide instead of facing her ticks Ivy off enough to pull her out of her pout and get her focus back on school, though she has developed an interesting new habit of mumbling man-hate whenever she thinks she's alone.

I've forgiven her for making me leave the Halloween party before I could spy Noah dancing, mostly because she let me pick the movies. Besides, it's given me something to look forward to needling Noah about today.

Despite the sunshine, a cold breeze again compels me to abandon my favorite tree in favor of the dreaded but warm math lab forty-five minutes early. Installing myself at our usual table, I pull out my math homework and make some lame attempts to tackle it but end up texting Ivy most of the time. It seems Professor Plum has finally moved past her prune fixation and on to fertility foods.

Stifled amusement at Ivy's latest comment fades when Noah shows up, deposits himself in a chair, and commandeers my assignment without so much as a hello. Forehead resting against his fingertips, he's taking this simple-for-him math far too seriously. I can't resist the temptation to tease him.

"Hey, Noah. Glad to see you too!"

"Number four requires a different formula than the one you used. Can you see why?" He points to my paper and picks up his pencil.

"It was a great weekend, thanks!" I'm pretty impressed with my approximation of Amy's enthusiastic chatter. "Especially seeing you dance at the Halloween party. Definitely the highlight of my week."

He levels me with dagger eyes, and I give him my brightest fake smile. "You didn't see me dance," he says.

"Oh, but I did! And can I say you were fantastic? Amy really brings out the—"

"Nice try, but I didn't dance with Amy."

Dang. Called my bluff. "You didn't?"

One eyebrow lifts to break the ice in his glare.

"You didn't. Huh. Amy was pretty convinced she could—"

He heaves a sigh, and his prickly expression turns . . . tired? "Look, I don't want to talk about it, okay? Amy could not convince me to . . . anything. There's nothing there. I've already had to have this discussion with her. Three times. So I would really appreciate *not* rehashing it again here. Can we just do the math?"

Huh.

What can I say to that? We do the math. It's fairly straightforward once Noah explains it, which is a good thing because I spend most of my mental energy trying to figure out what has him so down. It's not like he's normally a ball of laughs or anything, but he usually takes things in stride. Not so today.

We wrap up, and I'm disappointed to see that we haven't used the full hour. Not that I want to spend more time doing math, but I want Mom to get her money's worth, right?

And, maybe, I'm worried I've upset him.

"Hey," I say as he stands to leave. "I'm sorry if I—"

He cuts me off. "It's not you," he says. I'm shocked when, instead of bolting without a word, he meets my eye and holds for a beat. He starts to say something, stops himself, and settles on "See you next week" as he leaves.

I spend the walk home chastising myself for taking the teasing too far, worrying about Noah, and brainstorming something I can do with Ivy that will distract us both. Ice-skating seems promising—cheap entertainment plus moderate exercise—until I open the door to our apartment, straight into Ivy and Dave standing nose-to-nose. They step apart, embarrassed, then Dave pulls Ivy back in and whispers something in her ear before dashing out the door. I've just closed it and turned to get the lowdown when he bursts back in.

"Thanks, Grace," he says, accosting me with a quick hug before dashing out again.

"What on earth?" I demand, but Ivy is so giddy I can't get a word out of her. "Ivy! Explain!"

She pauses her twirling long enough to enlighten me. "You know how mad I was that he couldn't even face me on Sunday? Well, I shouldn't have been. He went home to talk to his dad, and his dad convinced him to give us a chance!"

I'm happy for Ivy, but there's more than a hint of envy tainting it. I squash the green monster into a corner and put on my happiest happy face. Ivy tells me how lucky she is, and I agree wholeheartedly. Seeing their affection brings a pang of regret at the loss of Ethan's attention, but my heart knows it wasn't going anywhere with him.

I ignore the refrain of the Harry Connick Jr. song "But Not for Me" from Mom's oldies playlist going through my head.

Chapter 15

ENDORPHINS

FUNNY, HOW EASILY I SLIPPED back into the Grace-Ivy duo for a few days. It's been much more difficult resuming my solo act now that she and Dave are officially dating. Luckily, I have a great deal of experience with flying solo and marrying off roommates. Not that Ivy's engaged. She's not, but that doesn't mean she won't be. It's only a matter of time.

Desperate times call for desperate measures—which explains why I'm out running in the biting November wind at a ridiculous nine in the morning instead of lazing happily beneath my comforter like usual. I am determined to make this a good day, and I'm calling in all the endorphin reinforcements I can muster. Remembering the stale donut that is my only breakfast option at home, I promise myself some real food on campus and push harder, lungs burning in the cold.

A quick hot shower when I'm done evens out my sweaty core and frozen extremities. I take a little extra time with my toilette today, pleased with the glow that running frigid brings to my cheeks, and chug some water as I make for campus and real food.

I have just enough time to scarf a taco salad before human development, in which we are currently examining Piaget's stages of cognitive development. I choose to continue thinking of this instead of the life story rough draft I'll have to finish over the weekend.

The library provides a good location during my break between classes to complete some meditation exercises for stress management—two birds with one stone and all that: finish an assignment and stop thinking about what I'm going to have to write later. The only drawback is the meditation writeup, but I whip that out in no time and head to the math lab.

Noah is already seated and glaring at the door when I walk in at precisely three o'clock. "You're late," he says.

Looks like I've drawn the tetchy Noah from last week again. "Right on time." I prove my point with my phone that reads 3:00 in bold.

"You're usually . . . never mind." He taps the table, as if that will raise my books from Trusty's depths.

No way am I letting him ruin my vibe. I gave up a warm bed and tortured myself for an hour in the cloudy cold to achieve good-mood status. "Couldn't wait to see me, huh?" I say, smiling. His thick brows converge, forming a crease between them that makes me laugh out loud, which makes the crease deepen. "It's November 11, Noah! Embrace it!" I pull some randomness from the social-media surfing I did during lunch. "Not only is this the day we remember the Armistice of 1918 and the veterans who served to protect our freedoms but it's also eleven eleven! That's a powerful number! Are you into numerology? Eleven eleven is all about new beginnings. And there's *snow* in the forecast!"

The other occupants of the math lab are looking at me like I'm crazy. Sheesh. You'd think, with their love of numbers, that they'd find numerology to be at least mildly entertaining, but no. Noah's expression is completely blank, other than one ridiculously high eyebrow and what might be a nervous twitch at one corner of his mouth. I want to keep teasing him, see if I can get him to smile, but after last week I'm hesitant to push too far. I back down with a sigh.

"I know, I know." I hold up my hands in surrender. "Let's do the math so you can get me out of your hair." With that, I pull out my books and follow him obediently through the assignment, which only confuses him further.

Funny, how that confused look—with his head tilted to one side—takes years off his face, making him look more like a little boy than my stoic tutor. And that little-boy look somehow makes me want to smile even more. I refrain from teasing him, because he isn't quite recovered from whatever was bugging him last week, but I can't help but smile at that expression. The more I do, the more confused he is, making a fascinating positive-feedback cycle that's definitely working in my favor. I haven't felt this light in weeks.

It must have been a better run than I thought.

Chapter 16

DON'T BOTHER ME WITH DETAILS

"SO . . . I'M CONFUSED." THE GUY holding my life story paper flips pages back and forth as I will my knee to stop bouncing. There's no desk to hide it under in the cavernous auditorium where my human-development class is currently engaged in the purgatory of peer review.

I didn't even want my *professor* to read this, let alone a peer.

Apparently I missed the fine print announcing today's activity, or I would have prepared myself. Or skipped class. At the very least, I would have left out certain sections until the final draft. Honestly, I was counting on the size of the class giving me some anonymity.

Instead I'm sitting face-to-face with a fresh-out-of-high-school debate king— it doesn't even look like he shaves yet—who is probably only in this particular class because someone told him it was a great place to meet girls. His cologne is suffocating. And he's peering into my deepest pain.

Peering and prodding.

"Benson is . . . your brother?"

"Yep." I haven't spoken aloud about Benson with anyone besides my family and Ivy since his death, and now *this* boy wants to be the first? He glances at my leg, which has gone spastic again. I stop it.

"You say he's 'gone,' but you don't say why or how, only how that changed you and your career path."

"It's my story, not his."

"True, but I think clarification would give your reader—"

"Look"—I glance at his paper in my lap for his name—"Aaron. This paper is not going to be read by anyone else but the grader. Ever. It's a reflection paper, something that helps *me* reflect on *my* life. I already know the details, so it isn't necessary to rehash them."

Aaron repositions his glasses with a sniff and consults the peer-review form we've been given. His pencil scratches out a few comments, including the suggestion to fill in the gaps I intentionally left, and he drops an empty compliment about my writing style in an unsuccessful attempt to assuage my irritation. It's a good thing we did his paper first, or I might have ripped him—I mean, *it*—to shreds.

The irritation sticks with me all the way back to my apartment. Discovering Ivy home and alone is nothing short of a blessing. I shut the door a little harder than necessary and flop onto the couch.

"Bad day at the math lab?" she asks from behind the pile of books and papers on the kitchen table.

"I don't have math on Thursdays."

She makes an affirmative sound and eyes me shrewdly, shutting her laptop. "So . . . what's up?"

I don't want to talk about this, even with Ivy. She's on the couch before I know it, her warmth easing the irritation that's covering my pain. I stare the other way and blink like mad.

"Life story?"

I nod, knocking one traitorous drop free. I ignore it since it's on the cheek opposite Ivy.

"Benson?" she asks.

I nod again. "I didn't know we were doing a peer review."

Ivy gifts me a groan of validation.

"Right?" I say. "Honestly, why do they do that? Anyway, in the paper, I . . . uh . . . mentioned Benson and my change of major, and my *peer* wanted me to fill in the details. He said it would help my reader understand better, but I told him, other than the grader, no one besides me is going to read this. Ever. I'm not filling in those details." My voice fails at this point, but Ivy waits for me to collect myself before she says anything.

"Gracie, hon," she says, "have you considered that, maybe, your reader—*you*—would benefit from taking a closer look at those details?"

And because she's the best friend ever, she doesn't ask anything else, just sits next to me and holds me together as I fall apart.

Chapter 17

DEMENTED ANALYSIS

MY PROFESSOR CALLED IT "DIMENSIONAL analysis."

I just think it's demented.

Noah insists it's the best thing since sliced bread, and he's determined to convert me. I'm not inclined to listen, especially since we're probably the only two people in town studying on the Tuesday afternoon before Thanksgiving break. The only other people in the lab are two employees, scrolling on their phones as they bide their time.

"You need to see how it applies to real life," he says, leaning back in his chair and removing his glasses long enough to rub the bridge of his nose. "Let's say you move to Germany—"

"That's not real life."

"—and you're having some friends over, and you want to make your favorite—do you have a dessert or something you like to make?"

"What if I don't cook?"

His eyes flash. They're more green than brown today. "Let's pretend."

"Fine," I say. "Brownies. Mom's recipe. Best ever."

"Okay, Mom's brownies. But all the measurements are in cups and English units—"

"Isn't it strange how we still use English units and the English don't?"

"—and your fully furnished flat only has a metric cooking scale. How are you going to measure?"

"Beats me. Guess I'll have to buy some strudel."

"No. You absolutely have to make your mom's brownies because you've bragged so much about them to your new friends."

With a voice completely deadpan, his dry humor is easy to miss, but I've spent enough hours with him now that I can see it peeking through at times. I wonder what his belly laugh sounds like—those smile lines insist that he has one—and what it would take to coax it out of him.

"So you google the conversion factor"—he pulls out his phone and has it in less than three seconds—"and you find that one cup of flour weighs one hundred fifty grams."

"But it's way more humid in Europe. What if the flour weighs more there because of increased water content? How do I take that into account? Also, more flour is required at higher altitude. So wouldn't I have to decrease it if Mom bakes at 5,800 feet and I'm baking near sea level?"

He tips his head in that rather charming way, though I'm pretty sure he's annoyed. "Did you ever consider going into STEM?"

"Pardon?"

"Science, technology—maybe not engineering or mathematics, but chemistry? Biology?"

I shake my head. "Too much math, but I've always loved the concepts. I was an English major for a while, before I changed to rec-man."

"Huh." His eyes narrow, and I prepare to deflect when he asks why I switched.

Everyone changes majors. It's common enough to be unremarkable, though mine was anything but. Maybe I'm paranoid after Aaron's nosy peer review, expecting Noah to press me for details.

But he doesn't.

Unpleasant memories slink back under my floorboards as he returns to math.

"Those are valid considerations, about the flour. But let's assume you're living near the Alps, so the altitude and climate are similar enough that we can just focus on the calculation. Agreed?"

"I don't know. You know what happens when you assume things."

His mouth quirks up a millimeter before he repeats sternly, "Agreed?"

I sigh my resignation.

"How many cups of flour in your mom's brownies?"

"I don't remember."

The muscles in his square jaw bunch, making the shadow of his stubble more apparent. "Okay, let's assume . . . I don't know . . . six cups."

I stifle a smirk and tuck a stray curl behind my ear. "There you go, assuming again. That's way too much. I don't have that many friends in Germany."

"Fine. Two?" The words sound through clenched teeth.

"Well, that's rude. I'm sure I have more than two friends."

"Cupssss," he says, drawing out the *s* like a snake.

"Oh, *cups*." I definitely enjoy needling him. "Sure, two sounds good."

He exhales and nudges my notebook back toward me. "Write down two cups, and then you need to multiply by your conversion factor."

"One hundred fifty grams per cup?"

"Yes, but remember this is all about keeping your units straight. You like fractions, right?"

"If you say so."

"You're good at fractions, so think of this that way."

I'm good at fractions? It's been a very long time since anyone complimented my math skills. Maybe since fourth grade. Consequently, I have a hard time concentrating on his next words, but I package the pleasure to savor at home.

"You have to remember you want to cancel out the units," he says, "so they always have to be top and bottom, like when you're multiplying fractions. Since you start with two cups, that means . . . ?"

"One hundred fifty grams goes on . . . top? Putting one cup on the bottom?" I wince, sure I'm wrong. I hate being wrong.

"Exactly," he says. Though there is no emotion in his voice, I feel like I've won the lottery. "After that it's only a matter of multiplying the numbers on top and dividing by those on the bottom. Easy."

The way he explains it, it is. However . . . "Most of these problems are way harder than that. How am I supposed to keep everything straight?"

"Let's try another." He leans back again and considers the ceiling. "How about this? You're planning a huge pre-finals party and you need to know if you can afford to buy pizza for everyone."

"Why don't I buy as much as I can, and the latecomers will just be out of luck?" I give him a cheesy grin.

He ignores me. "How many slices do you think people eat, on average?"

"My little brother can eat a whole large if we let him."

Noah closes his eyes for a second to fortify himself against my cheekiness. "Let's assume an average of two since most singles won't allow themselves to look like a pig in front of a large group. We need to know the cost for one pizza and how many slices are in each."

"If we go cheap, I can get a five-dollar pizza with eight slices."

"No one is expecting fancy at a student gathering, so cheap it is. How many people do you want to invite?"

I want to argue about the number, but he's sounding weary, so I rein in the teasing and play nice. "Forty?"

"Forty. Write down all our given information. What do we have?"

"Okay. Forty people, five dollars per pizza with eight slices each, and an average consumption of two slices."

"Now set up your equation."

"But this is where I get confused! I don't know which one to start with."

"So start at the end and work backward."

I give him my blankest stare.

He refuses to react. "What are we trying to determine?"

Sigh. "How much money I will spend."

"So we need to end with . . .?"

"Dollars?"

"Right, dollars on top at the end." He continues to coach me through every step, refusing to give me the answers while helping me discover that I already sort of know them.

He leans in, looking over my shoulder to make sure I set the calculations up right, and I can smell his shampoo or aftershave or something, and I'd really like to know if it's coming from his hair or his neck. I breathe deeply, considering. That smell is making it exceptionally difficult to identify the numbers on my calculator, so I inch away, and then he does too.

"I get . . ." I finish punching in the numbers and hit the equal sign. "Fifty dollars. Is that right?"

"Yes," he says, moving even farther away and taking that delicious smell with him. I'm expecting some kudos, but if anything, he looks annoyed. "Let's go back to your assignment now and see if it's any easier."

It is, and I'm almost disappointed.

Chapter 18

NO PLACE LIKE HOME

WEDNESDAY MORNING I STEP THROUGH the door of my childhood home and into nose heaven. Closing my eyes, I savor the warm scents and try to identify which pies Mom has finished baking. Definitely pumpkin, possibly berry. If she's done the apple, I can't detect it.

"Lou!" A voice debating between child- and manhood gives me a split-second warning before little Zach nearly bowls me over as I try to set my things on the floor. My twelve-year-old brother isn't so little anymore, his dark head no longer fitting neatly under my chin.

"Good grief, Zach! What has Mom been feeding you?" I say, squeezing him back. "You're not supposed to grow up while I'm away!"

"He eats everything in sight," Dad says, stepping out of his den and enveloping us both in a huge bear hug before Zach can escape. "How was your drive?"

"Uneventful," I say.

"Best kind," he says.

The ninety-minute drive from Oak Hills into the western slope of the Rockies where my parents live can turn ugly in a blink in late November. Thankfully, today's roads were dry and clear.

Dad motions with his chin for Zach to take my bags to my room and keeps one arm around my shoulders as we move to the kitchen.

Mom is up to her elbows in flour and pie crust, the oblique sunlight highlighting a few gray streaks in her dark hair. "There's my Gracie Lou!" she says, setting down her rolling pin and brushing her hands off on her apron before hugging me around the waist. I put my arms around her and soak up the comforting smells of home, marveling anew at how small she is. "We've missed you! Are you hungry? Y'all come and sit at the bar and talk to me while I finish up this crust." Her accent always thickens when she's baking. I guess it reminds her of her own childhood in North Carolina, though she's lived in the West since she was eighteen.

"Any leftovers?" I ask.

"Shepherd's pie, middle shelf," Mom says, pointing with a flour-coated finger.

"I'll be in the den," Dad says with a squeeze of my shoulder.

"Where's Kaden?" I ask Mom as I dish out a hearty portion of shepherd's pie and stick it in the microwave.

"Playin' ball down at his friend's church," she says, settling back into her crust.

"I thought there was a moratorium on holidays."

"Oh, there is. That only means they can't go to the school or have the coach there. Nothin' to stop them from playin'."

I stare into the microwave as the seconds tick by. *Are they really playing ball? Who is he with?* Round and round goes my plate, along with my thoughts. I open the door and stick a finger in the middle, then add another minute. Round and round.

Mom's rolling pin stops. "He's fine, Gracie. They're good boys."

That's what I thought about Benson.

The timer runs to zero, and I nearly burn my fingers on the hot plate as I hurry it to the bar. I fetch salt and pepper, seat myself, and take great interest in achieving a symmetrical spread of seasoning. But I'm not sure I have an appetite anymore.

"Gracie."

Mom's eyes bore into me, but I don't want to look up. I've been pushing the food around, removing the carrots. Now I take a bite, filling my mouth with food in lieu of words.

She sets her tools aside and leans across the bar toward me, putting her warm, floury hand on mine. "He's not Benson."

I slide my hand free to scoop up another bite I no longer want. "I just wanted to see him."

"He won't be long," she says. "We weren't sure when you'd get here."

Zach struts into the kitchen, shoulders back and head high, and rescues me.

"How's life, little man?" I ask, tousling his hair.

"Good, when there's no school," he says, grabbing an apple out of the fruit bowl, taking a huge, crackling bite, and talking around it. "How's college? You need me to help you with your math?"

I chuck a carrot at him, but he catches it easily and pops it into his mouth with a thank-you.

"Stop throwin' food in my kitchen," Mom says. She's smiling, though, so I toss another carrot, higher this time, and Zach catches it in his mouth.

"I mean it. Y'all won't be gettin' any pie tomorrow if you keep this up."

"Want to pepper?" I ask Zach.

"Volleyball's for girls. Besides, my arms are tired." His eyes brighten, and he pulls up one sleeve to show me his still-developing bicep. "Kaden let me lift with him this morning."

"Girls?" I squeeze the offered bicep. "I guess you'll fit right in, then. Where's the volleyball?"

"Hey!" he says, slugging me in the shoulder.

"I'm kidding!" I laugh. "Bring those big biceps of yours and hit some balls at me, manly man."

He grabs me around the waist, and I put him in a headlock.

"Out-out-out!" There's some real irritation creeping into Mom's voice, so I wrestle Zach into the family room and let him think he might win a few times before I manage to pin him. It won't be long until my baby brother passes me in strength and height. I'm not ready for him to grow up.

The door slams, and before I can release Zach, we're attacked by a sweaty, blond Kaden.

"Hiya, Gracie!" Strong fingers dig into my ribs and send me into a paroxysm of laughter and squealing.

Zach yelps and groans beneath the combined weight of two older, bigger siblings. I let him out so we can gang up on Kaden, but somehow Kaden manages to wrap Zach up with his legs and simultaneously pin me with his upper body.

I pull away from Kaden's armpit—thankfully, he's wearing sleeves—long enough to voice my protest. "Ugh, you smell like a gym rat! Gerroff!"

"Can't take your little brother anymore, can you?" Before he lets me up, he tousles my hair much like I did to Zach, destroying the minimal effort I made this morning. "Must really suck to get so old and useless!"

"Nothing little about you but your brain." I give his huge frame a good-natured shove and reach down to help Zach to his feet. Once Zach passes me up, I'll only be taller than Claire. It's a hard pill to swallow. I liked being first, oldest, biggest.

"Ha!" Kaden takes the jab in stride, though his chest swells to show me how big he is. "Tell that to Mr. Therman."

"Aw, how is old Thermy?" Our high school's chemistry teacher is an eccentric relic, a fixture at every home sporting event and a favorite among the students. "He let you blow anything up yet?"

"Nah, but he's shown us a few things. We won't get into exothermic reactions until third term."

"I miss that stinky coot. Smells like you've been seeing a lot of him. Remedial?"

"Hey!" He pauses to sniff an armpit. "That's just good, clean sweat. Besides, you probably wouldn't smell much better than him if you spent all your time in a room full of sulfur. And, just so you know, I set the curve on our last test. So I guess everything about me *is* bigger than you, including my brains."

"Well, you definitely have a big head."

Zach worms his way under my arm and into the conversation, half-wrestling, half-hugging me as he laughs at Kaden. "She got you!"

"Watch it, or you won't be lifting with the big boys anymore."

"Will he really let you blow things up?" Zach asks.

"Sure," Kaden says, collecting the bag he dropped when he tackled us and aiming for the kitchen. "Is there any shepherd's pie left?"

"Hey, leave some for me!" Zach says, close behind.

I follow them into the kitchen, watch as Kaden bends to give Mom a kiss on the cheek, and let the worry I've been carrying unwind a few notches as he attacks my abandoned plate.

Kaden's going to be fine.

For now.

Chapter 19

INTERROGATION

THANKSGIVING DAY IS WONDERFULLY GLUTTONOUS, with our annual neighborhood flag football turkey bowl in the morning, followed by finishing the cooking with Mom and a delicious extended-family feast in the early afternoon. Claire, her husband, Ryan, and their two kids are with Ryan's family for Thanksgiving, so there isn't anyone tiny for me to play with. At least we'll get to have them for Christmas.

Once the initial cleanup is done and the relatives are gone, Dad and the boys settle in front of the TV to digest while Mom and I wash the last few dishes. If I work hard enough in here, I might make room for another piece of pumpkin pie. Plus, it's nice to have some alone time with Mom.

Until she recognizes an opportunity to interrogate me.

"School goin' well?"

"Yeah, my load is pretty light. I've been putting in some extra hours with the after-school kids."

"I bet they love you."

"I love being there. It puts things in perspective, and the kids are great."

She agrees and hands me the electric frying pan, dribbling water down my arm and into my sleeve in the exchange. I shudder and rub my arm against my side to stop the stream.

"And what are you doing for fun?" she asks. "What trouble have you and Ivy made?"

"Not seeing much of Ivy these days."

"Oh?"

"She has a boyfriend," I say, bracing against the wedding bells I know this will set off in Mom's ears.

"That's great!" she says. "Are they—"

"They just started dating," I say, cutting her off before she can go any further.

The bells quiet, but there's a determined glint in her eyes. "And who are you datin'?"

Dang. Did I say the *d*-word? Maybe I can redirect her back to Ivy and we can dissect her relationship issues instead of mine. I throw a little more effort into drying the pot in my hands, scrambling for a deflection. Too late.

"*Are* you datin'?" she presses.

Does Noah's paid tutoring count? I mean, we see each other every week . . .

What about the impromptu celebration and attempted kiss from Ethan? Not really, but I'm using it since it's all I have besides the crappy first date with the guy who only wanted to talk football at the beginning of the semester. "Some," I say.

"And how's math?"

It's unnerving how she jumped right to that. And why was Noah the first person to pop into my mind when she asked about dating, anyway? "You know, it's not too bad. I think I'm pulling a C."

She does a happy little clap, sending a spray of bubbles into the air from her pickled hands. "I knew you could do it!"

"Mostly I think it's my tutor."

"It never hurts to have a good teacher. Is she nice?"

Dang. Again I've managed to give her an in where there wasn't one before. Can't lie to Mom though. "He's a he, and yeah, he's nice enough."

"Married?"

Here we go. "No."

"Engaged?"

"Not that I know of," I say, stacking a pie plate on the growing pile and dreading the glint I know I'll see if I slip and meet Mom's eyes.

"Well," she says. "That's good he's able to help you."

I can tell she's using the entire force of her will to hold back from asking all the questions now bouncing around her brain. Maybe if I meet the storm head-on, she'll let it drop.

"We're just friends, Mom. Not even friends—business acquaintances, more like. He's all business. We don't talk about anything but math."

She looks up from her sink of soapy water, and I swear I can see her literally biting her tongue. I grab another pan to dry. Still, over the running water and her silence, it's like I can hear the questions she's dying to ask.

Is he attractive? Do you enjoy your time with him? Look forward to it, even? Does he make you feel smarter than you really are? Is his aftershave distracting? Does it make you want to study his jawline instead of your assignment? Maybe run your fingers along that shadow of stubble?

Whoa! Where did that come from? No way Mom would be thinking that! She couldn't know how—

I pull myself back to the present only to realize I'm standing in front of the cabinet with a very dry pan, staring at nothing. I put it away quickly and reach for another.

But the dishes are all done, the sink is clean, the water is off, and Mom is looking at me like it's Christmas.

Chapter 20

ASTRONOMICAL DISCOVERIES

IT'S STRANGE HOW MOM HAS left me alone about the dating thing since the fiasco in the kitchen. It's been a whole day and she hasn't said a thing. She's uncannily perceptive, but even she couldn't hear me thinking those questions about Noah.

What on earth *was* I thinking, anyway? I wonder again why, when she asked me about dating, Noah was the first one to pop into my mind. Even before Ethan—the only male who has paid any semblance of romantic attention to me all semester. I guess I haven't thought of Ethan in weeks, and Noah is the only other guy I spend any amount of time with.

Am I developing some kind of crush on my tutor? I shudder. That's too cliché.

Also, I'm not attracted to him. I'm not.

He smells nice. That doesn't mean anything.

So what if his jawline is ruggedly shadowed by early afternoon?

"Looks like we've got a nice break in the clouds."

Dad's voice draws my attention from where I've been stewing, sitting in the living room window seat with a book while the boys watch TV and wishing I hadn't eaten so much of Mom's turkey noodle soup at dinner. Dad's annual Thanksgiving stargazing was foiled last night by the heavy cloud cover; today he's been glancing out the windows every five minutes since sundown.

"Moonset isn't until about one," he says, bouncing on his toes, "but it's only first quarter, so the seeing should still be decent. Saturn's too close to the sun, but Jupiter will rise right before midnight." He already has his winter coat on, along with the little-boy delight he wears stargazing. "We can check out craters until it's up. Who wants to come?"

"I'm in!" I say, abandoning the book I've been "reading" and scurrying to my room for warmer clothes so I can meet Dad at the shed. The boys aren't too far behind me as I grab my parka and go outside, pausing on the back steps to let my eyes adapt to the darkness before I make my way to the hill where Dad waits. I take in the crisp, clean air and feel some tension slide from my shoulders.

Open spaces have always calmed me. When I was ten and we moved to Cedar Ridge, Dad found this amazing land outside of town with a perfectly positioned hill for his favorite hobby. He always says he would have chosen astronomy if he hadn't been so darn good with computers.

Just don't ask him to fix anything mechanical. His talents lie in the abstract. When Mom insisted a few years back that he needed some kind of shelter if he was going to stare into space for hours on end regardless of the temperature, he insisted he would build one himself. Thankfully, she overruled him and hired a family friend to construct the shed—a dome-topped cube, complete with retractable roof panels and a slide-out platform for his second scope. In the end, I think Dad was relieved to hand over his vision for someone else to bring into reality.

Now that my eyesight has adjusted a little, I make my way across the yard, through the gate at the back of the garden, and up the trail to the hilltop. The faint strains of Vivaldi and the vague outline of Dad's shelter against a dim red glow beckon me forward. I've missed this.

I've missed him.

"Hey, Lou." He greets me without looking up from the six-inch Dobsonian telescope on the platform. His voice is hushed, though that isn't necessary. There aren't any neighbors close by, and stars don't get spooked. I think he does it subconsciously, out of respect for the heavens.

"How's the seeing?" I ask.

"Not bad," he says, rising from his chair and moving over to the larger ten-inch, which is centered in the building and aimed in a different direction through the open roof. "Take a look."

He's aimed the smaller scope at the moon, knowing how I love to view the craters. They look amazing tonight, the air calm and the image steady. I can hear him fiddling with the keyboard on the bigger scope, muttering to himself as he inputs whatever it is he's looking for. The motor whirs, adjusting the aim, and soon I hear the quiet sigh that means Dad has focused on his target.

"It never gets old," he says. "The longer I observe, the more I see to appreciate and the more I love it."

He spends most of his time viewing deep-sky objects, but I prefer things closer to home. Once I've sated my lunar appetite, I move to Jupiter rising in the east.

Before long my brothers join us, and we take turns viewing the Horsehead Nebula with Dad and watching Jupiter in the smaller scope, Dad chatting with whoever isn't viewing. As much as he loves his astronomy, I think he loves sharing it with us more. Mom even makes an appearance a few minutes before midnight, failing to contain her shivering, though she's wearing enough layers for a midwinter Arctic expedition.

"You'd better get back inside, sweetheart," Dad says after a short time.

"You know I love to be out here, but I don't know how y'all manage to stay warm," she says through chattering teeth. "I just hate to miss out."

Kaden stands up and throws an arm around her. "C'mon, Mom. I'll take you back in. I have to get to bed anyway if I'm going to make it to the gym by seven."

"Can I come?" Zach pipes up, abandoning his watch on Jupiter.

"If you can get yourself up, you can," Kaden says, spurring a good-natured argument about how impossible it is for Zach to wake up to an alarm versus the maturity required to work out with the big boys.

I hear Dad laugh as their voices fade and he settles back in at the ten-inch. I take Zach's place at the smaller scope and get comfortable for a longer look at Jupiter and its biggest moons, readjusting the aim every few minutes as the earth's rotation pulls them from my field of view.

"Did you hear about Comet Siding Spring?" Dad asks.

"I didn't. Armageddon?"

He chuckles. "Earth is safe for now, but it came pretty close to hitting Mars last month."

"Really?" The image in my scope fades away, and I pull back to see that clouds have rolled in. I switch to watching Dad instead. He's still bent into his scope, one hand on his knee and the other on the focus knob.

"Within ninety thousand miles—that's closer than the moon is to Earth—and it dumped a couple tons of space dust on Mars's surface." He extracts himself from his eyepiece and checks the sky. "Looks like that's it for tonight," he says with a sigh at the clouds, putting the cap on his eyepiece. "Luckily, we already had machines there to observe the comet."

"Yeah?"

He launches into an excited commentary about all the Mars rovers and orbiters and how they had been retasked to observe the once-in-a-lifetime comet encounter as he wheels the smaller scope back into the shed. His enthusiasm about the comet's flyby and everything the scientists have been learning from it carries us all the way through cleanup.

"Do you think we'll ever get people on Mars?" I ask as he locks the shed door and we stroll back toward the house.

"That sure would be something," he says. "There are just so many obstacles. Funding, fuel, radiation, supporting humans for extended periods in space, achieving Earth-independency in the spacecraft . . . I think it's possible, but we don't have anything like the focus we had during the race to the moon."

"How long would the trip take?" I ask, imagining what it would be like to go into space, live on another planet.

"Depends," he says. "Throwing a dart from one moving planet to another is no small feat. The distance between the two is anywhere from thirty-five to 250 million miles. It could take anywhere from five to ten months, with current propulsion tech."

How fast would the craft be moving to cover such a distance in such a time? My mind spins, numbers floating around and colliding like asteroids. Then, in a rare moment of mathematical clarity, they march together into a simple dimensional-analysis setup, distance and time clicking into position to yield miles per hour.

"Gracie? You coming?"

I'm standing stock-still in the middle of our backyard, eyes glazed and jaw hanging open. "Dad."

Worry on his face, he moves back to my side and takes a gentle hold on my arm. "What is it?"

"I can do math!"

Chapter 21

ANOTHER DIMENSION

TUESDAY DAWNS COLD AND CLOUDY. Regardless of the weather, there is a bounce in my step as I approach the math building. The guy in front of me gives me a strange look as I thank him enthusiastically for holding the door.

It's a good thing, for Noah, that I've had to wait four days to tell him about my math epiphany. My initial enthusiasm might have been overwhelming.

On the other hand, it's been a very bad thing for me. In the process of expounding my sudden appreciation for dimensional analysis, I have endured a disturbingly high occurrence of *the look*. You know, the one you always get as a young single person, even if you're describing a completely platonic situation?

That look.

I got it from Dad and Mom—which was predictable—but now that I'm back at school, I'm getting it from Ivy. She even went so far as to suggest I ask Noah out.

As if my excitement has anything to do with him!

First of all, he's my tutor. He is being *paid* to spend time with me. I'm sure I only enjoy the time so much because he excels at his job. Finally tackling my fear of this class has made me appreciate him, sure, but it's just because he's helping me clear such a giant hurdle.

I'm grateful, that's all.

It has nothing to do with attraction.

Second, I'm not attracted to him! Just because a person smells nice or you happen to notice the curious way he cocks his head when he's thinking or your thoughts scatter when he leans in to see your work, that doesn't mean you're attracted.

Right?

Third, even if I were attracted to him—which I'm not—he's made it quite clear that he isn't interested in getting to know me. Ivy insists this must be because he's shy or because, like Ethan, he deems the distance a necessity. I disagree.

My point is, because of the delay, I have way overthought today's tutoring session, and now it's making me nervous. But why shouldn't I be excited about math? Attempting to put all the knowing looks from my people behind me, I determine that I will not *act* like anything. True self and all that.

I take a cleansing breath, smile at a stranger passing me in the wide hallway, and open the door to the math lab.

Noah is at our table, scowling at his phone. As soon as I set Trusty down, he swaps his phone for a pencil and greets me with a lift of his chin and a marginal softening of his dour expression, though his eyes remain dark.

"Guess what!" I say, pulling my things out and setting them on the table.

He sits back in his chair but doesn't say anything.

I take this as an enthusiastic invitation to share. "I can do math!"

He folds his arms.

I laugh. "I'm serious!" I say, tempted to swat his arm like I would Kaden's if he were baiting me like this.

Noah is wearing a T-shirt with shorter sleeves than he normally wears even though it's freezing today. I can't help but notice that his arms are more toned than I'd expected.

"I gathered that from your laughter," he deadpans.

Don't think about his arms. "I can do *math!*" I insist.

"And . . . ?" He sounds anything but impressed.

"Like, real math. On my own!"

"I know," he says, picking up his pencil and tapping it against the tabletop.

"What do you mean you know? I haven't even told you my story yet!"

He blinks in slow-motion, and I wonder if it's more a suppression of eye-rolling than a blink. "I *mean* I know you can do math. I've known that from our first session."

This stumps me for a minute. He knew? How could he know? I was still struggling then. I set his statement aside for later analysis and press on with my story. "So I was home for Thanksgiving, and Dad and I were stargazing and talking about some comet and Mars exploration, and I thought, *How fast could a spacecraft get a human to Mars with current technology?* And the equation to figure it out just popped into my head!"

"Popped."

"Popped! I realize it's nothing like calculus or whatever, but I figured it out, just like that! At closest approach, if it takes five months to get to Mars, you're going almost 10,000 miles an hour! But if you could go as fast as the fastest probe—it left Earth's orbit at 36,000 miles an hour; I had to look that up—you could get there in as few as thirty-nine days! Even at that speed it would take nine months at the farthest approach. *Nine months* on recycled air in a tin can. Can you even imagine the calculations they'd have to do for a landing?"

I pause for air and notice that his eyes have narrowed.

"This came to you while you were stargazing?"

"Yeah, my dad's kind of star-crazy," I explain, brushing one hand to the side and wishing he'd focus on the point of my story. "He has a couple of scopes, and we always do that at Thanksgiving since Christmas is usually too cold for the rest of us."

His eyes dim a shade. "You're lucky," he says. "To have a dad like that."

There's pain behind the words, though he's doing his best to cover it. I vacillate for a second, wanting to get back to my epiphany, before remembering my vow to see people, really *see* them.

I don't want to overstep, but I ask anyway. "Do you spend much time with your dad?"

He shakes his head, focusing on a little piece of scratch paper he's picked up off the table. "He's dead."

Shock jolts my core. *Why did I ask, why did I ask, why did I ask?* "I'm so sorry," I say. So inadequate. But I mean it, and it's all I have.

"Don't be," he says. "It's probably for the best."

I have no response to this, not knowing what terrible circumstances would lead him to say such a thing, so I default to silence, hoping he'll feel safe enough to confide more. Unlike the last time I tried the wait-time strategy with him, today it works.

"Dad started drinking young and couldn't stop," he says, his eyes down as he puts a careful fold in the paper, creases it, then makes another. "He battled it for nearly twenty years. Got sober long enough to convince Mom to marry him, but the pressure of trying to take care of all of us sent him back to the bottle. I remember a few good times, from when I was little, but mostly I remember him as drunk or gone."

"That's so hard, Noah," I say, stunned, willing myself to hold it together for his sake.

"It didn't help that depression runs in the family," he says, almost meeting my gaze with a sideways glance before returning his focus to folding, creasing, and unfolding the paper in his hands. He sinks a little into the table as he speaks, his shoulders sagging and his elbows splaying wider as he talks and folds. "The drink just made that worse. Then one December, they found his car wrapped around the concrete pile of an overpass. There was ice, and his blood-alcohol was like twice the legal limit. They took him to the hospital, but they couldn't do anything. Mom picked up the slack and held us together."

I feel sick. He has no idea how well I can relate, but the last thing I want to do is make this about me. His voice is flat, like he's reciting dry history, but his hands show me how hard this is for him. I focus on my breathing, making sure my voice is soft but steady when I speak. "How old were you?" I ask.

There's a pause in the folding. "Twelve," he says, his voice finally betraying the weight he carries.

My heart sinks. Zach's age. So young to lose so much. No wonder he's closed off. "I'm so sorry you had to go through that," I say, reaching out with one hand to comfort him. He must see it coming, because he immediately stiffens, pulling his arms in and straightening in his chair. I can see his walls rebuilding, like Iron Man's armor, and I reel my arm back in, much like I did that first day.

"It's fine," he says. "Fourteen years ago this week, and my mom—" He clamps his mouth shut and glances down at his phone. "Sorry. I didn't mean to . . ." He trails off and rubs one hand through his hair.

"Thank you for telling me," I say. "Not the kind of anniversary you look forward to."

"Life goes on," he says, squaring his shoulders and placing the last piece of armor. "We have math to do."

Our eyes meet, and though he doesn't say anything outright, I can relate to his unspoken need to drop the subject and move on. So, again, we do the math.

And I don't say anything about how much I now know we have in common.

"His dad was an alcoholic?"

I nod at Ivy, still reeling from Noah's admission.

"I can't imagine having to deal with that," she says.

"Yeah." I think back on our tutoring session, remembering now what I wish I'd seen more clearly when I walked in: darkness under his eyes, slumped shoulders, rumpled T-shirt that was a little too small. He was definitely not in a good place.

"But it's good he opened up to you."

"Yeah," I say again, puzzling on that. Why *would* he open up to me about something this big when he's always been so careful to avoid personal talk? I shrug and find Ivy analyzing me. "What?" I ask.

She's giving me *the look* again.

"What?" I ask again.

"Don't you think it means something, that he opened up to *you*?"

No comment.

"Also that you have something in common?"

I get up from the couch, where we've been chatting, to unload the dishwasher.

"Does he know about Benson?"

Pushy roommate. I don't know why I put up with her. "Of course not. I don't talk about . . . that . . . with anyone."

She's followed me into our tiny kitchen. "I know." She sets a hand on my shoulder as I'm putting away the glasses. "I have to ask, Grace. Did you think about Benson when Noah was talking about his dad?"

I stop unloading and stand still, facing the cabinets, with Ivy's hand still on my shoulder. "Maybe."

Her hand does a little circle, rewarding me for talking at all. "Maybe you'd both benefit from sharing."

I can't help but stiffen at this suggestion.

"Or maybe he just needs a friend," she amends.

My heart pounds as I turn around. "Oh man, you know where to hit me."

A slightly apologetic smile is her answer. "Sorry."

"Not sorry," I argue.

She shrugs. "I'm pretty sure you'd regret it later if you didn't at least give him an opportunity at friendship."

I scoff. "He has rebuffed every effort I've made at anything resembling friendship."

"Mm-hmm," she says. "Until now."

I hate when she's right.

Ivy takes a breath, holds it for a second. "What if he *has* been holding back to maintain a professional distance?"

That what-if keeps me awake most of the night.

Chapter 22

MEAN

BUTTERFLIES TAKE UP RESIDENCE IN my gut as I wait in the packed-for-finals math lab, wondering how awkward it will be with Noah after last week's revelation. Things were oddly comfortable when we parted. Maybe I can build on that. It would sure make what I've promised Ivy easier. Regardless, I have to follow through. She said she'll kick me out of the apartment if I don't.

Noah walks in with only two minutes to spare, though he's looking much more put together than last week in spite of the shadows still under his eyes.

"How are you doing?" I ask.

"Fine." His enthusiasm is underwhelming.

I dish to him the one-brow skeptic he's so fond of using.

He exhales, lifts his glasses to rub the bridge of his nose. "Look, I'm sorry about my . . . about last week. Can we please forget that even happened?"

So much for him confiding in me. I want to push, but I can tell he's digging in. "Okay," I say, though I can't help worrying.

Our eyes meet and hold. He didn't expect acquiescence.

"Well," he says, recovering, "final next week. Lots to cover."

Forty-five minutes later we've reviewed everything and I'm feeling much more confident about the math than what I'm about to do.

The sun is setting—outside and on the tutor-student relationship. It's our last session, and I've procrastinated this . . . whatever it is . . . to the last possible moment.

I close my notebook and gather my courage, calling on all the encouragement—and threats—Ivy has given me over the past few days. Thankfully, Noah and I are alone at our small corner table amid the white noise of a full house.

"That should do it," Noah says. "Make sure you're relaxed going in, do some breathing exercises if you need to, and your final should be a breeze."

"Mental toughness," I say, zipping Trusty and wishing I could coax my butterflies in there with the books. "Listen, Noah, I want to thank you for helping me so much this semester. I couldn't have done it without you."

"That's my job," he says matter-of-factly, picking up his things and rising to leave. All business.

"It's more than that." My time has run out. I stand, swallow my pride, and take a leap. "I . . . I've struggled with math for years, but with you it makes sense for the first time since elementary school. I'd like—" I clear my throat. "I was wondering if I could take you out to dinner."

His expression tightens. Did I misread him? Did I say something stupid? He hasn't said anything, so my mouth runs to cover the silence.

"Just, you know, to show my appreciation. As friends. To say thank you." I become intensely interested in the floor, but I've made a pact to speak my appreciation, and I will do it. Maybe not with eye contact. "I don't think you realize how important passing this class is to me. Without it I couldn't graduate, and the job I have lined up would no longer be an option." I risk a glance, and he's wearing the blank face—the one he puts on any time I bring up anything personal. "I'll never forget how much you've helped me," I say.

His blank face cracks and his eyes harden. "Really?" Sarcasm drips from the word.

Does he not realize how much he's helped me? How much I appreciate it? I have to convince him. "Yes, really! I could never have done this—"

"You'll never forget?" His voice is bitter.

"Huh?" What's going on here? Maybe he doesn't want to go out to dinner, and that's disappointing but fine, but he doesn't believe I appreciate his help? All I can do is shake my head, confused.

"Forgive me if I doubt your memory and allow me to *re*introduce myself. My name is Noah Jennings." He holds his hand out, and mine is drawn into his in spite of his derisive tone.

Heart-pounding warmth spreads through my skin from his touch—a confusing sensation, considering the hostile squeeze he's putting on my hand. Like he did that first day, only now he's taken a step closer and his voice has lowered so I can barely hear the words in spite of his closeness. I feel calluses on his palm, smell cinnamon as he speaks.

"Noah. Jennings." He draws himself to his full height, gaze momentarily dipping before snapping up to look me straight in the eyes. His are more brown than green today, and my heart is hammering as he resumes his reintroduction.

"Between my freshman and sophomore years, I spent a summer building wells in Ghana." He pauses again, waiting. His eyes narrow, daring me as he did that first day.

That first day . . .

Wait.

Ghana? That's where Claire's husband—

Suddenly an image emerges from the depths of my memory, superimposing itself onto Noah's face in front of me. The fit is almost perfect, though the details have shifted considerably.

Stocky now instead of slender.

No beard.

Glasses.

But the same olive skin and square jawline, though that's less pronounced at his current weight. And those hazel eyes—staring straight into mine as we stand nearly nose-to-nose—sparking with anger and triumph as they expose my shame.

I take a step back, and he drops my hand, folding his arms across his broad chest and leaning against the table, waiting for my reply. Smug.

I am speechless. There are no words for the embarrassment burning through my memory, my face, my neck.

When I don't say anything, he continues. "I made friends with one of the guys."

Ryan. My sister's husband.

"And we got along so well that when we reconnected a few years later, he wanted to set me up with his wife's sister."

Oh, for a hole to swallow me. Is it not enough that I have relived my idiocy a million times since that night? That I have attempted, in all my interactions since, to be *present*, to *see* people?

No.

Noah—not a nameless first-date-gone-bad, and definitely not my semi-approachable math tutor—*Noah Jennings*, of the Great Shame, is relishing his victory.

"I don't enjoy setups—no one does." His lips curl, though there is nothing nice about this smile. "But Ryan knew me better than anyone, so I figured it couldn't be *that* bad."

"Please, stop." If my voice is a living thing, it is microscopic. If he hears, he doesn't listen; he can't help but see the pain that he's inflicting, that he chooses to ignore.

"Little did I know," he continues, "my 'date' had even less desire to be set up than I did. And when she discovered that I didn't fit her *requirements*, she didn't bother hiding her disappointment."

He knew about my height requirement? Had I said something to Claire? My stomach clenches.

"Yeah, I heard you," he confirms. "Then I watched as you did your best to ignore me, as you treated everyone around you with indifference or disdain—and in the case of your sister's friend, outright hostility."

My sister's friend? Ah yes. Mandy Miller. Hearing her name still triggers me, though the response now is more of sadness than aggression. I can't help but groan as I realize what *that* exchange must have looked like from his already biased and uninformed perspective.

"I don't think you understand—"

"Oh, I think I do." He isn't about to let me explain. "You were openly hostile to someone who was nothing but friendly."

"But—"

He holds his hands up to stop my words. "When I realized it was you I had agreed to tutor," he says, "I briefly hoped you had changed or that I *had* misunderstood. But—in addition to not even recognizing me—you proved yourself when you showed only irritation at the inconvenience a man's *death* had caused *you*."

"Is that really what you think?" I say, unable to mount any better defense.

"You've given me no reason to think otherwise."

My hands are fisted, my fingernails digging into my palms as I try to recall the thrill of skydiving to force angry thoughts from my head. But all I get is the sick feeling right before I jump.

I glance around, worried about how much attention we're attracting, but everyone is too stressed about finals to notice our quiet, if heated, exchange. "You don't know what you're talking about." Bells are going off between my ears, warning me to hold my tongue, my training reminding me that words spoken in anger don't heal.

"I know enough." His smugness is like an earthquake to a nuclear power plant, and suddenly there is a crack in my reactor and my embarrassment vaporizes in the heat.

"How dare you! You know nothing! Nothing of Mandy, nothing of my thoughts or feelings, nothing about me at all! How dare *you* judge *me* when you have deliberately baited and laughed at me for three months!"

If anything, his smugness intensifies at my outrage, but I'm past caring now. I'll have my say.

I step toward him. "My entire major is focused on helping others. You don't know anything about me but what you convinced yourself to see—because I insulted your pride *three years ago*!"

"Oh yeah. Your *major*." He laughs, ignoring my jab. "Recreation management. Do you really need a degree to go camping or run a zip line?"

My face heats at the stereotype, and before I can stop it, any semblance of containment fails and the toxicity possesses my tongue. "You know, you remind me of that Taylor Swift song," I say.

His head tilts to one side—in that way I don't find attractive—as he considers and throws his next barb. "What, the one where she moons over a guy that has no interest in her?"

"Hardly." I give him a venomous smile. "The one called 'Mean'."

His laugh is mirthless. "Oh, so now because *I* don't want to go on a date with *you*, I'm abusive. That's laying it pretty thick, don't you think?"

"Well, you haven't hit me, but the other words in the song? Liar? Pathetic? Alone? Yeah."

His sneer dims as my words hit their mark. Stepping back, I retrieve Trusty, taking slight comfort in the sight of the threadbare fabric, the pressure of the worn straps settling onto my shoulders as I stand as tall as I can. I might be leaning onto my toes as I stare down his arrogance. Anger checks the burning in my eyes. There will be time for that later. "I'm sorry to have taken so much of your time and for my many faults. I do appreciate you helping me graduate, but I won't trouble you any longer."

Or ever again.

Part Two

Chapter 23

GOOD RIDDANCE

NOAH LEANED AGAINST THE TABLE, watching Grace walk away and feeling rather proud of himself.

The pit in his stomach had to be hunger.

He sat back down in his chair, allowing plenty of time for Grace to clear the area and pretending to check his phone as his thoughts spun. She would pass her class and graduate, securing a job guiding rich people several yards from their fancy cars to some hardcore glamping, and never think of him again.

Usually Noah's first impressions were spot-on. He rarely expected anything from anyone, and they therefore rarely disappointed. Humans were a predictably unreliable lot. But Ryan had built up his expectations for Grace before their date, and the first time Noah had seen her—the very first time—it had been like sunshine after a long rain. Fresh. Warming. Hopeful.

There she'd been, playing with her sister's baby on the floor, smiling and laughing and blissfully unaware of his reaction to her. The clouds that typically shrouded his mind had parted as their eyes met. He smiled. She smiled. The fortifications around his heart had opened a little, to *possibility*.

Then she'd stood to meet him, and *SLAM*.

She had slapped her shutters closed and refused to let him see any more of that light, refused to connect with him, refused to acknowledge him as anything more than the flat tire on their double date. It was unexpected so soon in their acquaintance, but he knew what to do with rejection. He'd wrapped the hurt in a thick blanket of resentment and buried it with his other baggage.

Clearly, Ryan had been wrong about her.

The second time Noah had seen Grace was more like blinding winter sunlight through the fog of a developing inversion: indirect, glaring, more annoying than warm. His old, blanketed sliver of resentment had remembered Grace the moment she stepped into the math lab, though it had taken his eyes and brain longer to accept. When she'd refused to recognize him, the sliver had morphed into a living thing with an ugly head and a voracious appetite.

He had made a choice, in that moment when she'd unknowingly reintroduced herself and held out a self-serving-disguised-as-friendly hand. He would tutor her—he needed the money—but he would *not* like it, and he would definitely not let on that he knew her. He would use the time to catalog every lousy, miserable fault she had and feed it to his resentment.

Like her snarky playfulness. It *had* to be fake. No one felt that happy all the time. Even when the math had been exceptionally frustrating, she had always presented him with that irritating, definitely fake smile that somehow transformed her fairly average face into something more—especially when she teased him by pretending she understood less than she actually did. When that happened, the smile spread into her eyes and made them sparkle in a way Noah had thought was confined to cheap novels.

He didn't like it. He didn't.

Surely her attitude resulted directly from her idyllic background. Her life must have been so blissfully trial-free that she knew nothing of sadness or pain. That would explain the annoying good humor. Maintaining his dislike for her through all that cheerfulness hadn't been difficult since he considered bubbly people annoying as a matter of principle.

She's not annoying like Amy.

The thought rang true, but he shoved it aside, focusing on how spoiled Grace was, taking all those easy classes and not even holding a job. He knew from a few things Ryan had said that her family was well-off. Grace had enrolled in a bunch of meaningless classes to fill out her final semester around the required math with no worry over how to pay for such wastefulness. Noah cared too little about fashion to know what her clothes cost, but if he were a betting man, he'd wager that her understated style didn't come cheap. Her ridiculous named backpack *was* beaten and threadbare, but she probably kept it out of novelty rather than an inability to replace it. If anything, that proved even more how spoiled she was. Keeping something well past its expiration date was a choice for her, not a necessity. She'd never *wanted* for anything, let alone had to work for it.

Speaking of work, since when had *recreation* counted as a career? Grace was bright, even if she wasn't mathematically gifted. Only someone immature and spoiled would spend time and money pursuing a degree in having fun. Degrees should be difficult and demanding—like his own Master of Accounting program was.

Then there was her nosiness. Every week she had poked and prodded and provoked him, trying to force him into giving her information about his personal life that was none of her business. And all the details she'd dropped about herself—though he had paid as little attention as possible—were of no interest to him.

However, ignoring her details had become increasingly difficult when he'd bumped into her off campus. Forgetting how she'd looked trail running or in that Halloween getup was just not possible. Simple math became challenging when images of her strong legs or the dark-chocolate waves in her hair danced about in his head, taunting him. Even the stars mocked him, conjuring images of her huddled up against the cold around a telescope with her perfect father.

In spite of Grace's physical attractiveness, it was her dogged mental efforts in math that had really threatened Noah's armor of resentment. From the first day of tutoring it had been clear to him that she had no confidence in her ability to manipulate variables, regardless of the ease with which she managed calculations. Yet, unlike others he had tutored, she'd refused to settle for memorizing steps or simply arriving at the right answer, insisting on understanding *why* certain problems were approached certain ways, *why* she had to follow the order of operations, *why* she needed to learn algebra at all. He reluctantly conceded that she'd shown a remarkable level of determination for one so obviously coddled.

He could give her that, but no more.

Besides, in light of the self-centered and thoughtless behavior he'd witnessed on their date, even her determination became a fault. He'd never felt as invisible in his life as when she had resolved to ignore him that night, and that was saying something.

At least he'd made some money off the tutoring—enough to supplement what he'd earned working construction over the summer and generating some welcome slack in his tight budget.

If only he hadn't caved in a moment of weakness and talked about his father. That must have been why she'd asked him out—a courtesy date for the poor tutor with no dad to take him stargazing or anywhere else.

Well, Noah wasn't about to be anyone's charity case, least of all hers.

"Do you mind if we sit here?" A woman's voice brought him back to his senses.

"All yours," he said. More than enough time had passed for Grace to be gone by now. He stood, put on his jacket, pushed his chair under the table, and left the math lab. The door thumped shut behind him, an exclamation point closing the chapter of his life that Grace had invaded.

As he walked home, her last words echoed inside his head. His ears grew hot as he examined them.

"*Liar.*"

He may not have been forthcoming, but he'd never actually *lied* to her. So that, at least, was not entirely applicable.

"*Pathetic.*"

There had been no pity in her eyes, so she must have intended the "loser" definition of the word rather than "pitiable." Noah could deal with that. He didn't need her approval—or anyone else's.

It was the last dart she'd thrown that sank into his skin and festered.

"*Alone.*"

It took several days for that one to stop stinging, to fade to the dull ache it always was.

And then, on the last day of finals, her email arrived.

It sat in his inbox, unread, for several hours—the bright-red notification glaring at him every time he looked at his phone. His rising irritation outstripped his growing curiosity until he forced himself to swipe left and delete the email, unread. Then curiosity took over, and he brought it—and the annoying notification bubble—right back.

He didn't want to read it, but he couldn't just let it sit. What if there was something important in there?

Like what? he thought. There was no what-if scenario that could convince him it was necessary reading, no emergency situation that would require Grace to reach out to *him*. There were plenty of people left on Earth, and Noah was smart enough to know that he would be the very last one she'd ask for help.

For anything.

And yet, she *had* emailed him. So why?

He had no idea, and the little red dot gnawed at his peace of mind. Once finals were over and the unfilled downtime of Christmas break took hold, it became a nagging voice inside his head—one that threatened to drive him crazy.

Just read it.

    I don't want to.

Yes you do.

    No I don't.

Then why are you still thinking about it?

Eventually, a compromise was reached. Irritation demanded action, and curiosity dictated what it would be. With nothing better to hold his attention but the echoing silence of his empty apartment, Noah sat down on his twin bed and opened Grace's email.

Noah,

I promised I wouldn't trouble you any further, but as a means of getting some closure for myself, I feel compelled to write the defense you wouldn't allow me to speak.

Of course, you're just as likely to shut me down now as you did before, but at least I will have given myself the opportunity to explain, whether you hit the trash button before you read this or not.

First, please allow me to apologize for my treatment of you on our date. My behavior cannot be excused. I was immature, self-absorbed, rude. Claire let me have it after you left, and I did my best to take her words to heart. I realized that night that it's never okay to treat others poorly, that hurting others will only make my own hurts worse. I had always prided myself on my kindness, but that night I allowed my personal challenges to blind me and felt justified in doing so. I was wrong. I'm sorry.

In my efforts to improve, I did my best to learn from that night—to make changes but move on as if it never happened. I was too ashamed to think about it. Claire and Ryan could both see this and never brought it up again. We succeeded admirably because I really did not recognize you when we met again. In my defense, your appearance has altered, but that doesn't excuse my initial disregard, and for that I again apologize.

As for your charge that I responded with only irritation at the "inconvenience" of a man's death, may I first remind you that I had only spoken to Lupe Navarro once and never met her or her poor brother? I distinctly remember offering my condolences, but you cut me off before I could finish my sentence. At that point, I hastily assumed that it would be more comfortable for you to get to the business of tutoring. I was also panicking at the possibility of having to find another math tutor in a short amount of time for a class that I dreaded. Math in general stresses me out, as you know, and to have the added pressure of my graduation and employment hinging on a passing grade rendered me insensitive. I offer that as an explanation of my mistake, not justification. I know I was inconsiderate, and I'm sorry. Losing a sibling is one of life's most painful trials. I pray your friend is able to make peace with her brother's passing.

And then your comments about my major got my hackles up, and I said things I regret. Please forgive me for failing to curb my anger and hold my tongue. I'm trying to do better.

I would, however, like to explain a little about therapeutic recreation, not that you care. It's true that I might take people zip-lining or camping, but my training has focused on how I can use recreational activities to help people with illness or disability re-discover the joy of living. I've seen it work. I've seen how recreation brings light into the eyes of someone struggling with loss or depres-sion, how facing fears reduces anxiety and boosts confidence and facilitates connection, how accommodations can be made so that the physically limited can enjoy the exhilaration of extreme sports. It isn't just "glamping," although that doesn't sound too bad either. I hope you've had experiences in your life in which you were able to spend time outdoors, commune with nature, or try something you thought you never could or would do. If you haven't, maybe give it a shot. It's wonderful.

I'm rambling. I got on my soapbox. Sorry. Again.

As for the incident with Mandy Miller, I believe I can defend myself there, though I should have curbed my reaction during our date that night. Mandy grew up in the same neighborhood with Claire and me. She's a year younger than Claire, and we all played together when we were little. She moved away in junior high when her parents divorced, and we lost track of each other. By the time she got to high school, she was running with some pretty wild friends and wanted nothing to do with us. She was, however, very interested in my younger brother. Her influence led him into the same rough crowd and was instrumental in bringing more grief to our family than I can put into words. Mandy has her own story, though I don't know it, and for that I'm sure she deserves compassion. But running into her that night brought up a lot of unprocessed emotion in me. I like to think that my response to her now would be much different. That doesn't excuse my past mistakes, but maybe knowing the background will help you understand.

Well, I'm surprised if you're still reading at this point. Whether you are or not, I feel better for having written it. Again, I apologize for my sharpness. I will always remember and appreciate your patience and expertise in tutoring me. I wish only the best for you as you move forward.

Sincerely,
Grace Ebert

Noah closed his mail app, plugged his phone in, and tossed it to the floor.

Fantastic.

Grace had obviously found her closure by justifying everything she said. Now she could start her ridiculous job—*communing with nature*, Noah thought, rolling his eyes—with a clear conscience and go back to forgetting his existence.

He pulled his quilt up around his shoulders and swallowed against the tightness in the back of his throat, reminding himself that she was the first offender.

He would just have to forget about her too.

Chapter 24

ALONE

WEEKS PASSED, WINTER SEMESTER STARTED, and Noah could not get Grace's email out of his mind. School was going well enough, but any time he was away from his studies—and often when he wasn't—there it was in the back of his head. If that email had been on paper, it would have been ratty and torn from the frequency of his reading it.

January was always a struggle, with the lack of light and exercise, another long semester in front of him, and the holidays a too-recent memory. For Noah, family time necessitated recovery time. His older brother, Matt, made a few dutiful efforts to pull Noah from his shell via text, but Noah rarely responded. Likewise, his mom called regularly. Mostly, she talked to his voicemail, but he occasionally answered, gritting his teeth through complaints of not seeing enough of him and lengthy recaps of Matt's most recent success. Noah took his meds—thankful to have finally found some that worked without killing his appetite or making him gain weight—sat in front of his phototherapy light to study, and went for a walk when he felt low. It kept him functional. Barely.

The ski class at the small resort near Oak Hills helped. He had signed up for it on a whim, thinking it might make the dark weeks go faster.

It had nothing to do with Grace's email.

Besides, it filled what had been a wide-open day in his school schedule, and it was fairly inexpensive to do it through the school, though he could barely justify the added expense of the class, let alone new equipment. He'd bought an old, beat-up set of skis and boots from the classifieds for next to nothing that fit well enough.

He also took on another tutoring job, and although the material was much more challenging (calculus) and the student mathematically inclined (a freshman aiming to get into the engineering program), the sessions crept by in a way they never had with Grace. Noah had to drag himself to each appointment. The money was barely enough incentive for him to show up, which didn't make any sense at all. He had pointedly hated Grace through every session, yet he now found himself itching for someone to tease him as his new client silently did calculations.

How can I miss seeing someone I hate?

Everything about Grace had irritated Noah, but now that she was gone, he kept discovering things he'd taken for granted.

He hadn't even realized the pleasant, mildly flowery scent he'd associated with the math lab was actually *her*, until his new student sat down and smelled like, well, a guy.

A guy who never once shared anything personal or talked about life outside the math lab, who never made Noah want to laugh.

Grace was true to her word; he had to give her that. No matter how many times he checked his inbox, there was nothing new from her. That made sense. He hadn't sent a response, and her school email was probably defunct now that she'd graduated. He had composed many messages in his head, even typed out an email reply filled with more of the venom he'd spouted at their final meeting. That word—*alone*—still smarted. When he had finished spewing and almost pushed Send instead of the trash icon, he'd nearly had a heart attack.

Much as he didn't want to admit it, the repeated readings of her email had softened his perception of her. Maybe she wasn't that terrible. Maybe he'd judged her too harshly. But what did she mean by her "personal challenges" blinding her? What challenges could she possibly have? Her life was a cakewalk.

But then the issue of Lupe Navarro's brother's death crept back into his mind, and Noah was forced to admit Grace had completely justified her response. He could remember, now, that she *had* tried to express sympathy. And Noah had cut her off. Rudely.

The words in her email about losing a sibling being one of life's most painful trials reminded him that she, too, had lost a sibling—a brother, if his own faulty memory could be trusted. Ryan had mentioned it before their date. So maybe she had faced some personal challenges.

The frequency with which she continued to encroach on his thoughts was disturbing. When she started showing up in his dreams, teasing him about his grumpiness or asking him to help her with her homework, he knew he had to do something.

After his dad had died, the therapist Mom had forced him to see had assigned Noah to write letters to his dad. It had cracked his dam of anger and resentment, eventually allowing him to process some of the hurt.

Maybe it would help to do the same with Grace.

He drafted a new reply to her email—this time in a document so he couldn't accidentally send it. All it said was, *I'm sorry for being mean.* He almost felt he *should* send that one, but eating crow in private was hard enough. He convinced himself it would be better for her if she never heard from him again. Besides, he didn't have her new email address or any other way of contacting her.

At least, not one he was willing to use.

The next entry he wrote after a particularly vivid dream reliving their date. He filled it with all the bitterness he could summon, much of it having nothing to do with her, if he was honest. Like lancing a boil, getting all the hateful words out of his head cleared his mind for different thoughts.

As he read what he'd written, seeing for the first time how much of his anger at Grace stemmed from the rejection he'd felt as a child, he admitted to himself that he missed talking to her—or, well, *her* talking to *him*.

He missed her telling him all those little things about herself he had pretended to ignore. The writing helped, but he regretted all the times she had asked about his life and he had shut her down. Would it have been so bad to share? Blurting out that his dad had died an alcoholic had been strangely cathartic—even now, he wasn't sure how that had happened—and when he'd told her he didn't want to talk about it again, she'd respected that boundary without argument. Almost like she understood.

The snow fell on the plateau and in the mountains, his classes slogged on, and Noah somehow survived. His last ski class came and went, and those now-empty Tuesdays loomed as the longest day of the week. March brought some sunshine and slipped into a warmer April, but the usual lift he felt in the spring was missing.

Something had to change.

Chapter 25

PITCH

ONE COOL BUT SUNNY LATE-APRIL afternoon, after completing his last winter semester final, Noah zipped up his jacket and started home from campus. His dingy basement apartment on the west side, shared with three other single men, was less than homey—but it was in good repair, and it was cheap. He imagined what kind of apartment Grace lived in—he had only ever heard her mention one roommate, so she probably had a private room in one of the newer units farther from campus. The dream job had taken her nearer to Grand Junction, if he wasn't mistaken. He pictured her lounging comfortably after work in a sunlit living room, reading a novel, surrounded by glossy brochures for exotic outdoor adventures, her curly brown hair falling in front of her eyes—

"Hey, Noah!"

He startled at the voice next to him, looked around to get his bearings, found Amy's roommate at his side, and stifled a groan.

"Oh, hey . . ." He racked his brain for the girl's name but came up short and covered the fail with a nod. In addition to the Amy connection, he knew the woman was dating a guy he'd had a class with but couldn't remember his name either. A twinge of guilt niggled at him. He had railed at Grace for forgetting him, but his memory was clearly far from perfect.

"Jane," she said, providing the name he couldn't supply. "I'm Amy's—"

"Roommate," he finished, feeling like a heel on multiple levels. Maybe it was time he made an effort to be social again. "Yeah, I recognized you. I just couldn't . . ." Her boyfriend's name materialized. "Chad's your boyfriend, right?"

Her smile brightened. "Fiancé, actually. We were just talking about you the other day."

"Oh," he said, trying to smile as his stomach tightened. He thought the thing with Amy had been long since resolved. Was she sending her roommates to fetch him for her now?

Jane chuckled. "Don't worry," she said, "I'm not here on Amy's bidding."
Noah failed to hide his relief.

"Yeah, she can be . . . overenthusiastic, but she has a good heart. Anyway,"
she said, repositioning her backpack on her shoulders, "do you mind if I
walk with you?"

He shrugged and resumed his homeward trek as Jane continued talking.

"So Chad and I are going to volunteer at an orphanage in Mexico for a
week after finals."

What was he supposed to say to that? "Good for you"? "Way to be charitable"? He just nodded.

"There's this foundation that organizes teams to travel down and help—
I've gone a few times. Anyway, we've got a great group going this time, all
singles—except me and Chad, I guess—but one of our guys just had to bail."

"That's too bad," Noah said. What did this have to do with him? Surely,
she wasn't asking—

"We've got some other girls who might be able to go, but we could really use
another guy in the group, and Chad brought up your name. You work construction in the summers, right?"

"Yeah." How did Jane know that? He had talked to Chad a few times in
class, and he was a nice enough guy, but Noah barely knew him. Jane even
less.

"That's perfect!" she said. "I know it's spur-of-the-moment and you won't
know everyone, but I've done this a few times and it's amazing. Spending
time with the kids, improving their living situations, showing them that
there are people who care . . . I'll send you a link so you can check it out."

It did sound kind of amazing—just the kind of thing that might pull
him out of this latest funk—other than spending an entire week trapped in
another country with a bunch of people he didn't know. Fortunately, the fact
that he could barely pay his rent gave him an easy out.

"That does sound great, but I can't afford—"

"That's the best part!" Jane's eyes lit up. "My uncle has his own company,
and when he heard I was putting together another group, he offered to sponsor
us, so it's all paid for except for a few meals and gas. We're taking a van, so that
won't be much, and if you want to, you can bring food from home for the
drive so that won't even be an added expense."

Noah's mind reeled as Jane continued her high-speed sales pitch. They were
nearing his apartment now, and she could probably sense she was running out
of time. He couldn't just pick up and leave.

Could he? He did have over a week before his summer job and classes started, but was this what he wanted to do with it?

What else am I going to do with that week?

He tuned back in to Jane. She had mentioned something about work clothes and a day at the beach, and now she was covering logistics.

"—so we'll leave Monday morning, stay with my uncle in Tucson that night, and finish the drive into Mexico on Tuesday. You're going to be such an asset, with your building skills! Do you have a passport?"

"Yeah . . ." Thanks to his trip to Ghana, which like this opportunity, had been sponsored by a wealthy donor.

"Great! Can I get your phone number?"

Phone in hand, she walked away, leaving him bewildered at the top of the stairs that led to the bottom row of Grand Apartments. Had he really given his phone number to an engaged girl he hardly knew? A text buzzed in on his phone.

This is Jane ☺ *I'll text you the link to the foundation's website as soon as I get home. So excited to have you on board!!!*

Link? On board? Noah's face scrunched as he attempted to replay their conversation. Had he actually agreed to anything? Had she even asked? He put his hands in his pockets and made his way to the dungeon he called home.

Constructed in the age of dinosaurs, the bare concrete walls and rusted railings at the spuriously named Grand Apartments were as homey as anything had ever been for Noah. He'd made the mistake of looking around before choosing this place for its price. There were a few crazy-nice student apartments in Oak Hills—lofty names, new buildings, private bedrooms, spacious kitchens that didn't smell of mildew and old fridge, occupants who used Daddy's car and credit—but those weren't for Noah. His was the world of concrete slab and rusted railings and DIY schooling. The only way he could afford higher education without burying himself under a mountain of student debt was through scholarship, frugality, and hard work in the summers.

He unlocked the front door, wiping his feet on the outside welcome mat in deference to the thin brownish-gray interior floor covering that was more upholstery than carpet, and went straight to his shared room. Wyatt, his freshman roommate, was locked into some gaming world, as usual, and gave only the barest of head bobs in greeting. Wouldn't want to mess up the game for an in-person interaction. They had lived in this room together for four months, and he still didn't know the kid's last name.

Noah's phone buzzed as he sat on his neatly made bed. It was another text from Jane.

Here's the link! Let me know if you have any questions! See you Monday morning! ☺

He clicked the link only out of curiosity. No way could he take off for a week in Mexico. The screen loaded, and he wasn't surprised by what he saw: a pair of enormous inky eyes peeked out at him from behind a brightly colored kite. Youthful skin crinkled at the corners in what was surely an adorable smile, and Noah found himself pulled in.

He scrolled down and identified the boy's full face in another photo. A young woman held him in her arms and was surrounded by a small army of similarly dark-eyed children of varying ages, all smiling and laughing at the camera. Other pictures on the page showed volunteers working on various construction or maintenance projects, handing out food, and playing soccer with the children. Banners urged him from every corner of the site to GIVE, VOLUNTEER, and SHARE with the orphans.

Great marketing, Noah thought. Whoever had organized these materials knew what they were doing.

He picked through the carefully curated photos and spotted a few shots of Jane. But there was caution behind the older children's eyes—caution Noah could relate to. *What's the catch?* They seemed to say. *Why are you spending time with me?* Noah's throat caught as it sank in that his youth may not have been ideal, but at least he'd always had his mom and Matt. These kids had no one, no family to take care of them. What if he *could* go spend a week with them, build something for them that would make their difficult circumstances a little easier to bear?

Even as he reminded himself that picking up and leaving the country for a week on only a few days' notice was reckless, Noah's increased heart rate and the unmistakable calmness in his gut informed him that he was, as Jane had put it, on board.

Chapter 26

PACK UP, MOVE OUT

"Mexico?"

Noah smiled at the skepticism in his mother's voice.

"How on earth can you afford to go to Mexico?"

"Mom—"

"I mean, if you can, that's great, but if you're calling for money, you know I can't . . . I wish . . . maybe Matt—"

"Mom," he interrupted, "I'm not calling for money. The expenses will mostly be covered. I only have to pitch in on gas and pay for my own food."

"But where will you be staying? Are these good people you'll be with?" She sucked in a breath. "What if you run into one of those cartels?"

"Of course they're good people—a group of singles going down to volunteer at an orphanage run by nuns." Leave it to Mom to blow out of proportion any possible travel risk, real or contrived. She'd had a similar freak-out when he went to Ghana, and that trip had been planned well in advance with a group of people she knew and trusted. Noah was a paragon of optimism and confidence in comparison.

He gathered up some socks and piled them on the bed with the rest of his gear. "We'll be perfectly safe—the foundation sends groups down all the time. I'll send you a link so you can check it out for yourself, okay?"

"All right, but I just worry." She let out a sigh, then gasped. "Do you need to get shots or anything? Did you check the travel advisories from the State Department? Make sure you don't carry too much cash!"

As if he had enough cash for anyone to bother stealing. He chuckled at her exaggerated worries. "I promise, Mom, I'll be fine. I'll always be with other members of our team, but I won't be answering my phone for a few days because I won't have coverage down there. I don't want you to worry if you can't get ahold of me."

She took a couple of deep breaths. "What day will you be back?"

"I'll be able to call you by Sunday morning," he said, though the schedule said Saturday afternoon. Better to be a day early than have her worrying if they happened to get back late. "And I'll text you contact information for our group leader. She has coverage down there, so you can contact her if there's an emergency."

"Oh good! I'll—"

It took him at least five minutes to strictly define which situations she could classify as emergencies, followed by an interminable recap of his older brother's latest accomplishments.

"I'd better go," he said in an attempt to end her gushing. "Tell Matt I said hi."

"Aren't you going to call him yourself?"

Clenched teeth held a cynical answer on the tip of his tongue. He swallowed it and forced cheer into his voice. "He's so busy. I wouldn't want to bother him."

She pushed back, as mothers did. "He's not too busy to—"

"Just tell him hi for me, Mom. I have to finish packing." Throwing his few things into a duffel would only take a second, but she didn't need to know that. The disappointment was clear in her voice as they finished their goodbyes and hung up. That was nothing new.

Five minutes later Noah threw the duffel over his shoulder and left on foot for the nearby parking lot where Jane had told him to meet her, determined to leave his wallowing behind. This would be a great and inexpensive opportunity to serve others, visit another country, and possibly make some new friends. Small groups were much easier for Noah to navigate, and he was tired of being alone.

"Alone."

Grace's voice echoed in his head as he waited to cross the street. He'd made plenty of mistakes in his life—one of which, he now acknowledged, was being too hard on Grace and holding that grudge for so long—but he was determined to stop looking back.

"I was wondering if I could take you out to dinner."

Why had she asked him out? Pity. She knew enough to peg him as the loner he was.

Well, time to change that. He banished Grace's voice and rounded the last corner, spotting Jane and Chad near a fairly new-looking fifteen-passenger van ready and waiting in the parking lot, though Noah was ten minutes early.

Unlike Matt, who was consistently late. It drove Noah crazy—a constant reminder that his brother's time was more important than Noah's.

He headed for the van, watching as Jane and Chad loaded a bag of soccer balls into a rooftop cargo carrier. Chad saw Noah first and hollered a hello. "Bedding is going in the back," he said, "so put your bag in the van. There are only ten of us, so there should be plenty of room for gear."

Numbers and anxiety swirled through Noah's head. Ten people. Twelve driving hours today, an overnight stop at a stranger's house tonight in Tucson, six more hours in the van tomorrow, nine virtual strangers sharing his space, five nights on the floor in a country where he didn't speak the predominant language.

What if they can't stand me?

What if I can't stand them?

What if—

Pulling out an old anti-anxiety trick, Noah inhaled and focused his thoughts on his feet as he approached the van, wiggling his toes in the new socks he'd splurged on and noting how the old running shoes formed to his soles. He let out his breath and pushed the anxiety with it.

Silly, he thought. It was such a simple exercise, it shouldn't be able to calm him so quickly, but it usually did, even when he didn't believe it would. A few seconds of thinking about his feet, and he felt a little better. Silly but effective.

As he threw his duffel into the back seat of the van, he noticed a couple of guys collecting their gear from a dark-gray sedan parked nearby. He took another intentional breath and approached the car. "Need any help?" he asked.

The thinner of the two guys emerged from the trunk with a case of water bottles and handed it off to Noah with a friendly lift of his chin. "These go in the van. Maybe under a seat or something."

Relieved at the casual nonintroduction, Noah stashed the water and turned to find the second guy on his heels with another case. "Sorry," Noah said, stepping out of the way.

"No worries." Tall and broad-shouldered, the second guy stashed the water next to Noah's and stretched out a hand. "I'm Alec. You'll have to forgive Garth," he said with a smirk at the first guy. "He's not too social."

Noah met Alec's hand and returned the firm grip. "We ought to get along, then. I'm Noah."

They fished the rest of the gear out of the car, stowing it in the van as Alec kept a mostly one-sided conversation going with speculation about the trip. Garth mumbled a few monosyllables, while Noah contributed an occasional nod or grunt.

"I hope my Spanish can keep up," Alec said, frowning and running a hand through his blond hair as he assessed the remaining space in the cargo area. "I don't know if we've got enough room here for—"

A car screeched into the parking lot and stopped near the van, its doors opening to spill a gaggle of laughing females into the morning sunlight.

A girl with a honey-colored messy bun atop her head held a fist aloft and hollered, "I told you we'd make it!" before executing what must have been meant as a victory dance.

Alec belly laughed. "I knew you'd make it, Emily, just not on time."

Noah glanced at his watch, which showed they were already five minutes behind schedule, as Alec and Emily continued teasing each other.

Five women. By the sound of things, Noah doubted he'd have one moment of quiet in the van—or for the next week. Garth sighed, seeming to mirror Noah's thoughts, then stepped forward to help load all the new baggage.

Once things were stowed, Chad called the group together for some quick introductions. Other than Emily, the women's names sailed past Noah, though the blond, blue-eyed twins were hard to miss.

A girl with long black hair held her tongue but laughed readily at her louder friends. Mischievous eyes matched her hair and hinted at Asian ancestry. She caught him watching her and offered a smile before looking away.

The loudest of the group, after Emily, sported chin-length brown hair and bangs brushing light-green eyes that stuck on Alec. It figured. Athletic build, beach hair, outgoing personality—Noah had no doubt who would be the girls' favorite.

"Let's move!" Chad said when the introductions were complete.

"Only fifteen minutes behind schedule," Alec muttered loud enough for Emily to hear.

"Be nice!" she countered, swatting at his hair—no small feat, as she stood a good foot shorter than him.

"Maybe you can make up some of that time for us," Chad said to Alec, tossing him the keys.

"Can't say no to that," Alec said, snatching the keys out of the air and taking the driver's seat. "I've always wanted to drive one of these babies. I hear they corner like they're on rails."

Bangs let out a groan. "I'd better take shotgun if Alec's driving."

Quiet Girl smirked as Noah caught her eye. "Guess that means I'm in the back again," she said.

"Again?" Noah asked as they lined up for boarding.

She chuckled good-naturedly. "We've done a few road trips. I don't get carsick, so I always get the back."

"Taking one for the team, huh?"

Her smile broadened. "You could say that."

Noah relaxed a bit. "I'm sorry, I didn't catch your name."

"Vanessa," she supplied as she stepped into the van. "You're Noah, right? Our last-minute fill-in?"

"That's me," he said, following her. The twins—he didn't know their names—sat in the first passenger row, with Chad and Jane behind them.

Ahead of them, Garth stepped past Emily, who had claimed the third-row window, and planted himself in the rear. "Whose bag is this?" he asked with a nervous look at Vanessa.

"Mine," Noah said, stifling a laugh at Garth's obvious relief. At least the fourth row had four seats instead of three so he and Garth would have plenty of room to spread out.

Vanessa tossed a smile over her shoulder at Noah. "Guess that puts me with Emily."

Too bad. The thought surprised Noah.

"I'll take the aisle first, if you don't mind," Garth said. "We can switch off later so we each have a share of the extra leg room."

"Good plan." Noah scooted past Garth's long legs and boots, bending over the third seat to avoid hitting his head on the roof. Alec revved the engine and pulled out, taking a speed bump fast enough to send the rear passengers and all the gear zero-G and back down with a thump.

"Sorry, guys!" Alec hollered from the front. "Wasn't sure how this beauty would handle the bumps. I'll go faster next time so you can catch some real air."

The girl with bangs groaned again, but Alec laughed.

"Anyone have Dramamine?" Noah asked dryly.

Vanessa threw one elbow over the back of her seat, along with another smile. "You'll probably be fine, unless that's something you really struggle with. He'll calm down now, but Alec never turns down an opportunity to tease."

"Especially if it's Brianna," Emily added.

"Or any other female," Garth muttered.

"True that," Vanessa said. "He's never been one to discriminate."

Emily threw her head back and laughed, allowing a curl to escape the confines of her messy bun and reminding Noah of another woman—much taller and with darker curls—as she tucked it back behind her ear. He clenched his jaw and pulled up the map on his phone, inputting Tucson as the destination.

Eleven and a half hours. He should have brought something to occupy his mind. Anything to keep it from wandering back to Grace.

Chapter 27

ZONED

THE FIRST HOUR PASSED QUICKLY—AND more quietly than Noah had expected. He attempted to follow the steady stream of conversation between Emily and Vanessa with Chad and Jane sometimes joining in, but he had little to contribute. Up front, the twins started a movie on a laptop while Brianna entertained Alec and Garth dozed.

Noah was starting to nod off himself when the van slowed and the voices of his companions drew his attention.

"What are you doing?" Brianna asked.

"Giving you a reason to stop scrolling Instagram," Alec said.

"There's literally nothing to see!"

"And that's why we're taking the scenic route."

Brianna groaned along with several of the others.

"We really can't afford to add to the drive," Jane said.

"Trust me," Alec said.

"Not happening," Brianna said, pointing straight ahead to the interstate on-ramp. "Just get back on the highway."

Noah clenched his teeth. The last thing he needed was *more* time in the van.

"It only adds ten minutes!" Alec shouted from the front with a laugh. "And it's actually a few miles shorter because we don't have to backtrack. You're gonna love it!"

"What's in Cisco?" Garth asked, tipping his head at the name on a road sign as they passed under the interstate and turned onto a two-lane country road. Drab desert stretched into the distance on both sides.

"Trust me!" Alec insisted again.

"When you said 'scenic route,' were you talking about the landscape or the road conditions?" Brianna asked. "Because I'm seeing some pretty big valleys right here in the asphalt."

Alec swerved around several potholes in the narrow, unstriped, shoulderless road, taking her teasing in stride. "It all adds to the charm."

When the next sign announced Next Services 54 Miles, Noah pulled out his phone and opened his map app, watching the loading icon spin and spin until a thumping passage over a railroad crossing stirred his stomach and drew his eyes back to the road. A few buildings and a sign for Cisco Landing had popped up, but Alec stayed the course into another stretch of slightly rolling gravel hills and stark desert.

The map refused to load. Putting his phone away and wiping his hands on his jeans, Noah cleared his throat and tried to swallow the knot forming there. The desolation held a kind of barren beauty, but he hated not knowing where they were. *Not a big deal,* he thought, letting out a deep breath. *Alec knows where he's going. I hope.*

Vanessa turned to put one arm over the seat. "It really isn't much longer this way."

Noah wondered if she'd noticed his anxiety or if she was just making conversation. Hopefully the second. He made an effort to relax his hands, which were splayed aggressively on his thighs.

Vanessa continued. "And Alec is right. It's totally worth it."

Noah looked pointedly out the window before turning back to Vanessa with lifted brows.

She chuckled. "I promise! We're not that far from Moab. Look!" she said, gesturing to a bluish hint of snow-capped mountains on the horizon. "Those are the La Sals, the second-highest mountain range in Utah."

"Only second, huh?" Garth said. "Baby mountains compared to Colorado."

Vanessa's smile broadened as she turned her gaze to Garth. "They're close to 13,000 feet. Still nothing to sneeze at."

"I thought Moab was all about sandstone, not mountains," Emily said.

"That's just what made it famous," Vanessa said, "but pretty soon we should be—yeah, look!"

A line of bright green broke through the monotony, and the road brought them into a narrow valley bisected by the muddy water of the Colorado River. Bright-green fields stretched between red cliffs, the pavement occasionally hugging the walls, the river sometimes seeming to lap at their tires. An involuntary sigh escaped Noah, his worry easing away with it.

"Fantastic, isn't it?"

He pulled his gaze from the window and found Vanessa watching him. "Yeah," he said.

"Ever been to Moab?"

"Nope."

"If you ever get the chance, take it."

"Have you spent a lot of time here?" he asked.

Emily laughed. "She came once and ended up changing her major to geology."

"Really?" Noah asked.

"Yeah," Vanessa said with a wince. "I could live my whole life down here and never run out of places to explore."

"I bet," Noah said, turning his attention back to the scenery. Campgrounds sprouted in the floodplain as cliffs ranging beige to dark red slipped past, bright- and dark-green bushes growing directly out of the rock. As they drew nearer to Moab, the canyon walls rose nearly vertical on either side, dark streaks of desert "varnish," as Vanessa called it, painting their faces. Noah watched mountain and road bikers on a separate paved trail between road and river as the gorge widened, and before he knew it the cliffs had thrown their arms wide to reveal the verdant Moab valley.

Alec pulled into a park at the gorge's mouth, right next to the busy main highway bridging the river. "See?" he said to Jane. "Right on time and totally worth it."

Jane looked at her watch and smiled. "Not quite on time but, yes, worth it. We'll stop here for about ten minutes if anyone wants to stretch their legs or use the restrooms."

One of the twins hauled the side door open, allowing warm, dry air to seep into the van. Noah waited for the others to exit, then stepped into the sunshine and let the sun heat his back as he watched the river flow across the valley and into a gap in the cliffs on the other side.

"Nice, isn't it?" Vanessa said.

Noah nodded. "This valley looks different from the river gorge."

"That's because it wasn't cut by the river."

Noah gawked at the marvels around him, listening as Vanessa pointed out fault lines and explained how the valley was formed when an underlying layer of salt washed away.

"I'm boring you," she said, breaking into his thoughts.

Noah tore his eyes from the cliffs. "Not at all. I'm just—this is so amazing. I can't get over the magnitude of the forces it took to create all this—turning sand into solid rock, then lifting it up and washing it away over millions of years. It's incredible."

Vanessa's eyes were laughing.

"Did I get it wrong?" Heat blossomed in his cheeks.

"No, it's just—that's more than you've spoken the entire trip."

"It's only been a couple of hours."

She chuckled and he chuckled, and for a second Noah thought maybe . . .

"Hey, so . . ." Vanessa tossed a look around and lowered her voice. "Do you know if Garth is dating anyone?"

Oddly enough, being firmly friend-zoned by Vanessa helped Noah relax as Alec and Brianna traded places with Chad and Jane and their long drive resumed. He hadn't realized he was putting relationship pressure on himself again—not that it ever truly relented for a single guy his age—but her question about Garth helped him consciously decide against trying for any of the women on the trip. Better to just develop some new friendships.

With that in mind, along with Vanessa's comment about him barely speaking, engaging in the conversations around him grew easier. The girls were entertaining without being obnoxious—Emily with a ready laugh and expressive face, Vanessa more subdued but every bit as funny. Even Garth was drawn in with their rapid-fire Q&A game about hypotheticals relating to music.

"So the zombie apocalypse has arrived," Vanessa said, a hint of a smile on her lips, "and you have to choose which music to preserve for the remnants of mankind. Do you choose classical or modern?"

"Modern," Noah said. "No contest."

"Live or studio?" Emily asked him.

"Studio. Hate the screaming."

Vanessa asked next. "Jazz or rap?"

"Uh, neither?"

"No, you have to pick one," Vanessa said. "We're narrowing the field."

"Really. Neither."

"Noah!" Emily said.

"Fine. Jazz. But it's out on the next round."

Vanessa smirked and shot another question at him. "Folk music or country?"

"Can you not include something I actually like?"

"Hey, don't knock country," Garth said, adding a little extra twang to his rural accent. "I'm named after Garth Brooks, you know."

Emily practically jumped out of her seat. "Not true!"

"True. My parents are nuts about him." Garth clasped his hands over his heart and raised his pitch. "'Garth Brooks brought us together!'"

The girls laughed. "How?" Emily asked.

"They met country dancing, two-stepped to 'Two of a Kind, Workin' on a Full House' and never looked back."

"Oh, that's sweet!" Emily said.

Garth shook his head. "I guess, but really? They had to name me after him?"

Vanessa squinted at Noah. "You're a classic-rock guy," she said.

He hid his surprise behind a lifted eyebrow, neither confirming nor denying it as the van slowed and took an exit ramp.

Smug, she turned back to the front.

"Where are we?" Alec asked, rousing himself from sleep.

"North Phoenix," Jane said and then directed Chad through the heavy traffic.

"I'm starved," Garth said. "Are we eating soon?"

Noah's stomach grumbled in agreement as Jane answered. Any trace of the sack lunch he'd eaten as they drove was long gone. "There's an Indian place nearby that's supposed to be amazing."

"Mmm," one of the twins said. "Do you think it's as good as Prasanna Palace?"

Noah had heard people rave about the Indian restaurant in Oak Hills, but his budget didn't accommodate eating out often. Hopefully, he'd still have enough cash after this to get some authentic Mexican food south of the border.

Once the gas tank was filled, it was only a few blocks to the restaurant. Chad pulled the van into a strip mall and parked. Stepping out onto the piping-hot asphalt, Noah spotted the restaurant wedged between a hearing center and a hair salon. Bright-red letters above the door flickered against the afternoon sunlight, announcing the Indian cuisine that seasoned the air and made Noah's mouth water.

Once inside, Chad asked if they could combine several smaller tables to seat them all in the middle of the tiny restaurant, and Jane ordered a variety of dishes for them all to share. Noah tasted everything, from the mild shrimp korma to the hot chicken curry—that one lit a fire on his tongue that required a chocolate from Emily's stash to put it out. His favorite was the medium chicken tikka masala, with its delicate blend of spices and just enough heat to make it interesting.

They lingered over dinner, enjoying the food and waiting for the traffic to thin as the sun dipped closer to the horizon. Eventually, Jane deemed the roads passable.

"I am *not* ready to get back into that van," Brianna said with a groan.

"Remember," Alec said, grinning and putting an arm around her shoulder as they exited the restaurant, "it may only be another two hours tonight, but we get six more tomorrow!"

This prompted grumbling from the rest of the group, along with a slug in the arm from Garth, but Alec laughed it off. "Come on, guys! If you keep this up, I might start to think you don't enjoy my company."

Garth muttered something that sounded violent but refrained from hitting Alec again.

Emily offered herself as a guard against boredom once they were back in the van by relating some of her worst dating experiences. "So an hour later," she said on her third or fourth why-I'm-still-single story, "I'm standing with my friends, just talking, and I feel this *tap, tap, tap* on my shoulder again."

"No way," Alec said as he saw where the story was going.

"Same guy! Skinny as a straw, same exact line." Emily lowered her voice to a more manly range. "'Excuse me. I'm sorry to interrupt, but would you care to dance?'"

The twins let out matching groans.

"But wait! There's more!" Emily held out her hands, imitating an infomercial announcer. "He takes my hand and leads me onto the dance floor. And asks my name. Again."

"Stop!" Vanessa said through her laughing tears. "I can't!"

"What?" Emily asked. "You've already heard this one!"

"I know, I know! It's just"—she gasped for air—"it gets better every time!"

Emily swatted her playfully and continued. "I figure, okay, I'm not the most memorable face here, and he's probably danced with a lot of girls tonight, which is good—there are always girls waiting to get asked. And it's nice to just get on the floor sometimes, right? I mean, swing dancing is not good solo."

"So not good," Brianna agreed.

"Benefit of the doubt. I give him my name. No big deal. But then"—Emily paused for effect—"he proceeds to retell me the *whole story* of his driving the moving truck to Mississippi in twenty-four hours and how he ate chicken nuggets so he'd stay hungry because he has such a high metabolism and that would keep him awake."

More groans erupted from the group.

"Right as he's getting to the end of the story, he looks at me and says I look familiar and did we already dance tonight? Yes. Yessir, we did."

"That's terrible!" Brianna said.

Emily shook her head, making her now-even-messier bun wobble. "Nah. Being forgettable totally has perks." She waved off the contradictions from her captive audience, a smirk playing at the corners of her mouth. "If I ever need to rob a bank, I won't even have to wear a mask!"

Noah laughed along with the others, enjoying Emily's lightheartedness and the camaraderie of relationship failure, but he couldn't quite ignore the ease with which Emily laughed off the snub—another pointed reminder of how unfair he had been to Grace.

Chapter 28

HOTEL ARIZONA

THEY MADE GOOD TIME TO Tucson, entertained by Emily and having missed most of the evening traffic. Chad slowed the van and took an exit, then wove through the streets toward the rolling foothills.

"Why is it so dark?" Brianna asked, her voice high and whiny. "Don't they believe in streetlights here?"

"Tucson is a dark-sky city," Jane said, gesturing Chad straight through an intersection.

Brianna scoffed. "Well, obviously it's dark, but why?"

"It's to reduce light pollution so you can see the stars better." Jane frowned at the dark street, then consulted the map on her phone. "But it sure makes finding my uncle's house a challenge."

Noah could only imagine what Grace would say if she were present. Most likely, she would defend the dark-sky movement, waxing poetic about the night sky's beauty and encouraging all of them to get out and enjoy nature more. She might remind them of the harmful effects of light pollution on both humans and ecosystems, finishing off with a hearty endorsement of reducing energy consumption.

Either that or she would have played along with Brianna, encouraging further complaints while sending conspiratorial looks Noah's way.

"What's funny?" Vanessa asked.

"Huh? Oh, nothing." Noah crushed his smile and thoughts, fishing for a distraction out the window.

Headlights from passing cars revealed shopping districts and neighborhoods with more plant life than Noah had anticipated in addition to brief glimpses of wildflower-covered hillsides. The houses grew bigger and farther apart as they left the city behind, solar panels blanketing many of the sun-baked rooftops.

Following Jane's directions, Chad passed a golf course and wound through streets named for the hills' animal inhabitants—Fox Drive, Coyote Cove, Bighorn Lane—before pulling into a long driveway coming off a cul-de-sac. Dim landscape lighting illuminated the drive as they approached, turning off a few seconds after they passed. It was another hundred meters or more before Noah caught sight of the house, an adobe-style mansion with a semicircular portico guarding the front entrance. An archway next to the entry led to more garage doors than Noah could count in a glance, everything lit by dim, downward-aiming lights. The effect was stunning, like something you would see at the front of a hotel. A superfancy hotel.

His stomach clenched. What kind of person was this uncle of Jane's, anyway? What had Noah gotten himself into? Before he could work up a full panic, he found himself drawn from the van by the flow of stir-crazy companions, everyone thrilled at being free and gawking at their surroundings. The afternoon heat had diminished into a lovely evening. A burly middle-aged man in jeans and a T-shirt strode toward them from the one open garage, a giant grin on his face as he rubbed greasy hands on a towel.

Chauffeur? Mechanic on retainer? Noah fought an eye roll—thankfully so, because as soon as Jane saw the man, she squealed, "Uncle Frank!" and ran at him.

The man laughed and pulled her into a giant bear hug. "How's my Janie?" he said, drawing back and holding Jane by the shoulders to give her a once-over before catching Chad's eye. Releasing Jane, he gave her fiancé a firm handshake and back slap. "Chad! Good to see you again."

"Great to see you!" Chad said. "Still working on the Packard?"

The man's expression lit up. "She's a gem. You'll have to come see what I've done, but the car can wait. Who's doing introductions?"

Jane laughed and complied. "Uncle Frank, this is Brianna, Emily, Vanessa, Kaisley, and Kylie."

He repeated everyone's name as he shook their hands. "You two must be twins!" he said to Vanessa and Emily with a wink, triggering a cascade of laughter among the women. Then he turned his attention to the guys, straightening to maximize his substantial height and pulling his thick shoulders back. "And here's my competition—"

"Frank!" A woman's voice stopped him in his tracks.

"Uh-oh." He shrank into himself, looking to the girls. "Don't let her get me!"

A tiny woman stepped out from the house, her hands on hips covered by a frilly apron. Silver hair in a loose, thick braid hung to her waist. "Don't let him bother you," she said, stretching up to swat Frank's arm. "He's all bark."

He feigned a grunt and settled a huge, gentle hand around her shoulder. "Don't get any ideas, young bucks. She's taken." This earned him an elbow to the ribs.

"Aunt Leanne," Jane said, stepping forward.

"Oh! We've missed you!" Leanne hugged her niece and each of the girls as Jane introduced them. "And here's Chad!" Leanne said with another hug. "Thank you for bringing our Janie for a visit." She threaded her arm through Frank's and turned toward the other men. "Now, let's meet Frank's so-called competition."

Once the introductions were finished, Leanne waved them all toward the house. "I'm so happy you're all here," she said. "We figured you're probably sick of being cooped up in that van, so we set some food out by the pool. Jane, why don't you take everyone up to the guest house so they can change if they want to swim."

The smell of freshly baked bread greeted Noah as soon as they stepped into the house, which was decorated in an expensive-looking southwest style. Still, it felt homey, especially with the warm welcome they'd received.

Above the garage, the guest house had a huge common area and two big bathrooms in addition to several bedrooms. The girls would be sharing those rooms while the guys took the couches and floor. Noah stowed his things in one corner and dug his trunks and towel out of the bag. Once they had all changed, they followed Chad and Jane down to the pool.

The main house opened onto a beautifully designed deck area, lounge chairs lining one side of a huge rectangular pool while umbrella-clad tables flanked the other. A pavilion, complete with barbecue, fireplace, and a flat-screen TV mounted on the single wall, housed Leanne's idea of "some food"—a huge spread of fresh fruits and vegetables with hot-out-of-the-oven breadsticks. Noah had to keep reminding himself that he was at a home, not a resort.

Brianna and the twins dipped their feet into the pool, but Vanessa and Emily dove right into the deep end. A race to the other end found Vanessa winning easily, slipping through the water like a torpedo while Emily exerted twice as much effort for half the speed.

They came up for air at the side of the pool where Noah was about to get in, Garth uneasy at his shoulder.

"Rematch?" Vanessa said. "Maybe you weren't warm."

Emily scoffed. "As if that would help! You're either a mermaid or part fish!"

Vanessa answered with a deftly aimed spray of water from her clasped hands. "How about you, Garth?"

"Not me," he said. "I barely dog-paddle."

Noah thought he saw a blink of disappointment before she turned her smile on him. "I'm game," he said, his pulse picking up. "How many laps?"

"Are we racing?" Alec said, jumping up from his perch between the twins. "You're going down! Water or deck start?"

Noah fought the urge to groan under the weight of Alec's ego, thinking maybe he should bow out. Vanessa's eyes flitted to Alec and back to Noah, her smile mischievous. "What do you say, Noah?"

Though the pool was a big one, Noah had no idea whether Alec could swim a straight line, let alone dive one. And since none of them had goggles . . . "Water start, two laps?"

"You're on," Vanessa said, pushing off toward the deep end.

Alec executed a running cannonball that set the twins squealing. Noah slipped into the water unnoticed during the uproar and positioned himself on Vanessa's far side.

"Think you can take him?" Noah asked her.

Vanessa tipped her head to one side. "I've raced him before. It's you I'm not sure about."

Emily climbed out of the pool and took charge. "All right, you three, backs to the wall!"

Alec took his place on the other side of Vanessa. "You're going down, mermaid!"

She laughed and shoved him farther away. "Only if you grab my ankles! Swim nice, beach boy."

Noah let them banter, focusing instead on some deep breathing.

"On your marks," Emily's voice grabbed his attention, "get set, go!"

All three pushed off. Noah dove under, keeping his eyes open in the deliciously comfortable saline pool and watching his friends' blurry figures rise to the surface and begin stroking. He stayed comfortably underwater, concentrating on his dolphin kick and maintaining an efficient streamline while they battled it out up top. He doubted he could beat Vanessa in a freestyle, but she hadn't specified a stroke. Fortunately, he had always been able to hold his breath longer than the average person. He made the first underwater turn barely in front of the others, but by the time he made the second, he had them by half a body length. As he made the third turn, he could see Vanessa coming into the wall ahead of Alec's longer form. Lungs begging for air on the final stretch, Noah kicked harder, rising to the surface as he touched the wall. Vanessa lunged in after him, with Alec a split second behind. The cheers of the spectators grew louder as the water drained from his ears.

"Epic fail, beach boy!" Vanessa laughed.

Alec took her ribbing in stride. "Well, I gave it my best shot. I'm not ashamed to take second to a mermaid."

"Second?" Emily said from the deck. "Aquaman beat you both!"

Surprise registered on both his opponents' faces, but Vanessa's quickly changed to amusement. She challenged Noah to a strictly defined freestyle rematch and narrowly won, while Alec basked in consolation from Brianna and the twins. Jane strung a net across the pool for a rousing game of pool volleyball during which Alec successfully bolstered his ego. Noah couldn't help but think how being six inches taller than anyone else in the pool was a distinct advantage. All things considered, though, Alec seemed to be a nice enough guy. Noah wouldn't hold it against him that he was many things Noah was not.

As he laid down on his sleeping pad that night, he found himself grateful for Jane's pushiness. He never would have sought out or agreed to this trip on his own. Things had started out a little awkward, but his sneaky swim victory had established him as an accepted member of the group. Initially, he had regretted allowing his competitiveness to show, but with most of them calling him Aquaman for the duration of the evening, he had to acknowledge that it had been a good move.

It had been a long time since he'd felt he belonged.

Chapter 29

PRICKLES

THE NEXT MORNING DAWNED BRIGHT and hot. Successful integration notwithstanding, Noah dreaded another day in the van.

Jane's aunt and uncle treated them to an amazing breakfast of waffles and fruit, with a cheesy egg casserole Noah had difficulty not claiming entirely for himself. His full stomach combined with the previous night's short sleep on the floor rendered him nearly comatose once they passed the southern border. He awoke a couple of hours later to a painfully dead arm and a barren stretch of Mexican highway that looked the same as when he had fallen asleep. The group was quiet with the exception of Chad and Jane talking quietly in the front.

Arm prickling awake, Noah stared out the window and thought back on the previous night. How long had it been since he had fun like that? Too long. He wasn't sure when he'd fallen back into the habit of isolation, but it was becoming clear to him how deep he'd been. Apparently, he wasn't maintaining his mental health as well as he'd thought. Looking back, he felt he could trace his backslide to Thanksgiving.

He'd gone home for the long weekend on a high from helping Grace. It was obvious to him that she was better at math than she gave herself credit for and that her confidence grew each week. She had teased him more than usual during their session on dimensional analysis, her hair taunting him with its unruliness. He'd come dangerously close to craving a taste of her mom's brownies, wishing he could meet her brother or go to the pizza party they had hypothetically planned, tempted to throw out his resentments and touch one of those tantalizing brown curls . . . He had even allowed himself to lean a little closer than usual to check her calculations, but she had leaned away as if his proximity were disturbing. That had gone a long way to restoring his defenses, reminding him to keep his distance.

But a new thought struck him. What if it had been a *good* disturbing?

She *had* invited him to dinner at the end of the semester . . . Was it possible she'd moved away that day because *she* was attracted to *him*?

No.

This was Grace Ebert, he told himself. She had been repulsed by him from almost the moment they'd met. The dinner was merely a thank-you, as she'd said. A show of appreciation. Possibly pity.

Platonic.

Not a date.

In spite of his good mood going into the holiday, Thanksgiving had been a disaster, as usual. His mom had been a mess, striving to make everything perfect for his perfect brother and Matt's high-society, high-maintenance girlfriend, Anabella. Noah had struggled through a day and a half of his mother's special blend of anxiety and nonstop fawning over the power couple before he'd resorted to blaming schoolwork for an early departure. Unfortunately, Matt and Anabella had left around the same time, rendering his mother even more depressed and anxious and alone than she had been before the holiday. She had called Noah repeatedly that evening until he'd finally answered, and then she'd spent the call rethinking everything about the abbreviated visit and begging more than once for Noah's assurance that her future daughter-in-law wouldn't hate her. This had persisted throughout the weekend, until Noah had again stopped answering her calls. After that she had text-bombed him mercilessly.

Add into that mess the anniversary of his dad's death and his mom's insistence that he accompany her to the cemetery, and it became obvious why his walls had been so ineffective in his next meeting with Grace. He'd been reading a text from his mom, racking his brain for a legitimate-sounding excuse to avoid the cemetery when Grace had walked through the math lab doors, refreshed from her break with her perfect family and glowing with the belated discovery that, yes, she could do math. Her account of stargazing with her father had helped Noah understand where her interest in science originated from, sparking a flame of sadness and envy so strong he could hardly breathe.

And then he'd gone and spilled the beans about his alcoholic father.

To Grace.

After weeks and weeks of keeping his walls up, resisting her attractions, and maintaining his disinterest in all things personal, he had confided his deepest wound—one even Ryan didn't know the full story on—to Grace, of all people.

If she hadn't already been disgusted by him, that would have tipped things against him for good. What could she possibly know about such things, with her perfect life and family?

Only . . . she had asked him out *after* she knew. His past hadn't turned her away. It had brought them closer—or it might have, if Noah had allowed it.

What if, instead of berating Grace and throwing her dinner offer back in her face, he had accepted? A scene formed in his mind of them together at dinner, laughing about the awkwardness of their beginnings and the irony of his winding up as her tutor.

No.

He pulled his thoughts back to the barren sameness outside his window. There could be no rewriting of the past. He'd thoroughly burned that bridge, and there was nothing he could do about it.

Chapter 30

MURPHY'S LAW

SEVERAL HOURS LATER, WHEN THEY exited the dusty highway, the entire crew perked up. Banter and anticipation swelled, windows opened to let in the tangy ocean air, and James Taylor's "Mexico" played through the van's crackly speakers.

Noah drew in a lungful of the salty heat and listened to the lyrics. If only *he* could leave behind all the things that bothered him . . .

Why not? None of these people knew him. What better time would there be to step out of his shell? He had been a more personable version of himself at times in the past, like during his summer in Ghana. He could do it again. It might even stick this time.

Chad drove through the streets of a small town as Jane navigated, finally winding down a barely discernible, packed-dirt lane that deposited them in front of a tall, white iron fence. A large gate broke its lines, iron letters at its top declaring it *Hogar Para Niños*, which according to Noah's Sesame Street–learned Spanish skills, had something to do with children.

The group quieted as they got out of the van, not sure how to proceed. Noah stretched his cramped limbs, thankful to be cage free, and took stock of his surroundings.

An old Jeep Cherokee with Colorado plates sat next to the van, and Noah vaguely recalled Jane saying something about the rest of their group meeting them at the orphanage. Low, brightly painted buildings stretching back from either end of the white fence surrounded a large courtyard with a dry fountain at the center. Cement pathways marked the courtyard's covered perimeter and crossed the hard-packed earth to meet at the fountain. Everything was neat and tidy, the sandy soil freshly raked. A building at the far end of the courtyard rose higher than the others, a simple cross adorning its domed roof. Chattering children gathered in the shade, probably getting to know the earlier arrivals.

Noah followed the flow of his group into the courtyard, butterflies in his stomach. Alec launched immediately into Spanish, greeting the staff and ruffling a boy's hair as he spoke.

Jane embraced a petite Mexican woman in a simple light-blue dress with a dark-blue vest. The woman's countenance radiated kindness, her bronze face deeply lined with evidence of her good nature. A man in his fifties smiled at her side, reaching out to shake Jane's hand.

Noah stood with the other non-Spanish-speaking newbies, not sure what to do with himself until Jane reached out with introductions.

"Noah," she said, "this is Sister Margaretta, the leader of the orphanage. She speaks very little English. And this"—she smiled toward the man—"is Oscar. He'll be supervising the building project."

"Hola, señor Noah," Oscar said, shaking Noah's hand as Jane introduced them.

"Hola," Noah replied, exhausting his supply of Spanish.

"Noah will be a great help to you with the building," Jane explained to Oscar in English.

"Sí, sí," Oscar said, nodding enthusiastically. "We are so happy to have your help!"

A wave of relief and gratitude washed over Noah at hearing the words in lightly accented English. At least one of the locals would understand him. He wished he'd had more time to prepare and learn at least a few helpful phrases.

Musical laughter pulled at Noah and brought a smile to his face. In spite of the children's unfavorable circumstances, this felt like a happy place. A safe place. The laugh sounded again, followed by a string of Spanish in a voice that tugged at his memory.

His smile faltered. Scanning the courtyard, his eyes passed over the heads of the giggling orphans and around the volunteers, searching for the owner of that laugh, that voice. The crowd parted enough to reveal a far corner of the courtyard where several of the children had gathered around a dark-haired woman and were tickling her and rattling away in Spanish.

Noah's feet dragged him closer to the group, willing his eyes to disprove what his ears were hearing. Dark, curly hair tumbled about the woman's shoulders, her head ducked as she spoke to one of the smaller children. She looked up, and the mirth froze on her face, taking with it all of Noah's plans for fresh starts and reinvention.

Grace.

Of all the people. Grace. Nearly two hundred million square miles of surface area, over seven billion people occupying Earth, and now he would be trapped for five days on a couple of acres with the one person who hated him most.

Spectacular.

Noah's thoughts swirled with the contents of his stomach. Would she acknowledge they knew each other or pretend they'd never met? He could see her discomfort and hated knowing he'd caused it. If only he could leave.

She was obviously better suited for this adventure, with her friendliness and uncomplicated life and affinity for children, not to mention her Spanish. One of the boys climbed onto her lap and pressed her cheeks between his hands, pulling her attention away and evoking another laugh as she replied to the boy's rapid-fire entreaties. She agreed to whatever he was asking, wrapping her arms around him for a hug before setting him back on the ground and following him and several other children toward a swing set.

"You okay?" Vanessa pulled him from his blatant staring.

"Uh, yeah," he said, scrambling to excuse his gaping. "Just . . . a little overwhelmed." He hauled his eyes from Grace and her entourage, summoning a smile for Vanessa.

She took his arm and led him to a table where several of the children were coloring. "I don't speak the language either, but what matters is that you make the effort to engage the kids. It takes a little longer for them to open up to the English speakers, but they're very sweet."

He faked cheerfulness and sat down to color. Luckily, it didn't require much concentration, because his thoughts were stuck on Grace at the swings.

Thanks to the labeled crayons, Noah almost had his Spanish colors down when one of the nuns rang a triangle, prompting a migration of children toward a building at the back of the property.

"Volunteers," Jane called, motioning them in the opposite direction. In his peripheral vision Noah saw Grace disentangle herself, encouraging her fans to follow the other children before heading his way. Not that she was coming to *him*, but he did happen to be standing at the edge of their group. Their eyes met briefly, sending a zing of anxiety through his stomach.

"We'll be staying in the east dorms," Jane said. "Dinner is almost ready, so if you'll grab your stuff, we can get things put away and go get some food."

Noah picked up his bag and found himself face-to-face with Grace, who chuckled uncomfortably as they stepped in the same direction, twice, in an attempt to move past each other. He gave her a tight smile and motioned with one hand for her to go ahead, following in her familiar flowery-scented wake. Hopefully that would fade after a couple of days with limited showers.

Their accommodations consisted of one big room with a multicolored tile floor and six sets of neatly made bunk beds. "They've consolidated the kids in the other building, so we'll have this room while we're here. We'll sleep on the floor to save them from having to clean the bedding," Jane explained, "but we'll set up sleeping arrangements later. You can stow your stuff along the wall for now."

Noah took his time staking out a corner and arranging his things, stalling until Grace had left before following the other stragglers to the dining hall at the rear of the property. Right inside the door, the smell of soap and a row of sinks invited them to wash before lining up for fresh tortillas, beans, rice, salsa, and sliced watermelon set in a buffet. The children were already seated at several long cafeteria tables set in rows, but Jane encouraged the volunteers to disperse among them.

Last to arrive, Noah took the only seat available and ended up much closer to Grace than he would have chosen, their backs to each other at adjacent tables. He smiled at the children surrounding him but was unable to focus with the sound of Grace's voice prattling away in Spanish. The tone she used reminded him of her teasing. Unable to understand a word on either side, he imagined she was coaxing them to tell her about themselves, teasing them into sharing their thoughts with her.

His hand tightened on his fork and sent a piece of watermelon splattering across the table, drawing a giggle from a young neighbor. *Take it easy*, he thought, shrugging with a smile at the pig-tailed girl at his side. She laughed again and went back to eating.

He'd been looking forward to a clean slate—a getaway from his usual worries and a chance to reinvent himself. Now Grace's presence goaded him with reminders of his inadequacies. Limited options ran through his head as he ate without tasting the good food. He could pretend they didn't know each other. She'd probably prefer that. Maybe they would work on different crews, allowing them to avoid each other most of the time. Grace had never mentioned any construction skills. If that were the case, it shouldn't be too difficult to avoid her because she'd likely be assigned to other tasks. And his van-mates already knew he wasn't talkative. The easiest course would be to stay quiet and keep his distance. The harder part would be keeping Grace out of his thoughts.

So much for losing his load.

Chapter 31

FUN FACTS

THE LAST FEW CHILDREN SCRAPED their plates clean and piled them into a bin by the kitchen before scurrying out the door. Jane gave them knuckles as they left, then addressed the group of volunteers.

"Hey, everyone," she said, waiting for their chatter to die down. "I'm so glad we all made it here okay, and I want to thank you again for being a part of this amazing week, especially those who have agreed to do the evening devotionals for me. Marcus, you and Grace have tomorrow, Emily has Thursday, and Friday will be our farewell dinner party with the kids.

"Tonight I'd like to do introductions, even though most of us already know each other. Give us your name, why you're here, and one fun fact."

Jane went first, explaining that she'd started coming to the orphanage five years prior with the family of a friend. Chad followed her and emphasized their wedding date coming up in a few weeks as his fun fact. Garth shared the backstory on his name, Emily said she thought this trip would be a good way to kick-start a better perspective, and Vanessa expressed her love of country dancing. Alec was excited to polish his rusty Spanish while working with the kids.

One of the new guys stood and introduced himself as Marcus. With a full beard and light-brown hair working its way toward dreadlocks, Noah expected him to talk about the time they'd be spending on the beach or something, but Marcus was rather eloquent in explaining that he wanted to show these kids the kind of love he'd never felt as a child. "Fun fact is I nearly lost a limb to a shark," he said.

A chorus of amused disbelief mixed with several horrified gasps.

"Get out!" Alec said. "Were you surfing?"

Marcus chuckled and let the noise die down. "Well, I was on a field trip—"

"You went surfing on a field trip?" Alec asked.

Marcus shook his head. "Our teacher said we could feed the sharks."

More sounds of disbelief from the group provided backup for Alec's good-natured skepticism. "No way!"

"With shrimp," Marcus added. "I was slow on the draw and didn't get any shrimp out of the bucket before they were all gone, so I kind of stuck my finger into the tank and wiggled it around, trying to attract some sharks."

Skepticism switched to laughter as Marcus held up one hand and traced a jagged scar around his first finger. "Nearly lost my finger to the big guy. He was nearly *two feet* long."

Once the laughter subsided, it took a few minutes of ribbing and examination of the scar before the group calmed down enough for the next introduction. A guy named Devin was Marcus's polar opposite. Clean-cut and soft around the middle, his crisp khaki shorts and boat shoes looked like they came straight out of a fashion ad, but he, too, surprised Noah with his sincerity and desire to help the children. His fun fact was that he'd traveled to over forty countries with his family before his eighteenth birthday.

Next in the progression was Grace. Would she acknowledge that they knew each other? Would she tell them what a jerk Noah had been? His knee bounced under the table.

"I'm Grace Ebert," she said, standing up from the table next to his. "Marcus and I work together, and when he learned I speak Spanish, he invited me to come along. I love kids, and I love to travel"—she gave a nod to traveler Devin—"so I jumped at the chance."

Her eyes worked their way around the room as she spoke, coming to rest on Noah. She paused for a moment, watching. Debating? Noah dug his fingers into his legs.

"My fun fact is . . . I was surprised to discover I also know a couple of others in the group—Alec, who was my neighbor a few years ago, and Noah, who single-handedly enabled me to pass the last class I needed to get my degree." Her smile broadened, and she swiped her forehead in theatrical relief. "So if any of you need a math tutor"—she found his eyes again—"he's the best."

A compliment? He couldn't breathe.

The twins took their turns before Noah, giving him time to settle his nerves and pull his attention away from Grace's words. He hated speaking in front of a group of people almost as much as he hated talking about himself, but he stood up and tried to gather his thoughts, aiming to keep it short.

The room grew quiet. Too quiet. He plunged ahead. "I'm Noah. I'm in accounting school at Oak Hills, I'm here because someone else bailed and Chad knew about my work in construction, and my fun fact is . . ."

Why were the only things coming to mind things he couldn't share?

My dad was an alcoholic.

I don't really have friends.

The last time I saw Grace, she asked me out and I made fun of her for it.

His eyes jumped around the room, looking at everyone but Grace as he attempted to think of something—anything—interesting, striking out until they landed on Vanessa, who jumped in to save him.

"His fun fact," she said, "is that he can hold his breath and swim fast enough to be Aquaman."

All his van buddies laughed at the shared memory, and the tension that had mounted dissolved, leaving him more light-headed than he'd been after the race.

Jane thanked everyone again for coming, then explained some of the rules—don't flush the toilet paper, drink only bottled or filtered water—and encouraged all of them to head out to the playground to get better acquainted with the children.

A soft touch on his arm stopped Noah as he started to leave. He turned, and Grace pulled her hand back as if she'd been scalded. She waited for the others to disperse before speaking. "Hey," she said, voice low and face unreadable. "I hope it's okay that I said we knew each other. I thought it might be better to get that out in the open so we don't have to, uh, pretend, I guess?"

She expected a reply of some sort. Again his mouth sealed itself shut with responses he wouldn't speak.

Why are you being nice to me?

You smell like flowers.

I'm sorry.

"Sure," he managed.

A flush worked its way into her cheeks. "Okay, well, I guess I'll see you around." She nodded and walked away.

Noah watched, uncomfortably aware of the last time he'd seen her do that.

A quick trip to the bathroom gave him time to recover. It was probably good that Grace had acknowledged their prior association. Now he wouldn't have to pretend not to know her.

A thorough review of her faults—spoiled, nosy, self-centered, fake—shored up his defenses once again. He told himself that her physical attractions were tempting but manageable. A memory of her at Halloween—wavy hair, long legs, that T-shirt—surfaced and he quickly snuffed it.

Dangerous.

But her laugh, the understanding in her eyes, that glow she had around children?

Deadly.

His construction experience should keep them separated, he assured himself again. He didn't imagine they would allow the kids into the heavy work zone, and Grace's talents would most likely keep her with them.

Feeling marginally better, he meandered out to the playground. Swarming with children and volunteers, it looked like a well-worn throwback to the 1970s, sporting a geo dome for climbing, wooden teeter-totters, and several metal slides of varying height in addition to the swing sets. Noah secured an open position as swing-pusher that allowed him to keep his back to Grace, who was spotting a climbing toddler on the geo dome.

A revolving succession of swinging children kept his arms occupied. Though the job didn't require language skills, Noah quickly discerned that a squealed *"no tan alto"* meant to stop pushing, while an insistent *"más rápido"* meant to push harder. Once he learned that, his mind wandered back to Grace, whose soft tones as she encouraged her little charge slipped through the commotion to torment him from behind.

Chapter 32

WALLS

SPLAT!

Noah sent the mortar from his trowel onto the cement blocks with more force than strictly necessary. Alec and Marcus talked as they worked, getting to know each other, while Noah gratefully zoned out in the familiar and repetitive nature of the job—building concrete block walls for a new bathroom building.

He hadn't slept well, thanks to the combination of new surroundings, thin air mattress, and too many roommates.

One of whom was Grace.

Why had she spoken to him—about him—as she had?

He'd managed one ambiguous syllable.

Despite his troubled thoughts, he found a nice rhythm with his trowel, the movements coming back easily. He lifted a block into place on the fresh mortar and, wishing for a hat to shield the early-morning sun, checked to make sure the block was aligned, plumb, and level with the guide lines by tapping the butt of his trowel on one corner. Too bad social situations weren't as clear-cut as good construction technique: scoop the mortar, scrape it onto the block, set it, and tap it into place.

"You work with Grace?" Alec's question made Noah flinch as he reloaded his trowel.

"Yeah," Marcus answered.

"Some kind of boarding school?"

"Therapeutic boarding school."

"What's the difference?"

Marcus bent to pick up a block. "Most of our students come to us from intervention programs that have helped them out of crisis, so besides providing their academics, we have a psychiatrist, therapists, and support personnel on staff."

"What does Grace do?" Alec asked.

"She's part of the recreation team. They work with the boys after school and on weekends, take them on excursions and stuff."

"Sounds like babysitting."

Noah watched sideways as Marcus dipped into the bucket, pulling too much material and slopping half of it into the center of the block instead of on the top edge, where he'd been aiming. With a frown, Marcus attempted to retrieve some of the wasted material out of the center, then gave up and reached again for the bucket. "It might sound that way," he said, "but the recreation team is vital to the boys' success. They provide experiences and connect with the boys in a totally different way than the teachers and therapists can."

Alec made a sound that was not quite agreement as he placed a block.

"You knew her before, right?" Marcus asked.

Noah almost answered, but Marcus wasn't asking him.

"Yeah," Alec said, scooping some mortar of his own. "We lived in the same complex a few years ago. I didn't know her well, other than she likes volleyball."

"Oh yeah!" Marcus said. "She was playing with some of the guys at the school the other night."

Alec chuckled. "She used to come around to the sand courts all the time wanting to play. Hoping to get into the men's game, I guess." He paused as he grabbed a block. "Or maybe she was looking for a date, but I was seeing someone else. Anyway, I'd rather play with just guys, keep the level high, you know?"

Marcus paused in his work. "She's pretty good. Gave the boys some good pointers."

"Well," Alec said, nudging his block with one finger, "I never really saw her play. Might ask her out once we get back though."

"You're out of line." Noah's voice came out gruffer than he intended, and the other guys looked surprised.

"Huh?" Alec said.

"Sorry," Noah said, forcing a smile to cover his embarrassment. "Your block—it's not quite straight. See?" He pointed to the guide string. "It just needs a tap here and here. Now you're good." He returned to his own section of wall and scooped some mortar, regretting his interruption even though the correction had been necessary.

"So you were Grace's math tutor?" Marcus asked him.

Why did I talk? Why, why, why? "Mm-hmm," Noah said, praying Marcus wouldn't push for more.

Scoop. Scrape. Set. Tap.

"And you've worked some construction before, right?" Marcus asked.

"Yeah. Mostly summers," he said, spreading some mortar up the side of a block. "It's decent money, and I've always liked to work with my hands."

"It definitely shows," Alec said. "How do you get the mortar to stick on the side like that with only one stroke? Mine falls off every time."

Huh. Maybe Alec wasn't completely arrogant.

Noah relaxed. He could talk construction. "That usually happens when I go at it from the top. It's easier for me if I start at the bottom," he said, demonstrating, "then slide it up on an angle. See?" When he glanced up, Alec was nodding at the wall, but Marcus looked right at him.

"I see," he said.

Chapter 33

BEACH BOYS

Sweat dripped off Noah's head as he scooped the last of the mortar from the bucket. The walls had climbed as steadily as the scorching sun once the other guys had gotten the hang of it. He was about to mix another bag when Oscar came to check on them.

"Bien, bien," he said, running his hand along the walls and bending to check their lines. He glanced into the mortar bucket and smiled. "Muy bien! Good timing. Now we eat!"

"Yes," Alec said, drawing it out. "My stomach's been growling for at least an hour."

"Same here," Marcus said. "Nothing stokes my appetite like work and sun."

Oscar showed them where to clean their tools, and Noah stayed to hose out the bucket and rinse the sweat off his arms and face. He arrived at the dining hall behind the twins, whose names he still hadn't mastered, and Brianna as they waited to wash their hands.

"How was the painting?" he asked, noticing the splatters decorating their clothes and remembering his goal to be more outgoing. The rest of the volunteers had spent the morning painting the exterior of one of the buildings a bright yellow.

"Exciting," Brianna laughed.

"So I see," Noah said. "Did you get any on the walls?"

"Some," one of the twins said, "but it was a close call with the kids helping."

"Good thing we were outside," her sister said.

"Yeah," Brianna agreed, "or we would've had painted floors too."

"Did Jane say what time we're taking the kids to the beach?" the first twin asked.

"After lunch is all I know," Brianna replied, drying her hands and waiting for Noah to do likewise before following the twins into the cafeteria.

"Do we take all of the kids?" Noah asked her, his mind involuntarily dipping into worst-case scenarios involving the ocean, hordes of small children, and not enough adult supervision.

"I think they're keeping the younger ones here and maybe not sending all of the older kids," Brianna said.

Noah picked up a tray, wishing his thoughts didn't mirror his paranoid mother's so often. Of course they wouldn't send too many children to the beach with a bunch of strangers.

"How's the construction going?" Brianna asked.

"Not bad." Noah ladled some soup into a bowl—it looked like chicken soup but with a red broth and no noodles. Brianna added cilantro, cheese, and sour cream, so he copied her. "Do you know what this is?"

"Looks like pozole to me."

He'd never had it, but it smelled delicious. He followed her to a table and sat down amid the locals, wishing again that he could understand something of what they said. The first spoonful of soup surprised him with its spicy heat, but the children didn't even flinch.

An hour later, bellies settled and swimming suits on, the children were anxious to get to the beach. Jane and Chad led the way out the front gates and onto the dirt road that had brought their group here, turning west toward the beach. Emily was skipping along with some of the kids, belting the "Mexico" song. Noah couldn't help but smile at her enthusiasm, and neither could the kids.

Just then, two little hands wormed their way into his—a girl on his left and a boy on his right. He caught Vanessa's eye.

"I think you've been assimilated," she said.

"Miracles never cease." He lifted their hands with his own, bringing broader smiles to their faces. "Wish I knew their names."

Vanessa said something to the girl in what was unmistakably Spanish.

"Hey! I thought you didn't speak the language!" Noah said, indignant.

"It's not that hard to learn a few phrases." Vanessa laughed. "I wouldn't call that speaking the language."

Noah grunted. "What did you say?"

"I asked her name. Want me to teach you?"

Next thing he knew, Noah had some rudimentary Spanish skills. "*Yo soy* Noah." He squeezed the boy's hand. "*Cómo te llamas?*"

"Alejandro!"

He squeezed the girl's hand. "Cómo te llamas?"

"Teresa!" Her pigtails bounced as she skipped along at his side.

"Hola, Alejandro. Hola, Teresa." He looked at Vanessa. "I'll be fluent by Friday."

She laughed.

Their pace picked up as the road changed to sand.

"Man, I've missed the beach," a grinning Alec said as the water came into view.

Swimmer though Noah was, he had never spent time at the ocean. Alejandro and Teresa let go of his hands and stormed the beach while he took in the rough white sand, cloudless sky, and crying seabirds. Tension slipped away as he shed his glasses and T-shirt, relishing the heat on his chest. Mild waves slapped the shore, grinding seashells into sand.

Emily and Vanessa plowed into the water with the first wave of kids. Alec kicked a soccer ball around with Marcus, Devin, and a bunch of older kids. Brianna and the twins had plopped right into building sandcastles with some of the younger ones, and Garth was picking up seashells with several of the girls. Three staff members had accompanied them, but they stayed back and let the volunteers run the show.

Noah closed his eyes for a moment and inhaled the sea breeze. Something thumped into his leg, startling him.

"I am so sorry." Grace grimaced, stepping away and pulling at an enormous bag that had slipped from her shoulder. She straightened, the top of her cover-up—a loose-fitting tank dress—askew to reveal a bright, floral swimming suit and a smooth shoulder marked red from the heavy bag. "I wasn't watching where I was going. I was looking at the beach. And this"—she frowned at the bag—"is a little fuller than I'd like."

"Kitchen sink?" he asked.

The worry on her face melted into relief. She let go of the bag, reaching up to rub her shoulder. "Everything but," she said. "Half the kids left without their towels. Sister Margaretta caught me, but I couldn't catch the group with this load."

He nodded his understanding and looked back at the chaos. He hadn't noticed Grace's absence, and he'd managed two whole words to her.

Progress.

"It's nice to feel the sun again," she said with a happy sigh.

"Yeah." He dug his flip-flop-exposed toes into the sand, appreciating the cooler dampness under the heat.

Just as he was searching for something else to say, Alejandro and Teresa sprinted out of the water directly for him, grabbing his hands and pulling him toward the waves. Grace said something in Spanish that made them laugh and pull even harder. He abandoned his flip-flops in the sand, surrendering to preserve the skin on his hands and wrists.

They reached the water at a trot, sending cool spray up his legs. His escorts let go, jumping and splashing him with their hands. He bent to return the favor only to have Alejandro land on his back like a flying squirrel, sending them both to the ground right as a larger wave broke and soaked them all. The kids roared with laughter as Noah spluttered and spit and wiped his burning eyes.

"What happened, Aquaman? Someone give you kryptonite?" Vanessa laughed.

"Wrong superhero," Garth said, chasing the soccer ball and launching it back down the beach.

Noah spit again. "Nasty!"

Vanessa laughed harder. "Aquaman can't have a saltwater weakness!"

Noah glared at her, shielding his face with his hands and holding back his own laughter as the kids continued their assault. "I've never been in salt water before."

"You've never been to the ocean?" Vanessa asked.

"*To*, yes. *In*, no. I grew up in a landlocked state and never really traveled."

"But you had a passport?"

"Well-building trip to Ghana. We didn't go to the beach."

"Hmm," she said, swinging a girl with a crown of braids around and sending her off again. "Well, you'll get used to the salt."

Alejandro managed to give him a facial as Vanessa said this, proving the point. Growling, Noah grabbed the boy, hoisted him over his shoulder, and carried him to deeper water, where he tossed him in the air the way he'd seen dads throw their kids at pools. Alejandro squealed, splashed down in the surf, and came back for more. Several other boys lined up to take a turn, and soon Noah's arms were aching.

"No más, no más!" he said, using more of his excellent Spanish to ward off his attackers and making a face to show them how tired he was. They would have none of that, clinging to his legs and arms until, for self-preservation, he dove into the water, losing most of the cling-ons, and swam the rest of them off in two strokes. Squinting under the water, he noticed that his eyes didn't hurt so much now that he was used to the salt, then swam out farther before surfacing.

Alejandro spotted him and immediately gave chase. Gulping a lungful of air, Noah dove again, swimming parallel to the shore. This time when he came up, he saw Alejandro had given up the water chase and was running along the shore, followed by several others. The boy let out a string of Spanish, gesturing wildly.

Alec burst with laughter. "Dude, he's calling you out! You'd better come and get him!"

A grin split Noah's cheeks. He dove toward shore and swam until he could high-knee it through the shallows. All of the children screeched and scattered, but Noah zeroed in on Alejandro.

"You're it!" Noah called when he caught the boy, then ran away, children still skittering out of his path.

Alec rattled off some Spanish, and the game was on. Alejandro chased Noah first, but after several unsuccessful attempts, he sought an easier target in Teresa. Noah tried to jump out of the little girl's reach but was stopped in his tracks with an "Oof!" as he ran into someone, allowing Teresa to tag him. Noah grabbed hold of his victim and steadied them both, finding Grace in his arms, her hands on his shoulders.

Grace, in a swimming suit, her smiling face tanner than her arms and shoulders, her skin hot against his wet hands. Their eyes met, freezing both of their smiles. "No glasses?" she asked.

"No." Heat radiated from her hands into his shoulders.

"I'm it!" she shouted, running after Alejandro.

Rooted to the spot, Noah tried to catch his breath as he watched her longs legs churn the sand, her giggles mingling with the children's.

Not so much progress.

With an about-face, he returned to the collection of towels and water bottles in the sand, searching out his flask. Warm, metallic water was not quite the refreshment he sought, but it did ease his thirst. He grabbed his towel, dried his face, and ran a hand through his hair. His eyes drifted back to the game. Alec, with Teresa on his back, caught up to Grace and wrapped her in a bear hug. It shouldn't have made Noah jealous, but it did.

"Nice going," Vanessa said, searching out her own bottle.

Grace shoved Alec into the surf, his feet catching on a wave that sent him and Teresa into the water. Noah dragged his eyes away. "Huh?"

"Tag," Vanessa said, pointing with her chin. "They're having a great time. Why did you leave?"

"Thirsty." He lifted his flask to prove the point and went back to watching.

"Hmm." She took a drink.

The game dwindled into chaos. Grace circled the children up on the sand, she and Alec directing them in Spanish.

Vanessa shook her head at the pair, who had the full attention and cooperation of the children. "Unfair advantage, speaking Spanish. It would take me weeks to achieve that kind of rapport."

A girl with long braids ran up and wrapped her arms around Vanessa's leg, jabbering in Spanish and pointing at the sand toys. Noah looked pointedly at Vanessa.

"Okay, maybe not weeks." She asked the girl's name—Rosa, matching her bright-pink swimming suit—then pointed back to the sand toys. "You want to build a sandcastle?"

"Advantage nothing," Noah mumbled over the girl's enthusiastic response. He sat in the sand with them, digging and filling buckets while allowing his eyes to wander.

"You knew her from before, huh?"

How long had his attention rested in that particular direction? "Who, Grace?"

Vanessa chuckled. "Yeah. Did you guys date?"

"No," he said too quickly. "Well, yes. Actually, just one date." Their sandcastle definitely needed a moat. He dug it out, donating the wetter sand to fill the girls' buckets and forming a bridge reinforced with sticks and rocks.

His eyes landed again on Grace—she now led the group in a rousing game of what looked like duck, duck, goose; though it sounded like potato, potato, gonzo to his ears—but he pulled his gaze away and forced himself to focus on the sand like he would a complex differential equation.

Dig. Fill. Dump.

Vanessa was quiet, but he could *feel* her questions. He wasn't about to answer, especially if she didn't ask.

"It was a setup," he heard himself blurt anyway. Why was he volunteering information? Scrambling, he said the first unrelated thing that came to mind. "Hey, thanks for rescuing me yesterday," he said.

"She looks at you too, you know." Her expression acknowledged but allowed his clumsy redirect. "When did I rescue you?"

"Fun facts. Awkward silence."

"Oh, that. No problem."

"I hate talking in front of people, and I don't have any fun facts anyway."

Vanessa laughed. "Sure you do! Aquaman is a great fun fact."

"Thanks to you."

"Where did you learn to hold your breath so long?"

"Best method to escape my older brother in the pool."

"Ah," she said. "Good incentive to swim fast too."

Noah nodded. "Our family didn't do much during the summer, but one of our apartments had a pool. It was lame but wet. Matt and I were there almost every day."

"I bet."

Noah handed a bucket to Rosa and sent her to get some *agua* for the moat. "He loved to dunk me, but once I learned to hold my breath and swim away underwater, he mostly gave it up."

"Aren't older siblings a joy?"

"You have an older brother?"

"Sisters."

Noah agreed, as if he knew this would also be terrible, though he had no experience growing up with females. It had only ever been him and Matt. "How many?" he asked.

"Four," Vanessa said.

"Wow. That's a lot of—"

"Hand-me-downs," she finished. "I think I was twelve before I had a pair of new jeans all to myself. By then I was taller than the rest of them, so I got the new ones."

"They must not be very tall."

Vanessa laughed. "They aren't."

"I mean, you're only—" he looked at her, judging her height.

"Five-seven, on the nose. They're all five-three or less. I'm even a hair taller than my dad."

"Huh. Where did your height come from?"

"Beats me." She shrugged, taking the wall-form she had filled and setting it carefully next to the last one. "They called me Mutant."

Noah shook his head. "Nice."

"Yeah, they were always looking out for me," she said sarcastically, her gaze straying to the action on the beach—landing on Garth, if Noah wasn't mistaken.

"So . . . country dancing?" Noah said, referring to the fun fact she'd shared.

Vanessa's eyes narrowed as they returned to Noah. "Yeahhhh?" she said, drawing it out as a question.

"I never would have guessed," Noah said. He watched Garth, who looked a little strange without his boots, and remembered Grace saying something about John Wayne once. "What is it about cowboys, anyway?"

Vanessa closed her eyes and grinned. "Mmm, cowboys."

"I don't get it."

She opened her eyes, still smiling. "Broad shoulders, chivalry, horses, and that tip of the hat with a 'Howdy, ma'am'?" She sighed. "Gets me every time."

"So if I take some riding lessons and get a cowboy hat, that will improve my datability?"

She laughed. "I can't see you in a cowboy hat, somehow. Nah, you've got your own thing going."

"I do?"

"Sure, Aquaman." Vanessa's eyes flicked down to the beach to where Grace, Alec, and Garth were volleying a beach ball with the kids and then back to Noah. "You just have to let it show."

Let it show? How on earth was Noah supposed to do that when he didn't even know what "it" was?

They finished their sand castle just in time for duck, duck, goose to revert to tag, and soon their masterpiece was demolished by a stampede. Noah noticed Rosa welling up at the destruction, so he hauled her over his shoulder and joined the herd. Better to chase those tears away before they got started.

Besides, it allowed him to escape Vanessa and her knowing looks. She was clearly reading more into his acquaintance with Grace than was warranted. He would keep his distance, as planned, and take better control of his wandering eyes.

Chapter 34

PEACE

THE REST OF THE TIME at the beach flew by, the children's energy never waning. By the time everyone got back to the compound and changed into dry clothes, Noah was famished and dinner was waiting—quesadillas served with deliciously fresh guacamole and salsa.

"I'm impressed with how good the food is," Devin said, taking a seat by him.

Jane overheard from her spot down the table and joined the conversation. "They used to eat mostly rice and beans, but with the support of the foundation, they've been able to make some deals with local vendors to get more variety into their diets."

"And I'm sure they're best-foot-forward when they have visitors," Alec said.

Whatever the history, Noah's stomach was grateful, having worked up a hearty appetite playing in the water and sun. Everyone looked a little pink in the cheeks, except for Marcus and Grace, who looked more pink on their shoulders, thanks to the many hours they regularly spent outside for work.

Alec teased them mercilessly about getting paid to ski with a bunch of teenagers. The two took it in stride, though Grace's smile faltered when she caught Noah watching her. Noah's comments about her major in therapeutic recreation resurfaced in his head, making Alec's teasing sound tame by comparison. Grace obviously remembered the exchange too.

Following dinner, the staff coaxed the children to their rooms, leaving all the volunteers alone together for the first time that day. Jane asked them all to circle up, then stood at the front of the cafeteria and waited for their chatter to die down.

"Nice job today, everyone. I think the kids are really feeling the love. I'm sure everyone is tired, so we'll have a quick devotional, and after that you can hit the sack or whatever. I've asked Marcus and Grace to take the lead tonight." Jane smiled and yielded the floor, taking a seat next to Chad.

Marcus stood and smoothed his long hair away from his face. "My youth wasn't a happy one. Messed-up family, parents weren't around much. I got myself into some trouble. What would I have done differently if I'd had a good support system?" He fidgeted with something in his pocket. "Kids can be bullheaded, and I'm sure I still would have tested things, but I'll always wonder. At the same time, I don't know how much I'd take back, because it's made me who I am and brought me to a pretty good place. I've been working with young men in crisis for about eight years now . . ."

Noah's mind drifted as he wondered how old the guy was. He looked younger than Noah's twenty-six, but if Marcus had been working with kids for that long, he must be nearer thirty.

"One thing that really helps these boys," Marcus was saying, "is finding peace in hard circumstances. Eckhart Tolle has a lot of writings about this, but the underlying idea is that if we can accept where we are right now, we can not only have peace in the moment but also better work toward where we want to be.

"So many of these boys feel powerless, like there's nothing they can do to change anything. Or sometimes they fixate on changing what's in the past. Once we accept where we are and the things we *can't* change, that's when we find peace. Only then can we start changing things about ourselves that will actually make a difference. I've asked Grace to share a little about her journey."

Grace stood and ambled to the middle of the room, wringing her hands.

"As a kid I thought my family was perfect. I'm the oldest of five, and I prided myself on setting a good example, being obedient to our parents, and working hard at whatever I was involved in."

Noah fought an impulse to scoff, resting his elbows on his knees and scrutinizing the floor. But why should he scoff? Grace might have had an easy upbringing, but she had shown she was willing to put in the work in the math lab.

"My younger brother Benson was very different from me," Grace continued. "He struggled academically—and not just with math. He was a thrill seeker, he tested boundaries.

"Junior year he fell in with a rough crowd. His grades dropped, he lost interest in school, and he started drinking and staying out all night. One night—"

Noah's head came up and his heart pounded as he watched Grace fight for composure in the silent room. *"He fell in with a rough crowd,"* she had said. Grace was speaking of this brother in the past tense. Noah recalled the line from her email, explaining her reaction to the girl who had influenced her brother for the worse. Ryan had told Noah about Grace's sibling dying. Was that who Grace spoke of now?

She swallowed a couple of times, then sought out Marcus, who gave her a *You got this* look. Acknowledging his support, she continued, haltingly. "One night he didn't come home. He was seventeen, driving home drunk, and ran his car into a wall. He died instantly. I was away at college. I blamed myself. I should have stayed closer to home, been a better sister, not put so much pressure on him." She cleared her throat. "His death shook me. I changed my major from English to therapeutic recreation, hoping to help other boys who were struggling to overcome their problems. When that didn't feel like enough, I spent a year in Peru doing humanitarian work. Maybe if I worked hard enough, I'd be able to prevent anything similar from happening to my other brothers or anyone else I cared for.

"I learned so much, but I never dealt with the grief of losing Benson. I came home and went back to school. I took extra psychology classes, thinking that knowledge would enable me to help anyone I met. But I never talked about Benson. I thought I was fine."

Her gaze flicked up to Noah's for an instant before she continued. A drop of sweat ran down his back, his dinner churning in his stomach.

"About the time I graduated, it became clear to me that I had never taken the time to work through my own stuff, had never made peace with what happened, and I began to see how that reduced my awareness of others.

"Then I started working with the young men at our school"—she and Marcus exchanged a look—"and, boy, did they call me out. I was hiding my pain, trying to erase it by 'fixing' them, and they could see that. They helped me realize I needed to find my own peace before I'd be able to help anyone else."

She exhaled and wiped under her eyes, then smiled. "So I'm talking about Benson, sharing my story, and it's helping. I've learned I can't 'fix' other people; I can only love them. I'm learning to accept that Benson's death wasn't my fault. Maybe I could have done more to be involved in his life, but what's done is done, and ultimately it was *his* actions that led to his death.

"Our decisions determine our lives. Many of these boys were raised in circumstances of abuse or neglect, but once they can come to peace with where they are and assume accountability for their own actions, they can heal from the traumas in their lives and move on. That's what I'm doing with Benson. By talking about him, his life—the good and the bad—I'm letting go of my guilt and fear. All I can do is me. I can be kind. I can forgive. I can be loving.

I can make the effort to see others and hear their stories, and that will bring me peace."

Noah wished he could go back to the beach and bury his head in the sand. How could a devotional on peace throw him into such a tailspin? He barely managed to get out of the dining hall with his dignity intact, didn't say a word to anyone as he slunk out the door. Taking the coward's path, he went straight to bed and feigned sleep when the others filtered in some time later.

But Grace's words played on repeat in his mind, trying and convicting him as he stared at the gently sloped ceiling and listened to the not-so-gentle snoring of someone across the room.

Losing a sibling is one of life's most painful trials.

That's what Grace had said in her email about Lupe Navarro's brother. She *had* had compassion for Lupe's loss.

"One night he didn't come home," Grace had said tonight.

Her own brother had died in an alcohol-related accident, just like Noah's dad. That was why she'd been so understanding when Noah had spilled his own history. That was why she'd been so upset when she ran into Mandy—the girl had led Benson into the behavior that had brought about his death. Noah remembered seeing Grace yesterday with the same threadbare backpack she'd used in college and recalled the defiance in her eyes when he'd almost dared to mock it back then. He'd bet money that Benson was the brother who had given it to her. No wonder she hadn't replaced it.

Puzzle pieces clicked together in his head. Ryan had warned Noah—amid the glowing reports of Grace's many good qualities—that Claire's brother had recently passed and that Grace had taken it especially hard. The setup had taken place only a few months after Benson's passing, yet Noah had brushed the warning aside and immediately taken offense at Grace's standoffishness.

Yes, Grace had insulted and ignored him. But had he even *tried* to break through her walls?

No. He had embraced the role of victim. So much so, in fact, that it had led to a rift in his friendship with Ryan. He'd hardly spoken with his friend since. Not that they were intentionally not speaking—they just . . . didn't. Noah could have laughed the date off as the spectacular failure it was—like Emily and her twice-in-one-night dance partner—but he'd chosen to let the wound fester.

"About the time I graduated . . . I began to see how that reduced my awareness of others."

Noah crumpled under the weight of that one. In his accusations to Grace, he had unwittingly passed judgment on himself. How ironic that he had told her she was self-centered and rude, even as he'd judged her.

Cut her off.

Shunned her invitation.

Belittled her chosen occupation.

Yes, her behavior that night had been self-centered and rude, but his actions following had been just as bad or worse.

Yet, for all the abuse he'd dished to her, what had she given in return?

First, she'd called him out. Pointedly. Deservedly.

But then *she* had apologized to *him*. *Apologized.* Explained her actions while admitting that she had room for improvement. Asked for his forgiveness.

They'd both made mistakes, but Noah, from the comfort of his high horse, had responded to her apology with silence.

"I can be kind. I can forgive."

That was exactly what Grace had done when she'd seen him in Mexico, working to defuse the tension before anyone else noticed.

All he'd said in return was "Sure."

The knot in his throat—like an under-chewed shard of tortilla chip stuck just beyond his ability to swallow—ached and burned. How could he have been so blind?

"I had never taken the time to work through my own stuff."

A memory from his father's funeral arose in his head. Mom leaning on Matt, tears running down their faces as twelve-year-old Noah stood holding her hand, his cheeks dry.

"I needed to find my own peace."

That was what he was missing. Noah had never worked through his own issues or found peace with his father's drinking and death or the resulting baggage he'd been dragging around. There was so much he had to change, so much he had to answer for. Where to start?

"Accept the past. Apologize."

His heart rate picked up in confirmation that he needed to accept everything that had happened and stop wishing he could change the past. First thing in the morning, he would apologize to Grace. Once that was done, he'd think about what needed to come next. An appointment with his old therapist, for sure, and lots of changes in himself.

Anxiety shook his legs. He tried some deep breathing. Grounded himself by pressing his bare feet to the floor, concentrating on the cool tiles and the fine grit sand that had defied the broom. Held one hand to his head and closed his eyes for a backward count from fifty.

Nothing helped.

As a last-ditch effort, he did a five-senses assessment, hoping it would finally lead him to sleep.

Five things I see:
- *white-painted ceiling*
- *wiring running up the wall*
- *unlit fluorescent light bulbs*
- *dark-blue curtains moving in the breeze*
- *gecko on the windowsill*

Four things I hear:
- *snoring*
- *crickets*
- *someone rolling over*
- *my breath*

Three things I feel:
- *hard floor*
- *soft pillow*
- *breeze on my face*

Two things I smell:
- *sleeping bag*
- *Grace's hair*

That one couldn't possibly be accurate, but there it was. In his nose, in his mind, tormenting him with sweetness and kindness and patience, bringing back the knot of anxiety that had barely begun to dissolve.

What can I possibly say to her to make up for how I behaved?

He finished the exercise, but it only made things worse.

One thing I taste:
- *fear*

Chapter 35

MAY DAY

NOAH WOKE AT THE FIRST sign of dawn, anxious for the day to begin. It was Friday, the first of May—their last full day with the children and his last chance to talk to Grace.

He had spent all of Thursday worrying about how to approach her and what her reaction to his apology would be, only to have zero opportunity to act. His earlier wish to be mostly separated from her was coming back to haunt him. He had been assigned to the building crew again in the morning, and Grace hadn't.

The afternoon had been spent with a slightly different combination of children at a beach a short drive away, after which the children were taken home and the volunteers had gone to a local taco stand for dinner. Noah had ended up in a different mini-group than Grace for the driving and the eating, but she'd caught him watching her several times throughout the evening. He'd tried to convey with a look the gratitude he felt. She'd smiled a time or two in response, but there had been no chance for the kind of talking he needed to do. They arrived back at the orphanage late, and Grace had gone straight to bed. Falling asleep was once again a monumental effort for Noah, his worry warring with frustration. Fatigue had finally taken over in the wee hours, allowing some semblance of rest.

Now no one else stirred. Twenty minutes passed in slow motion before his nervous energy forced him out of his sleeping bag. Quietly, he collected his toiletries and took them to the bathroom. Lacking another occupation, he showered and shaved, nicking himself with an unsteady hand. He snuck back to his corner, put everything away, and grabbed the magazine he'd purchased on their long drive south. It was light enough that he might be able to read— or pretend to read—in the courtyard. Staying in the dorm and watching Grace until she woke up might send her running.

Eventually the sounds of kitchen workers and early-rising children drew the others from their slumber. Unable to maintain the pretense of reading any longer, he abandoned the magazine and decided to take a walk around the grounds, running into Oscar by the dining hall.

"Buenos días, Noah!" Oscar greeted him with a hearty handshake. "You are awake with the birds this morning."

Noah forced a chuckle. "Just, uh, can't wait to get to work," he said.

"Julio won't be back with materials for another hour," Oscar said, "but can you help with the breakfast? I usually get the flour for Sister Francisca, but my back . . ."

Noah readily agreed, happy to have any kind of physical outlet. Besides, he was as likely to find Grace in the kitchen as anywhere else. She had to eat.

Oscar showed him to a storage room where they kept the nonperishable food. Hefting a bag of flour over his shoulder, Noah carried it to the kitchen and dumped it into a giant mixing bowl as instructed by Sister Francisca. She poured in the rest of the ingredients and turned on the machine, then enlisted Noah to make the dough into balls. Once that was done, they ran each ball through a ringer to flatten it before tossing the raw tortilla onto an enormous grill to cook. The tortillas were flipped once, then piled onto a serving tray when they were done.

While he tended the tortillas and kept watch for Grace, Sister Francisca scrambled a quantity of eggs the size of a small child and set some beans to heat. His stomach growled at the smell of hot breakfast, his mouth watering at the sight of fresh salsa and guacamole, but he wasn't sure he would be able to eat anything until he could get the weight of his apology off his chest.

The children lined up, washed, and filed through the line. The volunteers followed. Noah kept flipping tortillas but saw no sign of Grace. The steaming mountain of tortillas dwindled, and Sister Francisca finally shooed him out of the kitchen to get his own breakfast. He lined up at the sinks behind the other volunteers, responded to their greetings as briefly as possible, and kinked his neck looking for Grace.

She didn't show.

He sat down at a table and took a few bites but mostly toyed with his food while he watched the door. Just as everyone else started clearing out, she finally entered the dining hall. He lingered, taking tiny bites and chewing longer than necessary. Soon only he, Jane, and Chad were left in the cafeteria. Grace filled her plate and came their way, hesitating when she saw Noah. Jane smiled and motioned for her to join them.

"Good morning," Grace said as she sat down by Jane, across the from him.

Jane and Chad both greeted her; Noah's good-morning caught in throat, but he managed a wobbly smile and a head bob.

How am I going to get an apology out if I can't even manage good mornin

"What's on tap today?" Grace asked.

Jane collected her dishes, looking around the hall. "I need to ask Oscar, but I'm sure they want us to wrap up the exterior painting and get the roof on the bathroom today. I'll go see if I can track him down," she said, standing. "Chad, will you go tell everyone we're meeting back here in ten minutes?"

That left Noah alone with Grace. His heart pounded in his throat. This was his chance. His metal fork became slippery in his hand as the awkward factor multiplied in the near-empty, near-silent room.

Now or never.

"Grace?" Her name caught in his constricted throat. He coughed, trying to clear his throat, and reached for his water. When he looked up she was waiting for him, amusement on her face.

"You okay?" she asked.

He let out an uneasy chuckle, taking courage. Some of his anxiety calmed, leaving a different sort of anticipation in its wake. He cleared his throat again. "I wanted to tell you I really appreciated what you said the other night. Your devotional with Marcus."

Surprise smothered her amusement. "You did?"

"You made some really good points."

"Thanks." Her voice was soft. She studied him. Her eyes were light-brown this morning, milk chocolate.

He swallowed. "I realized I have some things I need to . . . make peace with. Accept."

"We all do."

"My dad."

She nodded.

She *knew*. All those months ago, she had understood. Why hadn't he recognized it at the time?

Or had he?

Regardless, he needed to finish what he had to say. Time to eat crow. Strangely, it wasn't unappetizing. "I want to apologize for the things I said when you—"

"You were right," she said, returning attention to her plate and stabbing some egg with her fork. "I should never—"

Matt had been riding his road bike early that morning when a c
run into him from behind. The driver hadn't even seen Matt because th
was in his eyes. The proximity of the accident to the hospital had prob.
saved Matt's life.

Mom hadn't been able to specify injuries, but Matt was in critical cona
tion. She was barely holding it together. Noah knew he had to get home, bu
with no car and no phone and very little money, he had no idea how he would.
He doubted the limit on his single, never-used credit card was high enough to
cover the expense of last-minute air travel. Maybe there was a bus—but busing
through an unfamiliar country where he couldn't speak the language?

He was rolling up his sleeping pad, brainstorming other possibilities,
when Chad and Jane burst into the room.

"We have it all worked out," Jane said, as if reading his mind. "Marcus
will drive you north to Hermosillo—it's less than two hours, and his phone
has service. There's a flight at noon with one layover that should have you in
Denver by dinnertime, but you have to leave right now."

"What?" Noah said. "I can't—I don't have—"

"Don't worry about a thing," Chad said, picking up Noah's duffel and
ushering him toward the door. "We'll take care of your bedding. It's all settled."

"How?"

Jane hesitated. "I called my uncle. He's taking care of everything."

Relief and gratitude surged through Noah.

Yeah, Mom, he thought. *They're really good people.*

Chapter 36

FLY

NOAH WAS GRATEFUL THAT MARCUS didn't force small talk while driving. Unfortunately, that left Noah's mind free to play the worst-case-scenario game. Were Matt's injuries life-threatening? Was their mom holding up? Would Noah make it to the airport in time to catch his flight? Would the plane crash and put Noah out of his misery?

Guilt rushed in behind that thought. What would *that* do to his mother? He gritted his teeth, realizing he was catastrophizing every bit as much as she did.

In rare moments when he was able to sweep worry and guilt about Matt into a back corner of his mind, thoughts of his multiple failures with Grace took right over. How many times had he misjudged and mistreated her? He'd lost track of her in the craziness of leaving, and now he'd probably never see her again.

He blew out some frustration, drawing a look of concern from Marcus. "Want to talk about it?" he asked.

"I doubt it would help." One more reason Noah was an idiot. He should have contained that better. The last thing he wanted was a psych eval, but Marcus just nodded.

Though the drab scenery flew by, time crawled, his thoughts as churning and muddy as a midsummer flash flood. He successfully repressed another sigh of frustration but noticed Marcus glance at the rather insistent drumming Noah was doing on his knees.

"How are we doing on time?" Noah asked, pressing his hands into his legs to stop the motion.

Marcus looked at the clock on the dash. "We should hit the airport right around eleven, and your flight's at . . . ?"

"Noon."

_ and see what our ETA is. The connection wasn't
anage."

.e phone and pulled up the map, showing they had only
Navigating gave Noah something to occupy his thoughts
ratcheted up as they arrived at the airport curb. He retrieved
.n the back seat and turned to thank his driver.

us held out his hand. "Good luck. We'll be pulling for you."

andshake and forty minutes later, Noah was on the plane, envying all
calm passengers.

Maybe that was why his dad drank—to try to calm his anxieties.

The brief flight to Phoenix was uneventful. Noah had his phone in hand
long before they landed, powering it up as they approached the gate. He
stared at the screen, watching for notifications while he waited for everyone
in front of him to deplane, but nothing came up.

Knowing he had a couple hours of layover, he found a quiet corner and
sat down on the floor to call his mom.

"Noah?" She sounded terrible.

"Hi. I just landed in Phoenix."

"Landed? How—"

"Jane's uncle," Noah said, cutting her off. "I'll explain later. How's Matt?
How are you?" He leaned against the wall as she talked.

"He's torn up pretty bad, and his left leg is broken, but they're mostly
worried about his head."

"His head?"

"He hit hard enough to destroy his helmet."

"Skull fracture?"

"Yes, and they had to do surgery because there was"—she gulped—
"bleeding on his brain. He hasn't been conscious since I got here."

"When do they expect him to wake up?"

A pregnant pause drew sweat from Noah's palms.

"Mom?"

She sniffed into the phone. "They don't know."

Noah bought a sandwich after the phone call, but the combination of bad
news and stale airport food spoiled his appetite after a few bites. He spent
most of the short layover walking around looking for distractions. Usually he

enjoyed people watching, but not today. Everyone blurred together. Nothing could quiet the what-ifs.

What if Matt dies?

What if I never get to talk to him again?

What if I'm not strong enough to help Mom through it?

Physically and emotionally exhausted when he finally boarded, Noah passed out against his window for the slightly longer flight to Denver. He woke with the landing, texted his mom before the door was opened, and raced through the crowded terminal once it was. An Uber driver waiting curbside agreed to take him to the hospital. Thirty minutes dragged by like so many days and dropped Noah at another curb as twilight descended. He tossed a thank-you over his shoulder as he exited the car and jogged up to the entrance.

There his hurry ran out.

The automatic door slid open, and the unmistakable mix of disinfectant and medicine and fear poured out to engulf him.

The last time he'd been in a hospital was to say goodbye to his dad.

His feet deposited him at a desk, facing a harried-but-friendly older woman in a pink volunteer shirt.

"Can I help you?" she asked.

He blinked. "Uh, yeah. My brother, Matt Jennings, was brought in this morning. I'm not sure where he is now."

She smiled some pity his way. "Okay, hon. Do you have ID?"

He obliged and was given directions. Down the hall to the elevator, up to the third floor, show ID again at the ICU. Procedures were tighter, and it was a different hospital than his dad had been in, but it was still eerily familiar.

He stopped at the entrance to the ICU waiting area, petrified, then pushed through the door and the dread.

What if . . . ?

"Noah." His mom breathed out his name like he was her last hope.

He hurried over, wrapped his arms around her, and held her. "I'm here, Mom. I'm here."

Chapter 37

PUSH AND PULL

MATT DID NOT LOOK GOOD. He wore a typical hospital gown, his shoulders and arms showing above hospital blankets tucked into his armpits. An IV snaked into one arm, and a blood-pressure cuff clutched the other. Another tube in his mouth rested over his bruised and swollen upper lip, presumably delivering oxygen. A bandage wrapped around his head, covering his hair and forehead.

Noah stood outside the glass walls of his brother's hospital room with his mom, watching the steady rise and fall of Matt's chest, listening to the incessant beeping of monitors and the chatter of nurses, smelling the omnipresent disinfectant. He could barely spot his brother's nose and mouth among all the bandages and tubes and monitors. It had been only a few minutes since he'd arrived, but the weight of his brother's situation made Noah feel as though he'd aged a decade. He didn't know how his mom was holding herself together.

A soft hand crept around his waist. "I should have figured out how to get him a car."

Noah frowned. "He has a car."

"I mean when he was still in school. If he'd had a car, he never would have started cycling on the roads so much, and this never—"

"Mom," Noah said, reaching his arm around her shoulder and pulling her close. "He loves biking."

"I should have given him a ride to work."

"You live forty-five minutes away."

"I should have lived closer." Her voice broke. "I should have called him this morning, delayed him, anything."

Noah took her by the shoulders, her tears inviting a few of his own. "Mom. This is not your fault. There's nothing you could have done to prevent it."

Her face scrunched up as she gave in and burrowed into his shoulder. It was strange how much bigger he was than her. It didn't seem that long ago that he could sit on her lap. Patting her back, he looked over the top of her head at the city lights flickering through the waiting-room window.

"C'mon," he said when her tears had slowed. "Let's take a break and get something to eat."

They searched out the snack bar, which at this hour offered only drinks and a limited supply of unappetizing prepackaged sandwiches and desserts. They each chose a water and some sad-looking cookies, then sat at one of the little round tables.

"So where's Anabella?" Noah asked, more for conversation than anything else. He couldn't really picture his brother's girlfriend pulling an all-night hospital vigil.

His mother gave him an odd look. "They broke up months ago. Right after Christmas."

"Oh." It was May, for goodness' sake. Had it really been that long since he'd spoken to his brother? "Was he . . . pretty upset about it?"

"Not too much. She wasn't right for him, and I think he saw that."

"So he did the dumping?"

Mom shrugged. "From what he told me, it was mutual. I think he was more upset about starting over than breaking up."

Was Matt as worried about finding the right person as Noah was? Did the threat of winding up in a relationship like their parents' scare him too? Noah ground his teeth, remembering the many texts his brother had sent after the holidays. It had felt like forced charity at the time, and Noah had pushed against it, but maybe Matt had needed a friend.

Something else to add to Noah's list of changes to make: be a better brother.

If Matt recovered.

Mom shook her head. "You two were so close when you were little, and you used to get into so much trouble. Remember when he broke his arm?"

Noah smiled, thinking back to the summer they'd built a jump for their bikes from construction-site scraps. They'd started safe but kept making it bigger, going farther up the hill in front of their apartment to get more speed.

Matt, of course, had to be the test pilot each time they made an adjustment, and the jump had eventually grown too high and fast for him to handle. He had ended up with a broken arm, and Noah had been grounded from his bike for as long as Matt's arm was casted. At the time, he'd considered it terribly unfair—after all, the broken arm and the idea for the jump were both Matt's. Mom hadn't agreed with his reasoning, but she had allowed them to loaf in front of the TV more than usual until Matt's hard cast was on. After that she'd sent them back outside. Noah could still remember the pungent smell of the cast when it was removed after weeks of boyhood summer escapades.

How long had it been since he and Matt had done anything fun together? *Too long.*

And now . . .

"How old were we?" he asked.

Mom fiddled with the lid of her water bottle. "I think he was thirteen, so you would have been eleven."

Those had been good days.

And then Dad died.

After that everything had changed. Dad had worked when he was sober, but even with his sporadic contributions, they'd only been scraping by. After his death, Mom had taken a second job, which meant she was no longer home in the afternoons when school let out. It was almost like they'd lost both parents.

Summers were worse, the boys left to their own devices all day. She'd done her best—Noah had to give her that—and maybe if things had been different, he and his brother would have grown closer. As it was, with the removal of their primary source of fear and embarrassment and the absence of their mom to draw them together, they'd grown apart.

Matt was two years bigger, stronger, faster, smarter—and he'd made sure Noah never forgot it. At home, Matt had taken on a fathering role that Noah resented. Matt was always telling him what to do, empowered by their mom's words: *"You're the oldest, Matt. You're in charge."* Noah could never see how she'd thought those two short years made Matt the responsible one. If anything, he was the one who usually got them into trouble. Noah was more reserved, less of a risk-taker, although Matt had frequently teased him for his caution.

At least he could escape Matt's influence at school. On the odd years that they were in the same school, Matt had mostly ignored Noah—an infinitely better treatment than the few instances when he had made a fool of Noah in front of his friends.

There was less conflict once Matt had left for college, but then they'd both gone their own ways, seeing each other only briefly on holidays ever since. They'd kept in touch, but it was all superficial. The unwritten rule was that the Jennings family didn't talk about the hard things—Dad's alcohol, his death, the collateral damage they'd all suffered. Mom took comfort in her worrying, Matt overachieved, and Noah flew under the radar. It was easier that way for everyone.

Noah's teenage isolation had convinced his mom to find him a therapist. He had jumped through the hoops, opening up just enough to his therapist to assure everyone that he was *just fine.*

"He worries about you, you know." Mom broke into Noah's thoughts. Her water was nearly gone.

"Me? Why?"

She unscrewed the lid, took another sip. "He feels like he wasn't a good enough brother, like he should have been closer to you."

Noah scoffed, knowing who had done most of the pulling away. "He tried. It takes two." He reached for her wrappers, but she stopped his hand with hers.

"Thank you for being here now."

"I wouldn't be anywhere else."

Chapter 38

PROGNOSIS

THAT NIGHT NOAH MISSED THE bedding he'd internally complained about in Mexico. Mom insisted on staying at the hospital in case Matt woke up, and the waiting room chairs he'd created a makeshift bed out of left much to be desired. Once he pushed a few of them together with his duffel as a makeshift pillow, he was slightly more comfortable, but sleep wouldn't come.

His mind wandered to the Mexico crew. What had they done today? Were they able to get the roof on the new bathroom building? He knew Jane wanted it done before the crew left, and he'd been looking forward to the work. Of course, they had Oscar there, and the others would have picked up the slack with Noah being gone.

Had Grace been on the crew?

He'd probably never see her again. At least he'd been able to get his apology out before he left, and her reaction hadn't been terrible. He couldn't be sure, but he was fairly confident the tension between them would have eased.

Not that it mattered. His only means of contacting her before had been through her now-obsolete school email address.

Ryan has her number.

Noah's heart thumped in response. Was he willing to open *that* door? He hadn't even talked to Ryan in months—hadn't talked to him about Grace since their disastrous date.

No.

He wasn't that desperate for closure. Climbing into his collection of chairs, Noah brought out his phone and played the only game he had—a lame Tetris copycat—until he dozed off.

He woke up disoriented, embarrassed to find a solemn middle-aged woman in scrubs watching him from the doorway with a clipboard in hand.

Noah pushed one of the chairs away so he could stand, running his fingers through his hair and wishing for a shower. The clock on the wall read 6:05.

"Excuse me," the woman said. A stethoscope and ID tags hung around her neck. "Are you Matt Jennings's family?"

Mom stood, and Noah came to her side. "I'm his mom, Cynthia Jennings. Noah is his brother."

"I'm Ana Hoffman," the woman in scrubs said, reaching out a hand. "Neurosurgeon on call today. I just checked in on Matt and read through his charts."

"How is he?" Mom asked.

"We aren't seeing any changes yet," the doctor said, consulting her clipboard. "As you know, he suffered a skull fracture and epidural hematoma in the accident. We were able to remove the pressure on his brain in surgery yesterday, and now we're watching and waiting for him to wake up."

"How can you tell there's been no progress, if he's still out?" Noah asked.

"Good question," Dr. Hoffman said. "We assess his responsiveness to light and voices and mild pain—like pinching his hand—and his vitals are about the same today as they were yesterday."

Mom was wringing her hands. "How soon will he wake up?"

"We don't know. But we'll continue to monitor him closely."

"Will he be all right when he does?" Mom asked.

Dr. Hoffman offered her a weak smile. "There's no way to tell. The sooner we see some progress, the better his outlook will be."

"What are his odds?" Noah asked.

The doctor assessed him, as if determining how much he could handle hearing. "Recovery from a traumatic brain injury is difficult to predict, but he is young and healthy, and they got him here in a hurry. Those things work in his favor."

Noah noticed the growing worry lines on his mom's face and regretted asking his questions in front of her.

"Would you like to come see him now?" Dr. Hoffman asked, motioning with one hand.

"Yes," Mom said, jumping at the opportunity. "Can we both come?"

"Of course."

Mom and Noah followed the doctor into Matt's room. The beeping grew louder, more penetrating. Deep breathing only drew the antiseptic smell farther into Noah's lungs, tightening the knot in his throat. He'd handled all sorts of bleeding wounds as a lifeguard with no problem, but the confines and smells of the hospital unnerved him.

Mom went immediately to Matt's side, taking his hand in one of hers and stroking his arm with the other. "Matthew, honey, it's Mama. Noah is here too, and we want you to know we love you. You're going to get better, and we're going to stay right here by your side until you do."

She continued to talk to him, coercing Noah into a brief greeting of his own, after which he settled into the corner chair.

Eventually, his stomach growled loudly enough—along with the nurse's assurance that Matt would be well looked after—to convince his mom to take a food break. The cafeteria had a breakfast burrito that wasn't terrible, but it made him miss the fresh salsa he'd enjoyed only yesterday in Mexico. He finished quickly, then felt guilty for eating as his mom pushed her food around her plate.

"Mom? You have to eat something."

"Hmm? Oh. I'm not really hungry. How was your trip?" she asked, still staring at her plate.

"I don't really want to talk about it," Noah said, running his hands through his nasty hair.

His mom flinched and looked up, hurt.

"But I *will*"—he softened his words with a smile—"if you'll eat."

His very selective trip report distracted her enough to get a few bites in, but eventually she put her fork down and refused to eat any more.

"I need to get back up there," she said.

Noah nodded, dreading more hours in the tiny, beeping room.

"Why don't you go to his place and get cleaned up."

Noah huffed. "Do I smell that bad?"

Her mouth curved, though her eyes remained tired and sad. "I think you could use a break."

"I don't want to leave you alone."

"I'll be fine," she said, patting his arm. "Once you're cleaned up, you can sit with Matt and I'll take a break. It's more important that we don't leave *him* alone."

As much as Noah hated to leave his mom, he was thankful to escape for a while. She promised to call if there were any changes, giving him the keys to her car and Matt's apartment. He pocketed the keys and threw his duffel over his shoulder, then gave her another hug on his way out.

Dr. Hoffman was at the nurse's station and spotted him as he was leaving. "Hey, it's Noah, right?" she said, handing some orders to a nurse. She leaned back against the high countertop on one elbow, more relaxed than she had been earlier. "How are you doing?"

"Going to get cleaned up."

She smiled knowingly. "It gets a little rough hanging out here. I'm glad you're taking some time for yourself." With that, she pushed off and started away, but Noah wasn't ready for her to leave.

"Hey, uh," he said, "you didn't really answer my question about Matt's recovery."

Dr. Hoffman's eyes strayed to the windows of Matt's room, where his mom could be seen keeping vigil. "Let's walk." She gestured for him to lead the way, so he headed for the waiting room. "As I told you earlier, recovery from a brain injury is very difficult to predict. I don't want to get your hopes up, but I also don't want to discourage you."

Noah dug his hands into his pockets. "I understand, and for my mom, it's probably best she doesn't know more than she asks. But I'd appreciate it if you'd give it to me straight."

Her brows furrowed, revealing not-yet-permanent lines of worry as she surveyed the empty waiting room. "I don't know how things will go with Matt. He could make a full recovery, but right now, it doesn't look great. His numbers haven't changed much since he came out of surgery."

"What does that mean? Mom said there was a chance he won't wake up, but if the surgery went well . . ."

"It was successful, but yes, he might not wake up. Or he might recover fully or something in between."

"In between?"

"He could have some impairment, physically or mentally. Some individuals experience personality changes after brain trauma, some may have limited use of one side of their body, others experience chronic neuropsychological issues." She let out a tired sigh. "It's impossible to know at this stage what will happen, but I can tell you that positive thinking and a good support system will help ensure the best possible outcome. It's good that he's young and healthy. It's good that you and your mom are here to support him, and we will do everything we possibly can to help him."

Physical impairment? Personality changes? Neuropsychological issues? Noah's mind churned with horrific possibilities. Dr. Hoffman put a comforting hand on his shoulder.

"It's a lot to worry about, which is why I haven't said as much to your mom. She seems . . . sensitive."

"Yeah, that was the right call."

"Don't let the negative possibilities get you down. Remember, anything is possible at this point."

"Yeah."

The doctor stepped back and straightened her shoulders. "Let me know if you have any other questions."

His thank-you stuck in his throat, and he made his way slowly outside.

Without remote keyless entry to guide him, Noah may never have located his mom's tiny white car. Repeated pushing of the lock button on the key fob and the resultant tinny beeping led him to a corner of the enormous parking garage and the Hyundai's flashing lights. Vanilla air freshener assaulted his nose as he opened the door and tossed his duffel into the passenger seat, followed by a sharp pain when the steering wheel assaulted his knee. Biting off a curse, he adjusted the driver's seat and reminded himself to appreciate the moderate height he'd inherited from his dad instead of focusing on the pain in his knee.

The navigation app on his phone led him into the heart of the city, inspiring another wave of guilt. He hadn't even seen the apartment Matt had been so proud to move into when he'd landed his first lawyering job after graduating last year. *What a lousy brother I've been.*

Buildings rose up around him, blocking the sky and hemming him in. The last turn brought him to a newer apartment building near Denver's city center.

Noah drove into the tidy, well-lit underground parking lot and parked in the visitors' section, then grabbed his duffel off the passenger seat and sought out the elevator. Matt's apartment was on the top floor, at the end of a tastefully decorated hallway. Smiling at a passing neighbor lady and pretending he belonged, Noah dug out Matt's keys and opened his door. He couldn't help but chuckle at the sense of familiarity as the door swung open.

Tidiness wasn't one of Matt's virtues.

Closing the door behind him, Noah stepped over a bright-blue riding jacket on the floor and into his brother's home. The place still smelled faintly of new paint and carpet in spite of the many takeout containers littering the kitchen on his left and the clothes and papers strewn around the living room straight ahead.

Huge, unadorned windows dominating two of the living room walls looked south and west over the city. Matt had invested in a couch, coffee table, and flat-screen TV, but those were the only furnishings besides the clutter. An open door in the hall displayed a washer-dryer stack, and a stray sock pointed the way to the single bedroom. Noah followed it, in search of the shower.

A framed southwest sunset picture hung above the unmade bed, and Matt's mountain bike stood in the corner in a double bike stand. The empty slot in the stand had a narrower opening to accommodate Matt's missing road bike.

What happened to the bike? Noah thought. *Did it survive the wreck?*

He wasn't sure he wanted to know.

Turning his back on the remaining bike, Noah slid his duffel to the floor and collapsed onto the bed.

The pillow smelled like Matt.

A framed picture of their family on the nightstand caught his eye. It was grainy and off-center, having been taken with the cheap camera Matt had received for his fourteenth birthday. Mom had wanted a picture with all of them in it, and Dad—sober for the special occasion—had helped Matt figure out the timer. They'd piled up a few books to stabilize the camera, tilting the pile just right to get everyone in the frame. Matt had insisted on being the one to push the button, jumping in at the last second and throwing all of them out of line. Everyone was laughing.

It was the last picture of them all together. Dad had died two weeks later.

Noah had wasted so much time in self-imposed isolation. He hadn't been there for his brother in years. What if Matt never woke up?

Emotionally exhausted, sleep-deprived, and surrounded by memories of his brother, Noah finally relaxed his defenses and gave in to his grief.

Part Three

Chapter 39

THREE, TWO, ONE . . .

Me: *WHERE THE HECK ARE you when I need you?*

Ivy: *Umm . . . you're the one who left the country. Not a good trip? Kids roast you on a spit?*

Me: *Kids were great. Trip was great. Just crossed the border into AZ.*

Ivy: *What gives?*

Me: *Guess who else was in my group.*

Ivy: *Well . . . John Wayne is dead, so not him . . .*

Me: 🤦

Ivy: *That guy from the Easter brunch?*

Me: *Think worst-case scenario here. Who on the earth would be most opposed to spending a week with me in a small group setting?*

Ivy: *Girl, no way.*

Me: *Way.*

My phone buzzes with an incoming call, but I silence it and go back to frantically texting, ignoring the side-eyes and silent questions coming from a driving Marcus. I should have taken the back seat instead of letting Devin play the gentleman.

Me: *Can't talk. Witnesses.*

Ivy: *Noah?! In Mexico?*

Me: *Ten points for you.*

Ivy: *With you now?*

Me: *No, he left early yesterday because his brother was in an accident in Denver.*

Ivy: *You're killing me! Enough with the twenty questions. Not texting again until you fill me in.*

Me: *I had no idea he would be there. He had no idea I'd be there. He was a last-minute addition because someone bailed. I tried to clear the air early, but he pretty much stayed away and/or silent . . . until yesterday morning, when he*

APOLOGIZED and THANKED me for what I said in my devotional and told me how WRONG he was about things!

Ivy: *I CAN'T EVEN!*

Me: *But then had to leave and no one has heard anything and I'm really worried and I feel like I should reach out but I don't even have his number and I don't know what to do and WHERE ARE YOU WHEN I NEED YOU??!!!*

Ivy: *Deep breaths girl we got this.*

Me: *Aaaaaaaaaaaarrrrrrrrrrrrggggggggghhhhhhh!*

Ivy: *What happened to his brother?*

Me: *Hit by car while biking. Critical condition. That's all I know.*

Ivy: *Dang.*

Dave says you need to contact him.

Me: *#nonumber #alsoscary #whyisdaveinthisconversation #jkhidave*

Ivy: *Don't be so last century. There has to be a way. How did you communicate for tutoring? #chicken*

Me: *No-longer-a-student email #definitelychicken*

Ivy: *Social media?*

Me: *Please. You think Noah is on social media?*

Ivy: *So you stalked him and found nothing?*

Me: *. . .*

Ivy: *Ha! What about your bro-in-law?*

Me: *Die first*

Ivy: *Chicken*

I can't help the frustration that whooshes out, and Marcus catches my eye before I can dive back into my phone. He glances to the back seat, where Devin has donned headphones for a Netflix binge made possible by our border crossing.

"You sound an awful lot like Noah did on the way to the airport yesterday," Marcus says, his gaze back on the road.

I plead the fifth and stare out the window.

"He didn't want to talk either, which is understandable with the news about his brother—not to mention he barely knows me."

No comment.

"I hope his brother is okay. Kinda has me preoccupied, the not knowing. So I'd imagine you're probably dealing with that, too, only more so because you two were already connected."

"Pfff."

"Okay, maybe not *connected*, but there's definitely some connection there. Things always hit harder when they happen to someone you know."

I concede with a one-shoulder shrug.

"But I think this might go beyond that, considering the number of times I caught you two watching or avoiding each other."

"I wasn't—" I break off, realizing what he's said. "He . . . ?"

Marcus's cheeks stretch into a sly grin.

I sit back in my seat and fold my arms. "You're the worst."

"Guilty as charged."

He goes thoughtful for a few minutes, giving me false hope that he'll drop it.

"I just met him, but Noah seems like a nice guy." He pauses, weighing his words. "Was he mean to you?"

His word choice sends me into a nervous fit of laughter that has my eyes watering. Nipping it before the tears get real, I give him the CliffsNotes version of our history. I focus on the road; he drives and makes validating-therapist sounds, asking clarifying questions that make me think harder about all that's happened.

"Do you *like* him?" he asks when I've finished.

"I don't know." I sigh. "But this isn't about that. I'm worried about his brother. And him."

"So let him know. Be a friend."

"I don't have his number."

"Jane does."

"I don't have her number either."

"I do." He hands me his phone. "Text her."

Less than a minute later, Noah's contact information stews in my phone. In the meantime, Ivy has texted me a few hundred times, so I catch her up.

Ivy: *I like this Marcus. He's a good influence.*

Me: *You're both the worst. But yeah, he has mad skills. Now, what the heck do I say to Noah?*

Ivy: *Reach out. Ask about his brother. See what happens.*

Chapter 40

CONTACT

Noah woke in Matt's bed. He didn't remember falling asleep after his breakdown, but early-afternoon sun now lit the west-facing window. Panicking, he grabbed his phone, sighing in relief when there were no missed calls or messages. He sank back into the pillow, allowing his adrenaline to spool down while he stared at the ceiling.

Other than nap grogginess and some post-losing-it congestion, he felt better—slightly guilty for abandoning his mom but physically stronger.

He blew his nose, made the bed, and hauled himself into Matt's bathroom. The large, beveled mirror proved he looked as bad as he felt—greasy hair sticking up in all the wrong places, puffy eyes over dark circles, two days of beard. The smell was worse.

Counting himself lucky to find a clean towel under the sink—there were several used ones on the floor—he started the shower and cupped cold water from the sink against his eyes while the shower got hot.

Once in, the rain showerhead and spacious glass enclosure made him want to linger, but thinking of his mom alone at the hospital spurred him on. He hurried through his wash and shave, glad to have his own shampoo and razor from his duffel, and came up with a game plan as he finished his shower.

He would sleep at Matt's for now. He'd contact his boss and professors to let them know the situation and text his roommate so he wouldn't worry when Noah didn't come back to their apartment—not that he would. The clothes he'd packed for Mexico—supplemented by Matt's—would be all right for now, but he'd need to do some laundry soon. He could throw Matt's things in with his own and get the place tidied up for when his brother came home.

If.

When.

Reluctantly he turned off the water, dried, and dressed. He ran a comb through his hair and brushed his teeth, then gathered all the dirty clothes and towels into an empty laundry basket he found in the closet. Momentum carried him into the living room and kitchen, where he limited himself to collecting the trash. The rest of the cleaning would have to wait until later. Mom was alone.

Back in the bedroom, he grabbed both sets of keys and his phone, checking again for anything from his mom. There was nothing from her, but there was a text from an unknown number. Unlocking the phone, he opened the message.

And sat down hard on the bed.

Hey, Noah.

I got your number from Jane. I hope you don't mind too much. Just wanted to see how you're doing. How is your brother? I'm so sorry about the accident. Praying for you and your family in this difficult time. Take care.

—Grace

Noah's heart pounded in his ears. He wiped at his eyes and read the message again. And again. He should reply. But what would he say?

A notification banner pulled down as his thumbs hovered over the keyboard. It was from Mom: *Bring me a sweatshirt, please?*

He texted back, letting her know he would and that he was on his way. Hopefully he could figure out how to reply to Grace as he drove.

Back at the hospital, he tried to convince his mom to spend the night at Matt's, but she wouldn't listen to him. She remained doggedly bedside, until Noah caught her head-bobbing in her chair sometime after midnight and sent her out to the waiting room to get some better rest.

While she was gone, Noah sat at his brother's side, debating. Repeatedly he read Grace's text, felt the comfort it brought, and started to reply, only to shove the phone back into his pocket and argue with himself.

I shouldn't be thinking about Grace.

It would be rude not to reply.

My family needs me.

Grace deserves to be acknowledged.

I don't want to text her.

Yes, you do.

But I shouldn't want to!

Why not?

I need to be focused here.

On what? Staring at the walls? Watching TV?

I have no idea what to say to her.

You're putting walls up if you don't say something.

His mom had taken to reading aloud whenever she was in the room, insisting their voices would encourage Matt to wake up. Noah tried it but felt stupid, and Mom had been gone long enough that the machines' continuous beeping was drilling holes in his head.

Not a funny metaphor, considering what the surgeon had done to Matt.

Rereading the text, he again drafted replies in his head. That beeping was going to drive him crazy. It seemed, if anything, to be accelerating.

Accelerating?

Noah stood, scrutinizing the many monitors and wishing he understood what they meant.

A light rustling of bedsheets nearly gave Noah a heart attack.

"Matt?" he said, taking his brother's hand. "I'm here, Matt."

The beeping definitely sped up. Maybe it was monitoring heart rate. Noah's own accelerated as he tried to decide what to do. He couldn't reach the call button without letting go of Matt's hand. His cell was in the pocket opposite his free hand. He eventually worked it out, only to drop it on the floor in his haste. How could he get help without leaving Matt?

Finally, a nurse came bustling in the door. "How's it going in here?"

"I think he's waking up!"

"I noticed his heart rate picking up," she said. "Have you seen any movement?"

"I heard the sheets move but didn't see anything."

"Have you tried squeezing his hand? Maybe talking to him?"

Noah squeezed. "Hey, Matt. It's Noah."

Was it his imagination, or had Matt's hand moved? He squeezed again, rewarded by a slight fluttering of his brother's fingertips.

"He moved!"

"That's great!" She took Matt's other hand. "Was it strong?"

"Not really. More like a flicker."

"Hmm," she said noncommittally, donning the stethoscope slung around her neck and listening to Matt's chest.

"What's happening?" Mom's voice sounded panicky as she entered the room.

"Come here." Noah waved her to his side of the bed. "I think he might be waking up."

"Oh!" she said, rushing over. Noah moved out of the way to let her in. "Matt, honey? Can you hear me?"

Noah shifted to the foot of the bed so he could see better, taking hold of Matt's foot in a lame attempt to help without getting in the nurse's way. Mom brushed her hand across Matt's forehead, the way she'd always done when they were sick as children.

Matt's eyes fluttered open, met his mother's gaze, and slid shut again, leaving the ghost of a smile on his lips.

Chapter 41

BRUSH-OFF

Ivy: *STILL NOTHING?*

Me: *Nothing.*

Ivy: *Did he read it?*

Me: *I don't know. It just says delivered.*

Hours have passed since I texted Noah.

The car rounds a bend, blinding me with the setting sun and making my head spin. I swing the visor down and watch the road. I'm doubting the sanity of driving straight through. When we decided to go for it, it sounded like an adventure. Three young, healthy adults to share eighteen hours of driving? Easy.

Except now I'm ready to be anywhere but in a car.

Regardless, Marcus has to work tomorrow morning. Devin and I are just along to facilitate his safe arrival.

Slap!

When I look toward the sound, Devin is leaning into the steering wheel, glassy eyes blinking rapidly, a red mark that looks like fingers surfacing on his cheek.

"Hey, Dev," I say, "how about you find a nice turnout and I'll drive?"

"Oh good. I'm dying here," he says, coming to an abrupt stop in what is more a slight widening of the two-lane road than an actual turnout.

Marcus, formerly asleep in the back seat, pops up with a curse. "What?"

"Devin's sleepy," I explain, climbing across the middle as Dev runs around the front of Marcus's aged Jeep Cherokee. I buckle into the driver's seat and check my mirrors, praying no crazies come whipping up behind us before Dev gets in and I can get us back on the road.

Marcus rubs at his eyes. "Dude!" he says when Devin slams the door and I stomp on the gas. "You gotta be nicer to Cher. She's old."

"Sorry." Devin yawns, leaning against the passenger window.

In the rearview mirror I see Marcus frown. "You okay to drive?"

My assent encourages him to lie back down, leaving me alone with my thoughts and the rural highway for company. The road is far too quiet to shut out the worry, so I get Devin to start an audiobook for me and cross my fingers that the plot will be intense enough to override my worry.

My phone buzzes a few times, but when the road is straight enough to hazard a glance, I can see that all the texts are from Ivy. Hours pass, Marcus takes over driving, and still there is nothing from Noah. I haul myself into bed sometime after one in the morning, convinced he won't be texting back.

I leave my ringer on, just in case.

I don't think I even move until I wake up a little after ten to Mom's ringtone and the sun in my eyes. There are several older notifications from her below the one that woke me up—probably because I forgot to text her when I got home—and one from Ivy in the mix, but when I see the banner at the bottom, I nearly drop my phone.

It's a text from Noah.

My fumbling fingers get the code wrong twice before my phone finally unlocks. Crossing my fingers that the news is good, I take a deep breath, open the message, and read.

He's out of the coma and doing better. Thanks for asking.

A wave of relief flows over me. Noah's brother is recovering. I send a prayer of thanks heavenward and read the message again, thumbs ready to reply, but something about the tone stops me.

Thanks for asking.

What does that mean?

Hours later, I'm still trying to figure it out.

"It's clearly a brush-off," I say as I position an address label on a thick envelope and hand it off to Ivy from my place at the kitchen table.

"I don't know," Ivy says, sliding an announcement into the envelope. "I don't usually take the time to text a brush-off from my brother's hospital room at three in the morning."

Dave—leg three of our triangular Wedding Announcement Assembly Circuit and Crisis Support Group—agrees as he takes the envelope, wets the adhesive with a sponge, and seals the flap shut. "It's not a brush-off. He's a guy. If he responded, he's interested. If he wanted to get rid of you, he'd ghost you."

"Ghosting sucks," I say, thumping my fist down on the current label.

Dave stops what he's doing and catches Ivy's eye. "Do you think this activity might be contributing to Grace's negativity, or is it just trip-lag?"

Ivy chuckles. "Definitely not this. Nothing's more fun than marrying off another roommate."

"There is nothing about either of you that I like," I say. I don't mean it. They'll disappear into the Newlywed Abyss in less than a month, and then I'll have no one to hang out with.

Again.

For the moment, I'm embracing my role as wedding assistant and glorified third wheel.

"What I meant," Dave says, ignoring my salt, "is that you asked him something, and he answered it. Bare minimum, yes, but he gave you what you asked for. Maybe he doesn't like texting."

"But 'Thanks for asking'? That's a total brush-off!"

"What makes that a brush-off instead of an actual thank-you?" he asks.

I roll my eyes. "Seriously? You have to ask?"

"She has a point," Ivy says. "The way it's worded kind of sounds like he's over and out."

"So how *should* he have responded, if he wanted to keep it going?" Dave punctuates his question by slapping a finished envelope onto the growing pile.

"I don't know," Ivy says. "Maybe ask about her drive home? How the rest of the trip went?"

Dave huffs. "He's at the hospital with his critically injured brother. Not to mention it was three in the morning."

"True, but considering their history . . ."

"He's a math guy, right?" Dave asks me.

"Accountant."

He smiles as if that proves his point. "Notoriously bad with words."

"Valid," Ivy says.

"Stereotype." I shake my head at her flip-flopping. "Which side are you arguing? I can't keep track."

"I'm exploring all options. Besides, you *know* he doesn't like to talk, especially about himself."

Dave can't help but throw in another two cents. "I still say you're expecting too much from someone in his situation. What about his apology? That doesn't sound like someone who wants to avoid you at all costs."

"Guilt," I say. "He was mending fences."

"See?" Ivy says. "Good fences make good neighbors. He wants to be friends, at least."

I disagree. "Good fences keep people out." As much as I've told Ivy about Noah—and that's most of it—she still doesn't comprehend how closed-off he is. "Trust me. He doesn't want people climbing his fence or even looking through. I'm not texting back," I say.

"But—" Ivy starts.

I hold up one hand to stop them both. "Look, I reached out. I let him know I was worried about him, and he responded in a way that says, clearly, 'Nice of you to ask. My brother's going to be fine. Peace out.' I have to respect that boundary."

Especially because I don't want to.

Chapter 42

WORK

FOR THE FIRST TIME IN nearly two weeks, Noah woke up in his own bed. A horrendous week of bouncing between Matt's apartment and the hospital had drained him. Added to that were the residual fatigue from Mexico and the stress of missing the first week of his summer job and classes.

Reaching for his phone, he was astonished to find it was nearly noon. Lame as his apartment and twin bed were, his body had recognized the familiar surroundings and surrendered to fourteen uninterrupted hours of sleep. He hadn't even noticed when his roommate Wyatt came in or whether he had played video games half the night like usual.

Noah rolled onto his back and smiled at the ceiling as he stretched, feeling well-rested for the first time in ages. A growl from his stomach reminded him that he had chosen sleep over food last night, arriving home empty-handed to barren cupboards and a smelly fridge.

Dressing silently to prevent waking a still-sprawled-in-bed Wyatt, Noah snuck out of his room and into the kitchen to forage. Unfortunately, his room-mates were as woefully understocked as he was, though the stinky, piled-high sink told him they'd definitely been eating *something*. Finally, he unearthed a stray granola bar in the back of a drawer and, seeing that it was only a few months past its expiration, downed it in two bites. That would sustain him long enough for a grocery run.

He texted his mom for the latest update—Matt was doing fine and aiming to be home from the hospital in the next few days—and his eyes landed on the unnamed phone number below his mom's text thread. He tapped it.

Hey, Noah.

I got your number from Jane. I hope you don't mind too much. Just wanted to see how you're doing. How is your brother? I'm so sorry about the accident. Praying for you and your family in this difficult time. Take care.

—Grace

Grace hadn't texted back after his reply, but Noah hadn't really expected her to, as aloof as he'd been in Mexico. As mean as he'd been in December. Apologizing could only go so far. Time would have to do the rest.

Heart pounding, he selected Add New Contact, input Grace's name, and tapped Save.

His thoughts strayed to some advice he'd heard once about dating—something to the effect of becoming the kind of amazing person you would like to spend time with.

Who would want to spend time with Noah, as grumpy and withdrawn, sullen, and resentful as he was?

With a hmph of disgust and a surge of resolve, Noah scrolled through his contacts for the number he needed, hoping that he'd be able to get an appointment soon.

He had a lot of work to do.

Chapter 43

JUNE BRIDE

IF ANYONE DESERVES A PERFECT June wedding day, it's Ivy and Dave, and it looks to me like they have it. Blue sky, not too hot, lovely ceremony, lively reception. She is the quintessential June bride, he is completely smitten, and their confidence in each other envelops them. I'm so happy for them, I could cry.

It's all I can do not to.

Nearly a month has passed since Mexico, consumed by work and wedding preparations. One would think I've been busy enough not to be preoccupied with pointless wonderings.

Thinking some food might keep the wallowing at bay, I make my way to the refreshment table on the pretext of checking stock. A grandmotherly woman in a sage wedding-party dress approaches, and I touch up my happy-to-be-here look.

"Would you mind?" she asks, glaring at the glass beverage dispenser. "I can't twist that spigot for the life of me."

"Of course not," I say, noticing the swelling and displacement of her weathered knuckles as I take her cup.

"You must be Grace." She watches me with too-perceptive eyes. "I'm Ivy's nana." Her soft, warm hands wrap around mine as I return her cup, the subtle scent of roses reaching my nose.

"It's a pleasure to meet you," I say, remembering the stories Ivy shared about visiting her nana.

"Thank you for being such a friend to my Ivy. She's told me how much you've helped her, how supportive you've been."

Whether from the warmth of her hands or her words, I'm blinking rapidly and losing ground fast.

Nana's brows furrow over her blue eyes, but her lips hold a soft smile. "It's hard letting go, isn't it? Always easier to leave than to be left behind."

She gets it.

Five roommates I've married off, three of whom were especially good friends, Ivy the closest of them all. I'm tired of being alone—left behind, as Nana said—but I shake my head and refuse the self-pity. "I'm happy for her."

"Of course you are," she says, patting my hand, "but I can tell that's not all you're feeling. You have to feel your feelings, or they'll eat you up."

I swallow hard. I know she's right, but I don't want to feel them. Not right now.

Nana squeezes my hand. I clear my throat and wipe at my eyes as if I have allergies, and I redirect. "Ivy's an amazing person, and Dave is so good for her."

She's silent until I meet her gaze, and I'm surprised to see I'm not the only one tearing up. "He *is* good for her." The loose skin under her chin bobs with a swallow, and I remember Ivy telling me Nana wasn't married to Ivy's grandpa until she was in her late thirties. They had one child together—Ivy's mother— and he died young, leaving Nana alone for the past forty years or so in addition to the first thirty-odd.

"Let yourself feel," she repeats with a single determined, teary nod, "and then move on." She squeezes my hand once more, and then she's gone, taking my tears with her as warmth spreads through my chest.

I know she's right.

Chapter 44

AUGUST

"I HATE THAT I'VE MISSED a whole summer," Matt said, lifting a box. "I mean, I'm glad to be alive and healthy and everything—don't get me wrong. But a whole summer stuck in the safety zone?" He shook his head with an exaggerated sigh, smiling as he waited for Noah in the hall.

"Don't you complain about missing summer," Mom chimed in from the kitchen, where she was wiping out the shelves in Noah's cabinets. "I did it twice for you boys."

"Did what twice?" Noah asked, coming out of his room with a stack of folded bedding and towels.

"Missed summer." She looked up as they walked past, frowning at Matt. "Is that box too heavy?"

"Not for these arms." Matt staggered intentionally, then let go with one hand to show how light it was. All it contained was some photos and toilet paper.

She threw her rag at him, which he easily caught in his free hand and tossed right back. "Stinker," she said with a scowl.

Matt opened the apartment door for Noah to squeeze through. "Glad I don't ever have to be pregnant." He shuddered, drawing a laugh from Noah as they walked to his car in the August heat.

"You sure you won't reconsider?" Matt asked, popping the hatchback and loading his box. "Try to find something in Denver?"

Noah piled the bedding on top of his other belongings. "Tired as I am of driving over the mountains, I don't want to go back to the city. You could move west."

Matt chuckled. "We'll see. Kinda hard to leave my job."

Noah knew it was a long shot, but it didn't hurt to plant the idea. It would be great to have Matt closer, and if that happened, Noah knew their mom wouldn't be far behind.

"Thanks again for staying," he said, grateful they had opted to stick around after his graduation to help with the short move from Oak Hills to Grand Junction.

"Least I could do after all you've done over the summer. You excited for all the changes?"

"Should be good. Real job, new city, fresh start," Noah said, surprised at how much he meant it, especially the "fresh start" part, which he hadn't really discussed with Matt.

His therapist had agreed that the changes would be beneficial. They had made serious progress over the summer, meeting weekly to work through Noah's baggage. He felt a thousand pounds lighter, having shed the resentment and bitterness that had lingered from his childhood and festered after his father's death. Regular exercise and better nutrition had also gone a long way to improving his mental health. He was optimistic about the course of action they'd set for after his graduation from the accounting program.

Impatient to be finished with school, he'd had no plan to attend the smaller summer commencement ceremony, but Matt had talked him into it. The only thing Noah had expected to gain from the experience was closure, but the speaker's words had hit home. The bits about graduation being a joyful time and using one's degree to lift others were predictable, but the entreaty to value and give priority to family connections had sunk into Noah's heart, validating everything he'd done over the summer and motivating him to keep it up.

After Matt's initial wake-up and almost-smile, his improvement had been steady. It had taken time, but his mobility and coordination were approaching normal. He was still working on physical strength, but mentally he was as sharp as ever—only with an added measure of humility and caution that were greatly appreciated by his brother and mother, respectively.

Noah had spent all the time he could with Matt after the accident, doing coursework online and staying at Matt's apartment when he was in town, showing up at physical therapy to provide moral support whenever his schedule had allowed, and spending evenings with him and their mom. Matt was tenacious with his at-home exercises, motivating Noah to strive harder with his own goals. Instead of competing, they'd cheered each other on.

The summer had flown by. With only a couple of classes to finish up his master's degree, Noah had still been able to work construction three days a week. Between that and commuting back and forth across the mountains, there hadn't been time for a social life.

But now . . .

Nerves electrified his stomach as he thought about the next step in his plan.

A few weeks into Matt's recovery, Noah had received a text from Ryan, asking how things were progressing. Once Noah had given the update, it had occurred to him that he'd never actually *told* Ryan about the accident. How had Ryan known?

Grace.

Ryan had said she'd asked him if he knew anything, and when he didn't, it had come out that she had been with Noah in Mexico when the accident occurred. She'd made Ryan swear not to say anything to Claire, told him she only wanted to know how Matt was doing and didn't want to "bother" Noah, insisted it was nothing but friendly interest in Noah's brother's health.

Ryan had smelled a rat, and since Grace wouldn't talk, he had gone to Noah, not letting up until he had the whole story—*including* the tutoring, which she had conveniently not mentioned.

Ryan insisted Noah still had a shot with her. And so, with Ryan's confidence to lean on, Noah was taking a chance. A big one.

He didn't dare look beyond that.

Setting his worry aside and focusing on the task at hand, he went back into his old apartment to gather the last of his belongings and finish up the checkout cleaning. Though he and Matt would be living a couple of hours away from each other again, they planned to continue spending time together. One of the most amazing outcomes from Matt's accident was how much their mom's anxiety had calmed down from spending so much time with her boys and seeing them get along better than ever. Noah hadn't thought he'd ever get to the point that he looked forward to time with his family. Now he did.

And he owed it all to Grace.

He had accepted himself, his past, and his family, blemishes and all. Once he'd done that, the peace had come, and then the enjoyment.

It was time to move forward.

Chapter 45

TELEGRAPH

THERE ARE DEFINITE BENEFITS TO being on the planning committee for Young Christians Serve: knowing what's going on, meeting lots of people, and—best of all—you don't have to worry about looking like you have nothing better to do if you show up. Because, well, you kind of *have* to be there.

On the other hand, you have to show up to all the YCS activities.

I'm setting up for our fall social, and I'm 90 percent sure I wouldn't be here without my assignment.

I work my way back around the park, savoring the late-summer sun as it cools into evening and the smell of dutch-oven barbecue, making sure everyone is ready. Pastor Will Johnson, who started YCS as a part of his young-adult ministry, is doing all the food, so that's been an enormous load I haven't had to carry. I can't imagine where he found enough dutch ovens to feed this many people.

The giant blow-up Twister game is inflated and holding. I'm not sure what Melissa is thinking with this one: Twister—not my favorite to begin with—on what's basically a bouncy house without walls? I'm definitely steering clear, but she was excited about it, so whatever. Maybe someone will enjoy it.

Hudson has somehow procured a large number of six-foot-long PVC pipes and swears the game he's going to use them for is a winner. I'm skeptical but willing to give it a shot.

Chris is doing a variation of the telegraph game, in which he forces people who barely know each other to hold hands with their eyes closed so they can telegraph to the person at the end of the line to grab a spoon when the chosen card is shown to the person in front. I'm steering clear of that one too. Not feeling real touchy today. Or maybe I'm feeling *too* touchy. Who knows?

Another benefit of being in charge: "Sorry, I can't play because I have to go check on . . . something."

I'm a party pooper. I own it.

Originally I wanted to set up some volleyball nets, but I was outvoted. Convenient, in hindsight, because I'm not as enamored of the sport as I once was.

Jamie, my new roommate, is wrestling a water cooler onto the serving table next to the cups, plates, and utensils. She could never replace Ivy—who is still mostly lost to the Newlywed Abyss—but she's pretty awesome. Jamie isn't even on the committee, but she's here to help me.

See? Awesome.

"Good to go?" she asks, pulling her long brown hair to one side to get some air on her neck as I return from my circuit.

"Locked and loaded." Now I'm just worried no one will show up. I've met a ton of new people here in Grand Junction, and there's definitely a different vibe than in Oak Hills. There are more young professionals than college students, which helps, but sometimes that translates into less enthusiasm for activities. I'm mostly enjoying my new normal. It's just—all the prep for this activity and everything else that's been going on has made for a long week.

"Do you think—" I start, but Jamie interrupts me.

"Yes, people will come. Pastor Will's food—regardless of anything else—will bring most of the guys, and that—"

"Will bring the girls." She's right. It's my first activity as cochair of the committee, and I'm a little nervous, especially since the other cochair is out of town on business.

Jamie closes her eyes and inhales through her nose. "Yum. Can we eat yet?"

I check my watch; it's five minutes past the time we said we'd start, so people should be showing up any minute. Sure enough, a couple of cars are pulling into the parking area, twenty-something singles spilling out with happy chatter.

Here we go.

I spend the next half hour working the crowd and making sure the napkins don't blow away in the breeze. The turnout is excellent, which unfortunately means Jamie and I won't be getting leftovers of Pastor Will's amazing meat and potatoes.

I spot him and his wife, Elaine, talking to someone at the end of the line. They're probably in their midforties but they have the energy to really connect with the younger set. Elaine smiles and waves me over, and I decide I'd better get some food before it's all gone. I check the napkins one more time and greet a few people in line as I make my way to her.

"Tomas Financial?" Pastor Will asks, getting a nod from the guy they're talking to. "That's just off North Avenue, isn't it?"

"Yeah," the guy says, turning as I arrive to give me a heart attack.

Noah.

My brain goes full panic.

"Grace," he says, the social smile he's wearing for the Johnsons spreading into a real one.

I've never seen him with a full smile. Not directed at *me*, anyway. And now I can't think and I'm staring at him and my face is hot and I am a complete, dumb idiot.

Elaine covers for me with a grace I didn't receive with my name. "You know each other?"

She's waiting for my answer, but I'm still in shock. What do I say here? *Yeah, but only confrontationally . . .*

"We do," Noah says, touching my elbow with a cool hand, guaranteeing another lengthy, silent heart attack from me and a thousand questions in Elaine's eyes. "How are you?"

I can't answer that for a million dollars. I have no idea. He's the one who brushed me off. I'm speechless with no end in sight, but Jamie shows up in time to save me.

She takes stock of our group and the look on my face and helps out. "I'm Jamie Alvarez," she says, offering her hand to Noah.

He's still looking at me—head tilted to one side, throwing me back to our tutoring days—but he takes his eyes from mine to greet Jamie. "Noah Jennings," he says.

"Nice to meet you," she says, turning to me and sending some telepathic moral support with her big brown eyes. "Chris wanted me to come ask you how soon we're going to start the games."

"Uhh," I manage with exceptional eloquence, looking at the dwindling food line, "ten minutes?"

She bobs her head and leaves, with a glance at Noah and a telepathic *"hang in there"* for me.

"So how do you know each other?" Pastor Will asks.

Noah manages to summarize our past in one sentence that makes us sound like we're friendly acquaintances instead of awkward antagonists. "We met through her brother-in-law, and then I was her math tutor at Oak Hills, and we ended up in the same volunteer group this spring at an orphanage in Mexico." He's standing straighter than I remember, shoulders back instead of weighed down. Confident.

"It's always nice to run into old friends," Elaine says as we get to the food table. She somehow manages *not* to load that statement with expectation, for which I am eternally grateful.

Noah steps aside so they can go first, then grabs two plates and hands one to me. "So really. How are you?"

I can't help the confusion that must show on my face. He waits patiently.

"Fine?" I can't help make it a question because I'm not sure what's up or down right now.

Noah Jennings.

Here.

Making small talk.

With me.

"Are you . . . visiting . . . someone?" I ask.

"Actually, I just moved into Mesa View Apartments," he says. "I'm close enough to work that I could probably bike when the weather's good, but since Matt's accident, my mom really hates to hear about anyone biking on the road." He scoops up some cheesy potatoes for himself and lifts the spoon to ask if I want some.

I nod.

"She used to freak out about everything," he continues. "You should have heard her when I told her about the last-minute trip to Mexico." He barks out a fond laugh. "She's loosened up in a lot of ways since we've been spending so much more time together, but road biking still makes her stress."

"I can imagine," I say, struggling against my shock. All. Those. Words. More than I've ever heard him speak outside of mathematical explanations and hostile accusations. "How is Matt doing?" I ask, grateful to finally know his brother's name.

His expression softens. "So good. Almost a hundred percent. It's been incredible." We finish the buffet line and take our food to a long picnic table. He sits across from me and tells me about Matt's recovery and physical therapy, how he beat the odds and how hard he had to work to do it.

I'm not even sure I knew he had a brother, before Mexico. I watch him as he talks, and I'm amazed. He looks good, like he's shed some of the protective layers he always wore before. How many times did I try to break through? He only let me in once—briefly, when he told me about his dad—and now his words are running like the Colorado after a big spring thaw without me even pressing. The Noah I always thought I could see lurking behind his grumpiness has broken free.

I like it.

Not good.

He finishes off his potatoes and washes them down with a drink. I'm much too aware of the muscle in his temple as he chews, the bobbing of his Adam's apple, the careful way he folds his paper napkin. The familiar whiff of his aftershave.

Bad. Very bad.

He asks me if I'm still working with Marcus, how he's doing, how my boys are progressing at the school. I end up telling him about the kid that enrolled this week and the crazy-hard stuff he's dealing with, careful to leave out names and details for privacy. Noah's expression tells me he understands how hard it is for this kid—and for me. He doesn't brush it off as teenage angst or tell me to leave it at work. He just listens, and somehow that makes it lighter for me to carry.

This is the most uncomfortable-comfortable conversation ever. I can't reconcile this Noah with the one I knew before—the coldly analytical math tutor, the resentful date, the silent critic in Mexico.

We move on to less-serious topics, and I'm in the middle of pointing out and naming other YCS leaders when I feel an arm snake around my middle, followed by a quick peck on my cheek.

"Sorry I'm late," Alec whispers into my ear, sending a shiver down my arm.

Surprise erases Noah's easy smile.

My cheeks are hot. Alec knows I hate public displays. "Hey," I say, easing out of his grasp and taking a hand instead, "look who just moved into town!"

"Aquaman!" Alec lets go of my hand and steps around the table to Noah, who stands up to take part in a lopsided—in height and enthusiasm—handshake/bro-hug/backslap. "How's it going? Catching up with Grace?"

"Yeah," Noah says, smiling again, though it's not the same. "Good to see you." His tone doesn't match his words.

Right then, Chris materializes at my side, pulling me away because it's past time to start the games. He's right. I've been slightly distracted. I stand beside Chris and have him explain each of the stations, then watch as people meander to their game of choice, some choosing to stay at the tables to eat or visit.

"I thought you were going to have nets up," Alec says with a tip of his chin toward the games when I return.

I shrug. "Outvoted." I hear my name and see Chris beckoning wildly.

"We need more people!" he yells.

I'd love to decline, but duty calls. Noah hesitates, then, surprisingly, follows along, though his ease of manner has fizzled. And though I'm sure Alec would rather die than play a party game, he catches up and takes my hand.

"What's the game?" he asks, and when I remember, I know I should have declined, regardless of duty.

It's the telegraph game.

A couple of other people have come over from the tables, and Chris says we have enough to play now. He splits us into two teams and tells us to sit shoulder-to-shoulder, facing the other team and holding hands with our eyes closed. Alec lets go of my hand long enough for us to sit down, then reclaims it. Noah settles in on my other side, chatting with Alec across me, and my heart pounds so hard I can't think.

And it has nothing to do with the hand I'm already holding.

Chris goes on with the directions, but I'm not really paying attention until I hear Noah's voice in my ear.

"I won't bite."

I turn to look at him—our faces too close for comfort, cinnamon in the air between us—and he tips his head down to indicate his waiting hand.

"I promise," he says.

Chapter 46

AFTERMATH

IT MIGHT HAVE HELPED TO *know she had a boyfriend*, Noah texted, then punched his code into the keypad to the new apartment—new to him, that is. The door stayed firmly locked.

Ryan: *She doesn't.*

Noah: *Tell that to the guy holding her hand.*

Ryan: *Hand-holding isn't definitive. Besides, she asked about you!*

Noah: *He also kissed her cheek. At the YCS social.*

He punched in the code again, with the same result. Grumbling, he tried again. Apparently, the door's keypad preferred a soft touch. This place was a big step up from his old one, though it wasn't as nice as Matt's.

"Hey." Jake, his only roommate, looked up from the video game he was playing in the living room. "How was the social?"

It was a nice change to have a roommate who occasionally acknowledged the real world. "Not bad," Noah hedged, focusing on how good the food—and company—had been before Alec had shown up.

"Nice." Jake nodded, going back to his game.

"Oh, and someone told me to tell you hi," Noah said, remembering the girl he'd met during cleanup. They'd covered the usual get-to-know-you questions, and she'd recognized his roommate's name.

Jake pulled away again, curious. "Someone?"

"Yeah. Can't remember her name. Reddish-brown hair, dark eyes, short, athletic."

His eyebrows ticked up. "Melissa?"

"Yeah, that's it." Names were always hard for Noah, even when he wasn't drowning in failure.

"Huh," Jake said, his expression lighter. Several seconds ticked by before the sound of his game started back up, bringing a smile to Noah's face as he went to his room. Maybe Jake's luck would be better than his.

Having a private room was possibly the best thing about the new place. Noah closed his door and slumped onto the twin bed to take his shoes off. One more year, and then he would be able to afford a down payment on a place of his own. The first thing he'd buy after that would be a man-sized bed.

At least he wasn't six-five.

Like Alec.

Alec, who had swooped in and taken Grace when Noah wasn't looking. *"A day late and a dollar short,"* his mom would say. It felt like a personal insult.

Noah placed his shoes in the empty slot on his shoe rack, pulled out his phone, and flopped onto his back, checking to see if Ryan had replied.

He hadn't.

It had felt so good to see Grace again, in spite of a twinge of guilt for surprising her the way he had. In Mexico they'd both been shocked. This time he'd deliberately inserted himself into her world, catching her at a disadvantage. He'd tried to let her know his intentions were good with a reassuring touch on her arm and by carrying the conversation while she recovered. It had helped, and she had gradually relaxed, the conversation flowing until the unwelcome interruption.

Noah's phone buzzed twice in quick succession.

Ryan: *What???*

Sorry for delay. Escaped toddler interfering with baby feeding. But I asked Claire about Grace. She doesn't know about any boyfriend.

Ryan: *Don't worry. I didn't give you away.*

So much for research. Part of Noah wanted to cut his losses. Why hadn't he just texted her instead of committing himself by moving into her territory?

Some guys really enjoyed the dating scene. Not him. Granted, he hadn't really planned to enter the actual scene since his sights were set on Grace and Grace alone. But if things with Alec were as tight as they appeared . . .

Noah got up to brush his teeth. He might as well get ready for bed, though he doubted he'd be able to sleep.

Seeing her this evening had been different from before, because *he* was different. He hoped she could see the change. It had been hard to keep his amusement at her confusion in check as he'd talked about Matt and his mom and everything that had been going on. His openness had loosened her up in turn—until her boyfriend had claimed her.

Alec had pretended surprise when Grace had pointed Noah out, but the two men's eyes had met briefly *before* Alec had snuck up to kiss her cheek. He had been posturing.

Then there was the telegraph game.

Noah hadn't known what he was getting himself into. He'd wanted to prove he was out of his shell—to himself as much as to Grace. It would have been less complicated if it hadn't involved physical contact.

Holding her hand had been revealing, to say the least. He'd always known there was some attraction there—on his side, obviously. On her side, maybe?

The game had unnerved him. The last time he'd touched her hand—when he'd "reintroduced" himself during their big blowup—he'd been seething. Looking back, he could remember that contact affecting him even through his anger. For a split second as he'd railed against her, he'd wanted to kiss her.

What if he had?

But no, he hadn't been ready for any kind of relationship then.

Now? He was ready.

Sitting next to her, their eyes closed, hands clasped and resting in the air between their knees as they waited for the message to telegraph down the line through their teammates . . . the energy humming from the contact on Grace's side had made it tough to detect anything coming from his other hand.

He didn't know what the exact relationship status was with her and Alec. But he could have sworn that tonight, when he'd held out his hand and told her he wouldn't bite, she'd glanced at his lips.

Chapter 47

SMASH

WHY WASN'T HE AS SURPRISED as I was?

It's all I've been able to think about since seeing Noah last night, and that's a problem since I'm on my way to Pathfinder Academy, where I work. Not only do I need to be 100 percent invested in the job, I'll also be surrounded by people trained to recognize mental distress.

But Noah wasn't surprised to see me.

Okay, maybe, possibly, that's not the *only* thing I can think about.

Noah held my hand.

Yes, it was compulsory. No, there wasn't anything romantic about it. But there was *something*. Definitely something. And it wasn't coming from Alec's side.

Also a problem, since we're dating. Enjoying holding one guy's hand while simultaneously *not* enjoying holding my boyfriend's? Not okay.

That issue was accidental and unavoidable, but my other issue . . . I'm not sure I can rationalize feeling not-guilty about *not* wanting to kiss the boyfriend good night because the compulsory hand-holding with Noah was better than any kiss Alec's given me.

I am in so deep.

Alec and I have been seeing each other for a couple of months—it started with hanging out after Mexico and progressed to dating from there. At first, it didn't even register that he was interested in *me*, I was so preoccupied with worry about Noah and his brother.

Stooping to asking Ryan for an update on Matt had been more embarrassing than the BASHFUL T-shirt on Halloween. I made him swear not to tell Claire, for which he blackmailed me into unlimited babysitting. I tried to act like that would be a sacrifice.

Once Ryan acquired some details to set my mind at ease, I felt ready to move on.

And there was Alec: long-ago crush, finally paying attention to *me*.

A guy I like, liking me back? Who knew *that* could happen?

It was like a dream. His excitement for life made me feel alive and wanted and included for once, instead of inhabiting my usual place on the sidelines, cheering on whichever roommate was about to get engaged.

Not that we're talking marriage. It's only been a couple of months.

Finding time to spend together when our schedules are so at odds has been a challenge—he works conventional hours, and I work evenings and Saturdays, with Sunday and Monday off. I was flattered when he offered to attend Pastor Will's Sunday service instead of the one he'd been going to so that we could have more time together.

I didn't foresee the difficulties.

Alec is the quintessential California boy: tall and attractive and athletic and funny and a really good person to boot. His personality is so dynamic, he can't help but take center stage wherever he is, and that's been difficult to navigate. Not that I've ever wanted the spotlight, but I'm used to having my own space, doing things my way. Surely it's just the collateral damage of extended single-hood: the longer I'm alone, the more set in my ways I become. All couples have to adjust to each other, figure out how they work as a pair. As much as I enjoy being with someone, that part has been a little rough.

Maybe it would be easier if we stopped playing volleyball together.

As for the physical . . . clearly I've watched way too many chick flicks and my expectations are way out of line. I *like* holding his hand. I *like* kissing. Expecting magic is unrealistic, and basing a long-term relationship on the physical is like expecting one strip of firecrackers to keep you warm all winter.

I know that.

But holding Noah's hand was—

Stop.

I pull my thoughts back to reality, back to my driving to work.

I'm dating Alec. He's the one asking me out, telling me how much he enjoys being with me.

Although, sometimes I wonder if he likes the *idea* he's created of me more than the *real* me. Sometimes I think his interest only caught because—this time—I didn't chase after him like everyone else.

Like *I* did, before.

He's a good guy, and fun and handsome, and the thought of going back to being alone in my free time or third-wheeling with my married or dating friends smells like onions moldering in the back corner of the pantry. All relationships take work, and I'm willing to do my part.

If only he wouldn't be so affectionate in public.

I focus on the tricky left into the parking lot, park my car, and do some mindfulness exercises to clear my head. Knowing I'm walking into a building full of therapists is good motivation.

Of course it's Marcus that I meet on my way into the academy. I apparently throw too much cheer into my "Hi, Marcus!"

That or he's clairvoyant.

"Whoa," he says, making a U-turn from the front door and following me into the commons area. "What's up?"

Nobody loads that phrase like Marcus. Shoot. I keep a neutral expression for anyone who might walk past, but I know Marcus will see through any fabricated explanations. "Ran into Noah last night."

His eyebrows raise.

"Hey, Lars!" I give the lanky sixteen-year-old a fist bump and a big smile as he passes by.

Marcus narrows his eyes so he can bore into my head with his therapist laser vision, worrying the shark-bite scar on his finger like he always does when he's analyzing. "'Ran into'?"

I give him the lowdown of my Monday evening, including Noah's move-in and Alec's escalating PDA.

"What are you going to do?" he asks.

"Ask him to tone it down. Again."

"I meant about Noah."

"There's nothing to do. We're friends, I guess, but I'm with Alec."

Marcus is skeptical.

"What? That's all we've ever been. I'm focusing on making things work with Alec right now."

He winces. "How long have you been dating?"

"A couple of months."

"And you're 'making things work'?"

"Yeah. All relationships take work." Right? I've never really been in one, but I hear people say that all the time.

"True." The way he draws the word out tells me he means it shouldn't be this hard. Not yet. "You're all good people. You'll figure it out." He pats my shoulder and gives me a bolstering look as he leaves.

Easy for him to say. What does he mean, we're "all good people"? My relationship with Alec has nothing to do with Noah. I brush off whatever I felt last night as fleeting, purely physical, solidifying my resolve to invest in my relationship with Alec, and my head clears just enough to focus on my work.

Brad is working evening staff with me again tonight, along with three others. On weeknights we come in after the boys finish school, take them on outings, and shepherd them until bedtime when the night staff takes over. Alec views it as glorified babysitting, but I've seen how influential having a healthy connection—a good role model—can be for these guys. For some of them, we're like the loving, accepting older siblings they never had.

Like the one you should have been to Benson.

I pause, acknowledge the painful thought, and set it aside, replacing it with my mantra: *I did the best I could with the knowledge and skills I had at the time.* My experience with Benson—painful as it was to acquire—is what helps me connect with these guys now.

It also helps when they try my patience, as teenagers do.

We have a good-sized group tonight—twenty boys ranging in age from fourteen to seventeen—that have opted for the outdoor activity, so we load them into a couple of vans and drive to the park for the evening, taking advantage of the good weather while it lasts.

They gravitate to the activity that interests them most, some playing soccer on the wide lawns or volleyball in the sandpits, others walking around. The staffers split so there's good supervision in each group. I choose volleyball.

"Grace!"

I turn just in time to catch the ball Lars has tossed my way. "Aww, you were supposed to set it!"

"You have to give me a better toss than that!" I hit the ball back at him, and he digs it, giving me a pass I can work with. I set him up, and he gets a great smack down over the net. "Nice timing!"

His smile is as wide as the Grand Canyon. He's planning to join a club team back home when he leaves Pathfinder.

Most of the boys end up here because of their alcohol or marijuana use. Our job is to help them see what drove them to substances in the first place and work through it so they won't go back to using when they leave us. Every time I get a smile like that one from Lars, I know I'm in the right place at the right time. I like to think Benson approves.

A couple of other boys join me and Lars, and Brad lines up with three on the other side of the net. It's a close game. I'm able to get Lars some good sets, and he kills more of them than he shanks. His hitting has really improved over the summer. The other boys aren't as skilled as he is, but Lars is good about including them and offering encouragement. He even sets me up a couple of times, and it feels fantastic to hit something, even though we lose the game.

We pile back into the vans as the sun sinks toward the horizon. I'm sticky and tired and surrounded by loud, sweaty teenagers, and my heart is full of endorphins and love for these struggling guys.

It's a great job, and I'm reminded that I *do* love volleyball.

Just maybe not with Alec.

Chapter 48

DOOR OR WINDOW?

NOAH WATCHED FROM A DISTANCE, battling an overwhelming desire to cut and run as Alec sat with his arm around Grace's shoulder at church and held her hand in the hall. Escape won out in theory, but the pastor caught him as soon as meetings were over and asked if Noah could stay for a chat.

They sat down together in the pastor's office. After deflecting compliments about his dutch-oven cooking and some obligatory get-to-know-you questions, Pastor Will's next words surprised Noah.

"So you already know Grace Ebert?"

"Yeah, we've known each other for a while," Noah answered, wondering what this had to do with anything.

"That's great," Pastor Will said. "You've worked together before?"

"Mm-hmm."

"She had some great stories about Mexico. Said it was quite an experience."

"Yeah, it was." He left it at that, hoping the dead air would move them past the chitchat. He didn't want to talk about Grace.

"Well," Pastor Will said, slapping both hands on his knees, "I think you'd be a great addition to our YCS planning committee."

Noah repressed the urge to laugh out loud at the irony. Maybe he *should* have talked more about Grace. "Uhh . . ."

Pastor Will's smile faltered. "Grace is one of the cochairs, so that should be an easy transition since you already know each other."

Noah cleared his throat, fishing for some valid excuse to say no.

"It's a large committee," the pastor said, shoring up his smile, "so it shouldn't take up too much time. Would you be willing to help out?"

"Sure," Noah answered, his hook coming up bare.

Pastor Will thanked him profusely, let him know the first meeting would be next Sunday, and sent him on his way with an enthusiastic handshake.

It did nothing to settle the butterflies in Noah's stomach. *Maybe this is my chance*, he thought as he walked out of the building, trying to put a positive spin on it. Maybe Grace and Alec weren't serious, though Alec's attentions suggested otherwise.

Noah growled in irritation.

A car was pulling out, but it paused, the window rolling down to reveal a familiar face. "Hey, Noah!" the girl called out.

"Jamie, right?" he said, recognizing her from the activity as he came to her car. "Grace's roommate?" Probably the only reason he'd remembered her name.

"Yep." She smiled. "How was your first week?"

"Not bad," he said.

She put the car in park and folded her arms onto the open window. "You're an accountant, right?"

"Yeah. You?"

"I'm a nurse for a pediatrics office."

He shifted on his feet, sweating from the sun on his back and realizing her car was still running. "I don't mean to keep you. I'll just—" He motioned to the street, leaned that way to start his walk home.

"Do you want a ride?"

Grace's roommate. Hmm . . .

"That would be great," he said, scrapping his plan to walk in favor of some firsthand research.

Small talk as Jamie drove consisted of the usual who-where-when of his move and his roommate. She hadn't met Jake, as she'd been in town for only a couple of months herself. When she asked if Noah had done anything fun over the summer, he mentioned the Mexico trip. Physical therapy with Matt had been time well spent, but most people wouldn't label it as fun.

"Same trip as Grace?" She looked over while she waited at a red light.

"Yeah." Noah paused before adding, "Alec too."

"Right!" Jamie brightened. The light changed, and at Noah's direction, she turned onto his street. "It's so great how they reconnected there. Grace had a huge crush on him a few years ago, and now they're so cute together."

"Does he live by you guys?" Noah asked, striving to keep his voice neutral.

"No," Jamie said, gathering her hair to one shoulder. "He lives about twenty minutes from here, but he started coming to church with Grace a few weeks ago so they can spend more time together."

Noah *hmm*ed, hoping and dreading that Jamie would keep talking as he directed her to his apartment building.

"I guess their schedules don't line up, with her working evenings and Saturdays. I think it's sweet that he's willing to do that for her."

Noah agreed—out loud, at least—as she came to a stop. "Thanks for the ride," he said, opening the door. "I guess I'll be seeing you around."

"Anytime," Jamie said. "I think you'll really like it here. There's usually a group doing something on the weekends. I could"—she paused, tucking her hair behind her ear—"let you know."

Her offer of introduction to the local social life felt like being given a Band-Aid for a compound fracture. One of his mom's oft-repeated adages came to mind, something about God opening a window somewhere when a door closes.

Noah grumbled his thoughts on that as Jamie drove away. He'd been banking on the door, for a change.

Grace hadn't looked exactly thrilled with Alec at the social. But they were serious enough for public affection and altered church attendance—serious enough that Noah had to back off. Why *wouldn't* Grace be happy with Alec? He was good-looking. Outgoing. Fun.

Tall.

Whatever had been bothering her the other night must be something else.

What if it was her family—her brothers? He realized they hadn't talked at all about her family at the social. Why hadn't he asked?

He could text Ryan, ask if anything was happening.

No. It wouldn't do any good.

Discouraged feet dragged him up the stairs to his third-floor apartment and into his room. What had he expected? That he would move in and say hello and Grace would immediately want to be with him?

He should have known better, considering their history.

He should have texted before he made his decision to relocate here. He could have led with an update on Matt and seen where it went from there.

But he hadn't.

With his new YCS assignment, he thought maybe he'd been given an opportunity to spend time with Grace without any walls up, but Jamie's information confirmed that he'd have to build a new wall to hide his feelings behind instead.

Luckily, he had plenty of practice keeping things businesslike with Grace. He'd throw his hopes out the door and do his job and, once again, stay far enough away to resist her charms.

Chapter 49

HANGRY

IF BRAVING CONSTRUCTION TRAFFIC IS any indicator of relationship fitness, Alec and I are Olympians.

I hate, *hate* driving through construction, and the current juggernaut—combined with my car's barely-staying-ahead-of-the-August-heat air conditioning—has turned what's usually an easy twenty-minute drive into an exercise in anger management. I'm on my way to see Alec, stuck in a never-ending inchworm between my place and his, when Tony Ito, fellow cochair of the YCS planning committee, calls. I answer with my car's Bluetooth; no sense in delaying the inevitable.

"Grace," he says after my hello, "we need to schedule a committee meeting." He's not one for pleasantries.

"Hey, Tony!" I say, accelerating briefly with the rest of my worm segment. "How was your trip?"

"Pastor Will said we're getting some new committee members on Sunday, so I don't see any point in doing it before then, but we have to get things rolling."

The snarky reply I knew I wouldn't need—*I'm glad your trip was a success, and I'm doing very well, thank you*—blows away with the AC and a roll of my eyes. We have all our activities and projects mapped out until Christmas, but that won't stop Tony's worrying. "We should definitely meet with the new people," I say, slowing as I notice the cascade of brake lights moving my way.

"And we need a debrief on last week's activity: what worked, what didn't." Like the awful telegraph game.

A sensory flood—callused palm, hazel eyes, cinnamon—distracts me long enough that two cars sneak in front of me as we speed up again.

"Can you hear me?" Tony says, testing our line.

"I lost you for a second." True, if misleading. "What was that?"

"I said our numbers were down 4 percent from last year's fall social. We need to determine and address the cause."

He spends the rest of the traffic jam discussing strategies for better turnout while I make monosyllabic contributions. I resist reminding him that we don't get paid commission for higher anxiety or more people—don't get paid at all, in fact—not that I don't want to do the job well, but sheesh. His hypervigilant perfectionism has me fighting some serious passive aggression. Eventually, he gets back to setting a time for our next meeting. He really wants to have it before worship, but he settles for directly after.

Alec won't like how that cuts into our time together, but I don't see any way around it. My efforts in the traffic gauntlet should buy me some credit.

When the call ends, I bask in the silence and free-flowing traffic, and by the time I get to Alec's, the AC has pulled ahead and my mood has mellowed. I pull into one of many empty slots and run into Garth on my way up the stairs to their apartment. We exchange pleasantries and he walks back with me.

"Alec isn't home yet," he says, pulling out his keys and unlocking the door. "I can let you in if you want to wait."

"That would be great," I say, happy to get out of the afternoon heat.

"I'd stay," he says, "but I'm meeting someone for dinner." He tells me to make myself at home, and with that, he's gone.

I take a seat on the sofa and pull out my phone, but the only messages I have are from Tony on the committee group text, saying in several installments and too many words that we have a meeting Sunday. Nothing from Alec or anyone else.

I shoot off a message to Alec to let him know I'm here, then open my ebook. It's a good one, but it can't hold my attention in this too-quiet not-my-apartment. I check my messages again—nothing—and switch to a word game.

Several levels and a growling stomach later, there's still no sign of Alec. As insistent as he was about my being here right when he got home, my imagination is worrying its bounds. I hope everything is okay at work, that he didn't get into an accident.

He's nearly half an hour late when I finally hear him coming up the stairs, talking to someone in the courtyard. Pleasant surprise claims his handsome features when he opens the door and sees me.

"Hey!" he says, setting his keys on the table and wrapping me up with long arms. "This is nice to come home to!"

I relish the feeling of being held, kissed, wanted. "Traffic?" I ask, though the chances of that are slim since he's coming from this side of the construction.

"Straight shot," he says. "What should we do tonight?"

I'm confused. Didn't he have something planned? Why did I need to be here at a certain time if he didn't? I could have waited half an hour and missed the traffic. I could have had a snack. I bite off my irritation and give him the benefit of the doubt. I must have misunderstood. "Maybe . . . get some dinner and then go for a walk?"

"Nah," he says, flopping onto the couch and patting the cushion next to him. Suspecting that sitting too close might result in a serious delay of dinner, I leave some space between us, putting my hand on his knee as consolation when he pulls a face. "How about we order pizza and watch a movie?" he asks.

With the apartment to ourselves, I'm 90 percent sure that will translate into more of what might delay dinner if we were to go out. Not that it isn't nice, kissing him, but I'd rather focus on other aspects of our relationship. We've established that our lips are compatible.

"Wouldn't you like to get out, after working all day? Enjoy the warm weather while we can?"

"Mmm, good point," he says. We toss around a few ideas and decide on a nice counter-serve place close by. It takes him a few minutes to change clothes, my belly grumbling as I wait. He looks great when he comes out, and I'm ready to go, but he has other ideas. When I pull away, he asks if something is wrong.

"Not at all, but I'm hungry. I thought we'd be eating sooner."

"Well, I just got home, but I guess we can go now if you want."

"You're not hungry?"

"I can always eat," he says with a smile, "but they had some treats set out for someone's birthday. I guess that took the edge off."

"Is that why you were late?"

"Late?" he asks, confused.

Tamping down my rising irritation before I go postal-hangry, I casually usher him to the door. "You told me to be here forty-five minutes ago."

He throws a smolder my way. "Missed me, did you?"

I straight-arm the pass he makes at me, hide my clenched teeth behind a smirk, and look up into his eyes.

"You're forty-five minutes late," I say. "I'm hungry." *And the only thing I'm missing right now is food.*

Something clouds his eyes—disappointment? irritation? hurt?—but he shrugs it off, stepping under my block to get the door. "Let's get you something to eat," he says with a conciliatory smile.

"Thanks," I say, grateful to be moving.

I don't realize until we're in the car that he didn't apologize.

GLUTTON

RYAN: *HOW GOES THE HUNT?*
　Noah: *Out of season.*
　Ryan: *They can't be that serious if she hasn't mentioned him to Claire.*
　Noah: *That would be more convincing if I hadn't seen them. Or heard her roommate's glowing reports.*
　Ryan: *I'm serious. Sisters tell each other everything.*
　Noah: *Did she ever mention I was her tutor?*
　Ryan: *. . .*
　Noah: *Ha*
　Ryan: *Maybe I wasn't listening.*
　Noah: *If you had inside information from Ivy, that would be something.*
　Though Noah had only met her briefly on Halloween, Ivy's name had come up often in the math lab. He was sure she and Grace were close, and he was willing to bet his left pinky that Ivy knew more about Grace's current relationship status than anyone—with the possible exception of Jamie.
　Ryan: *Who's Ivy?*
　Any hopes Noah had had of gleaning even a particle of useful information from Ryan were quickly dwindling to nothing.
　Whether an optimist or a glutton for punishment, he had gone to last night's YCS service project hoping for an opportunity to talk to Grace without Alec present. Unfortunately, she hadn't come, so he'd spent most of the time with her roommate. As a result, he now knew everything Jamie did about the couple, including their dating habits and exactly how excited Grace had been the first time Alec kissed her.
　In spite of the too-much-information so willingly proffered, the optimist inside him argued that Jamie was more enthusiastic about the relationship than her roommate was. He was no psychologist, but Grace hadn't seemed all that taken with Alec.

Or maybe that was just wishful thinking.

Another text came through from Ryan. *Claire knows who Ivy is.*

Noah: *So do I. That doesn't mean she's sharing information with me.*

On the dark side of things, his time spent with Jamie was beginning to remind him of Amy's dogged pursuit. He might have to change his approach to prevent a disaster there, but as painful as it was to hear Jamie's Grace-and-Alec stories, he hated to give up the scoop. It would be a fine line to walk without hurting Jamie's feelings.

Maybe if he expressed interest in one of the other girls or invented an imaginary girlfriend . . .

Ryan: *Don't let Grace be your Marianne.*

Momentarily confused, Noah groaned when he caught the reference to the old Boston song, pulled himself out of bed, and changed into his running clothes. If he waited any longer, it would be too hot—the high for this first day of September was predicted at ninety-one. At not quite eight o'clock, it was still in the midseventies. Manageable.

It would have been cooler if he'd gone early, but Noah wasn't much of a morning person. That was one of the things that had helped him choose which of his three job offers to accept—flexible hours. As long as he got his time in and his work done sometime between seven a.m. and nine p.m., his boss didn't care what time he showed up or went home. Noah didn't miss getting up at the crack of dawn to work construction and had quickly adjusted to a routine of going to bed when he wanted and getting up when he woke.

His phone buzzed again as he left—Ryan had sent a link to the "More Than a Feeling" music video. With a humph, Noah slid the phone into his armband and made for the gravel path that formed one side of the parking lot and flanked a canal. The waterway was one of several that snaked through the city, delivering river water to fields, orchards, and vineyards in Grand Valley.

The flat trail beckoned him to increase his pace and made him grateful to be off the streets. Lingering paranoia from Matt's accident wasn't overwhelming, but it was enough to make the bland route palatable. If he'd had the time, he would have tried a hike in Monument Canyon. He started his run playlist and zoned out, staying to the right in case anyone caught up with him from behind.

As he rounded a bend in the trail, he noticed a runner in the distance going the same direction. Another minute or so brought recognition—the form, the long legs, the swinging ponytail of dark, curly hair—along with a surge of speed and focus.

Definitely a glutton.

He caught up in a few minutes, slowing his pace when he neared so he wouldn't overtake her in an overeager sprint. As he eased up on her left side, she heard his steps and slid right to let him pass. Instead he matched pace and watched her sideways with what was probably a goofy grin. *Blame the runner's high*, he thought.

Grace ran on for a few more strides, her brows furrowed in concentration, before she shot an oblique glance at the weirdo matching her pace. When she recognized him, she smiled. "Hey!" she said.

"Hey!" he said back, pausing his music and removing the headphone on her side while reining in his grin. *Don't screw this up.*

"Day off?" she asked in the shortened clips of run-talk.

"Flexible hours. You?" He knew very well—thanks to Jamie—what Grace's hours were, but he thought it best to feign ignorance.

"Evenings."

"You like it?"

"I do." She looked left as they came to a street crossing. The furrows had taken hold again. "It's not ideal for social life, but I enjoy my free mornings."

"How's the new kid?" he asked, remembering her worry at the social.

Her face relaxed as they crossed the empty street. "Doing better. His guide is really helping."

"Guide?"

"Fellow student," she said between breaths. "Further along in the program."

"Ah. That's good. And the dream job—is it everything you wanted?"

Her eyes narrowed.

Noah wanted to kick himself. She probably thought he was mocking her work again. "I mean, it sounds like you can make a big impact there. Do you enjoy it?"

Her tension eased. "It's different than I expected. Harder." She waved at a baby being pushed in a stroller by a woman walking the other direction. "Things are always different in reality than theory."

"True." Like placing himself in a position to pursue Grace, only to find she had a serious boyfriend.

"How about you?" she asked.

"Huh?"

"New job, right? Accountant?"

"Oh," he said, recalling the drift of their conversation. "So far, so good. Healthy culture. Good people. Not as intense as the other firms I interviewed with." Noah eased in behind Grace for a few strides to give an oncoming biker room to pass. "How's your family?"

They settled into a nice rhythm as she chattered about her brothers' sports and the harvest from her parents' massive garden.

"Honestly, I don't know why they plant so much. They have a hard time finding enough neighbors to eat it all."

"How's Claire's baby?" he asked.

Grace's steps sputtered.

Apparently she'd planned on ignoring their original connection, but the question had just slipped out. Choosing to act as though they were nothing more than old friends—and hoping Ryan hadn't let slip to Grace that Noah had been asking about her—he went on. "Ryan mentioned a while back that they had a boy."

Their eyes caught as he glanced sideways, and he tried to convey nothing more than friendly interest with his. That seemed to reassure her, and with another question or two from him, her face lit up as she talked about her niece and nephew.

She was complaining about how little time she got to spend with them when another street cut across the trail. "Oh!" she said, looking around. "I didn't realize how far we'd come. I usually turn around before this."

"Sorry," Noah said, doing an about-face. "I probably threw off your groove."

"Not at all." She smiled. "It's been a nice distraction. Besides, more mileage isn't a bad thing. I don't have to be to work until this afternoon. Are you going to be late?"

"Nah, I'm good." He might have to work through lunch and into the evening, but if that was what it took to get some alone time with Grace, it was worth it.

Chapter 51

CHAFING

IT'S DISTURBING, THE WAR INSIDE me.

Alec's hand slips around my waist, pulling me closer as we look for a seat in the chapel. "Let's go up a little closer," he whispers into my ear.

I fight the urge to pull away. Honestly, can he not just make a hand gesture or something? Choosing a seat for worship service is not a romantic endeavor. I grit my teeth, tell myself how lucky I am to have *someone*, and let him guide me.

For which I am blessed since I catch a glimpse of Noah sitting in the pew I almost sat in.

A rush of guilt washes over me. I haven't mentioned to Alec that I ran with Noah several times last week. I doubt he'd care, but I probably shouldn't be spending time alone with a guy other than my boyfriend. Still, it's not like it was planned. Noah's schedule happens to be similar to mine, and we've accidentally bumped into each other every day since the first time—sometimes on my way out, sometimes on the way back—but always for a few minutes, we run and talk.

Pastor Will finishes his opening remarks as we get settled and invites us to join him in opening the scriptures. Alec eases his arm around my shoulders and rests his open Bible half on my lap, half on his. It's a show of affection, a compliment—not a demand for attention.

Right?

I focus on the sermon, not hard to do with Pastor Will. He always manages to make things simple and deep at the same time.

I feel a tap on my shoulder and accept a folded paper from someone behind me. It's a note from Tony, sitting a few rows behind us, reminding me that I agreed to share a verse to begin our committee meeting after church today. I'd be irritated if I hadn't forgotten. It also says he's contacted the new people to make sure they'll be there. Other than Jamie—who told me before church that she'll be there—I'll have to wait and see who they are when I get there.

I keep one ear tuned to the service as I think over my week in search of something to share, but Alec keeps toying with a curl at the base of my messy bun, sending shivers down my arm as I listen. Attention is nice, but this is not the time. I bend down to adjust the strap on my sandals, using the shift to capture his hand with my own. The look he gives me makes it clear he knows what I'm doing, but he settles for making circles on my hand with his thumb when I sit back.

By the end of the meeting, I'm in need of some space and possibly some ointment for the chafing.

I manage to extricate myself as we get up to leave, but his hand finds my waist again and guides me toward the outer door.

"I have a meeting, remember?" I say, gesturing to the small classroom off the foyer.

"Can't you skip it?"

It baffles me why I have to explain this to him. Again. "I'm sorry, but I need to be there, and this is the best time for everyone else."

Playing with my hand again, he pulls me out of the stream of people and lowers his voice. "Are you okay?"

I nod.

"You seem . . . I don't know . . . off today."

I squeeze his hand and step closer even though it kinks my neck, hoping without hope that no one is listening to our relationship discussion right here in the middle of the crowded entryway. "I'm fine. We'll still have plenty of time after the meeting."

He huffs. "What am I supposed to do in the meantime?"

"Come with me?"

His lack of enthusiasm is monumental.

"I'm sorry," I repeat. "I'll be as fast as I can. You can go to my apartment, or you can wait here." The crowd has mostly cleared, so I soften the blow with a kiss to his cheek.

His hand presses mine, confirming the tactic's efficacy. "I'll go to your place. Can you get a ride?"

"I'll ride back with Jamie," I say. I hand him my keys, watching as he walks to his car. He's everything I ever thought I wanted. It's surreal that we're together.

So why am I annoyed?

Chapter 52

GREEN

Noah took the seat Jamie waved him to in the small classroom, not thinking about the kiss he'd seen Grace plant on Alec's cheek, the way he'd guided her to a seat with his hand on her back as they'd come late into the church, the way he'd toyed with her hair during the sermon.

Clenching his jaw, Noah smiled while Jamie introduced him to the other committee members and chattered on about how excited she was to be involved. He recognized Melissa from the fall social, but there was no way his brain would remember the other names—it took all his brain power just to appear civil.

The guy with the laptop and expression of doom was probably the other cochair, judging by the way he kept checking his watch and straining to see out into the hallway. When Grace finally came in, he didn't even wait for her to sit before he started. "Thanks, everyone, for coming on short notice. We have a ton to cover, so I'll offer a prayer, and then Grace has a verse for us."

It wasn't until Grace said amen that she saw Noah, if her expression when their eyes met was any indication.

Calm, friendly disinterest, he told himself, smiling and lifting his chin in greeting. Her face now bore her usual friendly smile, though slightly pinched. Apparently, she hadn't known about his assignment. *Great.*

"Thanks, Tony," she said. She read a verse in Hebrews, in which Paul tells the people to meet together and encourage each other in good works. "Our aim," she said, "is to come up with activities that draw us together while serving those around us who may be in need. Through our outreach and service, other people can feel the goodness of God and be drawn to Him."

Noah kept his eyes in his lap, thoughts wandering to the gratitude he'd felt when Grace reached out after Matt's accident. She had only sent a text, but simply knowing that she was concerned had brought comfort.

That led him to replaying the conversations they'd had on the trail. With no prior intention of becoming a daily runner, he suddenly found himself counting the minutes until he could go. Caution was warranted, and he'd varied his time of departure just enough that he still had a chance of running into Grace without being creepy, but even a short hello was worth the effort. He couldn't remember ever looking forward to exercise more. Like a cup with a hole in the bottom, he felt he could never know enough about her—her work, life, family, interests.

It was driving him crazy.

"Absolutely not." The sharpness of the voice brought Noah's attention back to the meeting. It was Laptop Guy—Tony—that had spoken, his comments directed at a guy with white-blond hair styled like Albert Einstein's.

Tony inhaled to say more, but Grace intervened. "I think a trip to Moab sounds fantastic, Chris," she said, her tone backing her words. "But I think what Tony means is that an overnight activity with no service doesn't really fit our mission."

Chris slumped in his chair, several gravity-defying blond corkscrews swaying with the motion. Noah wondered idly if he leaned more physicist or beach bum.

"Getting back on track—let's review assignments for tomorrow night," Tony said, reclaiming the meeting as Grace tossed an apologetic look Chris's way.

The feeling it prompted wasn't envy. Grace wasn't dating *that* guy.

The meeting dragged on, the only thing of note being that when Noah volunteered to pick up the food for their Labor Day activity, Jamie volunteered herself as well.

Troubled by Jamie's forwardness—or was she just being helpful?—Noah caught up to Chris in the parking lot after the meeting, an idea simmering in his mind. "So when are you going to Moab?"

Chris shot him a look of confusion. "That got shot down."

"Why not do it on your own? Get a group together?"

Dejected shoulders lifted. "I've always wanted to go down there . . ."

They talked it over, and Chris decided he could pull it all together in a week if he could convince a few people to go. "You're in, right?" he asked.

Nervous excitement bubbled up as Noah thought about getting to explore the beautiful landscape he'd only seen through the Mexico van's window and on their brief stops along the way. "I'll see if I can get a day off."

Chapter 53

LABOR DAY

ME: *HEY*

Ivy: *Hey!*

Me: *That was fast! You're awake!*

Ivy: *Dave's asleep, but I just had a nap. What's up?*

I roll onto my back, careful not to upset the giant bowl of extra-butter popcorn at my elbow, and stare at my bedroom ceiling lit by streetlights and passing cars. It's late enough that I should be asleep since my Labor Day cover shift starts at eight tomorrow morning, but I need to talk to someone. I'm relieved Ivy is available—I never know with her these days. Where do I even start?

Me: *Miss you. How are things?*

Ivy: *Miss me? What about Adonis?*

Ivy and her nicknames. I have to chuckle, but it makes me miss her even more. I'm still pondering what to tell her when she texts again.

Ivy: *I'm getting a vibe. Spill.*

Me: *Maybe I'm not right for him . . .*

Ivy: *Girl, you're killing me, but I can't call or move or Dave will wake up. SPILL.*

To facilitate faster thumbs and more efficient eating of popcorn, I sit up and lean my pillow against the wall, stretching my legs out on my twin bed as I unfold my day and week to Ivy in one big, long text—how Alec was late on Monday, his irritation at my attending my meeting today, his frustration that I have to work tomorrow and with my work in general—pausing occasionally to shovel another handful of buttery comfort into my mouth.

Ivy: *Hang on. Why is he irritated with you for going to your meeting?*

Me: *Sunday is our only day together, and he drove all the way here.*

Ivy: 🤦

And you drove all the way there on Monday, only to have him leave you waiting without explanation. You had a good excuse. He didn't.

Me: *He wants to be able to spend more time together. He was already disappointed because of the Labor Day thing.*

She sends me a full screen of face-palms in reply, but I can't really blame Alec for being frustrated that I have to work tomorrow on one of his few days off. The thing is, I took Independence Day in exchange for agreeing to work Labor Day. I can't call in sick, though I think that's what he wants.

Ivy: *You can't blow off work commitments.*

Me: *I know. But he said it feels like I'm more committed to my work than to him. He wants me to ask for different hours. Or look for a different job.*

Ivy: *And you said . . . ?*

Me: *I didn't say no . . .*

But I also didn't agree with him. He was in such a foul mood when I came back from my meeting, I had a hard time keeping my own temper in check. And I'm not sure I want to rearrange or leave a job I love for a relationship that is this difficult to navigate. Even basic conversation is becoming a challenge, making my brain itch like flea-ridden eczema rolled in stinging nettle.

If this relationship were *the one*, shouldn't conversation flow? Like it does with—

Ivy: *Tell me what else you've been up to.*

I tell Ivy a little about work and mention that instead of running every day this week, I want to get a couple of bike rides in so I won't be saddle-sore on the Moab trip a friend of mine is planning.

Ivy: *You? Have been running DAILY? Are you okay?*

Whoops.

Ivy knows me as the intermittent runner I usually am. Honestly, it's only been the last week that I've gone every day. If I happen to see Noah every time, that doesn't mean he's the *reason* I'm going.

It just . . . feels good.

To run.

Lately.

Ivy: *Hello?*

She's not going to let this go, and she'll see right through me if I try to dodge the bullet that's coming.

Me: *Don't freak out, but yes, I've been running every day. And . . . maybe I might usually happen to run into Noah while I'm out there.*

Ivy: *FREAKING OUT!*

Me: *Don't. It's not like we're running together. We happen to run at about the same time, and sometimes we talk for a minute. It's nothing.*

It's a good thing I proof the text before I send it. All the exclamation points would not have made the point I'm going for.

Ivy: *Why is Noah running where you are?*

Me: *He moved here a few weeks ago.*

Judging by the number of angry, swearing, and eye-rolling emojis she sends, I should have informed her sooner. I explain why I didn't.

Me: *It doesn't matter. I'm with Alec.*

Ivy: *My dear, you're being stupid. Dump Adonis.*

Me: *There's nothing between me and Noah. I'm. With. Alec.*

She sends a GIF of one of those enormous dump trucks they use in mining excavations, with wheels the size of a car. My heart pounds.

I can't dump Alec.

Ivy: *There was a time when I didn't want you to interfere and you did it anyway. I'm going to repay that blessing by asking you some questions that are pretty obvious to me but you're not seeing. You don't have to answer me. Think about them and be honest with yourself. Okay?*

I send her an unenthusiastic thumbs-up and wait. It takes a while, and when her text arrives I can see why. It's several screens long, and all of the questions make me think. But three of them prick my skin like the popcorn husks in my sheets.

Who could you talk to for hours on end?

Who lightens your load and makes you want to be a better person?

Who do you think about when you're not thinking about anything?

Those three keep me awake long after I've signed off and turned out the lights.

Considering the lack of sleep, my working Labor Day goes pretty well. The boys at Pathfinder still have a half day of school in the morning, but most are content with an afternoon off from their usual routine. After a slow morning with shortened classes, we eat a quick lunch, load the boys up, and take them to the local outdoor pool.

The weather has cooled enough to keep some of the crowds away, and it's great to sit and watch my boys interacting with each other. The other staff and I are confined to the deck chairs, each of us responsible for a defined area of the pool complex. I'm glad I draw the deep end. Diving-board antics keep me entertained until it's time to leave.

Once the guys are settled and we've handed them off to the evening staff, I check my phone and head for the parking lot. It's five o'clock, and the YCS group text has blown up while I was working. I take a minute to scroll through the panic, cracking my windows and cranking the air to combat the oven that is my car while confirming that all last-minute issues have been resolved. I make a quick stop at the grocery store for my contribution to the salad table. A caesar kit will have to do. I don't have time for anything fancy.

I swing past my apartment long enough to do a camp-bath, reapply deodorant, and throw on a new shirt to subdue the sitting-in-the-sun-all-day smell I've cultivated. My salad bowl has popcorn in it from last night's pity party, so I do a quick wash and dry on it before I run out the door. Halfway down the stairwell, I remember the salad kit I brought in because I didn't want to leave it in the hot car. Sprinting back up the stairs does not help my lateness or my appearance.

By the time I get to the park, it's nearly six, and I can feel Tony's angst from the parking lot. He's in the pavilion with Chris, counting soda cans and rearranging paper goods and wearing worry lines into his forehead. I attempt to summon enough inner calmness for both of us and hurry his way.

"Hey, Tony! Everything looks great!" I say.

He startles, then heaves a sigh of relief. "Glad you made it."

"Sorry about that—just got off work. Salads?" I point to the mostly empty table next to the paper goods. He nods. I break out my kit and assemble my salad.

Jamie pulls into the parking slot closest to our pavilion and gets out, reaching the trunk as Noah parks next to her and jumps out to help. She hands him a stack of pizza boxes, giving him a broad grin as they make the exchange and sending a violent surge through my core.

What the heck?

"Where do you want these?" Noah asks Tony, tossing a head bob my way.

I shove the weird feeling aside. So what if they're friends? Or more? It has nothing to do with me.

"That's a lot of pizza," Chris says approvingly.

"More in the trunk." Noah gestures back to Jamie's car, and Chris gets there in time to balance the stack of pizzas that started to slide out of her hands.

Tony opens one box, letting out a steamy whiff of meat and cheese, and counts the slices. "I hope we have enough."

"We calculated," Noah says, fixing the lid Tony failed to shut properly and straightening the boxes. His brows are furrowed, but I swear he's holding back a smile. "Two slices each and an expected attendance of fifty." His eyes flash to mine, and my heart rate picks up.

Is he thinking what I'm thinking? "What if we have latecomers?" I ask, testing him.

"They're out of luck, I guess." His smile surfaces, softening his thick brows. "They'll have to make do with your mom's brownies."

Laughter escapes me, releasing with it a week's worth of stress. I vaguely register Jamie puzzling at me.

"Didn't you bring a salad?" she asks.

Noah's answering belly laugh—deep and throaty—dissolves me even further, and I realize I've been waiting to hear that sound for as long as I've known him. It's been a year since he accidentally became my tutor.

"Did I miss something?" Jamie asks Chris, and I realize I'd better rein this in.

I press my aching cheeks and shake my head. "It's nothing, just an—"

"Inside joke," Noah finishes for me. Our eyes meet again, and his smile eases into something lopsided and dangerous.

Warmth blossoms in my chest in what must be an awkward silence for those around us, and suddenly I'm hankering for a run. With Noah.

What is wrong with me?

My wayward brain is forming a plan to ditch this party when I'm quite literally swept off my feet.

It's Alec.

And he's brought his net.

KILL

NOAH WATCHED, HELPLESS, AS GRACE'S boyfriend—*her boyfriend!*—swung her around, severing their connection with a jolt. He looked away, unwilling to see any more.

Had she felt it too?

He'd been pleased to see Grace there alone, intentionally letting his guard down when the pizza link had presented itself and communicating with his eyes what he couldn't bring himself to say.

Then? Alec.

Noah knew he'd question his connection with Grace later, but in the moment, he was sure she'd welcomed it.

But whatever link there had been—imagined or real or one-sided—didn't matter now. Alec had arrived, Grace was with him, and the pizza was going fast. Noah grabbed a paper plate, slapping down three pieces of pizza and no salad to spite himself. Caution to the wind, he added cookies from one of the dessert plates—the brownies someone else had brought didn't appeal—and took a seat near Jamie. The Couple was seated a few tables away, leaning in, talking.

Painting on a happy mask, Noah channeled his frustration into the conversation at his table and even teased Jamie about the amount of salad she'd piled on her plate. She laughed and teased back—reassurance that his act was convincing.

Once the eating was done, they were supposed to play some group games under the pavilion—four on a couch and the like—before doing a full park cleanup, but Alec quickly claimed Grace for himself and extended an exclusive invitation to two worthy opponents to join them at his net.

So much for "drawing together," as Grace had suggested in their committee meeting.

Concentration on the group game proved impossible since Noah ended up on the boring side of the four-on-a-couch circle and his name was never called. Eventually he stopped trying and observed the play at the net instead.

Maybe a heavy dose of reality would kill his interest.

Alec and Grace held their own against two guys Noah didn't know—he labeled them Tall and Taller. The Couple had better ball skills, but their opponents were no slouches. It was a tough matchup.

Alec dug Tall's hit out of the grass with a pass that sent Grace scrambling. She reached the ball just in time, sending a high set to the middle of the court for Alec to attack. He opted for the safe hit instead of a hard swing. Taller dug it easily, and his partner set him up nicely at the net for a kill.

Alec wasn't pleased.

He met Grace backcourt, frustration evident in his features as he gestured at what she should have done. They were both in profile to Noah, and though he couldn't hear their words, he could see the tension in her folded arms even as she smiled and nodded. Finally, Alec gave her a patronizing shoulder pat and they prepared to receive the serve. Grace passed the ball right to him. Instead of setting her up, he took the pass over himself with another subpar attack and stationed himself off the net to dig. Tall sent the ball sky-high, right in the middle of the net. Grace positioned her block well, but with springs for legs and a significant height advantage, Taller hit right over her, smashing the ball well in front of Alec's defensive position.

This time as Alec coached his partner, Noah clearly heard Grace ask why he wasn't blocking. He said something about needing to pass so he could hit before resuming his position. Grace stared after him, her fingers digging into her hips.

The group game distracted Noah momentarily when Jamie ended up in the seat next to him, but once she moved, he tuned back out—right in time to see Grace get a hard kill around Tall's block. She whooped, and her opponent slapped her hand under the net.

Alec called for the ball and went back to serve, but Noah didn't watch him. He had eyes only for Grace. She was quick. And strong. And . . . graceful. She never surrendered a ball, her long legs straining as she chased and kept it in play and then hustled back.

The volleyball was still going when the group game ended, Noah having participated not at all. Guilt drove him to pay attention as groups were arranged for the cleanup, keeping his back to the ongoing match, though hearing the players' exclamations couldn't be helped. It was difficult not to take Alec's repeated criticisms of Grace personally. Noah had seen how they played. Alec's ego was a burden heavier than his skill could carry, while Grace was a hardworking team player.

Working his way through the crowd, he forced himself away from the net, ending up in a group with Jamie and Chris discussing the Moab trip for next weekend.

"Are you going?" Noah asked Jamie.

"No," she said with a nervous smile.

"Come on," Chris said. "It's going to be great!"

"I . . . don't have a bike, and I've never been before."

"You can always rent, and it won't be that hard. You can totally walk the tough spots!" Chris went on and on, shooting down each of Jamie's excuses as she grew more and more flustered.

"Moab might not be the best place to learn," Noah interjected. "I've heard Slickrock can be brutal."

Jamie threw him a grateful glance. "Maybe I should start with some beginner trails around here."

"Sure," Chris said, obviously disappointed.

"I've only been a few times myself," Noah said. "I hope Slickrock doesn't eat me alive."

"Did you get a bike?" Chris asked.

"I'm borrowing my brother's." Ah, the guilt, borrowing Matt's bike when he still couldn't ride. "How long is the drive?"

This launched them into logistics of who was willing to drive and how many bikes they could carry, Jamie watching the conversation between the two men like a tennis match.

Noah picked out Grace's voice behind him, though no one else took notice.

"You know I'm not a setter." She sounded annoyed, her voice low.

"Neither am I, but you have to give the ball to the stronger hitter."

"At the expense of the block."

"The best defense is good offense."

Footsteps approached, and Grace muttered, "Hard to have an offense when you can't get a pass," before addressing Noah's group in an entirely different tone. "Hey, guys! Sorry I bailed. Who needs help?" Seeing there were plenty of people willing to collect the trash, she threw herself into wiping down tables with a chipper fury that melted the leadership stress from Tony's face.

Alec took down his net.

Jamie invited Noah to help her at the children's playground, filling the time with pediatrics anecdotes. By the time their area was clean, most of the people had left. Tony thanked everyone again for pitching in and headed for the parking lot.

Noah followed, patting his pockets to locate his keys as he reached his car.

"Noah?"

He took his hand off the door and found Jamie on his heels.

"Thanks for saving me back there."

"Huh?" The garbage pickup hadn't been that strenuous.

"With the mountain biking?" She glanced over her shoulder as if to make sure they were alone. "I'm not good at saying no to people, and I appreciate you getting Chris to back off."

Noah smiled. "He's pretty excited about this trip."

"Yeah." She laughed uneasily. "Anyway, I just wanted to say thanks, and I'm glad we're, um, friends." With that, she threw her arms around him for a quick hug. He barely had time to clumsily reciprocate before she backed away.

"See ya!" she said, getting into her car.

Noah squinted after her.

Crap.

TRUCE

"I'M SO SORRY."

It's noteworthy how surprised I am to hear those words from Alec. We're sitting in his car in the back of my apartment parking lot, and he's holding my hand in a way that feels much more sincere than the cloying affection he shovels out at church.

Still, I struggle to contain my anger. My emotions have been all over the board tonight.

When I arrived at the party, I was looking forward to a night off from relationship issues. Then Noah and Jamie showed up together, and I actually felt jealous. Of nothing. Or something. Either way, I have no right.

That dissolved when he joked with me—Noah! Joking!—about the pizza and brownies, only to be replaced with shock when Alec grabbed me.

I'm ashamed to say, I was *not* happy to see him.

Or his net.

As usual, he bulldozed my objections and guilted me into playing when I should have been—wanted to be—with the group.

He did go out of his way to spend time with me. How could I not humor him?

If only he had texted to let me know he was coming, I would have had time to prepare myself—and my objections—before he arrived. Maybe then I would have been able to withstand the force of his personality.

I was furious when the match ended—coerced into neglecting my duties, blamed for nearly every point we lost, condescendingly "instructed" throughout—and when I'd finally worked most of the frustration out on the poor tables, I saw Jamie hugging Noah in the parking lot.

I was still convincing myself I didn't care, that I was happy for them, when Alec accosted me again, wrapping me up from behind and laying a kiss on my neck.

Sometimes I feel like I'm dating a well-meaning tornado. I wouldn't mind if he occasionally opened with "Hey" instead of trying to sweep me off my feet. He was pretty shocked when I didn't just melt into his arms after that.

But apologizing? Completely unprecedented.

"It was selfish of me to give you a hard time about not getting the day off, and I wanted to make it up to you tonight." He watches someone get into their car a few slots away from us. "I thought volleyball would be fun—it *was* fun! You're a good partner!" He looks at our hands with a sad smile. "But I let myself get too into the game."

"It's okay," I say.

"You're still irritated."

I'm working on something to say that isn't cutting. It's difficult.

He sighs heavily and stares out his side window, his free hand wringing the steering wheel.

Several snide remarks are stewing on the tip of my tongue when he turns back. They die of shame when they see the emotion in his eyes. I may have managed not to lash out, but I've hurt him with my silence.

Idiot.

"Grace," he says, holding tighter to my hand. "I screwed up."

I take a deep breath and look at things from his side. He made a big effort to be here with me tonight, and I'm sure it didn't feel great that I wasn't thrilled with his surprise. "It's okay." I mean it this time, but he shakes his head.

"I know I have a lot to work on." He blinks a few times, clears his throat. "I don't want to mess this up. You're . . . different from other girls I've dated. This will sound cocky—I don't mean it that way—but I never really had to *work* for a girlfriend. The thing is, it was always so shallow. I feel like *this*"—he lifts our entwined hands—"*we*—could be different."

Different? Is he saying what I think he is?

"Look, this trip Chris is planning—I want to come with you. I'll get Monday off, and we can have two whole days together. What do you think?"

I'm processing, debating, when he lets go of my hand, cupping my chin gently to turn my face to his.

"Please, Grace. Give me another chance?"

Noah hugging Jamie replays in my head, and I realize that—whatever Ivy's questions made me think—I need to give Alec another shot. I've been holding back, daydreaming about something that is never going to happen with Noah. All we're ever going to be is friends.

I want more than that.

And so does Alec.

HUNTED

"Were you able to finish up the Allred account?" Noah's boss leaned against the cubicle doorway.

Noah nodded, buying time as he swallowed a bite of sweet-potato fries before answering. "Printing now. I'll have it ready for signatures before I leave today."

"Nice work. Still planning on the biking trip?"

"Yep. We're leaving Sunday, and I'll be back to work Tuesday."

"I hope you can still walk when you get back." His boss chuckled. "I got talked into biking Moab once. Never again. Although, I've heard those e-bikes are fun." He slapped his hand on top of the cubicle wall in farewell. "See you Tuesday."

Noah looked at the tray of fries—only a couple of wilty ones remained. When he'd joked with Matt about not eating much because of the long hours he was working, his brother had arranged for a delivery service to bring him dinner. Noah dunked the last two fries into the sauce, wiped his hands with a paper napkin, and tossed his trash into the can at the side of his desk before getting back to work.

It was nice of Matt to send him dinner. Even nicer of him to insist that Noah take his Volkswagen Tiguan and bike rack along with the bike, claiming he was living vicariously through Noah. Matt was nearly strong enough to mountain bike again, but he couldn't afford to take any time off work after losing so much of the summer months to his injury.

Besides, Moab probably wasn't the best place for a rebound ride.

When Noah had approached his boss about taking a day off, he'd been pleasantly surprised. Expecting a definite no since he had yet to accrue any vacation time, his boss's offer to let him work a couple of extra hours each day before the trip had seemed like a no-brainer. But those extra hours had come at the expense of his morning run.

He hadn't seen Grace in the few days since the activity. That was probably a good thing.

He also hadn't seen Jamie.

Definitely a good thing.

That hug in the parking lot had undeniably had more-than-friendly under-tones. Overt-tones, more like. If it weren't for Noah's having just signed a year-long contract, he'd be tempted to move again. If worse came to worst, he would sell his contract.

It would be best to avoid both women for a time.

In addition to loaning his bike, car, rack, and other gear, Matt had offered to meet Noah in the middle to exchange vehicles. He stood leaning against his car at the gas station in the little town of Gypsum when Noah pulled in.

Matt was tugging on Noah's door before the car had stopped. "I'm so excited for you!" He gazed lovingly at the top-of-the-line, full-suspension, barely used mountain bike strapped to the back of his SUV, beaming like a proud parent. "I wish you could have had a couple of weeks to get used to everything, but at least you'll have tomorrow."

Noah got out of his car and followed Matt over to the bike. "I'm sure I can figure it out Monday. It's like riding a bike, right?"

Matt's smile slipped. "You *are* taking it out tomorrow."

Noah hedged. "Won't that make me saddle-sore for Slickrock?"

Matt shrugged. "A long ride would, so don't do that. But you have to take it out on a trail to get the feel of it. Can't have my brother showing up at the most famous trail in the world on a bike he doesn't even know how to shift."

Noah acknowledged the point with a grunt. "Show me the ropes?"

Matt spent longer than Noah thought necessary running him through the bike's features, some basic maintenance and repair, and how to load the rest of the bikes onto the rack. "Everything is tight right now," he said, handing Noah a wrench, "but check whenever you stop to make sure nothing's wiggled loose."

Noah stowed the wrench in the back of the car, excitement and guilt battling for control. "Look, I know you've always wanted to do Slickrock, and I really appreciate—"

Matt shook his head. "I'm just glad someone's getting to ride. You scope it out, and next year we can go together."

"I'd like that."

"Better start saving for your own bike."

Noah did take the bike out early Saturday morning, amazed at how smoothly it shifted, how the shocks absorbed the bumps, how uncomfortable the seat was. Lacking enough time to get up into the hills, he opted for the canal trail, using the occasional curb as a test for the shocks and taking the bumpiest lines he could find. Once he was comfortable with the super-touchy brakes and the dropper seat post, he decided to head back.

Unfortunately, his timing led him directly into the path of one of the two women he was avoiding. He knew he was safe from seeing Grace since she worked Saturdays; he hadn't known Jamie used the trail too.

"Hey, Noah!" she called as she stepped onto the trail.

If only he'd come back one minute sooner. "Hey, Jamie!"

"You're out early!"

"Yeah, testing out the bike."

"Your brother's, right?"

"Mm-hmm."

"Where's your helmet? You have one, don't you?"

Noah ran a hand through his hair, tamping down the guilt he'd squashed earlier, when he'd realized his test run would be either helmetless for an earlier ride or in the heat of the day if he delayed to get a helmet. He'd opted for cooler weather, reasoning that there was hardly any traffic and he'd stay on the trail. "I'm picking one up later today. My brother's . . ." He trailed off, trying not to think of what had happened to Matt's old helmet or the panic attack his mother would have if she saw either of them on a bike without one.

"How's he doing?" Jamie asked.

"Great! Just not biking yet."

"Makes sense. I'm glad he's doing well."

Noah scrambled for a graceful exit. "I'd better—"

"When do you guys leave?"

"After church tomorrow."

"And you'll be back . . . ?"

"Monday evening, I guess, depending on how long the ride takes." Or maybe he could convince everyone to hang out in Moab afterward so there would be no chance of seeing Jamie when they returned. *I'm terrible.*

"It sounds like so much fun!" Jamie smiled at him. "I sure wish I was coming."

Noah frowned. "I thought you didn't want to."

"I don't want to *bike*. I'd love to come on the trip, but I have to work."

"Dang." Noah ignored the obvious explanation for her wanting to come on a quick biking trip as a non-biker. "Well—"

"But maybe I could call someone to cover for me since it's only one workday."

Oh, please no. "Pretty late notice," he said, trying to discourage her without being too obvious.

"Who's driving?"

"I am. We're taking my brother's SUV."

"With Chris and Jake and Melissa?"

Noah reached for his water bottle, his brain spinning. "Right. I hope we can fit all our gear in." *Hint, hint.*

"Hmm." Jamie's brows furrowed. "I guess I could ride with Grace and Alec, but that might be awkward."

Noah nearly choked. Grace was coming? And Alec? He took another drink.

Jamie's mouth pulled to one side as she thought it through. She really was cute, but Noah wasn't *drawn* to her like he was—

He cleared his throat.

Jamie startled, her smile returning. "But your brother's car is a five-seater, right?"

"Yeah."

"Well," she said as if something had been decided, "I don't mean to keep you. Good luck helmet hunting!"

With that, she abandoned her run and turned back the way she'd come, a frightening spring in her step.

Chapter 57

ONE BIRD

"I really wish I could go."

It's the eleventy-first time Jamie has made this declaration. I make a conciliatory sound and continue packing. Where did I put my gloves?

"I mean, I wouldn't do the biking regardless, but it would be so fun if I could come down."

"Anyone you could ask?" I know she has tried everyone to cover her shift, having witnessed her many phone, text, and voicemail rejections yesterday, but she'll enjoy telling me again.

"No one. It's so last minute."

"Yeah." It's Sunday, and we're supposed to be leaving here in ten minutes. Yesterday morning as I was leaving for work, she returned from a five-minute walk all hot and bothered, determined to find a way to Moab. She even hinted at getting a ride down with me and Alec, but there won't be room in the car with our bikes taking up the back seat and trunk. Not ideal, but neither of us has an SUV or a rack.

Speaking of which—Alec, bless his heart, is outside in the heat squeezing both our bikes in while I gather up the last of my things.

I've mostly tuned out Jamie's monologue exploring road trips as an ideal opportunity to strengthen relationships when I finally locate my gloves stuck between the wall and the edge of my bed.

"Yes!" I say as I zip them into the front pocket of Trusty, being extra careful where another tiny hole has opened up the seam. It might be time to invest in a new pack, but I hate to retire the last present Benson ever gave me. Maybe I can get Mom to show me how to stitch it back up next time I'm home.

"—because I really feel like there might be something there, you know?"

I tune back into Jamie, scolding myself for drifting. It's hard to stay mentally present when a roommate is rambling.

"This would have been a great way to see where it's going," she says. "Especially after he rescued me last week at the activity. What do you think? Is missing the trip going to hurt my chances with him? Do you think he's interested?"

Rescued? I sift through impressions as Jamie flops onto my bed, playing with the quilt ties. Personally, I wouldn't call stabilizing pizza boxes a "rescue," but if that's how she wants to see it, I'm not going to argue. Chris definitely paid Jamie a lot of attention at the activity—she told me how much he was pressuring her to come on the trip and give mountain biking a try. And I noticed he made a point of talking to her at church today. Maybe he *is* interested. I hate giving relationship advice. I pull a therapist move and throw the question to her.

"Do *you* think he's interested?"

Her cheeks flush, and she smiles. "Maybe? I *think* so. I mean, I felt like he was pretty disappointed yesterday when we talked about me having to work. But you know him better than I do."

"Huh? I only met him a couple of months ago."

Jamie's smile scrunches into confusion. "But I thought—"

"I didn't meet him until I moved in here. In fact, I think it was you who introduced us my first week at church, remember?"

"Who are you talking about?"

"Chris," I say, my heart sinking. "Did I miss something?"

"Not Chris!" Jamie laughs. "I'm talking about Noah!"

Noah.

She's been talking about Noah the whole time.

I should have known.

I probably *did* know. *The hug.* Of course she's talking about Noah.

I think I might be sick.

I can only hope Alec's interruption to announce that the car is ready covers my confusion and embarrassment and failure to speak after Jamie's revelation. I collect myself enough to rush a forced cheerful goodbye and hurry Alec to the car so I can make my escape.

I'm thankful, for a change, that Alec prefers loud music while he's driving. An hour into the drive, my head is still spinning from the conversation with Jamie.

How can I be such a jerk? Jamie has been nothing but kind to me, and although some of her roommate quirks are making me crazy—like her insistence that all the spices, including mine, be arranged alphabetically together—she's a sweetheart. What right do I have to be annoyed that she's crushing on a guy who wants nothing more than a casual friendship with me, who has seen me at my worst, most shallow, and most inconsiderate? Especially when—hello!—I'm in a relationship! I should be happy that two good people are interested in each other.

Alec cuts the volume in half and reaches for my hand with a smile. "You okay?" His bright blue eyes show concern; his warm hand offers reassurance and comfort.

Happiness is a choice, right?

Time to choose.

The not-so-gentle reminder of a budding relationship between Noah and Jamie will be exactly the thing I need to help me focus on Alec.

So what if Ivy's questions all made me think of Noah?

Alec is here, now, and as the saying goes, one bird in the hand . . .

Chapter 58

SEEING STARS

NOAH STASHED THE LAST OF the bags in the cargo area, checked the hitch and the bikes on the rack for the fifth time, and climbed into the driver's seat.

"Everyone ready?" he asked.

"So ready," Chris said from the front passenger seat. Jake and Melissa—the girl who'd asked Noah about Jake at the fall social—gave enthusiastic nods without pausing their conversation in the back.

Passing the Cisco/Moab scenic-route exit less than an hour later gave Noah an odd sense of déjà vu; he wasn't driving the same route from the Mexico trip, but the scenery was still starkly beautiful. He wondered how Vanessa and the others were doing. He hadn't had a chance to say goodbye, under the circumstances. Maybe he could reconnect with some of them if he ended up moving again.

"I'm happy to drive if you get tired," Chris said, his wild hair brushing the car's headliner.

"I think I'm good," Noah said, "but I'll let you know if I do." It wasn't likely. Not only was he hesitant to let anyone else drive his brother's car, but the prospect of two days with Grace and Alec had him wide awake. At least he knew what he was getting into this time, unlike in Mexico.

Not that knowing made it any more appealing.

Chris kept him entertained during the drive with a running commentary on all rides Moab, lamenting that they could do only one.

"Honestly," Noah said, "I doubt I'd be able to handle more than one day in the saddle—I haven't been biking much."

"It does take some getting used to." Chris chuckled. "Hey, I think we're getting close!"

Noah's excitement to go adventuring in the town that had captured his imagination in the spring spiked as they passed highway signs for the

Canyonlands and Arches National Parks and descended into the red cliffs and green valley of Moab. It seemed to welcome him back, and Noah's spirits lifted in spite of his worries.

"I've heard the float trips out of Moab are awesome," Jake said as they crossed the Colorado River bridge. The high canyon walls streaked with desert varnish called for Noah's attention and made him wish someone else were driving, but Main Street and heavier traffic soon refocused him.

Tricked out ATVs, lifted Jeeps, and trucks loaded with dirt-coated motorcycles rolled past T-shirt boutiques, motels, bike shops, and breweries. People of all ages roamed the sidewalks, enjoying the warm evening and relaxed atmosphere.

"Wow," Melissa said, pointing out yet another adventure-touting billboard. "If we hadn't already decided what we were doing here, I don't know how I'd ever choose."

"Right?" Jake agreed.

Chris directed Noah onto a side street through a more residential-looking area, then up into the foothills east of town. The narrow, steep road put them right onto the rim of the sandstone cliffs, drawing a gasp of delight from Melissa as she looked back at the city below them. Noah caught only a glimpse as he drove.

An entrance station announced their arrival at the Sand Flats Recreation Area. They paid their fees and continued uphill past trailheads for Hell's Revenge and Baby Lion's Back.

"Look at that!" Jake said, pointing to the latter. A Jeep crept up a fin of sandstone steep enough that the vehicle appeared on the verge of rolling off the narrow ridge.

Melissa leaned across him to get a better look. "Ah! I don't think I'd want to be inside there!"

The guys chuckled, and Jake assured her the ride was safer than it looked.

"Besides," Chris said, "they have roll bars. Even if they roll, they'll probably be fine."

"Maybe," she said, "but what about the poor Jeep?"

As they rounded a corner, domes of sandstone rose out of the desert soil, looking like great whales surfacing in a sandy ocean. Campgrounds surrounded by sagebrush and sparse trees dotted the flat areas near the road.

"There it is," Chris said, voice reverent as they passed a large, nearly empty parking lot signed *Slickrock Bike Trail*. The sun setting on the western horizon behind the lot highlighted the Colorado Plateau and Moab Valley stretching before them and reminded Noah of the framed landscape in Matt's apartment. They definitely needed to come back here together.

Much as Chris wanted to go check out the trail, they figured they'd better get a campsite first. The weekend crowd hadn't thinned much, but they lucked out and found a site with a few trees big enough for hammocks and a bit of shade. Jake and Melissa clambered out and lowered the back seats so the gear could be unloaded without taking the bikes off the rack.

"Looks like the lovebirds are about an hour away," Chris said, getting out of the car and slipping his phone back into his pocket. "I sent them a pin."

One hour, Noah thought, annoyed by Chris's label.

Setting up camp occupied his hands, if not his mind. Once the car was unloaded, they hung their hammocks and set up chairs around the firepit. Melissa was almost finished staking the tent she and Grace would share—with some unneeded but apparently welcome help from Jake—when The Couple arrived.

Alec hopped out first. "Party's here!" he said, working his way around to Grace's door just as she opened it.

Noah braced himself for the worst, but things weren't completely terrible as they finished setting up and Chris lit a fire for their tinfoil dinners. He could almost pretend everyone was *just friends*, until the food was ready and Alec claimed Grace with an arm around her back as they sat together on a log.

Regardless, conversation flowed easily around everyone's different adventures and travels, eventually landing on the trip to Mexico half the group had shared.

"That day at the beach was the best," Alec said.

Grace agreed. "I think that's where we really started connecting."

Alec smirked. "I guess I shouldn't have waited so long to ask you out after we got back."

She smiled but wedged an elbow into his ribs, drawing a little grunt from him. "I meant with the *kids*."

Everyone else laughed, including Alec, though his hold on her eased. It could have been the firelight, but Noah thought she flushed as she tucked a curl behind her ear and dropped her gaze into her lap.

Alec recovered quickly. "They *were* pretty great. What about—what was his name?—Alejandro?" He looked at Noah, who nodded. "You sure impressed him with your swimming, but I can't believe what he was saying to you."

"Good thing the nuns weren't there to hear him," Noah said.

Grace chuckled. "He did have a mouth, that one, but I'm sure it was all bravado. Lots of people hide their pain that way."

"You work with troubled boys, right?" Melissa asked. "I bet some of them are rough."

Alec squirmed.

"Our guys are pretty tame," Grace said. "They get worked up once in a while, but the program rewards them for pro-social behaviors—like talking things out instead of punching a wall or another human—and all their privileges are tied to good behavior, so they learn to toe the line. We make sure they get exercise, enough rest, good food. All those things go a long way to promoting a safe environment—physically and emotionally—for everyone. And hopefully they form habits that stick after they leave and keep them from turning to alcohol or drugs when things get tough."

Chris asked some questions about the outdoor experiences they provided for the boys, which Grace answered enthusiastically. Her love for her job and the boys was as obvious as Alec's discomfort. Usually a force in any conversation, he remained silent.

At a lull in the conversation, Grace looked at Alec, who was staring resolutely into the fire, and then caught Noah watching her. Rather than look away as he ought to, Noah tried to convey with a smile how much he admired her work.

Her.

The worried expression Alec's distraction had brought to her face softened for a moment before she threw a sidelong glance at her boyfriend and changed the subject. "Stars sure are bright."

Melissa looked like she had another question about Grace's work on the tip of her tongue, but she followed Grace's lead and looked up. "Wow! Yeah, they are!"

"There's the Big Dipper." Grace pointed.

"Where?"

Grace leaned over so Melissa could follow the line of her pointing arm. "And if you follow the line of these two," she said, "it leads you right to the North Star."

"I can see it! That's awesome!"

"And that leads you to the Little Dipper, right?" Chris asked.

"Right," Grace said.

Jake leaned in on Melissa's other side as Grace identified the Little Dipper and showed how Draco sat between Big and Little. Noah tried to follow along, but it was hard from the other side of the campfire, and he didn't think Alec would appreciate him weaseling in next to Grace for a better angle.

Alec looked into the sky, though he didn't seem too interested, and that gave Noah the opportunity to continue to watch Grace. The dying firelight highlighted her cheekbones and the contours of her smooth neck. Face alight, her eyes crinkled in pleasure as she guided her listeners through another constellation. Noah pictured how *he* would sit, were he the one next to Grace, his arm behind her back, her curls against his cheek—

Alec's chin lowered, his attention landing squarely on Noah, who yanked his eyes off Grace a moment too late. "Well," Alec said with an affected stretch, "I think that's about all my neck can take."

"It does get a little painful like this," Grace said, rubbing a hand under her curly hair. "The best way to learn constellations is to lie down in a circle with your heads together and use a focused-beam flashlight, but I didn't bring one."

"Short walk before we turn in?" Alec asked her, reaching out his hand.

"Oh," Grace said. "I guess it *is* about time, isn't it?" She took Alec's hand and stood, smiling apologetically at Jake and Melissa. "Sorry. I get carried away sometimes."

"No, no," Melissa said. "We shouldn't have kept you so long. Thanks for the lesson!"

"Yeah, thanks!" Jake agreed, waving a good night as The Couple left, then asking Melissa to show him again what they'd learned. Their enthusiasm bore a marked contrast to Alec's.

The fire popped, startling the remaining four. Melissa giggled and leaned back against Jake, their conversation quieting.

"Welp," Noah said with a pointed look at Chris and a clap of his hands, "I guess I'll turn in."

Chris fake-yawned. "Big day tomorrow." He joined Noah, walking away from the fire, and muttered, "Awkward."

"Ha. No kidding."

"See you in the morning," Chris said, beelining to his hammock.

Noah lifted a hand and made a trip to the bathroom before sliding into his own hammock—another loan from Matt. The air was still warm, so he stayed on top of his bag, wondering how many years it would take for the stars to stop reminding him of Grace. He thumped his head a few times with his fist before allowing it to rest there, his arm stretched across his head.

His resolve was slipping.

Without the possibility of being with Grace to motivate him, it would be so easy to slip back into old habits. He gritted his teeth, promising himself he wouldn't let that happen. She might have been the inspiration behind all the progress he'd made over the summer, but he hadn't done it *for* her.

He'd done it for himself.

As hard as it would be to get her out of his head and heart, he resolved to stay the course without her.

Make it through tomorrow, he thought, *and then I'll figure out how.*

Chapter 59

POSSUM

Too hot to get inside my sleeping bag, I'm zoning out on a stupid phone game in an attempt to quiet my thoughts when a text comes through.

Alec: *All tucked in? Need anything?*

Me: *I'm good! Thanks. Hope you get some good rest. G'night!*

Alec: *You too! We're going to need it!*

I doubt I'll get it.

At the sound of Melissa approaching our tent, I lock my phone and feign sleep. The hushed conversation and quiet laughter at the fire died down a while ago, but I'm still wide awake. She eases the zipper closed and slips into her own bag with a contented sigh.

Have I ever felt that content with Alec?

Noah's smile from tonight flits unsummoned into my head, and knowing I shouldn't, I let it linger. That brief connection—the depth of understanding he conveyed with one short look—warmed me more than the fire. More than Alec's aloof form had, pressed against my side.

With a mental slap, I chase the image away. I flood my head with Alec, trying to put myself to sleep with a list of his many great qualities, replaying moments of kindness and sincerity and fun, reminding myself how good and strong and handsome he is and how *he* wants to work things out with *me*.

Even though we don't always get along. Even though our primary shared interest is a conflicting volleyball ideology. Even though he hates the job I love.

Chapter 60

LET'S RIDE

NOAH TOSSED OFF HIS BLANKET, making a mental note to remove *hammock* from his growing wish list of adventure gear, and eased out of the torture device. It might be nice for lounging, but for a belly sleeper like himself, a whole night in a hammock was awful.

Pale-pink light illuminated the few clouds in a clear blue sky, complementing the pink-orange rocks and sparse vegetation on the sand flats. Noah tiptoed past his companions on his way to the facilities, wishing they'd wake up but not wanting to be the reason. The other guys had yet to move from their hammocks, and the girls' tent sat silent.

Back at the car, he fished through his duffel for Matt's biking gear and changed in the back seat, watching with vigilance for anyone who might wander by at an inopportune moment even though the windows were tinted. Once changed, he dug a protein bar and water bottle out of his food stash and decided to go for a walk to loosen up.

The diaperlike pad in the biking shorts felt strange and bulky as he walked, but if it prevented serious damage from the torturous seat, it would be worth it. Thankfully, Matt had included a pair of trail shorts to wear over the spandex. Stretchy pants in public was not a fashion statement Noah was ready to make.

He wondered if Grace felt the same.

With a growl, he sank his teeth into the protein bar, cringing at the texture. Matt had insisted that this particular bar was best, but maybe he hadn't been talking about taste. A long draw on Noah's water washed down the lump of almost-chocolate-tasting, chewy, grainy protein and left him wishing he'd packed some cereal.

Though the sun had yet to dawn, most of the campers at other sites he passed were up and moving, checking gear and eating breakfast. It was already warm; that slickrock would be blistering hot by midday.

A slight breeze ruffled Noah's wrapper, reminding him that he needed the fuel regardless of its appeal. At least his water was good. He finished off the bar and washed it down, tamping down his pre-ride jitters by focusing on the now-cool air, the low hum of prepping campers, the smell of the trees and last night's campfires, the feel of the rocks under his shoes, and the water slipping down his throat.

By the time he got back from his walk, his water bottle was empty and everyone was awake.

"Morning!" Chris called, rolling up his hammock. "You ready for this?"

"I'm game," Noah said more confidently than he felt. He tossed the empty bottle into the Tiguan and grabbed another, taking a long drag to keep his eyes off Grace in her sleeveless riding top and snug-fitting biking shorts. Thank heaven she, too, wore trail shorts over her spandex.

It was still a struggle not to gawk.

"I hope I can do this!" Melissa said, drawing Noah's attention and gratitude.

"You'll be great." Jake buckled the chin strap on his helmet and adjusted his fingerless riding gloves. "Sandstone is different from the terrain we've been riding, but you'll love how grippy it is."

"Yeah," Chris said, taking his bike off the rack, "until you land on it."

Noah caught his eye.

"Nothing like taking a spill on forty-grit sandstone," Chris said. "Talk about exfoliation!"

Melissa's eyes widened.

"We'll be fine," Noah said with another dose of false confidence. The bulk of the first-aid kit sitting in his pack gave him some reassurance, but there wasn't anything for increased coordination or endurance in there.

He lifted his bike off the rack, checked the tires and brakes, set the suspension like Matt had shown him, and inventoried the small under-saddle tool kit. Once that was done, he took out Matt's riding glasses, debating whether to wear them or his regular sunglasses with his contacts. His brother had insisted the yellowish lenses were a necessity.

"High contrast?" Chris asked as he walked by. "Nice!"

Figuring two endorsements were better than his own guessing, he put them on, then shouldered his backpack.

"Does everyone have enough water?" Melissa asked, squinting in the bright sunlight.

"Looks like Noah's carrying some extra," Alec said, patting Noah's pack with a laugh. "What all do you have in there? That's a big pack for a nine-mile ride!"

Not as big as the ego you're packing, Noah thought, forcing a chuckle. His pack *was* a little bulky, but everything except the water was fairly light. If they were lucky, they wouldn't need the first aid, but he wasn't about to leave it behind. As Alec turned away, Noah caught Grace watching him, her expression unreadable.

Chris threw a leg over his own bike, slapped his helmet, and rubbed his hands together. "Let's ride!"

"I'll lead out," Alec said, "since none of you have ridden this before."

"Sounds good to me," Chris said, right on his heels.

That suited Noah just fine. He motioned the others forward and followed them back to the trailhead parking lot, knowing that if he brought up the rear, he wouldn't have to hear another word from Alec before the ride was done.

Chapter 61

FALLING FLAT

Togetherness?

Ha.

I'm stranded in one of the sandy washes tucked into the slickrock, fixing a front-tire pinch flat and holding back a scream of frustration. It's hot and sandy, and I can hear Alec's voice in my head, teasing me for not going tubeless like he told me I should. Instead I'm stuck here changing my tube and praying someone with a pump comes along soon because I forgot that my compressed air cartridge is empty.

Alec has air, but he and Chris are long gone. Jake and Melissa passed me right after I stopped—I told them I was fine before I knew I wasn't—and I haven't seen Noah since we started. Maybe he passed me when I wasn't paying attention.

I sigh, summoning positive thoughts as I put the wheel back on and screw the axle into place. All I need is air. It's a well-traveled trail. Someone with air or a pump should come along soon.

Grinding gears announce the approach of a rider before he crests the ridge and makes the descent into the wash. It's Noah, though I can't imagine why he'd be so far behind, judging by the confident way he navigates the ledges coming down the hill. He has skills. And strong quads.

Not that I'm looking.

He glances up at the bottom of the slope, catching my eye right as his front wheel bogs down in the soft sand and derails him. He hops over his handlebars and stumbles into the sand, leaving his bike behind.

"Well, that was . . . smooth," he says, winded and glaring at the sand. When he faces me, I can't help laughing at his expression: surprised, mostly, with some embarrassment and a dash of frustration.

I clear my laughter. "I mean, the dismount was excellent."

He grins and does a mocking bow. "I did land on my feet."

"True." I smile back.

He notices my bike and tools. "You okay?"

"Yeah. Pinch flat, thanks to that boulder before the sand."

He nods back at the trail. "Did you get it fixed? Or do you—"

"It's all fixed, but please tell me you have a full cartridge. Or a pump."

He pulls his bike off the trail and rummages in the tool kit under his seat. "What happened to everyone else?" he says, pulling out the silver tube—like a tiny helium tank—that will save my ride.

"Ahead," I say, tamping down my frustration. It isn't Alec's fault that I was unprepared. "Jake and Melissa offered help, but I thought I had everything I needed."

He waits for me to say something about Alec, his eyes narrowing when I don't. Realizing he still has the cartridge, he holds it out. "Do you want me to . . . ?" he says with a jerk of his chin at my tire.

"Nah, I'm good," I say.

He sits down on a rock to take a drink.

"What held you back?" I ask as I fill the tire, making sure the bead seats on the rim.

He looks down at his water bottle and chuckles. "Let's just say I went a little overboard with my hydration this morning."

"Well, that's . . . a relief."

"No pun intended?"

"Never," I say, tossing his now-empty cartridge back. "Thanks for the air."

"Happy to help." He stands and packs his water bottle and the empty cartridge, refusing to go first when we resume our ride.

It takes a while to work past the discomfort of having Noah riding behind me, but he leaves a comfortable gap, and now the trail is speaking to me.

I drive my handlebars into a dip, then pull them up again as the back end follows, my bike's suspension smoothing out the bumps in synchrony with my joints. Relishing the flow, I lean into the stony hillside to guide my tires around a determined sage growing from a pocket of sand in the slickrock before attacking the next hill.

It's a steep one, the path marked by a darker-than-elsewhere tire line chronicling previous attempts of thousands of riders to ascend the insane slope. I thread my pedals through a narrow slot, the rocks on either side scratched white by the mistakes of my predecessors. With a mental pat on the back, I set my pedals to work, but I'm in too high a gear.

Uh-oh.

Already engaged on the slope, I back off the pressure enough to shift into granny gear, but the slope is so steep that I can't maintain momentum. Noah has almost caught me from behind, and if I don't get moving, I'll ruin his approach. I push harder, understanding what I'm asking of my bike, hoping chain and derailleur will hold. With grinding complaint, they shift. I double the pressure on my feet to regain some momentum.

Too soon.

With a terminal crunch, all resistance gives way, and my pedals spin out from under my feet, gouging into one shin and upsetting the delicate balance I have on the slope. Instinctively, I jerk my handlebars into the fall, trying to steer out of it, but it's too steep. I stretch out a foot, knowing I'm going down, but can't reach the ground because of the decline.

Sandstone rushes to meet me. Unforgiving and gritty. Great for tires, not skin.

And that determined sage I noticed earlier? I am about to revisit it, up close and personal.

I think I manage not to swear in the slow-motion time warp of impending pain, though there is definitely some hissing and grunting. Possibly a girly screech.

I absently wonder what it sounds like in real time.

Next thing I know, I'm on my back, bike on top of me, a pungent fog of sage swirling between me and the blinding sun in a cloudless blue sky. I wait for the pain to register.

"Grace!"

Noah's voice. Bike clattering to the ground. Rapid footsteps. A shadow briefly obscuring the sun.

"Are you okay?"

I think I'm okay . . . I hear the ticking of my rear wheel as it spins.

The sun blinds me again, and I try to inhale but can't. Pain shoots through my torso, towing panic.

"Talk to me." Noah moves to my side, his voice calm, steady. "Where does it hurt?"

His eyes meet mine, and he sees the panic there. A warm hand settles on my arm, soothing me.

"It's going to be okay," he says. "Looks like you got the wind knocked out of you. I'm going to lift your bike off, okay? Let go of the bar."

Bar? I blink against the pain and panic and realize I'm holding my bike, the top tube resting in my hands and across my chest.

"Let go," he says. "I have it."

I obey, and he sets my bike down next to his, off the trail, as I flounder for air. Again his helmet shades my watering eyes. He still has his sunglasses on—those goofy, high-contrast yellow-lensed jobs. Concern etches his face.

His warm hand on my forehead feels fabulous. I close my eyes and count, praying I can breathe again before I pass out.

"Just a spasm of the diaphragm," he says, voice calm. He gently moves my arms—looking for wounds, I assume. I don't really care why he's touching me. It's a balm for my panic, and finally I can inhale.

He smiles at the sound and congratulates me with a soft touch on my shoulder. "There you go. How's your head? Any pain?"

I move a little, and a hot knife slices up my leg. "Calf," I say.

He moves to my leg and takes a look, then takes off his helmet and backpack and starts rummaging. The pain levels off until he moves my leg again.

I suck in. "Warn me, will you?"

"Sorry," he says, and after that he talks me through everything. That lovely, sword-bearing bush has torn a gash across my right calf, but it's not deep enough to need stitches. He cleans it and pulls it back together with butterfly Band-Aids, then systematically rinses the pedal gouges on my shin and all the spots where my skin has been sanded away. I'm stinging in so many places as he rinses my wounds that I can't localize the pain.

Don't cry, don't cry, don't cry.

"Almost done," he says. "Hang in there." He finishes up the water torture and starts applying Band-Aids and ointment to all my abrasions, taking the stinging to a new level.

"You using lemon juice?" I say through my teeth, pulling my head up to see how far we have to go.

His hands pull back momentarily. "Antibiotic. Sorry. It stings."

"Well," I say, "I think lemon juice would be an improvement. It has great disinfecting properties."

One eyebrow ticks up, softening the worry lines in his forehead.

I lay my head back. "That's why there's less sickness in the summer."

"How so?"

I brace myself as he resumes his doctoring. "All that lemonade."

His chuckle takes some of the pain away, and I smile through my grimace.

When he's done wallpapering my legs, he helps me sit up. "Take it slow," he says. "Do you feel faint?" He takes my face in his hands, his hazel eyes searching mine as he leans to bring my face in and out of his shadow.

If I do feel faint, I'm fairly sure it's not from the fall. "Concussion?" I ask.

He startles, releasing me. "Hard to tell, but your pupils are both responsive and the same size, as far as I can see. Does your head hurt?"

I swivel it side to side, shake it a little. "Seems okay."

He nods, his lips pulling up, though he still looks worried.

"What are you, an EMT?" I ask.

He huffs, getting out a few more Band-Aids for my arms. "I was a lifeguard in high school."

"You're good at this."

His hands still for a moment before he replies. "My mom wanted me to be a doctor."

"But you didn't?"

He shakes his head, gently applying the last Band-Aid. I disregard the warmth that blooms where his skin touches mine, focusing on the rocks. "I'm better with numbers than people." He puts the lid back on the ointment and closes the Ziplock from his first-aid kit. He gathers up all the wrappers, then does another assessment, asking about my pain, scrutinizing my face, checking my eyes.

What if he didn't hate me? I remind myself that I have no right to enjoy this platonic, charitable attention, that Jamie is after him and he's encouraging her, and that I have a boyfriend and Noah wouldn't date me if I were the last woman on Earth anyway. Would he?

Needing an escape from my thoughts, I start to get up, but he won't let me until I've had a bite of some nasty bar he forces on me and a few sips of a sports drink from his pack.

Finally, he deems me ready. He reaches down to help me stand, keeping hold of my forearms to stabilize me. My heart is pounding, though I'm sure it's not from my injuries. Our eyes meet and hold, and the what-ifs run through my head again. What if I hadn't made some flimsy excuse to push him away the first time?

"I'm taller than you." The words are out before I can stop them.

His gaze flits back and forth between my eyes. "No, you aren't."

I smell cinnamon.

"I'm looking right at you," he says. "Our eyes are level."

"The ground isn't." An urgency has crept into my voice. He can't be taller than me. He isn't!

His eyes narrow, stray downward for an instant, and snap back up. Almost imperceptibly he closes the space between us and touches my nose with his, his breath on my lips for an instant that feels much longer than it is. I close my eyes and tell myself I don't like him that way, don't want him to brush his lips against mine, because he can't stand me and I was stupid and he was mean and there's all that history.

Too soon, he retreats, just far enough that I can feel him staring. Daring.

The intensity when I open my eyes nearly has me back on the rocks. Energy snaps around him like electricity on a Faraday cage. His grip tightens as I sway.

"We're even," he says.

Is he still talking about height? I hold my breath, unable to read his expression. What does he mean, "even"?

He releases one of my arms, and I lean into the remaining support as his free hand lifts to my face. His thumb sweeps the skin right below my cheekbone, sending a delightful shiver down my neck and arm.

Does he feel this too?

Does it scare him like it's scaring me?

Is it worth the risk?

I exhale and his hand freezes. He steps back, releasing me, his features pinching into a frown.

He clears his throat. "You had some dirt. There." His jaw clenches, enhancing the shadow of his cheekbones. "Are you good? Steady?"

What is he talking about? How could I be steady after that?

"Can you ride?" The warmth is gone from his voice, Benevolent Lifeguard Noah stowed securely behind Tetchy Tutor.

I manage to nod. So confused.

He dons his helmet and pack, looks around, checks his phone. "It'll be shorter to finish the loop than go back the way we came. We have about three miles left." He waits, but I'm still trying to figure out what just happened. Taking my silence for acceptance, he stands my bike up and signals for me to take it. "Ready?" he asks.

Frustration finally infuses some energy into my legs, and I take the few steps toward my bike. "Thank you," I say, and he offers a curt nod.

Retrieving his own bike, he jerks his handlebars off the ground, throws a leg over, and motions for me to go ahead with a tight Tutor smile.

It's going to be a long ride back.

Chapter 62

REJECT

STUPID, STUPID, STUPID!

The word played on repeat as Noah waited for Grace to put some space between them.

Much-needed space—space for his idiot brain to stop noticing her legs, her buttery voice, the way her eyes sparkled when she was joking around—to retreat so logic could take hold.

She has a boyfriend.

She's not attracted to me.

I'm moving on.

Anger surged into his legs and propelled him up the next incline. At least he hadn't *actually* kissed her. For a second there, he'd thought she wanted him to.

Why she'd brought up his height—the first conflict in their volatile history—he had no idea. It was almost as if she'd been talking to herself, not him. Thinking back on her stupid rule about only dating tall guys had triggered him—as if a man had any control over his height! He'd set out to tease her, show her that he was, in fact, taller.

In retrospect, going nose-to-nose had been a terrible idea. He'd been surprised to find that his nose *wasn't* higher, although she'd had a point about the uneven terrain. If they were barefoot and on even ground—

Noah shook it off. It didn't matter.

The rest of the ride was a blur of pain both physical and mental, the end of the trail as brutal as the beginning. Up one insanely steep, bumpy slope and down another, with ledges and sand thrown in for variety. The ups weren't long, but the downs were correspondingly brief in distance and even shorter in duration, thanks to gravity.

It was nothing like the mountain trails he'd ridden before—usually a long, mostly uphill climb followed by an exhilarating descent. He longed for a nice downhill to rest his lungs, but Slickrock never let up. The grueling climbs and the difficulty of the terrain did keep him from thinking too deeply about the stinging rejection that had settled around his heart.

Finally, blessedly, the trail rose and leveled out, allowing him to spot Grace pulling into the parking lot ahead of him. Exhaustion and relief threatened to overwhelm him as rolling, knobby sandstone gave way to strangely smooth asphalt.

Surrounded by the others, a concerned Alec looked over her wounds. Conversation and a whiff of the vault toilets reached Noah as he coasted to a stop at the outside edge of the group, but their words didn't register.

How had he misread her so badly? Even if he hadn't misread her, how could he have allowed himself to even consider making a pass at another guy's girl-friend? Thank heaven he hadn't kissed her. Besides, she'd made it painfully obvi-ous that she couldn't stand his touch—shuddering and holding her breath as she had when he'd wiped the dirt off her cheek.

Maybe he stunk.

Pretending to inspect his bike, he snuck a sniff, relieved when he detected nothing particularly offensive—only normal levels of outside exercise and camping smell. His gum was a little old, but he could still taste the cinnamon.

So why had she held her breath? Was his proximity so disgusting?

"You're sure you're okay to ride?" Alec asked Grace. "I can go get the car."

"I'm good," Grace said, the cheerfulness in her voice forced. "I mean, I don't really want to do another loop, but I think I can make it a couple hundred yards to the campsite." With that, she pushed off, leaving Alec and the others to catch up.

"Noah." Alec's voice had never been so annoying.

Glad the guy was speaking to his back, Noah spent some extra time checking his tires and drummed up a pleasant expression as he straightened. Alec had the decency to look contrite.

"I wanted to say, uh, thanks. For taking care of Grace back there."

"No problem," Noah said, clapping a hand on Alec's shoulder.

"I should have—"

"Anything for a friend." Noah had no desire to hear Alec "should" on him-self. He put a foot on one pedal and waited for Alec to mount before rolling. "How was your ride? Any mishaps with the rest of you?"

"Nothing major," Alec said, frowning. "A few bumps and scrapes."

"Did you have to wait long?"

"A half hour or so. I was about to come check on Grace, but—"

"Glad we saved you a second trip," Noah interrupted, sick at the idea of Alec witnessing his pass and humiliation. "Hey, Chris!" Noah said as he caught up. "What did you think?"

"Awesome!" Chris said. "Everything I expected and more. I hear you had some excitement."

"Yeah," Noah scoffed.

If only they knew how little it had had to do with the ride.

FREAK OUT

FREAKING OUT, FREAKING OUT, DON'T freak out, I'm fine, it's fine, everything is fine, freaking out!

Ten minutes into our drive, Alec's voice cuts through the car's audio and my hopefully calm exterior to interrupt my internal chanting. "You okay?"

"Mm-hmm," I say, opening my eyes and turning my head—gently, because it's already getting stiff from my fall—to give him a smile. I want to text Ivy so bad I can't stand it, but I was going for feigned sleep on the drive so I wouldn't have to talk to Alec or rudely ignore him while I text.

Besides, I'm not quite ready to tell Ivy she was right.

"I'm so sorry," he says again.

I've lost count, he's apologized so many times about leaving me to fend for myself, but it's me who should be apologizing. If I can find the words. Guilt buys me some patience for his repetition.

"I'm fine," I say. Putting my hand on his would give my words more weight, but I can't bring myself to do it. "It's fine. I wasn't expecting you to stick to my back tire and watch over me for the whole ride." *Like Noah did.* "I'm not mad." *Not at you.*

"I know. You're strong. But I should have waited."

"Everything worked out. I'm just a little worn out. Aren't you? You guys killed that ride!" Playing to his ego is cheap, but I'm scrambling here. I'll do anything not to talk about what's bugging me.

I can't. Not yet.

He smiles a knowing smile, then reaches forward to turn up—no, down—no, off!—his music.

Shoot.

"It was a great ride, and I'm glad we came down, but I can tell something's bothering you. Can we talk?"

He knows, he knows, he knows!

I nod, get a drink for my crackling-dry throat. If only I could transfer some of the water from my palms to there. It's so strange how the throat gets dry and the palms wet. What purpose does that serve, anyway? It's not like it *helps*, when you're nervous, to have a dry throat and wet palms and nausea, although I suppose the racing heart does help, like if I could run away right now, I'd have plenty of blood flow to my legs—

"Grace?"

Shoot.

As I reach to put my water bottle back in the center-console cup holder, he captures my hand, drawing my eyes to his before they settle back on the road.

"This isn't working for you, is it?" he says.

"I don't think so."

He glances my way long enough to throw me a resigned smirk. "Maybe we've been forcing things."

"Maybe."

He squeezes my hand once before returning his to the steering wheel. "I'm sorry," he says.

"Me too," I say. "I really thought we could . . . that this might . . ."

"Yeah." He exhales some frustration. "But it's not going to, is it?"

"No, it isn't. Which really sucks."

"Yeah, it does." He shakes his head, then laughs. "I thought this trip was going to help us work things out."

"Well," I say, smiling as calm seeps through the car, "I think it did. Are you good?"

He looks at me and smiles back. "I'm good. You?"

"Yeah." And I am.

It's late afternoon by the time we get back to my apartment. Alec helps me get my bike and all my gear up the stairs before he leaves. I don't even bother with a shower once he's gone, I'm so desperate for Ivy's help. I barricade myself in my room, hoping Jamie has to work late tonight.

Me: *Hey.*

Ivy: *Look what the cat dragged in!*

Me: *I know. I'm terrible.*

Ivy: *Groveling accepted. What's up?*

Me: *Welllllllllllll . . . you were right.*

Ivy: *Oh yeah, totally accepted. Also, to which instance are we specifically referring?*

Me: *Alec.*

Ivy: *YESSSSSSS! Kicked Adonis to the curb, did we?*

I fill Ivy in on the details, making it clear that the breakup was mutually agreeable. We'll definitely be better off as friends. As relieved as I am for myself, I'm equally relieved for him. He's a good guy. He'll find someone who fits.

Me: *I'm glad it ended friendly. He even helped me get my bike and all my gear back up to the apartment.*

Ivy: *Very nice. Now, when are you asking Noah out?*

Never one to waste time, Ivy. I explain to her that I'm not sure he's open to that, recounting—minus a few details—my wipeout and Benevolent Lifeguard's appearance, followed by a jarring return to Tetchy Tutor.

Ivy: *I approve the appellations, but I think you're being paranoid. He couldn't have been that grumpy.*

Me: *He didn't say another word to me.*

Ivy: *Paranoid.*

Me: *Also, there's the roommate code to consider.*

Ivy: *WHAT?! Jamie?*

Me: *Yeah. She's liked him for a while. I suspected, but she confirmed before the trip. I can't straight-up ask him out after that.*

Ivy: *Code shmode.*

Me: *Also, I already asked him out once at your insistence. Remember how well that went?*

Ivy: *That was entirely different. But I can tell you're digging in, so let's make a plan.*

Chapter 64

REVOLTING

NOT WANTING TO KILL THE post-ride euphoria of his traveling companions, Noah agreed to hang out in Moab for the afternoon once they'd packed up.

It proved harder than expected to maintain a happy face, especially after Boston's "More Than a Feeling" had sounded in his head as Alec drove off with Grace. Surely, *Marianne* had had a good reason for walking away.

If only it were so easy for Grace to walk out of his thoughts.

An afternoon flirtation might have been an effective distraction, but since the trending crowd in Moab was both sparse and leaning to the retiree demographic, that wasn't really an option. Instead Noah dug up some people skills and set Chris to talking about himself as they walked Main Street and hunted for T-shirts before grabbing a bite to eat at Pasta Jay's.

Melissa and Jake kept the conversation lively during dinner with a recap of their leap-frogging a biker from Hungary on the trail several times.

"We got to the first river overlook," Melissa said, "and decided to stop for a drink and some pictures." She looked to Jake, who continued the story.

"This guy was already there, trying to take a selfie with the Colorado River in the background." He threw it back to Melissa with his eyes.

"So of course I offered to take the picture because I—"

"—hate selfies," she and Jake said together, breaking into laughter.

Chris and Noah shared a look across the table from the newly established couple and their cuteness, joining in awkwardly with the over-the-top laughter. That kind of thing was always more fun when you were part of the inside joke.

Like it was with Grace and the pizza.

Melissa caught her breath and wiped her eyes. "The guy was super excited to hand off his phone. Then he backed his bike up closer to the rim and lifted it upside down over his head."

Jake chuckled. "I thought, 'Nice pose. I like it.'"

"He asked us again at the next lookout," Melissa said. "I was looking forward to seeing his new pose. I thought maybe he'd change it up, but no. Every single time, he lifted his bike overhead." Melissa chuckled.

"I don't know," Jake said. "Maybe it's a thing."

"If it isn't, he's hoping to make it one." Melissa shook her head with a smile for Jake. "What about you, Chris? Anything interesting happen with you or Alec? We already know about Grace's washout."

Chris offered a couple of anecdotes, but Noah didn't listen, tucking into his food instead as he prayed that no one—besides himself—would speculate about the state of The Couple's relationship after Alec had basically abandoned her on the trail.

Not fair.

Maybe *abandoned* was too strong a word.

Even Noah knew Grace wasn't one who wanted coddling, though she had accepted his first aid willingly enough.

Maybe she has a concussion after all! Maybe she held her breath because she was feeling light-headed. What if she had a serious injury that I didn't catch?

Noah fought the urge to smack the Mom part of himself. Grace would be fine. She had no serious injury. But if she did, Alec would take care of her.

She had shuddered because she found Noah revolting, just as she had on their first date.

Must. Move. On.

Chapter 65

THE BEST-LAID PLANS

Ivy: *WELL???*

I set Trusty in the passenger seat of my car and double-check that I have everything for my drive east. It's Mom's birthday on Sunday, and I'm expected for the weekend, along with Claire and family, but I'd better update Ivy before I leave, or I'll never hear the end of it.

Me: *Well. If nothing else, I'll soon be in the best cardio condition of my life.*

She sends me a gigantic face-palm. If I had a dollar for every one of those she's sent me lately, I could probably afford a new car.

Ivy: *Enough with the sneaky plan! You. Have. His. NUMBER!!*

The liberation I felt after confessing to Ivy has been obliterated by her constant nagging since.

It's been nearly two weeks since Moab, and I have yet to catch the slightest glimpse of Noah. He wasn't at church last week, and we haven't had any YCS meetings because Tony is out of town again. I've been exercising religiously, trying and failing to run into him like before—I even biked the trail once, thinking I could cover more ground that way. Ivy insists I need to take a more direct approach.

Like texting him.

Considering what happened the last time Ivy convinced me to take a direct approach with Noah, I'm not optimistic about my chances. Besides, I want it to feel natural when we see each other again, not forced.

I mean, semistalking him by spending hours on the trail he runs isn't exactly organic, but I could still *pretend* we just happened to be exercising at the same time. If I straight-up text him, that's no happy accident.

I text Ivy instead. *No phone. I told you I need to see him in person.*

Ivy: *Thank him for all the Band-Aids. Easy opening. See where it goes.*

Me: *Too late for that. It's been two weeks! There's no easy opening now.*

Ivy: *Isn't there a pickup line about needing help with your chemistry?*

Now it's me sending the face-palms. She sends hysterical laughter back.

I wish there were a way, but nothing's coming to me. It's like he's disappeared, although Jamie mentioned she saw him Saturday when a bunch of people got together at the park.

That's the other thing.

I'm not ready to risk the wrath of a good roommate for another rejection. I'm trying not to be annoyed that Jamie is decidedly more disappointed about my breakup than I am. The contemptible part of me wonders how much of that is because of my friendship with Noah.

Not that we're friends lately. I'm beginning to think he's intentionally avoiding me, and that makes anything overt even riskier.

Me: *I have to hit the road. I promise I'll let you know if there are any developments.*

Ivy: *Right. Like there's any chance of you seeing him at your parents' house. Ugh. Drive safe.*

Buckling in for the longish haul, I hit play on an audiobook, and the drive passes without incident. Soon enough, I'm happily distracted by the cutest niece and nephew ever born. So distracted that when Claire asks me about the angry new scar on my calf, I let it slip how much worse it would have been if Noah hadn't been there with his first-aid kit.

"Noah?" she says. "As in Noah Jennings?"

I see the sideways communication she throws at Ryan. Before I can say anything else, he's scooped up Ava from where we've been playing on the floor and airplaned her out of the room.

It's awfully quiet with only me, Claire, and a nursing baby Clark. Deprived of my entertainment, I'm reduced to drawing patterns in Mom's plush carpet and contemplating the merits of background music until Claire breaks the silence.

"You went on a trip to Moab. With *Noah Jennings*."

"It's not what you think. I was actually there with Alec—"

"Hot Alec? Volleyball Alec?" Clark startles at Claire's sharp tone, giving me some time to gather myself. The look she gives me when he's soothed is hurt and confused. I haven't been terribly communicative lately.

"We were dating."

"You and Alec?"

I nod.

"*Were?* Past tense?"

"Were," I say.

"And why was Noah there?"

Embellishing the carpet drawings, I dive in. Before I know it, I've spilled everything, from tutoring and Mexico to YCS and running and Jamie's crush and Moab. Even the weird, wonderful, conflicting things I feel from him—like the understanding he gifted me over the campfire and the almost-kiss and the angry look that ended our latest charged interaction.

More than I told Ivy.

The telling takes long enough that Clark is contentedly sleeping on Claire's shoulder when I finish. "I'm sorry I didn't tell you before."

She waves off my concern. "Water under the bridge. I'm glad we're talking now." Clark fusses a bit, so she bounces him with reassuring pats on his back. "Do you think . . . ?"

"I don't know," I say, slumping against the couch. "Mostly, I think there's too much history between us. I just need to get over it."

Chapter 66

GAME ON

RYAN: *DUDE. I HAVE CLASSIFIED info.*
    Noah: *You don't even know Ivy.*

Chapter 67

REBOOT

I HATE DATING.

It's exhausting.

I'm socially exhausted.

Not for the first time, I contemplate how peaceful a life alone could be. I've always wanted a family, but honestly, at this point, I'm not sure it's worth the effort of trying to find one.

It was such a relief to tell Claire everything last night. I've missed her.

I haven't missed her tenacity. I thought Ivy was bad.

Thanks to small children who must be put to bed, she waited overnight to start lobbying me for another chance at setting me up. I held strong until she pulled out her big gun: I didn't give it a fair shot the only other time she tried, so I owe her another attempt. And the guy she has in mind will only be in town today.

Ah, the arm-twisting power of guilt.

Thus, I find myself dutifully entrenched at the prescribed corner table in a hometown eatery as Claire has instructed, fiddling with the straw in my glass of ice water and waiting for my date to show up for lunch. Butterflies battle with what must be an army of angry snakes in my gut.

But.

For longer than I care to admit, I have been reminded on a near-daily basis how badly I failed at Claire's last setup, and I am determined to give this one my best effort. I can't help ruminating on all the mistakes I made that night.

I am not that person anymore.

I own my pain and acknowledge my past.

I will be kind and attentive and—

The bell on the restaurant door jingles, and my nerves ratchet up in response. This might be my date.

I can't look. I stare at my menu.

Maybe it isn't my date.

Maybe he isn't coming.

Footsteps approach and slow. Keeping my eyes down, I cast up a prayer that he isn't creepy.

"Grace." It's not a question. The voice is deep and attractive and excruciatingly familiar.

My head lifts so my eyes can confirm what my ears already know.

"Noah?" It's all I can get out.

His face is inscrutable, his jaw covered in the same roguish three-day beard that he wore on our first date, his brows furrowed the way they do when he's translating math into English. "I think my friend and your sister have sadistic tendencies." He tips his head, and his hazel eyes soften, questioning.

My heart is pounding. It is so good to see him here. So good. I still haven't recovered my ability to speak.

"Would you rather . . . not?" One side of his mouth ticks up, nervous, self-mocking against my silence.

With a mental slap to myself, I recover my ability to speak. "No! I'm so sorry. I just wasn't expecting . . ."

"Me."

"No. Yes. I mean, I wasn't expecting you, but I—" I can sense his walls going up, and I scramble to steal some of his bricks. "Please stay. I'd love it if you would stay." I pull my menu toward me and motion for him to sit across from me in the booth.

He hesitates, so I smile, though it probably looks pinched, with my emotions all haywire.

Noah.

Claire set me up with Noah.

Again.

"Can I get you something to drink?" our server says.

Noah asks for a water, and she leaves.

I pretend to focus on my menu until I can't handle the quiet. He's watching me when I look up.

"I'm sorry about you and Alec."

I can tell he's waiting to see how sorry *I* am about it. "I'm not," I say. Some of his worry eases, but I feel a flash of guilt. "I mean, he's a great guy. Just not for me. I mean, we weren't right for each other." Such eloquence.

He tilts his head and is about to say something, but I interrupt.

"So what about Jamie?"

He's confused. "Jamie?"

I shrug.

"We never . . ." He clears his throat. "Just friends."

Containing my sigh of relief is a feat of strength I'll always be proud of, though I have to bite my lips together to keep it in.

The waitress returns to relieve our awkwardness. I look down at my menu again, my hands white-knuckled as they rest against the table. A little bubble of hope squirms its way through some hitherto unknown breach in the prison I built for it. Between that and the warring butterflies and snakes, nothing on the menu is very appealing. I hear Noah order, listening more to the rumble of his deep voice than the words, and decide on a random salad because it's cheap and I'm probably going to waste it.

Now I don't even have the menu to hide behind. I take a sip of water.

"Grace?"

My name on his lips. Oh, the way he says my name.

"Can we start over?"

I close my eyes and squeak out a "Please."

"I had a long talk with Ryan."

Our eyes connect.

"He told me about your breakup, said I should ask you out." He huffs and examines the paper napkin he's mangling with his hands. "I told him there couldn't be anything between us. Too many hard feelings, too many misunderstandings. Too much history."

Maybe I don't like openness. I start to shove that little hope bubble back into its cell, but he keeps talking.

"He said I needed a fresh start."

"I hate setups." How did I end up here? Again? I clasp my hands together on the table, dig a hidden fingernail into my palm.

"I'm sorry," he says.

"Not your fault. Claire insisted she had one more shot since I'm the one who messed up her first time."

"You didn't mess up."

"Ha." I roll my eyes. "You know I did."

He concedes with a shrug. "I wasn't ready for you anyway."

"You? Weren't?"

He shakes his head. "I had a lot to figure out. And you helped me."

"I did? But I was—"

"Struggling. Stubborn." He half-smiles, his eyebrows worrying his forehead. "Hurt. And later, when I could finally see it, forgiving and kind and open. But even the first time I saw you—"

I grimace. I'd been blowing raspberries on Ava's belly on the floor. Not my best angle.

His smile widens as if he read my thoughts. "I watched you, playing with Ava. When you smiled at me, I was a goner."

"Huh?"

"Did you ever wonder why I was so bothered by that night?"

I can only shake my head. What is he saying?

"Ryan had told me so much about you, built you up, shown me pictures. I was just coming out of a rough spell, thought I was ready to move on." He scoffs, resumes his napkin torture. "But I had some more work to do." He sits up a little taller. "I wouldn't have been so upset if I hadn't seen immediately that you were even better in person than he'd led me to believe. I watched you, in those few moments before you stood up, and I convinced myself it was going to be a great night."

I wince, slump in my seat. "And I . . ."

He slides one hand across the table and covers both of mine with his warmth. "You let me know the timing wasn't quite right. It was arrogant of me to expect you to be interested as instantly as I was."

"I was." The words are out before I know they're coming. His hand freezes on mine, skepticism in his eyes coaxing me to unclasp my hands and meet his palm with my own. It is frightening to expose myself to him, but it's time to take a leap—and to give him something in return for what he's offered. The squirming things shrink against the pounding of my heart.

"You had the beard then too." My eyes wander his jawline, studiously avoiding his mouth though I can see his lips curving up under my perusal. His thumb brushes the back of my knuckles, his jaw clenching as I visually trace its line. "It looks good on you. I don't know why I was so . . . I guess I wasn't ready either."

"But you didn't recognize me when we met again."

"I was an idiot, but you did look pretty different. Glasses, short hair, no beard . . ." I pause, thinking how much healthier he looked with some weight on him but not wanting to offend him.

His head tips in concession.

Our waitress shows up with the food, and our hands slink apart. Loaded silence reigns as we eat. I miss the warmth of his hand.

My salad is surprisingly good—I guess I was hungry under all that anxiety—but the aroma of his roast beef is torture to my inner carnivore. It's thin-sliced and piled high on what looks like a sourdough bun, melty cheese overflowing the sides.

My mouth waters around another mouthful of lettuce.

"Want a bite?" He smirks.

"No, I'm good."

"So you say, but I don't think I'll be able to get your attention again until you taste this." He dunks the layers of his French dip into the steaming bowl of au jus and takes a big bite, chuckling around it as I glare at him. Possibly at his food.

He cuts a thick slice from the untouched half of his sandwich, dips it, and holds it out to me. "Go on," he says when I hesitate.

The handoff sends shivers up my arm, and I'm hyperaware of his gaze as I bite into the melt-in-your-mouth deliciousness. "Mmmm."

"Good?"

I nod and finish it off, wiping my mouth of the drippy, savory goodness. "I'll have to order that next time." His brows lift, and a flush works its way up my neck. "I mean—"

"I'm game," he says, holding my eyes.

My flush fades against the possibilities. "Claire ripped me apart after you left that night," I say.

He frowns around a mouthful, but I shake my head.

"Every word hit its mark. It was a wake-up call. I did everything I could to leave that night behind and not to make the same mistakes again. And I took a step away from dating for a while. I knew my head wasn't where it needed to be. I had to move past losing Benson." I gather the dregs of my salad, clear my throat, take the last boring bite, and dispatch it.

I don't know how Ivy survives without meat. Is she always hungry?

Noah takes my hand again, trails his thumb once across the back of my hand.

I appreciate the anchor, but it still takes several swallows and a lot of blinking before I'm ready to talk again. Four years, and I still have a hard time talking about my brother. But Noah's empathy eases the pain. "Thanks," I say.

He gives my hand a little departing squeeze and goes back to eating, though I can feel him watching me.

"I volunteered for a year in Peru," I say, "came back, looked for my new normal, and searched for who I wanted to be. A big part of who I am now came from the mistakes I made with you that night, so as painful as the memories are, I'm grateful for them."

His eyes are waiting for mine. "I'm sorry I didn't accept your offer of dinner. I'm sorry I was so resentful."

"Don't be. I deserved it."

"No one deserves that kind of treatment."

He gives me the last bite of his sandwich. A stillness settles over the table.

"You amazed me in Mexico," he says, leaning back from his empty plate. "The way you were with the kids there, what you said in your devotional, the work you do at your school . . . You were so different from what I had led myself to believe."

I amazed him? "But you were always glaring at me!"

Now *he* winces. "Not glaring. Staring, maybe."

I lift an eyebrow.

"Okay, maybe glaring at first," he admits with a laugh. "I still had a hold on that grudge, and I was a little embarrassed at my outburst in the math lab. I couldn't imagine what awful fate had doomed me to spend an entire week pretending we could get along. Besides," he says, his gaze sweeping my face, "I was still attracted to you, and that annoyed me."

"Still?"

His eyes narrow. I can see his wheels spinning, though I can't imagine what he's thinking. Eventually, a smirk slips through the fog. "Maybe it's a good thing I had that grudge to ground me, or I never would have been able to focus on helping you with your math."

I chuckle. "So I owe my graduation to my own stupidity from four years ago."

"I guess so," he says. His smirk dims. "What if we hadn't met until . . . later?"

The waitress approaches with our check, breaking the moment before I can tell him I've wondered the same thing.

"Cashier's at the front," she says, clearing the table with practiced efficiency and leaving us to battle it out over paying rights.

Noah slides out of his seat and holds out a hand—for the check, I think. It surprises him when I slip my hand into his instead.

"That's almost worth letting you pay," he says, helping me up and easing his hand to the small of my back.

"Either way, I'm paying," I say, leaning into his hand, though I'm moving forward. "I still owe you a dinner."

"Not keeping track, but if it makes you feel better . . ."

"It does."

A group moves toward us, and his hand migrates to my waist as we make room for them to pass. He stays close at the register, leaning on an elbow and pulling a couple of wrapped candies from his pocket as I make small talk with the cashier.

"Want one?" he offers as we leave.

I pop it into my mouth.

Cinnamon.

Chapter 68

UNDER THE INFLUENCE

Being with Grace was intoxicating.

For months—years, really—Noah had held himself well outside her personal space, smothering every fleeting impulse to lean closer, touch her arm, brush a curl off her face.

Now, having indulged just a little, he couldn't get enough.

Following her out of the restaurant, he stretched out his arm to hold the door, seizing the opportunity to keep one hand on her waist. The supersoft material of her shirt begged for more attention, her curls grazing his cheek as she passed through the door. A whiff of what he used to associate with the math lab assaulted his self-control, begging him to bury his face in her hair for more.

Intoxicating.

"So where have you been?" she asked, space forcing itself between them as they moved beyond the exit.

"Huh?" he asked. *Smooth. Idiot.*

"It's been a while since I've seen you . . . around."

How could he explain? He rubbed his hand across his jaw, but that only reminded him how she'd studied his whiskers at the table.

"Noah?"

"Sorry," he said, shaking off the pleasant buzz of being near her. "Just, uh, processing." She looked worried. He scrambled to put some processing power toward logical thought and conversation. It was difficult. He looked around the parking lot, realizing he had no idea where he'd parked. He barely remembered the drive there, he'd been so nervous.

She was still waiting for him to answer.

He laughed to cover his embarrassment. "Do you want to go . . . do something? I don't know what there is to do here."

"Why *are* you here?" Her eyes narrowed like they did when she tackled algebra, widening as the pieces clicked together. "You drove all the way here for this. For me."

Noah shrugged, looking down and shoving his hands into his pockets.

"How long have you and Ryan been . . . talking?" Her voice was soft.

He couldn't tell if she was impressed or angry. Avoiding her gaze, he gestured to some big trees across the road. "Is that a park? Can we go over there?"

She nodded, gears still clicking, judgment pending.

I'd better get this right.

Chapter 69

RESEARCH

I FALL INTO STEP AT Noah's side, wishing he'd take my hand again. The clear skies and midday sun make it a little warm on the asphalt, but a steady breeze keeps it comfortable. We make our way through the parking lot and cross the street, heading for the park on Main. There's a group of teens playing frisbee in the open space.

I didn't realize asking Noah where he'd been was a loaded question. But I'm more than ready to listen when he finally starts to talk.

"When I got home from Mexico—even with the accident and everything—I couldn't get you out of my head. I tried." He offers an apologetic smile, his gaze caressing my hair, face, neck. "You were so different from what I'd built up in my mind. I was working construction, finishing up my degree, helping Matt." He pauses, uncomfortable, quiet. "Going to therapy."

"That's important," I say, touching his arm. It seems to calm him. "Everyone deserves a good therapist."

He walks a little taller. "I kept thinking about you, wondering how you were doing." With a huff, he says, "I sound like a stalker."

I chuckle uncomfortably, thinking of my recent two-week stakeout on the trail and the marked increase in my running after our first accidental workout together.

"It gets worse." He blows out, hard. "When you reached out to Ryan to ask about Matt—"

"What? He promised not to—"

He holds up both hands, turning toward me as we walk. "He promised not to tell *Claire*. You didn't make him promise not to say anything to *me*."

I open my mouth to protest, but it's a legitimate loophole.

I'm going to hurt Ryan.

Then possibly hug him, depending on how this pans out.

He slides his hands back into his pockets, squints against the midday sun as if it can tell him how to proceed.

"Should we sit?" I point to a solitary picnic table in the shade of a huge maple.

He gestures for me to sit first, then settles next to me, leaning back with his elbows on the tabletop and his eyes on the frisbee game. "Ryan's a curious guy."

"Understatement."

He smiles. "You didn't give him much, so once I opened the conversation with him, he didn't let up until I'd filled in the sizable gaps in our history." He levels me with an accusatory look.

"Um . . ." I never *had* told my family who my tutor was. Or anything else about Noah.

"Annnd . . ." He draws out the *n* like a full sentence, letting me off the hook momentarily for hiding him from my family. "Then I asked him about you. He put two and two together, and since he hadn't heard of you dating anyone . . ."

He scolds me again with his eyes. I show him some teeth and try to look innocent.

"He convinced me I should make a move."

"Huh?" He never asked me out.

"Literally."

Ohhhhhh. That's why he wasn't surprised to see me at the YCS activity.

"So I moved, sought you out, and found—"

"Alec," I whisper.

His nose scrunches in adorable distaste. "Not exactly what I was expecting. You really ought to work on communicating with your family." Another visual scolding. "But . . . I was kind of committed at that point, so I just laid low." He tips his head. "Mostly."

"Running," I say.

"My one indulgence. It gave me appreciation for a sport I didn't previously enjoy."

I can't contain my laughter. He's looking at me like I'm a little crazy, which clearly, I am.

"Are you laughing at me?" he asks, half-amused, half-worried.

I shake my head and wipe my eyes. "I've been on that running trail *every day* for the past two weeks! I *hate* running!" I ask him again, "Where have you been?"

"You've been running? You hate running?" He's grinning like this is the best news ever.

I slap him on the thigh, successfully retrieving my hand before it gets ideas and sets up camp. *"Where have you been?"*

"Hiding," he says. "I didn't know you'd broken up until Ryan called last night."

"But you saw Jamie—"

"Who conveniently neglected to tell me about the breakup. I wasn't about to ask about you and Alec." He groans. "I should have known from the non-update."

"Huh?"

"She's always telling me how good you guys are together, how much fun you have, how much you enjoy—" He cuts off. His eyes fall to my lips, and I fill in the blank.

I cringe, dropping my head into my hands. What else has she told him? When I sit back up, my arm rests against the back of Noah's hand.

"Embellishment?" He sounds hopeful.

I cough-laugh. I'm so not going to discuss kissing *Alec* with *Noah*. I mean, it was nice at first, but the longer we were together . . . so yeah, embellishment. Time to change the subject. "What happened in Moab?"

That gets his attention. "Huh?"

"That look over the campfire."

A frown plays on his lips as a player sprints across our end of the field. "Alec was—" He stops himself. "I wanted to tell you how good your work is, how much I admire it."

"I felt it," I say, remembering the reassurance he'd conveyed compared to Alec's indifference. "It meant a lot." I don't know how to ask the next part, but I give it a shot. "But then, after my wipeout?"

He feigns ignorance, though I'm sure he can see where I'm going with this.

"When you helped me up?" I press.

Staring contest.

I blink first. "I thought you were going to . . ." Maybe he wasn't. Maybe I was reading too much into it. Oh, shoot. Why did I bring this up?

There goes his one eyebrow. "Kiss you?"

I shrug.

"I almost did," he says, brushing the back of his hand against my arm, opening his palm to warm my skin.

"But you didn't. And then you were . . . angry."

"I didn't think you wanted me to. Besides—"

I sigh. Much as I had wanted it, I am glad he resisted. "Alec."

The name brings a grimace to Noah's face.

"Why did you think I didn't want you to?"

His hand freezes against my arm, and I realize that—even with Ryan's assurances and the encouragement I thought I'd been giving, Noah's still unsure how I'm taking this. The risks he's taken for me—moving into my neighborhood, driving all the way down here today—are huge.

It's time for some payback, and that three-day beard is begging for investigation.

I raise one hand to his face and trail my fingertips along the line of his jaw, his whiskers catching lightly on my nails. His eyes close and he leans into my hand, the contrasting softness of his lips brushing against my palm.

"You like it?" he whispers.

"It's definitely a good look on you, but . . ."

His eyes pop open. "But?"

"I've never . . . I mean I've . . . but not with . . ." Words are stupid, so I ease a little closer, bypassing his tempting lips to place my own, lightly, into the whiskers near the corner of his mouth. I hear his breath catch, feel his hand tighten on my arm, smell cinnamon candy as I pull back enough to gauge his reaction.

His other hand seeks out my waist, warmth rippling outward from the contact. "And?" His voice is husky, eyes sparking.

I'm reminded of the fun I had teasing him during our tutoring sessions. "Hmm," I say, leaning in to try the other side. His hand presses gentle encouragement into my back, so I make my way slowly to his ear. "Inconclusive."

His chuckle rumbles against me, one hand moving up into my hair. "Further research?" he whispers against my cheek.

"Definitely," I say, brushing my lips against the scruff. "I might even need a tutor."

"Mmm," he says, his hand sending delightful shivers down my back. He pulls away enough to meet my gaze, then leans in and inches his lips to mine for a leisurely display that puts the shivers to shame. "Grace," he says a few divine moments later, leaning his forehead against mine.

"Hmm?" Heart racing. Can't form words.

"You don't need a tutor," he says, warm hand against my neck, thumb skimming my cheek.

I tap his nose with mine, as he did mine in Moab. "How about a research partner?"

"I like the sound of that."

Thwak! An overthrown frisbee hits the base of a tree nearby, startling us apart and reminding me we're not alone and I'm staunchly opposed to public displays.

Except, right now, I don't really care.

Epilogue

It's Thanksgiving, and we're stargazing with my family. It's pretty cold, so the others don't last long. I'm glued to my chair and Dad's six-inch telescope—waiting for the reemergence of the giant red star Aldebaran from its occultation behind the moon—when a warm hand slips beneath my curls to heat my neck.

"You're cold," Noah says.

"Not anymore." Two months together—two months of talking and running and laughing and kissing—and his touch still warms me like the summer sun. Maybe it's only because it took us so long to get together, but I find myself wishing there were more hours in the day so I could spend them all with him. I reach down and back to pull him closer with a hand on his calf, keeping my eyes on the scope. His body blocks the breeze, warming me even more. I'm tempted to leave the scope, but Aldebaran should show up any second.

Besides, Dad is out here too.

After our second, infinitely-more-successful setup, I took Noah home to meet my family. Though separating to drive our two cars back to the house was painful, it did allow me time to call Claire and give fair warning. I'm not sure what leverage she used to threaten everyone; it must have been powerful. My parents didn't wink, Kaden didn't posture, Zach didn't show off.

Frankly, it was a little unnerving how easily Noah slid into the family dynamics.

Mom even convinced him to stay over for her birthday party the next day, which suited me fine. She says my neglect of her for Noah that weekend was the best present she's received in years.

Explaining to Jamie when I got home Sunday night was more than a little uncomfortable, but she took it like a trooper. It didn't hurt that she'd finally noticed Chris's attention. Even so, Noah and I still spend more time at his apartment than mine.

Finally, Aldebaran emerges, peeking out from behind the full moon like a shy child shielded by his mother's skirt. I watch for a few more seconds, reveling in the sight and Noah's patience as he continues to shield me from the breeze, before standing up to share the view. I stretch my back while I wait for my sight to adjust from the brightness of the magnified moon.

"Do you want a turn?" I ask.

"I'm good." He lifts the binoculars he's been using, then sets them on my abandoned chair and unzips his coat, holding it open in invitation.

I look over my shoulder to check how zoned out my dad is at his scope, surprised to see that he's not there. "Where's Dad?" I ask.

Noah takes my hands and slips them beneath his coat, coaxing me into his warmth.

"When did he go in? Is he okay?" I ask, confused. Dad's always the last one to leave.

"A while ago. He's fine," he says, laughter in his eyes.

"Why—"

"Grace." His thumb brushes across my lips. "Don't worry about it." He wraps his arms around me gently.

Dad's classical music has given way to . . . "Boston?" I ask.

He smirks. It's a little lopsided.

My heart pounds. Is he . . . ? I mean, we've talked, but I hadn't allowed myself to hope that he'd do anything so soon.

"The first time I saw you, you took my breath away."

I start to say something. He silences me with a featherlight kiss that leaves me wanting more.

"I had a feeling about you, but neither of us was ready. I've watched you walk out of my life more than once, and I don't ever want that to happen again."

He tucks an errant curl behind my ear, trailing unsteady fingers down my cheek, and taunts me with another quick kiss. "I know we haven't been together that long, but I don't want to waste any more time. You've brought peace back into my life, motivated me to regain my family and myself, taught me so much. I want to share every moment with you, spend the rest of my life and beyond learning with you."

His knees shake against mine. I tighten my hold, willing him to say the words I'm aching to hear.

"I love you, Grace," he says, his eyes shining in the moonlight. "Marry me?"

"I love you too," I say, overwhelmed with joy and belonging and acceptance, "and I would love to marry you." I close the distance between us to seal my answer with another kiss. "You know," I say, retreating just enough to speak, "equivalent height is pretty convenient."

His lips tighten into a smile against mine. "It's true," he mumbles back.

About the Author

BARBARA J. ADAMSON GREW UP in Idaho and received a degree in biology education, teaching high school science for a time before leaving to raise a family. She and her husband have six children, two children-in-law, one grandchild, and a very sweet Labrador.

Barbara prefers books to food (other than chocolate), sports to shopping, and mountain biking to almost anything else. *Tutored in Love* is her first published novel.

Learn more at barbarajadamson.com, and follow her on social media.
Facebook: Barbara J Adamson
Instagram: @barbarajadamson